INFILTRATION
POWERS LEGACY BOOK 2
STARR Z. DAVIES

CHARACTER ASSASSIN BOOKS

BOOKS BY STARR Z. DAVIES

Divica Stormborn Chronicles

Stormvalor

Stormveil

Stormcrown

Divica War of Two Crowns

Volume 1: Darkness Falls

Powers Series

Ordinary

Unique

(extra)ordinary

Superior

Powers Origins

Miller: Origin

Enid: Origin

Celeste: Origin

Powers Legacy

Powers Legacy: The Prequel

Desolation

Infiltration

Insurrection

Invasion

Fractured Empire Saga

Daughter of the Yellow Dragon

Lords of the Black Banner

Mother of the Blue Wolf

Empress of the Jade Realm

Prosperous Eternity

Stand-Alone Stories

Stones: A Steampunk Short Story

This book is dedicated to dedication. Because it took a lot of it to write when my heart broke for these characters. Enjoy!

Author Note

DESOLATION INTRODUCED READERS TO some sensitive topics that some struggle to handle: alcoholism, child abuse, same-sex couples, and social disorders. *Infiltration* will certainly continue addressing some of these sensitive topics in a little more depth.

But *Infiltration* focuses on another topic that I know some readers might find upsetting or disrespectful: the age-old debate of science versus religion.

In particular, two characters stand on opposite sides of this topic until it comes to a head. Once more, I feel it's important to help readers understand I am not taking a firm stance in one direction or another. When these two characters launch into a debate, each arguing their own side, I don't intend to make people accept one view or another—just as these characters learn not to do. I hope the result is clear. There is no one acceptable answer, and that's okay. The important thing is that they learn to coexist *despite* these differences of principles.

Also, I feel like it's important to point out that, while pieces of faith in this book are based on numerous real-life religions, the *Book of the Prophet* and beliefs of the people who follow it are my own creation. It is *not* meant as an attack or a degradation against any faith. Please take this aspect of the story in stride as fiction.

I am a person of faith, and I would *never* target anyone else for theirs.

Cast of Characters

Elpis

Paige Powers — Somatic Muscle Memory; Psionic Precognition/Dreaming (and more to come…)

Gavin Powers — Psionic Perfect Memory & Psychic Navigation; Naturalist Matter Manipulation, Mutation, Environment Creation, Electromancy (and more to come…)

Easton Sinclaire — Somatic Strongarm; Kingdom recruit

Harper — FlexVision; returned to Elpis

Doctor Adams — Healing Hands; returned to Elpis

Olivia — Tracker; died in the Battle of Old St. Louis

Ugene Powers — Powerless; Paige/Gavin's dad; current Minister of Elpis

Enid Powers — Environmental Creation; Paige/Gavin's mom

Aron — Visual Linking; data analyst & Gavin's co-worker

Tudor — Parabolic Hearing; Department of Security Specialist; Paige's ex

Higbee — Natural Mutation; Gavin's boss

Bianca Pond — Super Somatic; Department of Security Colonel; Paige/Gavin's adopted Aunt

Director Levi — Levitation; Director of Department of Security

Alex Miller — Electromancy; Paige/Gavin's adopted uncle

Councilwoman Howser — Telekinetic; councilor of Elpis

Director Perlberg — Psychometry; Director of Department of Science & Technology

Captain Wilson — Department of Security Captain

Mat, Carlos, Nate, Sam, Benny, Elly, First Sergent Camden — Specialist training team with Easton/Paige/Tudor

THE HAVEN

Drake — Silencer

Emil — Lie Detector

Minister Charles Garraty — Influencer; Senior Elder

Carmen — Matter Mutation; Resource Elder

Ally — Strongarm; Guardian Elder

Luke — Telepathy; Education Elder

Julia — Healing Hands; Medical Elder

April — Wind Dancer

Dani — Transmutation Conversion

Pippen — Powerless

Mrs. Garraty — Powerless

THE KINGDOM

Alric Strong the Third — former king; deceased

Alric Strong the Fourth — former Crown Prince; deceased

Queen Elena Strong — Lie Detector; mother of Alric the Fourth, Bronwyn, Cypress, and Dominic

Lady Emry — Blood Cleansing; former king's consort; Zephyr's mother

Lord Baron Strong — Elemental Control; Admiral of Tides; brother of Alric the Third

Bronwyn Strong — Telepathy; princess; second-born child

King Cypress Strong — Item Tracing; third-born child; King of the Kingdom of Tides

Dominic Strong — Influencer; forth-born child; Keeper of Tides

Zephyr Strong — Power Negation; only child of Lady Emry; Captain of Tides

Lord Vincent Greene — Operator; oversees horse breeding and sales

Nat — Energy Absorbtion; friend to Zephyr and his First Mate

Ingrid, Mariah, Helen, & Maddy — Paige's maids/stylists

Officer Cante — Hematology; Zephyr's friend; Easton's trainer

Officer Ody — Scopic Vision; Zephyr's friend; Easton's trainer

Finrik — Operator; mainland recruit

Ian — Aurology; mainland recruit

Jeff — Stealth; fort guard

TRIBUTES

Alice — Environment Manipulation; mainlander

Bella Greene — Nature Manipulation; islander; Lord Greene's daughter

Everly — Telekinesis; islander

Holly — Futuresight; mainlander; left behind her one true love

Ivy — Mimic; mainlander

January — Cellular Manipulation; mainlander

Layla — Psychic Navigation; mainlander

Maeve — Organic Mutation; islander; father operates farmlands on the island

Nora — Hematology; islander; formerly engaged to Alric the Fourth and close with the family

River — Shriek; mainlander

Summer — Sound Amplification; mainlander

POWERS WORLD MAP
WASTELANDS
ELPIS
DEATH VALLEY

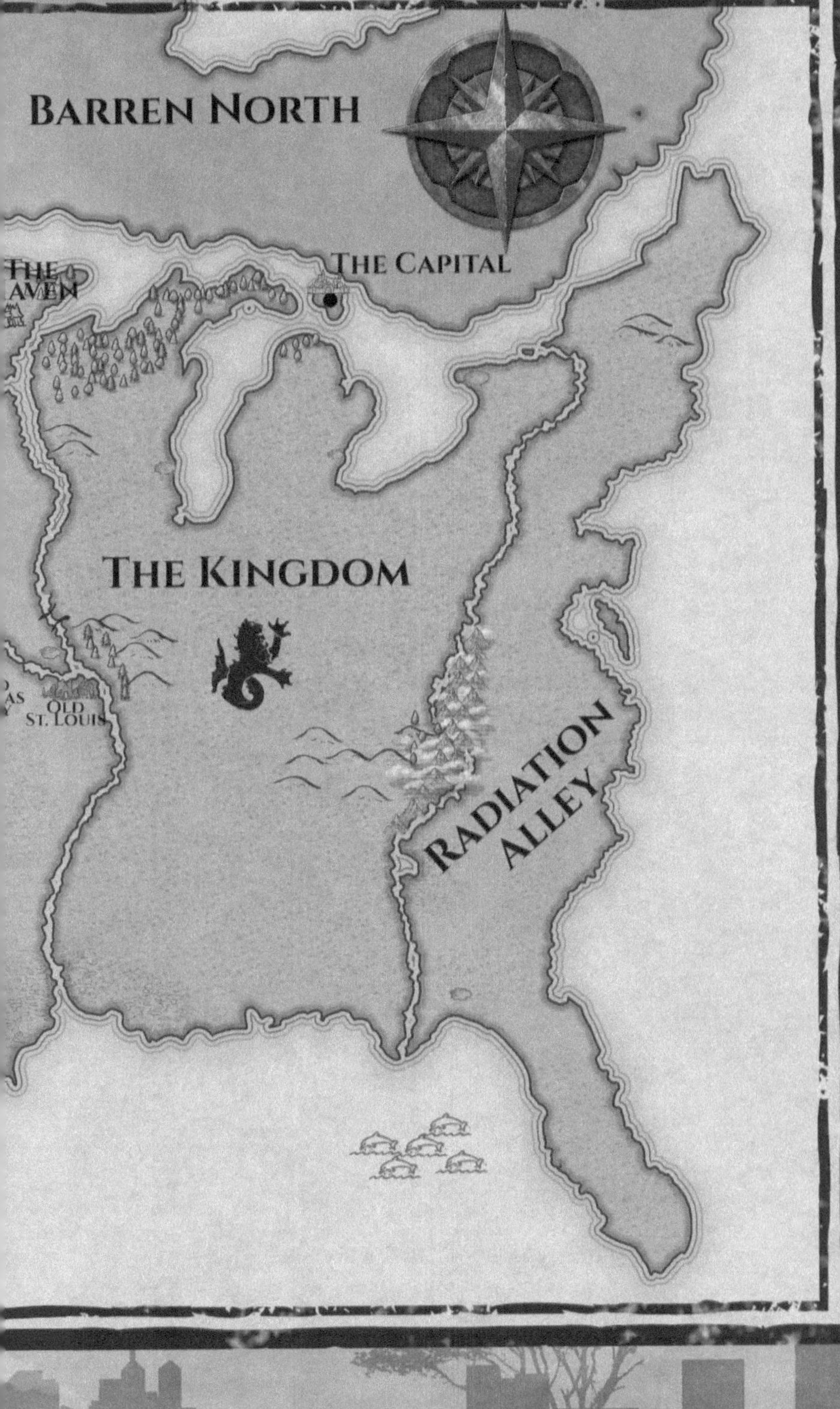

BARREN NORTH
THE CAPITAL
THE RAVEN
THE KINGDOM
AS
OLD ST. LOUIS
RADIATION ALLEY

KINGDOM OF TIDES
FIRST ROYAL DECREE

EVER SINCE THE COLLAPSE of the known world, humanity has struggled to survive in a desolate world. To the east, the former states have been irradiated. No life beyond that which grows green survives beyond the river and mountain. To the west, the grassland gradually dies out into a desolate wasteland. To the far north, unpredictable climates make the land barren of sustainable life.

Throughout the surviving grassland between the two rivers, lawlessness has taken hold.

No longer.

To protect those beyond our island, the Kingdom of Tides will expand toward outer communities. We will protect those incapable of protecting themselves. In exchange for our protection, communities will present all magic-wielding women and children to the Kingdom of Tides. We will train the boys to become the next generation of protectors for the communities. The women will have a chance to become wives to the most powerful men in the Kingdom of Tides, and their children shall inherit the reins to the Kingdom.

In exchange for the services rendered by the boys and women, each community shall be sent parcels of supplies to help sustain life. Soldiers will be sent to protect these communities from the lawless barbarians roaming the grasslands. We will continue to grow, expand, serve, and protect the people of this kingdom.

The Capital will become a stronghold of hope and protection for all our people.

A new structure of tradition and order has been created and *must* be maintained by the royal family and its' descendants.

KING OF TIDES

Only the eldest heir to the current king and his direct descendants have claim to this title. As King of Tides, he assumes the responsibility for maintaining order in the Kingdom of Tides, protecting the people, and ensuring growth which allows the Kingdom to repopulate the earth.

PRINCE OF TIDES

Only the eldest son of the current King of Tides may hold this position. He will be raised and trained to assume the crown upon his father's death or abdication. When the times comes to take a wife, he will have first pick of the magic-wielding women offered as Tributes by the outer communities. This ensures unbroken magical strength in the royal line to allow the Kingdom of Tides to continue offering protection to the people.

In the event there are *no* royal sons to carry on this position, the King may select his successor from among the noble lords in the Capital. They will then take up the mantle and assume a position as the new royal family.

ADMIRAL AND CAPTAIN OF TIDES

Upon maturity, the second-born son shall assume the position of Captain of Tides, where he will learn to take over military operations that offer necessary protection to the mainland communities of the Kingdom of Tides. Upon the Admiral's retirement or death, the Captain will become the next Admiral.

In the event there are no royal second-born sons to assume this position, the King may select his successor from among the noble lords in the Capital with military training. They will hold this position until a royal son can resume the title.

KEEPER AND DEVOTEE OF TIDES

To maintain our history, culture, traditions, and longevity of the Kingdom of Tides, the youngest royal son shall assume the position of Devotee of Tides, where he will study our history, traditions, and laws so that he can serve as the King's primary council. Upon the Keeper's retirement or death, the Devotee will become the next Keeper.

A Keeper and Devotee shall be sworn to devote every aspect of their lives to these positions, and shall vow to live completely in service to the King and Kingdom until their retirement or death. To keep them devoted utterly to their positions and avoid outside distractions, they shall never marry. They live to serve the Kingdom.

In the event there are no royal last-born sons to assume this position, the King may select his successor from among the noble lords in the Capital with military training. They will hold this position until a royal son can resume the title.

By royal decree, as the first king of the Kingdom of Tides, I hereby swear myself and my descendants to this noble endeavor. We live in service to protecting what remains of humankind.

Signed,
King Alric the First

1

UGENE

THE WORLD AROUND ME slows as I digest the news. Heaviness in my chest threatens to drag me under. My eyes burn and my vision blurs. I blink rapidly a few times to fight off the anguish, the tears.

Enid has no such reservations. Tears roll silently down her pale cheeks, but she doesn't make a sound. I can see it on her face: the news has broken her. I can't bear facing her grief. It would be the end of me, my final undoing.

The call for us to report to the Department of Security building had created a pit in my stomach that slowly grew larger the closer we drove to the building. I tried to tell myself that the team was back, and they just wanted me there to greet my kids. Enid and me.

I knew better, but I couldn't accept what the truth may be. Now, I can't think straight. I can't imagine the next step forward. I can barely breathe.

"Ugene?" Bianca furrows her brows. How can she be so calm? I want to punch her. Not that it's her fault.

I did this. I proposed Project Restoration. I set up the parameters for selection. I knew Gavin, at least, would be selected—though I had expected him to refuse. He hates change.

Now he's gone. A lump lodges in my throat. I fight to force it down, but it only makes matters worse.

And Paige. I didn't think her performance in the Specialist program was anything exceptional. But after her selection, I reviewed her records, stunned to see how high her performance scores were. I didn't expect them to choose her. And once they did, nothing I said or did would have stopped her. She's too stubborn.

Enid fights off a sob, gripping the arms of her chair until her knuckles turn white. I reach over and wrap my hand over hers. She jerks it away, and my heart breaks all over again.

The meeting room is warm, inviting, and makes me sick to my stomach. Across the conference table, Doctor Adams slouches in his seat, fidgeting with his hands on the tabletop. Harper won't stop crying and hugging herself. The sound grates on my nerves. I clench my jaw. *What does* she *have to grieve over? These are* my *children!* The thought isn't fair, but I can't help my anger.

Miller leans forward in the chair beside me, eyeing Bianca, then Levi, who stands on the other side, behind the remaining two team members. "So, what's the next step?" Miller asks.

Bianca and Levi exchange glances I can read all too easily.

"Nothing." The bitter anger in my voice makes Bianca flinch.

Miller scoffs, shaking his head. His blond locks wave with the motion. He needs a haircut. "Bullshit," he snaps. "Put together another team. Send them to the last known location and have them search from there. We know where that signal came from. We know where we need to go. Covert ops, right? You have it. Send it out and get those kids home."

An argument ensues. I can't seem to focus on their words. Instead, I watch Doctor Adams. I don't know what I'm looking for—if I'm even looking for anything at all. My stare makes him shift uneasily in his seat.

Their report fills me with both hope and grief. Easton sent a message to the two of them while they were guarding the truck. About the Haven, and a warning about the Kingdom and what they wanted—girls like Paige and boys like Gavin. The next morning, Easton reported they were under attack. He did everything by the book: coordinating a rendezvous, setting a limit, sending survivors back once that limit passed no matter what. We don't know anything beyond that. Except that no one made the rendezvous.

Harper and Doctor Adams waited an extra day, and all they found was Olivia's body.

Paige and Gavin could be dead, along with Easton. Or they could be captive.

"You don't know shit!" Miller surges to his feet, startling me. The lights in the room flicker, a sign of Miller's barely contained rage.

Enid startles, raising her gaze for the first time since they told us the news.

Miller slams his fist against the tabletop. Sparks fly out of the nearby outlets. He stabs an accusatory finger at Bianca and Levi. "They could be on their way back on foot, for all we know! They could have escaped!"

Levi flinches. I should be angry—I'm glad Miller is thinking straight because I certainly can't—but I can't blame Levi or Bianca, either. Their hands are tied. And they love my kids just as much as Miller does. This isn't easy for any of us.

"Sit down, Miller," I say, my voice empty of emotion.

He waves a hand in their direction, turning his fierce blue-gray eyes on me. "You're just going to sit there and let this go?"

Enid pulls her arms tighter to her sides but says nothing. What could we say or do?

"We are working on a plan of action," Levi reassures us. "But we have to pass it through the Council of Representatives. The truth is, we have no clue what the Kingdom is capable of. But if they seek Powers, then we have to assume their force is formidable. We can't just launch a rescue mission without examining the potential dangers to the entire city."

"We love those kids. We care about them," Bianca reassures us, "and we will do everything we can to bring them home."

Miller snorts, crossing his arms. "What a crock of fucking bureaucratic bullshit." Then he snatches his jacket off the back of the chair and storms toward the door.

Enid rises and follows him out like a wraith. I rise as well, but watching my wife turn inward without a single response makes my legs weak. I have to be the strong one. I must help her through this.

Bianca edges cautiously toward me, as if afraid I will lash out. Funny. She's the one with unfathomable strength. "Ugene, I promise we will figure something out. And I will organize a team to listen to the radio waves for any signs of s—" She chokes on the last word.

I clench my fists. "Say it."

She pales.

"Say it, Bianca. Say *survivors*."

Her jaw slackens as if she wants to comply, but she can't get the word out. Agony shines in her copper eyes. She and Paige were—*are*—close. How can she just stand there and act so clinically about this?

I shake my head in disgust and storm out of the room.

I can't deal with this right now.

I have to get my kids back.

Somehow.

2

PAIGE

AS THE SHIP DOCKS, the men aboard launch into action. They move to unload the carriages and tie off the ship to the dock. I stand on the rear observation deck, taking in the Capital as we back into place. A gust of wind sweeps across the deck, but I barely feel it. My Department of Security uniform is designed to keep me warm despite the chilly wind.

White flakes swirl gently along the crystalized beach as the wind picks up. Two, three, and four-story buildings line the waterfront flanking several massive docks. Up on a hill, overlooking the water and the sprawling waterfront, is a walled complex with watchtowers that clearly mark out the fort. That is where their military trains. My gaze sweeps over the view in front of me again, but I can no longer see the palace Zephyr had pointed out to me earlier.

"Time to go," Zephyr calls to me from the stairwell.

I give the Capital one more glance before jogging to the stairs.

"What do you think?" he asks as we descend.

"I would rather be at home."

He chuckles. "Your home is better than here? I find that hard to believe." His accent is curious, something I can't quite place. The words are all the same, but his inflections and emphasis differ from those in Elpis.

I shrug. This man abducted me and tossed me into a rolling cell. I'm not about to treat him like a friend.

Alice and Holly are waiting on the lower deck. Both were taken from their homes, too. Holly left behind her one true love after

Seeing his death if she resisted. Alice came along with little fight. Her mother begged her to stay, but Alice knew tragedy waited for her people if she resisted. Once, I asked her for a few more details but she said little else. Both have been standoffish ever since the men mutinied against Zephyr and attempted to steal us. Since then, they keep their distance and only give me cursory peeks.

I glance apprehensively at the boxed carriage. Moving around on the deck had been nice. I'm not looking forward to being locked in that thing again. The walls are oppressive, blocking off our Powers.

I take a couple of steps toward the carriage before Zephyr's hand clamps down on my shoulder.

"Where are you going?"

"To the..." I falter, glancing at the carriage. "Wait. Where is Easton?"

"He is in the carriage. You'll go that way with me." He points toward the ramp being lowered on the dock.

We are being separated. My stomach twists as this reality presses down on me. Easton is the only piece of home I have left. I don't want to be separated from him. Going alone terrifies me. And what will they do to him? "Can I say goodbye to him?"

Zephyr's lips thin, but he gives a tight nod, then escorts me to the carriage and opens the door.

Easton looks up as the door opens, and his face lights up when he sees me. It's an odd look for him.

"Paige!" He shuffles closer, then hesitates when he sees Zephyr holding the door open. His broad shoulders slump.

I don't need to ask. I already know we won't get any privacy. Easton seems to understand. What can I say to him that he will understand? What do I even *want* to say to him? I just wanted to see his dumb face one last time before we are finally driven apart. How long will it be before I get to see him again? *Will I ever see him again?*

Easton must sense some of my worry. He doesn't reach for me. His dark eyes sweep over me like he is trying to memorize everything about me in just a few moments. "This is fine," he attempts to reassure me. "Remember what we talked about? Stay safe and don't do anything stupid."

I snort and roll my eyes. "*Right*. You're the idiot here."

He smirks and shrugs. "If you say so." He swallows and, for just a second, his eyes dart to Zephyr. "I can handle this if you remember what I told you. Can you promise me that much?"

I remember our conversation right before our kiss distinctly. Be careful. Protect myself. Use my position to save us both. I couldn't give that promise to him then. Now, seeing the worry in his eyes, I can't deny him.

"I promise."

He nods and steps back.

Zephyr seems to understand our conversation is over. He closes the doors and locks them again. His first mate, Nat, nods in some unspoken understanding.

We walk off the ship with the other two girls trailing behind us. He doesn't say anything, but I can sense some regret.

A carriage waits at the end of the dock. It's much nicer than anything we have ridden in up to this point. Holly and Alice climb in with little prompting. I grab the rail to pull myself up but hesitate when I hear the clacking hooves of the horse pulling Easton's carriage away from us. It turns right and disappears behind the line of buildings.

"Paige." Zephyr's gentle command pulls my gaze away. I meet his dark eyes. He nods inside.

Unsure of what else to do, I climb in. The carriage lurches into motion the moment Zephyr climbs in with us. We turn left on the main street—the opposite direction from where Easton has gone. My stomach sinks. Part of me had hoped we would at least be in the same building. I should have known better. The fort was visible from the ship.

As our plush carriage trundles along the main street, I watch the people going about their lives. They seem happy enough. There are no cars here like in Elpis, but they have some technology like functioning electricity. People walk or ride bicycles to get about.

A couple of carriages travel down the street in the opposite direction. I assume they belong to the upper class, since keeping horses can't be cheap or easy. I mean—I would assume. We don't have horses in Elpis. Once upon a time, we had stables, but the resources to keep the animals outweighed their usefulness long before I was born. The creatures are magnificent, though. And much larger than I imagined.

Considering the destruction we saw in the crumbling old cities on the mainland, the immaculate condition of the island takes me by surprise. It's almost as if what happened to the rest of the world didn't touch them here at all. The homes are all in great condition, with clean windows and siding, intact roofs, and perfectly maintained paint. The roads are smooth, and the shops still glow with LED lights. The clothing the people wear is a strange mixture of an ancient world style and pre-collapse coats. I'm not sure what to make of it.

The carriage turns a couple of corners. I try to keep track of where we are heading—just in case. We pass a fenced-in stable yard with a few gigantic horses grazing peacefully in the small pasture.

People ride *those things?* I shake my head dubiously as we roll past.

It only takes a few minutes for the palace to come into view from its perch on the hill.

Alice and Holly murmur their admiration at the view out the side window. I lean over Zephyr to see what they see. An open field of dead grass lightly dusted with snow. And beyond sits the lake, its blue waters a sharp contrast to the snow. It is a stunning view, but I can't fully appreciate it under these circumstances.

Once more, the scent of lake water fills my senses, crisp with a hint of fishiness. The warmth from Zephyr's body seeps into me. I'm too close, and my stomach twists in knots.

Instead of fawning over the scenery like the other two girls—and not at all because of how close I am to Zephyr—I slump back in my seat and cross my arms, watching people out my window as we pass. They bow at the carriage. *Who do they think is inside?*

Houses half a mile across a field to my right stand impressive and immaculate against the landscape, visible only through a host of barren trees.

The road forks ahead. Instead of heading to the palace, as I expected, we continue past. *Where are we going?* I straighten on the bench, leaning closer to my window. The carriage finally turns through a short tunnel at the back of the palace and stops just on the other side.

Zephyr steps out first, closing the door behind him. A hushed exchange takes place outside, then he opens the door again and motions for us to exit.

I peer up at the impressive height of the palace to my left. It's *huge*, dwarfing the new government building in Elpis shamefully. Though it can't be over six stories tall, it stretches to the side across the block like a sprawling mammoth. The pristine white walls show no signs of age or wear. It's a well-maintained building.

Alice and Holly huddle close to one another. Their jaws slacken in awe as they stare at the back of the palace as well. *Is that what I look like?* I focus on clearing the amazement from my expression.

Zephyr calls for us to follow, then starts up a manicured path that heads away from the palace—in the backyard as my best explanation.

"You will stay in the cottage for the time being," Zephyr explains.

The cottage on the other side of the path is much smaller than the palace. Two stories tall, with many hips, gables, and dormers along the roof. It must be nearly as big as my parents' house in Elpis.

"Tomorrow, the physician will come to perform exams. It's standard just to make sure you are in good health. Nothing to worry about. The other girls are already here and have already done their physicals. We are a little late arriving. I apologize for that." He doesn't seem sorry. He *does* look worried, though. "I must warn you that using your magic against anyone else while you are here is against the law." His gaze pointedly meets mine. "The punishment is severe, so do your best to avoid it."

Though he is warning all of us, the way he stares into me makes me feel like it's meant mostly for me. He is worried about what I will do. *As he should.*

Zephyr opens the door and leads us inside.

A chorus of female voices hits me the moment I step inside. The chatter and laughter are at odds with our situation. How can these girls be happy?

He glances at me only a second before closing the door behind us.

Just off the entryway, two girls clean up dishes in the kitchen, working in amicable silence. I offer them a weak smile. They return it just as hesitantly, their curious gazes sweeping over the three of us.

Alice and Holly edge into the parlor, where three more girls sit at a long dining table. Their conversation lulls as we enter.

"Ladies, sorry to interrupt," Zephyr says. "Alice, Holly, and Paige will join you here."

"There are only four rooms and already five of us," a busty girl complains.

"Two to a room, then," he says, fixing her with a hard glare. An air of command surrounds him, as if he is used to this sort of thing and knows he has the power to force his will on others.

She clenches her jaw, then turns her defiant gaze to the tabletop.

"How much longer are we going to be here?" another girl with a youthful face and thin frame asks.

Zephyr says nothing. He simply turns and marches to the door.

"Jerk," the girl mutters not the least bit quietly.

His shoulders tense, but he doesn't respond.

I rush after him. "Wait! That's it?"

"For now. That's my job. Get cleaned up tonight. The physician will be here first thing in the morning." Zephyr ends the conversation there, closing the door before I can say more. A lock clicks into place.

I stare at the door, dumbfounded. While I knew this was a mission they had sent him on, hearing him dismiss me like that wounds me. I don't know anyone here except Alice and Holly, who haven't said more than a word or two to me since the mutiny.

I'm separated from Easton. Now Zephyr is gone. The only two girls I know don't like me. My stomach twists in sickening knots. I've never felt so alone. And to make matters worse, the sound of the lock clicking into place on the door makes the walls of the cottage suddenly seem much closer together. I need to get out of the entryway into a larger space.

I edge into the parlor where the rest of the girls are congregating. Already, they are sorting out sleeping arrangements as the two girls from the kitchen bring out leftovers for Alice, Holly, and me. I examine the other girls. They are a variety of heights, shapes, eye color, hair color, and skin tones. Whatever the King prefers, someone here will probably strike his interest. My gut churns at the prospect. I hope it isn't me.

After some discussion, the slim, graceful girl, Layla, agrees to share a room with Ivy so Alice and Holly can share a room. The busty girl, January, mutters something under her breath while glaring at me. It's obvious she doesn't want to share a room. Funny, this isn't my ideal situation, either.

The parlor is large enough for a long table with eight cushioned chairs. A blue crystal chandelier hangs from the high ceiling above the table. Four white pillars support the sloping pale blue ceiling. A mixture of blue and white furniture lines the outer edges of the octagonal room. It's an elegant space. But a prison is still a prison, no matter how gilded.

Once I finish eating a meal far too small for how many calories my Somatic muscles need, January pushes away from the table and plants her hands on her hips.

"Come on then," she snaps. "Looks like we're sharing, and you need a shower or you're sleeping on the couch. I'll show you to our room."

I follow her along a hallway lined with full bookshelves. My gaze sweeps the titles. All relics from before the Collapse.

She turns into the first door on the right and waves me inside. I edge past and peer into the room. Canary yellow walls. A full bathroom. A *single* queen-size bed. We have to share a bed? I glance at January, and her sneer makes it clear she doesn't like this any more than I do. Maybe less, even.

"There's a closet behind the bedroom door that has a few dresses in it," January explains. Her eyes sweep over me. "Hopefully, something fits over those muscles."

I murmur my thanks. She mutters something I choose not to catch and closes the door behind her.

The shower feels incredible after weeks on the road. I close my eyes and revel in the hot water as it soaks into my hair and rolls down my back. I want to spend all night in this shower but am aware that I have to share with seven other girls. They won't thank me for using all the hot water.

Once I'm clean, I wipe off the mirror and peer at my reflection. An angry, scared girl gazes back at me. Is that really what I look like? Face drawn. Thick lips pinched tight. Brows permanently knitted together. I must be a terrifying sight to these girls. I'll be honest, I'm a little startled myself. I suck in a deep breath.

Easton is counting on me. I need to pull myself together. I need to find a way out of this. And for now, that means I have to make the best of this.

I pick through the dresses in the closet after brushing my hair. All of them are knee-length. I have no interest in wearing a dress, but luckily, I find a few pairs of pajamas in the dresser. Satisfied, I slip them on.

For a moment, I linger at the door, debating whether to venture back out to learn more about the other girls. But I don't want to be social. I just want to crawl into a hole.

It's hard to imagine that one month ago, I left the safety of Elpis, certain I would change the world and return home with proof that I'm worthy of being the daughter of the Hero of Elpis.

Now, I'm stuck on an island over a thousand miles from home with no one I trust around me and no escape plan.

This reality weighs down on me. Instead of going into the other room to join the girls, I climb under the blankets and let the fear and grief swallow me.

Dad never wanted me to leave. He knew this would happen. He knew this was dangerous. Yet I had been too stubborn to listen. I close my eyes as tears threaten to spill.

The day we left, Dad had spoken privately with Easton as we climbed into the solar truck. What had he said to Easton? Will I ever find out? And what was in that black, zippered pouch they found in Easton's pocket? It wasn't standard-issue Department of Security gear. *Did Dad give it to him?*

Fear for Easton overwhelms me. He was right that night in the carriage. They will want information, and I have too much value for them in this ridiculous pageant. They will question him. Perhaps torture him.

Our training included captive interrogation resistance, so that we would know how to withstand torture and how to answer questions without giving too much away. I had been terrible at it. Easton had done far better than the rest of the team, a fact I had resented him for at the time. Now, I'm grateful for his resilience in training. He can handle himself until I can break us out. He must. For now.

And what about Gavin? What happened to him? Where is my brother now? Is he safe? Is he alive?

These fears crash down on me all at once, and I cry myself into a troubled sleep.

I dream of Easton tied to a chair, withstanding the burning of a heat lamp as they question him. Of a man in a white lab coat taking skin and blood samples against Easton's will. Of a man in the shadows observing it all, his mouth twisted in an evil smirk, and his arms crossed over his chest in satisfaction.

3

ZEPHYR

THE BETRAYAL IN PAIGE'S eyes as I shut the door in her face sticks with me as I enter the palace. It shouldn't matter. It shouldn't bother me. It's just another successful mission. Gather Tributes. Return them to the cottage. Simple as that. Holly and Alice didn't seem to care, and it doesn't bother me in the least that neither of them gave me a second glance once they stepped inside. But Paige isn't like those other girls. In fact, she isn't like any girl I've ever met before.

I worry about leaving her unguarded from using her magic. What she did in that forest remains vivid in my memory. According to Holly and Alice, Paige used some sort of magic to turn everything around them—including the mutineers—into ash. She burned everything to the ground in seconds. Yet Paige doesn't remember anything about it. Easton didn't seem to know what she was capable of, either. *So, what does that mean?* I can only hope that Paige remains ignorant of this immense magical strength a little longer.

The palace was once a grand hotel with hundreds of suites before the Collapse. After the Collapse, it became a refuge until the first King of Tides took command of the Capital and turned his eye toward the grand hotel. From that day on, it was the seat of the royal family.

As I round a corner to head up to my suite, a familiar voice draws me up to a sharp stop.

"You better have a good explanation for what happened, Captain."

My stomach drops. I draw in a breath and turn to face Uncle Baron. His thick brows are knitted so tight they look like a solid line across his forehead. The set of his square jaw tells me all I need to know.

Uh oh.

"Can we do this in private, please?" I glance around the hallway. A few servants rush to finish evening tasks farther down the hall. None of them look our way, but I know they hear everything.

Baron nods for me to follow, then pivots and marches to the elevator doors, leaving me with no choice but to follow him. We ride up to the top floor in silence, and he leads the way to his suite in the far corner of the palace. He prefers this suite over any other because, not only is it one of the largest in the palace, but it also offers him a view of almost all the palace grounds.

"You were supposed to return when you received my message," Baron says as he marches across the massive room to his desk. "What you did could be considered treason, Zephyr." He settles in his high-back leather chair and steeples his fingers together on the desktop.

I wince, stopping in front of his desk and folding my hands behind my back in resting attention. "Peppers didn't call for us to return. I didn't get a sense that it was a command."

Baron's jaw twitches. I've always respected my uncle. His disapproval cuts deeper than most. But how much of what happened in old St. Louis years ago does he know about? How much of it is he responsible for?

How much can I trust him? I loathe the rogue thought as it jumps to the surface.

I sigh. "Is Cypress angry?"

"The King? No. He's dying to know why you disobeyed. Queen Elena is another matter altogether, though." The way he levels his dark eyes on me makes my insides twist in a knot. I dealt with my father's anger for years. But Baron's disappointment cuts deeper. "What happened?"

How do I explain to him I wanted to see my mother's birthplace, and perhaps even meet people who knew her before she came to the island? That I wanted to see if they received any of the bounty for her position. But he didn't ask *why* I went to old St. Louis. I lick my suddenly dry lips. Whatever I tell Baron will sway Queen Elena. She has hated me all my life. I can't give her an excuse to kick me out of the palace.

For a moment, I fumble for the right words. "Something compelled me to go to old St. Louis."

"Something." His tone is as flat as his lips.

"The night before we crossed the river, I had a dream. About one of the girls."

Baron groans and sinks back, dropping his arms on the arms of his chair. "Zephyr..."

"Not like that." My face flushes. "She was trapped in a cage. I tried to help her when..." I hesitate. Telling them too much about Paige could put her in danger. I think fast. "...when everything started shaking."

"In the dream?"

I shake my head. "In our camp. We took shelter in some rubble under the bridge, out of the cold. But an earthquake struck. The shelter collapsed." I can't tell him about how Paige's magic drew me right to her. How I've felt nothing like it before. It was so strong...

Baron is family, but I'm uncertain what he would do if he knew the truth. For now, it's best if no one knows anything until I'm sure how to handle this.

"So, you carried on with the mission across the river during an earthquake?" Baron huffs.

"No, it was over by then. And I figured after the cave-in, I couldn't come back here with nothing to show for it. I knew there were people in the city, so I went to find them. And it didn't take long, but they were armed."

Baron frowns, eyes widening slightly in alarm. Which part of that surprised him? I can't linger on the thought.

I slide Easton's pack off my shoulder and drop it on the desktop. "This was his pack."

"Whose?" Baron leans over the bag, opening the flap and loosening the ties holding it closed.

"There was a young man with the girl. He volunteered as a recruit." I wave a hand at the bag. "This was his."

Baron pulls out a gun, eyes widening in shock. "Military?"

"I think so. He clearly had training already. And he has quite a bit of strength magic." I watch the way Baron examines the gun. We haven't had anything like this in our own arsenal in decades. We left the guns abandoned like most things. Those that had been gathered were rusted and faulty, unsafe for use. That's why we use swords and magic in combat.

"Where is he now?" Baron asks, peering into the bag again.

"At the fort with the rest of the new recruits."

"And the girl?"

"In the cottage."

Baron falls silent as he continues riffling through the contents of the bag. I wait as patiently as I can.

"This type of technology clears up how they put up such a fight against so many of our men," Baron says at last. "Where did they come from?"

The question isn't really directed at me. He seems to mull something over in his own head. I don't have an answer, anyway, so I stay quiet. Hopefully, Easton can provide us with something.

"Tell me more about the girl." Baron finally meets my gaze. "The men said she is quite a fighter as well."

I lick my lips. There is one piece of information I can't hide from Baron. He will hear the truth at some point. "On the way to the *Wave Slicer*, some men mutinied against me. I don't know what they hoped to gain. They wouldn't tell me. But anyway, they took the three girls and locked me in the box. When Nat came around, he got me out. And...that was when another earthquake struck. We followed a trail to the girls and found them surrounded by fire and ash."

Baron's brows shoot up his forehead. "Fire and ash," he echoed, awed.

"Alice and Holly insist Paige burned the men alive. I...I don't know if that's entirely true, but the ash around them..." I shudder at the memory. "Paige was unconscious."

Baron taps his fingers against the edge of the desk, studying me. "You think Paige did it?"

"That's what the girls say." I shrug, trying to play it off as no big deal.

"Hysterical, I'm sure."

I nod. There's no denying those two girls were hysterical when we arrived. Any of my men would attest to that.

"You are dismissed, Zephyr. For now." Baron rises to his feet and rounds the desk, placing a firm hand on my shoulder. "Stay in your quarters until I come get you. Is that clear?"

"Yes, sir," I mutter.

As I leave his suite, I suppose I should be grateful that my father is dead. Cypress might be curious about what happened, but my father wouldn't be afraid to beat me bloody. Not that I'm out of the woods yet. Confining me to my quarters when he mentioned treason doesn't settle well in my gut. Will they really punish me for what happened? I don't know what kind of king Cypress will be yet. Showing leniency toward me might make him look weak in the future. I need to watch my back.

I slam the door to my suit and march straight for the wet bar. A drink will help calm my nerves before I shower.

"Zeph?" Mom shuffles out of her room on the far side of the parlor. A frail smile carves its way up her thin face. *Has she lost more weight?* My heart sinks at the thought.

"Mom." I turn away from the wet bar to approach her.

She slides her arms around me. "Thank goodness you're okay. I was so worried."

"Worried? Why?" I give her a brief hug, then walk her over to a chair. Standing too long tires her out quickly.

Mom eases down in the blue velvet chair. "First, I worried when the others returned and you didn't. No one knew where you were. Then I worried when I heard your ship docked with only a fraction of your men. What happened?"

I pour her a glass of water, eyeing the whiskey bottle. My hands shake slightly, but I wait to pour a glass. She murmurs thanks as she accepts the water.

"If I tell you something, will you promise to keep it just between us?" I ask. If I can't trust my mother, I'm in serious trouble.

She frowns. "What did you do?"

"Mom." The firmness of my tone must change her mind. "Just for now, until I know what to do. Please."

Mom studies me for a moment with those dark, gentle eyes, then nods. "Okay. I promise."

I drag in a deep breath, then release it in a rush. "I went to old St. Louis to find your birth community."

The color drains from her already pale face. "Zephyr!"

"They lied to us, Mom!"

Her hand trembles. She sets the glass on the chairside table. "I wish you hadn't done that. Zephyr—"

"—Are you even listening to me? *There isn't a community!* It's gone, Mom. It's gone." I lean forward, silently pleading for her to understand. I'm not sure even I do yet. "They told us your community was receiving a bounty for your position. I've loaded the goods on the ships myself. But I went to old St. Louis. I found the broken arch and shelter you told me stories about. There had been a fire. Everything inside was destroyed. The only people we encountered were definitely *not* from old St. Louis."

Mom's hands fidget in her lap. Her face grows paler as worry creases her forehead. "Where do you think are the goods going, then?"

I shake my head. That's a good question.

Her chest rises and falls with quick breaths, gaze darting to the darkening sky to her left in some mysterious calculation. Tears well in her eyes and my heart sinks. I rush over and kneel in front of her, taking my mother's clammy hands in my own.

"I'm sorry. I didn't mean to upset—"

"What happened to my brother?" she whispers to herself. Mom shakes out of her inner thoughts and meets my gaze. Tears shimmer in her dark eyes, but they firmly fixate on me. "Baron told me my brother was alive," she says resolutely. "He wouldn't lie to me." Pain etches through every word.

I rub her hands to try warming them. "Maybe he didn't. Mom, it's been years. We don't know where they went, or why they're not around anymore. Maybe there was a fire and they moved shelters. Maybe they moved well before the fire happened."

"You're right, Zephyr," she says, anger blazing in her firm tone. "You can't tell anyone about this until we know more. I will see if I can learn anything more from Baron."

I want to tell her not to do this, but even in her weakened state, she is far more stubborn than I know how to deal with. She touches my cheek tenderly, then raises her trembling body and floats back to her room.

4

GAVIN

The Havenites dock the sailboat using April's Wind Dancing to guild the boat safely into a marina slip. Emil lowers the sails and sets to work making it look like every other boat tethered to the docks—abandoned. A few of the boats slowly sink into the waters or have already capsized. Dani and Drake join me on deck with their packs of scavenged supplies already strapped on their backs. Drake smirks at me as he hops off the boat onto the unstable dock.

I swallow, glancing at the rocking, rusting metal. It might hold his weight, but what about all of us?

"We got a long way to go, Gavin," Drake teases. "Need a hand?"

"I'm fine." I'm not sure why I feel the need to lie to him. Summoning courage, I awkwardly step over the edge of the boat onto the dock to join the others along the shore.

Then we walk. So far. All day. Paige would love the land around the Haven. A dense forest of pine, oak, ash, and maple surround us. The trees glow with autumn colors. Vibrant hues of red, yellow, and orange spotted with the occasional purple tree.

My feet scream at me by the time we arrive. It's going to take a while for the blisters on top of blisters to heal. I don't realize we've reached our destination until Drake leads me through a doorway hidden behind a mess of vines. It's no wonder they stayed out of the Kingdom's sights for so long, buried deep in the woods, off the beaten path, hidden from sight.

The city itself—if I can call it such—is nestled inside a series of hills that roll through the forest. They constructed the Haven entirely underground. That part Paige would hate.

The ground slopes downward from the entrance. Drake leads us on without comment. Lines of lights highlight the path. A few of them have burned out. When I ask Drake in a hushed whisper, he informs me they could not find replacements, and no one has the right gifts to fix them.

Gifts. That's what the Havenites call Powers. Their knowledge of Powers is an almost borderline ritualistic religious reverence.

Without thinking much of it, I extend the tips of my fingers down and reach out with my Mutation Power until I can sense the corrosion in the wires. With a few twitches of my fingers as we go, I create cleaner connections in the wires. Lights flicker on, then remain steady. Drake misses a step, his eyes wide as he glances at the lights, and then at my hand. He raises a brow at me but says nothing about it.

Once we've ventured deep enough, the path opens into a massive underground town square. Off the square, they attached signs to the wall beside doorways. I glance at a few of them as we pass. Medical. Apothecary. Smokehouse. Wood storage. Wares are on display through open doors or glassless windowpanes. What do they use for currency here?

Leading off the square, more tunnels head deeper into the Haven—no doubt to the homes.

In the center of the square, dozens of rustic, handmade tables scatter throughout the open space. String lights illuminate the area. Where they are getting power from, I don't know. It can't be solar, not with them living underground. Maybe I can get Drake to tell me more.

People wearing various handmade, piecemeal clothing occupy the tables. It makes me all too aware of how much my well-crafted Elpis clothing must make me stand out, dirty as it is. Dani and April bid me a quick farewell be for darting off to join people they know. I shift closer to Drake, worried that he, too, will abandon me.

Our arrival catches a lot of attention. Hundreds of sets of eyes lock on me. Despite the warm greeting the Havenites receive upon return, the people eye me warily, instantly marking me out as a stranger and a threat. I want to run and hide.

Emil whispers something to a man in brown robes. Both watch me as they maintain their hushed conversation.

"Drake, you're back!" A girl our age barrels into him, giving Drake a tight hug.

He grins and hugs her back. A flash of jealousy rushes through me. "Hey, Pip."

I adjust my pack on my shoulder, staring at my shoes. Maybe if I don't make eye contact, people will ignore me.

"We were so worried when we heard the Kingdom was prowling for Tributes," Pip says in a rush.

The reminder of my sister makes me flinch. My grip on the strap of my pack tightens and I fight off the wave of grief that rushes through me.

"Who's your new friend?" she asks.

I can feel her eyes weighing me. It makes me even more anxious. I shuffle my feet, wanting to flee but having nowhere to run.

"This is Gavin." Drake pats me on the shoulder. "Gavin, this is my friend Pip."

I offer her a shy smile, but my heart isn't in it. All I can think of is Paige. And the thousands of eyes on me. I want to melt into the floor. But I also don't want to be rude.

Before offering her my hand, I wipe the sweat off on my pants. Her smile is warm and welcoming—much different from everyone else around us.

"Nice to meet you, Pip," I say.

"You made it back just in time for dinner," Pip says, turning her attention to Drake. "I should have known you would."

He grins, running his hand through his dark hair. "You know me." He elbows me in the arm. "Come on. Let's get some food."

I want to ask where I can get some rest, just so I can escape all the people staring at me, but my stomach rumbles loudly as the smell of hearty spices reaches me.

The three of us collect our bowls of stew and bread, then settle at a table. The others already sitting shoot me a curious look but say nothing. It takes great effort to eat around the lump in my throat.

Pip is a curious girl. She asks dozens of questions about home, all of which I carefully answer. Easton seemed to think that telling others too much might be dangerous to the city. The Haven is small by comparison, but who knows how many other communities are out there, let alone ones they have connections with? Until I know more, caution is my ally.

Drake interjects in the conversation a few times. When she asks about his trip, he tells her about their failed attempt to find what they were looking for in old Minneapolis, so they moved downriver to old St. Louis, which was where they met me. I make a mental note of the city names. Maybe if I can map out the old world in relation to this one, Elpis might find more communities like the Haven.

When Pip brings up the Kingdom again, Drake steers the conversation away, watching me from the corner of his eyes. I appreciate his efforts, but I will have no choice but to face the bitter truth. Paige is gone, and I must get her back. Ignoring that won't solve anything, even if the wound is still fresh and very painful.

Emil stops beside me. A hush falls over everyone at our table. "Gavin?"

I set down my spoon and lift my gaze to meet his. My hands are shaking. Hopefully, no one notices.

"The Elders would like to speak with you," Emil says.

So soon? I'm not ready. Suddenly, eating doesn't seem like such a great idea. The stew turns into lead in my gut. I had some time on the boat to consider what I would say to them, but I'm not like Dad. I can write a mean proposal, but when I have to present it, I fall apart from the pressure. What a terrible idea.

Yet what choice do I really have? If I refuse, will they kick me out the door? If they did that, I'm not sure I could find my way back alone. Never mind that I don't know what is out there waiting for me to stumble across it.

Drake shifts to stand. Emil presses a hand down on his shoulder, pinning him to the bench. Instead, Drake slides my nearly empty bowl toward his own. "I'll take care of this for you."

"Thanks," I mumble.

As I rise, my toe catches on the bench. I stumble. Drake catches me with one hand on my chest. I catch myself on his shoulder, and heat rushes to my face, painfully aware of his hand.

Emil leads me through the square. All eyes watch me for sure now. My heart races and my mouth goes dry. I avoid eye contact with anyone, strolling alongside Emil with my gaze fixed on his shoes to predict when we are turning. Sweat prickles my neck. Every part of my body trembles now, making each movement short and jerky.

We turn down another lit tunnel for exactly nineteen steps—along which I count another five lights burned out, but I don't have the courage to focus on fixing them—before Emil walks through an open doorway. I pause at the door and take a moment to collect myself. Confidence. I need to tap into whatever scraps of my dad's confidence I have within me. The fate of the city—and my sister—depend on me.

Squaring my shoulders and raising my chin, I stride into the room.

Five sets of eyes lock on me the moment I step through the doorway. One of the men motions toward the door. For a moment, it confuses me. I glance back, alarmed that I hadn't even noticed the two men guarding the door. They pull two heavy wooden doors closed as they back out, sealing me in the chamber.

Stunning wood panels engraved with elaborate images cover the walls. They fascinate me. I wish I had time to study those images, to learn what they mean to these people, but a soothing male voice calls me to attention.

"Take a seat, please, Gavin," he says. "I'm Charles Garraty, the Minister."

So, he's like my dad, then? This might not be so bad, after all.

He motions down the line, making introductions as he does so. "This is Luke, Julia, Ally, and Carmen."

I lick my lips and step around the only chair facing the five Elders. They remind me of the Council of Representatives. Are they elected officials like our council?

Their chairs have high backs made from wood—like everything in this place seems to be—but each seat has a unique symbol carved in the center of the high back. I may not know what those symbols mean, but I understand they must represent different aspects of life each Elder oversees.

The Minister in the center folds his hands in his lap. I mimic him, hoping it makes me appear as calm as he does. The truth is my hands are sweating profusely and I can't stop them from shaking.

"Emil informs us you are eager to forge an alliance with your own community," the Minister says.

I swallow the lump in my throat and nod. "Yes, sir." Should I wait for them to ask me questions, or launch in some sort of explanation now?

My gaze sweeps along the line of Elders. Three women and two men, all varying ages. I match up the names to the faces for later. I had expected them all to be graying, since they are called Elders, but the young woman, Ally, doesn't look much older than me. Once more, I examine the symbols on their seats. Something about them feels familiar, like I should know what they mean.

"For the moment, we have just a few questions for you," the Minister says. I almost breathe a sigh of relief that I won't have to come up with some way to start this conversation. "Then you will be shown to your quarters."

Once again, I nod, worried that speaking will give my anxiety away.

"You don't appear old enough to be an ambassador for your people," Luke says. His chair bears a teardrop shape housing an eye atop a "t". I know I have seen that somewhere before. Before my mind can muse over where, he asks, "How old are you, Gavin?"

"Nineteen," I say, fighting to keep my voice steady. "Where I come from, we enter the workforce and are considered full adults at seventeen."

"You must be wise to be chosen for this task," Luke says.

Wise... Wait, that's it! The symbol above his head is the ancient Egyptian symbol for wisdom. I read about it in one of Dad's books years ago. Does that mean he has Perfect Memory, like I do? Or is he a Telepath? Does one need a Power to sit on the Elder Council?

"Wisdom and knowledge are two different beasts," I reply. "I'm not sure I would call myself wise as much as knowledgeable."

He glances at the woman, Carmen, beside him. Her seat bears a rolling wave. Naturalist Power?

"That alone is a wise answer," Carmen says. "Emil also mentioned you had three others with you when you met. One of whom was your sister?"

"*Is* my sister," I correct.

Paige is still out there. And I will find her.

But pointing that out at this moment feels like overplaying my intentions too quickly. They also don't know about the other two who weren't with us—Harper and Doctor Adams. For the moment, I will keep them out of this.

"There were four of us in the group he met, yes. Some soldiers took my sister. Olivia left just before the attack. And I don't know what happened to Easton. Hopefully, he escaped with Olivia."

The Minister offers me a sympathetic smile. The crest on his chair is a six-spoked wheel with a six-pointed star in the center.

"We are sorry to hear about your sister," he says. "We have been fortunate enough to avoid the Kingdom for a very long time, but we have heard stories from other communities. No one who leaves with them is ever seen again."

I avert my gaze to my hands as I tighten my grip on my lap. Empty hands. A dull ache presses into my chest. "I cannot allow myself to believe that."

"So say all who suffer these circumstances," Luke says sadly.

The words draw my gaze back up to them sharply. The ache bursts into a fire. They want me to give up on Paige. I won't. I *never* will.

"I appreciate the sentiment, but the Kingdom has not met my family." The heat in my belly burns in my voice, daring them to challenge me. "Historically speaking, absolutist monarchies all suffer the same fate in the end."

"And what fate would that be?" Ally asks. Her symbol looks like an anvil.

I set my jaw, exuding a calm focus. "Insurrection."

This draws scattered amusement from all five. It infuriates me, but then I realize why they are so amused. They think *I* intend to oppose the Kingdom. I'm not that foolish.

"I would like to focus on why I'm here. Not why my sister isn't."

The last woman, Julia, finally breaks her studious silence. Her symbol is a rod and a serpent. *Medical?* She leans forward in her seat, fingers steepled together as she meets my gaze. "Why *are* you here, then, Gavin?"

"The Minister of my community put our group together and sent us out for two reasons," I say, gaining confidence as I speak. "One is to learn whether we can begin restoring the world broken by war and Powers, and the other is to prove, beyond a doubt, that we are not alone. Our own council is prepared to take the first steps toward building a new global economy by establishing alliances with communities like yours."

"And what will they expect from us in exchange?" Carmen asks.

"I, uh..." This is a question I should have been prepared for, but our first mission for Project Restoration was not meant to establish these connections as much as determine if there *were* other people out in the world. They did not brief us about this.

Something I overheard Dad say years ago surfaces and before I can stop myself, I spout it out. "The only way we can fix the world and truly rebuild is together. The resources and Powers we have could provide the groundwork for a stronger, unified world. To do that, we need to find a common ground, some means of peace that benefits everyone. And—"

"Hold on, boy," Luke says, holding out a hand. My jaw snaps shut. "What kind of resources and Powers are you talking about?"

I work my jaw, trying to figure out how to answer that. Did I say too much already? "You *do* have Powers here. Emil and Drake and the girls—"

"You want to take them from us?" he snaps.

"No, no!" I backpedal. "That's not what I mean. I just mean—"

"Emil told us what you did with your gifts," Ally says. "It was some magnificent display, from what he says."

"It was a fluke." But they don't seem to hear me. Or maybe they don't believe me.

"How many others like you are there in your community?" Carmen asks. So much for getting to these details later.

"We could really use more people with gifts," Luke says to Carmen beside him. "We don't have enough to carry the load any longer. If they will trade people, we might work something out."

People? This stuns me into silence. My jaw slackens as I fumble for some response. They seem content to forget I'm in the room as they continue their conversation. My gaze bounces back and forth as they debate the merits of "acquiring" a few of our most powerful people for several minutes. But the *way* they say it harkens more to slavery than any sort of peaceful unity.

"Excuse me," I raise my voice above the din, firm like Dad when he commands a room. "People are not goods to be traded. What makes you any better than the Kingdom?"

All eyes fall on me. Their anger burns into me as surely as my own. I rise from my seat, hands balled into fists at my sides.

Before they can speak, I barrel on. "You are talking about my people like they're commodities. How do you think those leaders in the Kingdom talk about you? Stealing your children and women, forcing them to serve. That is exactly what you are talking about doing to my people right now! I may not always be able to tell when I've made mistakes or when people are angry with me, but I *always* know how I should treat them."

"We will continue this conversation at a later date," the Minister says dismissively.

The doors open, as if aware that the meeting is over. Emil strolls in.

"Emil will show you to your quarters," the Minister says. His gentle gaze turns to Emil and hardens. "He is not to go outside the Haven without permission."

Emil takes my arm, pulling me toward the door.

I jerk it free. "So now I'm a prisoner?"

"No, Gavin, you're our guest," the Minister says coldly. "It is wise of you to remember that."

Emil moves closer and takes my arm again, leaning toward my ear. "Stop," he hisses under his breath.

I let him guide me toward the door. *Guest. What a joke.* If they think they can stop me from leaving, they will learn their mistake.

Emil directs me firmly away from the Elders' council chamber and down a series of winding hallways. Resisting is pointless. Where would I even go?

"You can let go of my arm now," I snap.

Emil drops his grip. I adjust the strap of my pack on my shoulder. The contents of the bag aren't much, and certainly won't help me in this place. But they are the last pieces of home I have to work with. They are now my most prized possessions.

As we reach an empty hallway, Emil steps closer. I edge away.

"Whatever you do, Gavin, don't fight the Elders," Emil says under his breath. His dark eyes dart around the hallway as if worried someone will overhear him. "I've been down your road before. I tried leaving to look for my sister. Do you know what they did?"

I shake my head. How could I know?

"They locked me up in the temple with the young acolytes until I saw reason." He shudders at the memory. "Stay away from that place as long as you can manage."

"How long did they lock you in there?" I ask, keeping my voice just as low as Emil's. He's being cautious. I will as well.

"Two years."

I stumble over my own feet for a few steps. When I right myself, my eyes widen. "*What?!*"

Emil glances around again. "It was another five years before they would let me out the Haven doors. If you want to get out of here any time soon to find your sister, I suggest you play their game."

My stomach sinks like lead. *Seven years* before he was allowed outside the Haven? No wonder he never found his sister again.

"How close to the island have you gotten before?" I ask.

If there is even a chance I might get to Paige, I need data.

Emil grimaces. "They have soldiers all around the waterways and bordering the nearest part of the mainland to the island. Even if you made it to the water, the soldier stations on the mainland would catch you long before you reached her."

Not an answer to my question, but still good information to store for later. If they control the waterways, then commandeering a ship and sailing there isn't likely to work. But turning myself over to the soldiers might get me closer.

First things first... I need to infiltrate the Haven society, then gather at least a few people to help me on my mission to rescue Paige. Someone who knows how to sail will be critical. I eye Emil, chewing my lower lip. Maybe I can convince him to take me if he thinks he can find his sister there. Where else would she be but on the island?

I also came here on a mission: to establish peaceful relations between Elpis and the Haven. If it is even slightly possible, I can't overlook the chance to run off and rescue my sister. Drake insisted Paige would be safe on the island as a Tribute for now. I need to believe that.

Emil knocks on a door.

It opens and a kindly woman with a warm smile greets us. "Emil! We are so glad to have you back. Elder Ally worried you tangled with the Kingdom."

He grimaces, then nods at me. "This is Gavin."

"Of course!" She opens the door wider, motioning me inside. "We are thrilled to share our spare bedroom with you, Gavin."

My chambers are not my own. Emil casts me a warning glance before bidding us farewell and stomping away. The message is obvious. I am being watched.

The main living space is wide open and comfortable. A functional kitchen to one side. A gray sectional sofa and wooden coffee table occupy the main space. Concrete walls match the sofa. A plush teal rug covers the living room floor. The space is inviting and homey. But it's nothing like my home.

Pip bounces out of a room. When she sees me, her face lights up. "He's here!" She rushes over, taking my hand and pulling me toward a room. "I'll show you to your room. Come on."

I have little choice but to come along. "You live here?"

She nods, stabbing a finger at the door of the room she just bounced out from. "That's my room there. My parents are across the living room." She nods at a mostly closed door across the living space. "We even have a private bathroom. Few homes have that."

We step into the bedroom. It's small, but functional. A full-size bed, closet, desk. The bag slides off my shoulder onto the desk. This space will have to do. I have little choice.

It's this or being a prisoner in the temple with the acolytes.

Though this room feels just like a prison, though.

5

Paige

THE PHYSICIAN CLAIMS ONE bedroom on the second floor so that he can use the outer room as a waiting room. Alice is the first to enter. After showering and running a brush through her hair, the natural luster of Alice's creamy skin rises to the surface. I hadn't realized how much dirt was on her skin until she cleaned herself up. She's even prettier than I thought.

As she shuffles into the bedroom on shaking legs, Holly and I wait together in the sitting room. Much like Alice, the shower and a good night of sleep did Holly some good. But the deep sadness in her eyes is hard to miss. Holly misses her boyfriend.

Not that she will talk to me about anything. I try to engage her in conversation as we wait together, but she averts her gaze and clamps her lips tight each time.

"What have I done to upset you, Holly?" I ask. I need someone to befriend in this strange place. Before the mutiny, we were getting along wonderfully—her heartbroken sorrow aside.

Her knees bounce. She taps her fingers on the arm of the chair, gaze fixed on the closed bedroom door.

I sigh. "Whatever it was, I'm sorry."

"I don't think you are," she murmurs.

I flinch. "What?"

For the first time, she looks at me. Really *looks* at me. And it isn't anger or resentment in her gaze. It's terror. She fears me.

"Is this about what happened with the mutineers?" I ask. Not that I fully recall what happened.

She licks her lips, opens her mouth, then snaps it shut again as the door to the bedroom opens.

Alice marches out, significantly paler and seeming much more uncomfortable than she had been when she entered the room.

"Holly..." I lamely attempt to call the girl back, but she is already marching into the bedroom.

"I would like to go next," she says.

The door closes, leaving me alone and dumbfounded.

Holly just went in to avoid speaking to me. I don't understand. What did I do?

"Alice, do you—?"

"I don't wanna talk," she whimpers as she rushes down the steps to her room. A moment later, her door slams shut.

Waiting alone is long and cruel. I fidget, rise and pace, then sit again. I've had regular doctor exams over the years. No big deal. Part of my job requires me to see a physician regularly to ensure my health.

But hearing the occasional whimpers of Holly from the bedroom has me wondering if this is a normal exam. Or maybe it is. The other girls have probably never seen a doctor before. They don't know what to expect. This is all old hat for me.

It seems an insanely long time before the door opens and Holly waddles out. Much like Alice, she rushes through the waiting room, pale, trembling, and tear streaked.

I enter the bedroom, glancing back over my shoulder. What don't I know about this exam?

"There's a gown for you to wear on the bed," the physician says, his back to me as he makes notes on a tablet. It's the first piece of modern technology I've seen since arriving—electricity aside.

I wish now that I had worn a dress. He clearly expects me to change with him in the room. Even if he isn't looking, I would rather do this privately. I could at least slide a dress off under the gown. I work quickly out of my pajamas and slip the gown on.

"Underwear as well," he says, still not looking at me.

My heart skips. "Why?"

He pauses and turns to me. There is no malice or anger in his eyes, though I note a hint of frustration. "Do as you are told, Lady Paige."

My jaw twitches. "Turn around again."

He rolls his eyes but obliges.

I quickly shimmy out of the underwear. Gripping the gown closed at the back, I sit on the edge of the bed.

The doctor rises from his seat.

The first part of the exam is normal. Blood pressure. Heart and lung check. During the reaction test, I accidentally punch him in the face. I slap my hands over my mouth.

"I'm so sorry! I didn't mean to. It's part of my Muscle Memory."

He raises his brows, probing tenderly at his face. "Not bleeding. I'll live. Lie back on the bed, please."

I flush a deep shade of crimson. Holly and Alice's reactions as they left the room make much more sense now. They have probably never had such a procedure. Still, I can't help asking the dumb question. "Why?"

"To become a Tribute, you must pass a fertility test," he explains. "It would do the King little good to choose a wife who cannot bear his children."

I don't want to do this. I know what it means. I had to have a similar exam before being given birth control. The test is uncomfortable and very invasive. Will he be able to tell I am on birth control?

Taking a deep breath, I remember what Easton said. Play along. Find a way out of this. Both of our fates are in my hands. This isn't anything I haven't done before.

I do as he commands and close my eyes. I would rather not see what happens as he prods in places I don't let anyone prod. Even with experience in this sort of thing, it's uncomfortable.

"You can relax, Lady Paige," he says at long last. "You did wonderfully."

I try to relax, but the ache between my legs won't let me. And the fear that he will either think I'm infertile or will know I'm on birth control overwhelms me. I can't let it stop me from getting closer to the King.

"Um, not sure if it shows on your tests, but I have a birth control insert," I tell him.

He pulls his gloves off and tosses them in a trashcan beside the bed. "Is that so? How?"

I swallow. How do I explain to him we are way more advanced than the Kingdom without giving anything away? "It's not really common." Except that it is. "They gave it to me when I left the community."

He narrows his eyes. It's only partly a lie. Can he tell? Does he have a Power? I would guess it's Divinic Healing Power if he is a doctor. "Can it be removed?"

"Yes."

"Do you know how?"

I bite my lip. There is only one way I know to get it out, and it isn't fun. "Yes."

He nods once. "I will make a note of it, then. We can follow up later if it becomes necessary."

The implication of that statement is clear enough. If the King doesn't choose me, it won't matter, anyway.

He turns back to his medical bag and pulls out a set of vials. I know without asking what comes next, and panic grips me.

"You aren't drawing my blood," I say, shuffling off the far side of the bed. I press my back to the wall. How far can I get before he catches me?

"Then you can stay here in the cottage until the royal family decides what to do with you."

Would they let me go home? Not likely. "Why do you need it?" My heart races. Dad has been very explicit that we should allow no one to take our blood without his permission.

My brother and I are not like others. Our blood, our very DNA, is unique. If anyone learned what we carry within us, we could be hunted, used for experiments, or worse. Dad is Powerless, but he carries the potential to produce offspring that can control not only one Power, but many. Perhaps all of them. While I only ended up with Muscle Memory, the potential to carry those genetics remains in my DNA just as surely as it's in Dad's.

Allowing that sort of Power to fall into the Kingdom's hands feels like the worst idea of the century.

"For the same reasons we check for fertility. Diseases and genetic illnesses are unworthy of our king. Now, please take a seat, Lady Paige."

Genetic... No. I can't let them see my genetic makeup. Dad was explicit about this. I dash for the door as the doctor approaches me with the equipment.

Before I make it to the top of the stairs, a set of guards cut me off. *Where did they come from?*

The window. I can use the window in the nearby room to jump out and escape. I don't know where I will go, but I can't let them take my blood.

I pivot as a hand grasps my arm. I twist the arm away in a reflexive breakaway move and run, no longer caring that the back of my gown flaps open.

In the other second-floor bedroom, I snatch a trinket off the dresser and hurl it at the window to break the glass. There won't be time to open it.

"Stop her!" the physician shouts.

The trinket halts in the air, then thumps to the floor. *Telekinetic!* I should have known.

"Use this," the physician instructs.

Before I can take another step, my body floats into the air, then slams down on the mattress. The bedframe cracks but doesn't break. Two guards have turned into six, all pinning me down as I struggle to break free from their grip. My efforts, while valiant, are pointless. Whenever I buck one or two off, the others just take their place.

Something plunges into my neck.

I slump, fighting off sleep.
They tranquilized me.
I'm powerless to stop the drug.

WHEN I WAKE, IT takes a moment to remember where I am. A bandage covers the pinprick where they took my blood. I am on my bed in my room, tucked under the blankets. Tears well in my eyes. The one thing Dad has always warned me never to allow, and I was powerless to stop them.

How long before they learn the truth?

My stomach grumbles, so I make my way to the kitchen. The rest of the girls all sit in the parlor, chatting with one another. I grab an apple and a blueberry muffin from the counter, then wander into the room to join them.

Layla seems to have positioned herself as the ringleader of this group. As I settle in a chair, Layla offers me a smile that's far too sweet to be sincere.

"About time you woke up," she says. "What did you do, anyway? It was quite alarming to have so many guards storming this place."

I subconsciously rub at the bandage in the crook of my arm. "I don't like needles." There's no way I'm telling these vultures the truth.

River and Summer sit together on the sofa, eyeing Layla. I can tell the two of them don't care for her, but they don't say anything either. Ivy stares at the floor, lost in her own thoughts. Her skin seems...clammy. It's hard to tell with her darker complexion, but she almost looks ill. No one else sits anywhere near her, either. January studies me curiously. I'm not sure what to make of her. She's hot and cold on a whim.

"Where are Holly and Alice?" I ask, scanning the open space.

"Still in their room." River glances at the door across the hall from my own.

I suppose I can't blame them. The procedure is uncomfortable even when you're prepared for it.

Layla is happy to change the subject to revolve around herself. I munch on my apple and muffin without comment. She seems the sort of girl who puts herself in a position to win. Does that mean she *wants* to marry their king? She can have him.

They talk about home, but I can't handle thinking about Gavin or my parents. They must be beside themselves with worry. I finish my meager meal in silence, then slink away before they can ask me questions.

Gavin would already know what to do in this situation. He would have information and a plan. I could use his big brain. Thinking of my brother sends another wave of sorrow through me. What is he doing now? Has he returned home to tell Mom and Dad the bad news? I'm worried about his mental state. Gavin doesn't handle stress very well.

Without my brother, I feel adrift. It hadn't really occurred to me until I lie in bed that, until being kidnapped by the Kingdom, I have never spent a day away from my brother. I depend on him far more than I knew.

Now I'm lost at sea without my life preserver.

Agony grips me, and I cry myself to sleep, thinking about Gavin.

And I dream of a sea of stars. One pulses, drawing me closer. I reach out, hold the star in the palm of my hand, then see my brother. He sits in his bedroom back in Elpis, head in his hands. I approach, sliding my arm around his shoulders. The move is just as comforting to me as it is for him.

Gavin peers up at me from reddened eyes. "Paige?"

"I miss your stupid face," I say.

Gavin throws his arms around me, and the hug feels so real. I cling to him, to the feel of this moment, wanting to seal it away in my heart for my waking moments.

"I've been so worried about you," he cries into my shoulder.

I rub his back. "And I you. But this is a dream. It isn't real."

He pulls back, frowning and wiping tears from his eyes. "Does that mean you're not real?"

The smile I offer him holds no reassurance. "This is my dream. You are the one who isn't real."

He shakes his head. "No. This is my dream. I missed home, and I wanted to see you and Dad and Mom. When I fell asleep, I was here. With you."

The words sound so sincere but make no sense. I wanted to see him when I fell asleep. Remembering my dreams of Zephyr before I even met him, I wonder if I've had Dreaming Powers for years and never knew it. That could explain my insomnia issues.

The dream fades. Our time is up. "I love you, Gavin. I will find my way home again."

6

ZEPHYR

THE ENTIRE REASON I left on a mission to gather Tributes is because of Cypress. And the death of my father and eldest half-brother in a rockslide. While I don't mourn the loss of a father who never loved me, I wonder why Cypress is in such a hurry to marry, just like he was in a hurry to take the crown.

The swift coronation left me feeling unsettled. Pair that with a swift Tribute season, and I can't help feeling like something is going on that I don't understand. Elena all but pushed that crown on Cypress' head on the Day of Mourning as everyone came to pay respects to my father. Is she the one responsible for Cypress pushing for early Tributes?

I had asked Dominic if it was normal—before leaving on my Tribute quest—and he shook his head. His job as Keeper of Tides is to ensure the continuity of knowledge and our history, as well as serving the King. Dominic is married to his position. He even served Dad for a short while. I think it was part of the reason the two of them bonded so tightly together.

Dominic had informed me that only once in the Kingdom's history had a Tribute season been called early, after the very first crown prince died almost a hundred years ago. The new crown prince had wanted a wife quickly since there were no more suitable heirs. And only once had a king been crowned so quickly.

Right before a war against some of the heathen mainlanders.

But we have no one to go to war against. Unless they now know the location of the Haven and are preparing for a spring invasion. As Captain of Tides, I would think I would be part of that conversation.

Yet without the haste, I never would have learned about old St. Louis or met Paige.

These events clash with one another for control in my reeling mind as I pace the parlor in my fourth-floor palace suite. The waiting is getting unnerving.

Shortly after breakfast, Baron arrives with Dominic. I have to retell the entire story of my journey for Dominic's benefit.

I relay detailed accounts of the battle in old St. Louis repeatedly. Dominic picks apart the story with questions, asking for details I don't even know. Did the weather change during the battle? What caused the earthquake? How did the men get swallowed up by the earth?

I suspect Paige is at fault for some of what happened to our men—aside from those she killed with her gun—but I don't want to tell Dominic the truth. Something is going on in the palace and someone in my family must know the truth. Sadly, I don't know who to trust. I can trust Dominic. He's too softhearted to plot anything. But that also means he is soft enough to tell his mother or Cypress the truth if I give too many details. Which I can't risk right now.

Baron launches into a lecture on why princes are not allowed to return to their mother's communities. But I've never considered myself a prince. Nor would anyone else in the family.

The apologetic look on Dominic's face as he explains what happened last time a prince did return—he was killed—rings false. Did that prince *really* die? Or maybe he just chose not to return. Not that I would understand that choice, either. As much as I hate certain aspects of life in the palace, I do like the security living on this island provides.

"I just don't see what the big deal is," I say, throwing up my hands. "I was curious. I came home."

"With only a fraction of the men you left with," Baron snaps.

"It had nothing to do with my—"

"This is over, Zephyr!" Baron roars. "I have gone out of my way to protect you, and you repeatedly get yourself into these situations. I can't do this forever."

"I never asked you to."

His lips thin. He gives a tight nod. "That's true. You didn't." For a quick second, his gaze flicks to my mother's closed door.

I sense his anger. Not like normal anger. Baron's anger is a hammer of his magic against me. His Atmospheric magic works amazingly on open waters, but there in the palace it serves little good.

No doubt Mother's listening to every word, but she wouldn't dare emerge under these circumstances. Nor do I want her to. Did *she* ask Baron to protect me?

"You are lucky, boy," Baron hisses, edging toward me.

I flinch back. His movements remind me too much of my father, and I don't like that look in his eyes. Nor the insistent press of his magic against my own.

"I convinced your brother your acts weren't treason, but simply you being...*you*."

Again, I flinch. What does *that* mean?

"Bringing that Paige girl here as Tribute eased some of his tension. He is looking forward to the assessments in two weeks."

Dominic's gaze flicks to Baron for a moment, as if surprised the assessments will happen so soon.

"We agreed on one thing." Baron stops so close it takes everything in me not to retreat. If he punched me now, I could never stop him. "You will take a week of leave from service."

A week? What will I do with myself for a week? My gaze flicks to the wet bar.

"Wait, what about Easton?" I ask.

Baron bares his teeth and marches toward the door. "What about him?"

"I assume we will question him about their community," I say. "I want to be there."

Baron pauses at the door, glaring at me. "No."

"But—"

"Thank your lucky stars you aren't facing punishment right now, Zephyr! You will have nothing to do with the questioning of that recruit. And you will not step foot in that cottage to talk to any of the girls."

Baron jerks the door open.

I rush toward him. "I know things that might be helpful during questioning."

"I think we can handle him without you." Baron stomps out and slams the door shut behind him.

I spin on my heel, throwing my hands in the air. "Thanks for the help, Dom."

Dominic flinches, sinking down on the sofa. "I don't understand why you're mad at me. Zeph, he's right. You are lucky that Cy wasn't mad. He thought your rebellion was amusing. But Mom... She and Baron went rounds with one another last night and again this morning. You may not see it, but he really is trying to help you."

"He has a funny way of showing it." I stride toward the wet bar to pour a glass of whiskey. I need a potent drink.

"Don't do that." His tone isn't sharp. He sounds more worried than anything.

I glance back, glass in hand. Dominic eyes the glass with desperate pleading in his eyes. And sorrow.

"What else is there to do? I've just been told to sit around and do nothing for a week."

Dominic rises and glides toward me. His movements are so smooth I don't even notice him take the glass from my hand until it's gone.

"No. He gave you a week off to do whatever you want. Spend time with your mom. Go into town. Meet some girls." Envy flashes in his blue eyes. I feel sorry for my brother. He is married to his job, forbidden to have a wife. "Get a new suit. Do something *fun*."

I stab a finger at the glass. "I'm trying."

"*This* isn't fun." He pours it into the sink. "It's a heavy blanket that's slowly smothering you." Dominic pats my shoulder. "Take care of yourself, Zeph. I need you."

He needs me. As if I'm not standing right here. What does he think I'll do if I drink?

But those big, puppy-dog eyes soften my heart. My shoulders slump and I heave out a sigh.

Maybe Dominic has a point. I can't work as usual, but I can try finding answers to my questions.

And I have so many questions.

7

GAVIN

Pip takes me under her wing. Her name is short for Pip-pen—a family name, she tells me. Over the next several days, she helps me get better acquainted with life here in the Haven. Her bubbly personality is infectious. Despite my best efforts to remain guarded about whom I trust, Pip quickly wears me down.

The Haven is much larger than I expected. The engineering set up to operate the entire underground community had to be created using Powers. Pip shows me the air filtration system, a complex series of turbines that pull fresh air from outside, filter it through purifiers, and pump it throughout the Haven. Above ground, they hide the ducts that pull in the fresh air and push out the old air inside hollowed-out trees.

While we are in the maintenance room, a crew of men and women work to fix one of the broken duct turbines. A piece from the engine has corroded and broken, and they don't have a replacement. I listen to them argue about alternatives to fix the engine. Without that engine, a whole series of homes are without fresh air. I step toward them, but Pip takes my arm and pulls me back.

"Don't interrupt."

"I can help." I gently shake her off and stroll toward the crew, hands deep in my pockets. They glance at me, irritated by the interruption. "Can I take a look?"

They exchange uneasy glances, but nod. I peek my head in the gap they had been using for access. The output shaft crumbled to pieces—old and in need of replacement long ago.

"What do you have to spare?" I ask, still studying the complex machine. With my Matter Creation and Mutation Powers, I can easily identify the mechanisms of the machine. It's as natural to me as the nerve endings under my skin.

"Just more broken parts," the foreman says. He nudges a box of parts toward me.

I pull back, crouching in front of the box and flicking a finger through it until I find an old steel pipe with a hairline crack down the side. I slide my hand over it, pulling the molecules back together around the facture.

"'That's broken," the foreman says.

"Is it?" I hold it up for him to see the fracture gone.

The entire crew leans closer, eyes wide in shock.

Before they can stop me, I reach into the turbine casing and use my Powers to pull the pieces apart harmlessly. Then I slip the replacement piece into place and stitch everything back together. For good measure, I give it a little jolt of electricity to kick it into gear.

The turbine hums. The crew shuffles backward. Pip's jaw hangs slack as she gapes at me.

I wipe my hands with a towel and shrug. That was simple compared to some of the other mechanical work I've done, but I don't tell them as much.

The foreman stutters his thanks, dumbfounded. I dip my head and allow Pip to guide me away.

"That was amazing," she breathes, glancing back as we round the corner.

"It was nothing."

Pip drops the subject and continues with the tour.

The water comes from a treatment plant that resembles the Greenhouse water treatment center so much the same person could have designed it. It pulls water from a reservoir above ground, filters it through the massive tanks, and sends it through the pipes inside the Haven walls.

But when she shows me the tanks, something sickening crawls over my skin. Not literally. It's more like a sludge that makes my stomach twist. I saunter toward tanks and the sensation intensifies.

I slide my hand along a tank until I can't stomach the feeling any longer. My hand stops right over the filters. Biting my lip, I pull the filter out and peer at it closely. "When's the last time they replaced these?"

"Ten years ago."

Ten years? "Pip, this water may not be safe."

"We don't know what else to do. Either we use the old filters and hope they hold out a little longer, or we remove them and know there's nothing we can do to treat the water." She shrugs. "Dad says they have no choice."

I close my eyes, sensing the decade of sludge built up over the filter's carbon granules. It requires a bit of concentration to remove such microscopic bits of contamination. My stomach churns with acid. Then I pull the contaminates out of the filter cartridge in a long chain.

Pip blanches. "Gross!"

"That's in your water." I look around for somewhere to drop it and find a bucket nearby. Then I replace the filter.

By the time I've replaced the tenth cartridge, I've gathered a small audience from the water treatment workers. The bucket emits a rancid scent of rot. I nudge it when I finish.

"Please have someone dispose of that. Don't burn it or let it get back into the water."

The workers murmur to one another as Pip and I leave. Before I wash my hands, I run the water for several minutes just to be sure the old, nasty contaminated water has flushed from the pipes.

We tour the living quarters of the Havenites. The original section of the Haven—the area founded by the Prophet—was created over a hundred years ago with impressive Powers. It's the reason they can have such massive chambers without supports. The Powers reinforced the ceilings. Not that Pip understands this. To her, what the Prophet and his original acolytes did to create the Haven was miraculous. But I can see the bonds with my Powers.

"Without the Prophet, none of us would have survived," she explains as we walk the residential halls. "The original Havenites chosen by the Prophet had no gifts. He brought them together here and promised that one day we could emerge into a new world."

Her religious zeal makes me uncomfortable, but I don't interrupt her.

They assign the homes based on class and family size, according to Pip. While radioactivity had been dangerous a century ago, it no longer seemed that way. So why not just return to the surface?

I suppose if you establish a society like this one, leaving it behind would be hard. Even if the surface is safe. But they could still expand above ground. *And risk the Kingdom discovering them.*

They created most of the homes in the residential sector based on need as time passed. The Builders worked in coordination with the Elder of Expansion and the Minister to develop using gifts.

"But we don't really have anyone able to complete the work any longer," Pip says solemnly. "We haven't had any new Builders in a couple generations and things are getting crowded. That's why you are staying with my family. There wasn't anywhere else for you to go."

"How many Elders are there in total?" I ask.

"Five. There used to be seven, but we don't have anyone to fill those other two positions right now. It requires the right gift to hold the spot." Her bright eyes sweep me up and down. "Maybe you could become an Elder. I've watched you do some pretty amazing stuff lately. And Drake told me what you did in old St. Louis. You could be the new Elder of Expansion."

The prospect sends the gears in my head spinning. While the last thing I want is to lead in this place, such a position might help me expand the Haven toward Elpis. It might open that door if I can't find another way.

"How does one become an Elder?"

Pip shrugs. "Not really sure. They keep their selection process to themselves. I'm sure if you approached an elder with actual interest, he or she might share more with you."

Somehow, I doubt that is the case. First, I need to earn their trust. The Elders made it clear they don't know if they trust me. Without that, there is no way they will even consider me for the position.

"Is there anyone in charge of the Elder council?"

"Usually the Minister." Pip pauses outside the door to her family home, staring up at me through long lashes. "At least, that's how it's been since the death of the Prophet."

Their religious order runs this entire society. That does nothing to settle my unease.

Pip offers me a shy smile, then slips inside. I follow, wishing I could see Drake. I wonder what he is up to.

We settle into the sectional. Pip curls her legs under her and turns sideways to face me, launching into an explanation of how the Haven society runs.

Everyone has a job, most of which involve finding or making the most of the resources. The Guardian Elder runs Guardian rotations. It seems to be their version of the military. The Education Elder selects teachers to run their schooling system. I assume this must be Luke. He also handles job placement alongside the Minister, since they don't currently have an Organization Elder.

They send those who have the gifts to heal straight to medical training, overseen by Elder Julia.

"The Minister chooses his own acolytes to help carry on the future of the Haven and spread the teachings in the *Book of the Prophet*," Pip says. Sadness weighs down on her as she picks at the sleeve of her shirt.

Despite wanting to ask why this upsets her, I hold my tongue. Maybe I'm reading her wrong.

I quickly discern that the best positions are for the elite members of the community who receive the better job placement. And those elite members often pass those jobs down to their children. It hardly seems like an equal or fair system.

I lounge back, hands folded behind my head. "How many people here have gifts?"

"Not enough." She shrugs. "It's always been that way, though. The Elders have been trying to figure out a way to increase the numbers, but it's hard when we're restricted by the space available. There's no way to know until we reach puberty. Another giftless mouth to feed and house could risk crowding."

The implication of her words comes across clearly. With limited space, the Elders have no choice but to restrict the population. Which means imposing birth limits.

"Are there limits for each family on childbearing?" I ask, already knowing the answer.

Pip shakes her hand in a so-so motion. "There are limits, but not per family. A couple who want to have a child has to petition the Elders. Then current resources are reviewed before a decision is given."

"What happens if there is an accidental pregnancy?" I can't help my curious mind. "If there aren't resources and an accidental pregnancy happens, how would they deal with it?"

Pip flushes, averting her gaze. What is that reaction about? "Relations before marriage are forbidden. Once a couple is married, we put them on an herbal remedy that prevents conception."

I blink. That hardly ensures no accidents happen. What kind of accountability do they have in place to prevent couples from "forgetting" to take their remedy? A desperate couple might take the risk.

"So there has never been an unapproved birth?"

Her eyes widen and she shakes her head, as if scandalized by the very idea.

But I find it impossible to believe that, in over a century, there hasn't been a single accidental conception. So how is it covered up? Do they gain approval in retrospect? That wouldn't make sense either. Desperate couples would just ask forgiveness instead of permission.

"How do they handle it where you come from?" Pip asks.

"We don't have to worry about it." Though only five years ago my dad had worried that it would be necessary when the Greenhouse suffered a near-catastrophic crop failure.

"Not at all?" The very idea of free birth stiffens her spine. Her bright eyes peer deep into my own as if seeking some lie.

"No. Boys and girls can get birth control implants when they are fifteen. That prevents anything unexpected. But it's optional and removable whenever." Getting an implant had never made sense to me. The chances of getting anyone pregnant are zero. Not unless men can suddenly conceive.

Pip glances past me toward the entrance to the home, then leans closer and lowers her voice as if worried someone is listening. "Does that mean where you come from people don't have to wait for marriage? Do you have the implant?"

"No. On both counts." I rise, uncomfortable with where this conversation is headed. "I think I'll get some rest. Thanks for showing me around."

Pip jumps to her feet and follows me as far as my door, where she freezes. Her cheeks burn red. "Rest well, Gavin."

I return the sentiment, perplexed by her embarrassment. Was she ashamed that she asked at all?

Curling my fingers around the comforter, I pull it tight over me and close my eyes, willing myself to sleep, thinking of home, of my parents and sister.

8

PAIGE

THE DAYS COOPED UP in the cottage are so painfully long. The girls are getting snippy with one another, forming factions. Were it not for the access to the porch over the steeply sloped lawn in front of the cottage, my claustrophobia would have crushed me long ago. It's my sanctuary.

River and Summer share a room and spend more time in it than out of it. When they emerge, they whisper to one another as if none of the rest of us can hear. Their interest in this king is minimal. They spend more time making fun of the idea of a king and badmouthing him when they think no one is listening than they spend doing anything else around us. I wouldn't call myself a fan of these tactics for Tributes, but I'm not sure how they can badmouth someone they don't know. Aside from the whole kidnapping thing—which is no small thing, to be fair.

Layla and January have both attempted asserting their dominance as the alpha of the group. It's increasingly apparent that these two girls might be the only ones genuinely interested in this entire pageant. It's hard to tell with January, though. Some days, she doubts whether the King is worth all of this. Other days, she and Layla all but pull each other's hair out over the very idea of being queen. Their behavior is pathological.

Holly spends a lot of time disinterested in everything. She's been throwing up a lot lately, which causes the other girls to give her space. No one wants to risk getting sick right now.

Sometimes they talk to one another. Sometimes they just sit in amicable silence. Ivy often rolls her eyes at Layla or January, but she is also one of the first to offer agreement with either of them.

Alice gravitates around Layla. All the time. I liked Alice well enough at first, but she's diving me crazy.

I'm not sure how much longer I can spend cooped up in this cottage with the girls. They post guards everywhere around the cottage day and night. We can use the porch, but that's the extent of our outdoor recreational space.

The other girls slowly distance themselves from me. I didn't notice it at first. Alice and Holly maintain their distance and say very little that isn't necessary. But they have been whispering to the others. And whatever they are saying is turning the other girls against me. The only time the girls ever want to talk to me is when they need me to break a tie to settle an argument.

To my surprise, the girls' treatment makes me miss Easton even more. His snide comments were clearly a cover for feelings he wanted to hide. Not that I'm even sure if I share those same feelings for him. Kissing him felt nice, but I now know it was more of a desperate act for connection than genuine desire. What I wouldn't give for a snarky comment about my father. Or Easton's comforting hand over mine.

I dreamed of kissing him again tonight. It hadn't been passionate. In fact, it felt forced, like I was supposed to want it even when I didn't. The dream is so vivid, so real. Just like the dream I had where I talked to Gavin in his room at home. When I wake up, tears roll down my cheeks and into my pillow.

I'm surrounded by people and feel utterly alone.

I roll over and watch January sleep for a moment to convince myself she really is out. I need to get out of here, even if only for a night. Maybe I can use my training and skills to sneak into the fort and find Easton. There's no way I will get back to sleep. Insomnia has taken hold.

After sliding my feet into my boots, I tiptoe to the door and slip out as quietly as possible.

The main door is locked from the outside. I've tried it before. There are guards posted by it.

The porch door is unlocked, though. I've been on the porch several times this past week just to escape the bickering inside and keep the cottage walls from crushing me. The hill below the porch gently slopes downward, but not so much that I can't manage catching my balance if I lose my footing. A tiny yard with white furniture rests on the slope beside the porch.

I slide my arms into the thick down coat I found in the closet and ease the porch door open, then close it silently behind me.

Cold air hits my lungs. My breath rolls out in waves and my cheeks sting. But I revel in it all. This is freedom.

Near the side of the cottage, the porch opens onto the sloped lawn. After a quick glance around, I edge out onto the dead, frozen grass. It crunches under my boots and I wince.

A few more steps, and I should be able to slip through the trees undetected. If I can just make it to the street, no one will know it's me. As long as I'm back in before the sun rises.

I duck low to the railing, hoping to use it for cover as I make my way down the slope.

"Stop right there!" a stern male voice calls out from only a few feet to my right.

I freeze, eyeing him.

He stands in the shadows beneath the porch, along the sloping hillside. A clever place to keep watch out of sight and away from the wind.

"Lady Paige, you shouldn't be this far out. Go back into the cottage."

Damn. He knows who I am. Even if I could outfight him, which judging by his slight frame is a possibility, he could still report me. The alternative is killing him, but I have no desire to do that.

"I just need to stretch my legs. There are too many girls packed in that place." I stab a thumb over my shoulder. "And I've never been good at making friends with girls."

He takes a few steps closer but hesitates. Is he afraid of touching me? "You can use the porch if need be." He takes another cautious step closer. "Orders are orders, my lady. Please don't make me call it in."

Would that bring Zephyr here? I could ask him about Easton. "And who comes if you call it in? The Captain?"

He shakes his head. "Captain is on vacation."

I flinch. *Vacation?* Capturing girls rewards him with vacation while I'm packed in this cottage with a basket full of hissing cats? I snort and roll my eyes. "Figures."

"My lady." He motions back up the slope.

"Yeah, yeah." I stalk away and step out onto the porch instead. I have no desire to get this poor guy into trouble for doing his job. For all I know, he was stolen from his parents as a boy like these girls were stolen from their families. "For the record," I say, calling down to him. "The books in this cottage are incredibly boring. See if you can have them send in some spicy romance or something."

He chuckles below the porch.

———————

I STRETCH ON THE sofa the next morning. Someone placed a blanket over me once I came in and passed out here. I wonder which of the girls it was as I head into the kitchen to find something to eat.

The cottage door opens. I squeak, jumping and spinning toward the door. No one comes in here!

A man close to my father's age with deep brown eyes and a chiseled jaw enters. He looks so much like Zephyr that I can't help wondering if this is his father. Would his father be the King? No. That doesn't make sense. He said his brother was the King. Who is this man?

The man secures a medical mask over his face the second he spots me in the kitchen. With a flick of his fingers, six guards

march through the cottage. I try not to be startled by their presence, but this can't bode well. They pass the kitchen and head
toward the rooms.

The man eyes me up and down. "Lady Paige. Just the girl I was
looking for."

I doubt that. My gaze flits toward the rooms as two of the girls
scream and beg.

I shuffle involuntarily backward. "Why?"

"They informed me this morning that you attempted sneaking
out last night."

"Are you the King?" I ask.

He makes a noise in his throat and shakes his head. "No."

"Then I don't care," I say before he can explain. I turn away to
head to my room, hoping to escape him. He makes me uneasy.

An iron grip seizes my arm, pulling me back. "I think you need
to understand the rules in this place, miss."

"And I think you need to take your hand off me before I make
you."

The corners of his eyes lift. Is he smiling at that? "Try it and
these men will be all over you in seconds. These men all answer to
me."

"So a general, then," I say.

"Admiral."

"Huh. Then you can tell me how my friend Easton is doing."

"Is he why you were sneaking out?" the Admiral asks. He releases my arm.

I hate that the grip hurts and hate even more that I rub at it to
ease some of the pain. "I just want to know how he is."

The Admiral leans against the counter and crosses his arms.
"Your friend is fine. He's quite a fighter. More skilled than some
of my men. If I could trust him, he might rise quickly among the
ranks. Does that make you feel better?"

What more can I say? If he is telling me the truth—and he
has every reason to lie to me—then there's nothing more I need

to know now. Unfortunately, I don't believe he is telling me the whole truth. I nod anyway.

"You cannot sneak out of here," he says, satisfied with my nod. "You are all under quarantine."

"Is someone sick?" My heart skips. Holly spends a lot of time in her room. But her sickness is of the heart. No one can help her with that.

As if on cue, the guards muscle a struggling Ivy toward the door with a mask secured over her face. "No. Please. Please!"

My heart seizes. "What's happening to her?"

"Her tests revealed some illnesses which eliminate her from being a Tribute." The Admiral shrugs. "We can't risk infecting the royal family. Most illnesses will play out in a couple of weeks, so you need to stay put until that time is up."

I lean closer to him. He shifts away.

"Between you and me, I'm not sure I can handle living in this place with these girls for that long," I whisper. "Not without killing one of them."

The Admiral chuckles and shakes his head. He thinks I'm joking. He has no idea how close I have come to strangling any of these girls each day.

"Hang in there," he says as he makes his way to the door. I notice the gloves on his hands for the first time. Is he from the royal family? That would explain the resemblance to Zephyr. "Just a couple more weeks and you will have space all to yourself."

"Thank goodness for that." I offer him my most sly smile as he opens the door.

Then what he said hits me. "Wait, *two more weeks?*"

But he closes the door. The lock engages.

There is no way I will survive two more weeks in this place with these girls! There's no way they will survive in here with me.

9

ZEPHYR

DAYS OFF. WHOEVER WANTED them doesn't know how incredibly dull doing nothing can be. Especially in the winter. The golf course is closed for the season. So is the pool. In the morning, I sit with Mom, playing card games until she can't stand my presence any longer. Her insistence that I leave isn't founded in real annoyance. She wants me to go out, be eighteen, experience life. Not sit in a stuffy room with her all day.

I spend one day riding the trails on the island. It gives me time to think.

Cypress hasn't given any hints that he might have orchestrated our father and brother's deaths. I don't want to suspect my brother of killing them to take over. Cypress is a lot of things, but he isn't that devious. If anyone orchestrated it, Queen Elena is more of a suspect than Cypress. But why would she want her husband and son dead? And how do I prove it was her? Do I even know it *was* her?

No one could see the bodies. Except Cypress. He must have. He was there with them. But I can't just ask him about this. He may have forgiven my treason for disobeying Baron's orders to return to the island, but he won't forgive me if it sounds like I am accusing him or his mother of conspiracy.

Baron had kept the bodies under lock and key. Was it to protect us, or did he have more nefarious designs? And if so, what role does Cypress, as the King, play?

Then there are the missing supplies. Queen Elena is an islander: her family still lives here. But Mom's people are supposed to receive resources for her service to the crown. Just like the recruits, only the resources are more generous for queens and consorts. I know we have loaded those supplies on the ships. But one community implied that they never get what's promised. And Mom's community is gone.

So where do all the missing goods go? Where did Mom's people go?

Someone must know. Again, Baron is the one with access to the manifests and the resources. He controls the ships and their movements, as well as what goes on and off them. I need to see his records at the fort.

It seems like the better place to start, so the next day, I walk to the fort.

At the north entrance, the guards bar my passage.

"No offense, Captain," Jeff says. I've shared a lot of drinks with him in the past couple of years. "Admiral's orders."

"Come on, Jeff." I flash him a crooked smile. "What'd you think I'm gonna do? Let me slip past, and I will pay your outstanding tab."

Jeff works his jaw, eyes darting back and forth as he considers this. He owes a lot of money to the tearoom. So much so that I often buy his drinks.

Sam, the second entrance guard, shakes his head. "Sorry, Captain. The Admiral was extremely clear about what would happen if you stepped foot in the fort this week. Nothing is worth that trouble."

I inwardly sigh. There's no sweet talking my way inside. If Baron threatened court marshaling or worse, these men won't let me in, no matter what I offer them. My shoulders slump and I march away from the gate, muttering to them that it's fine.

But if I can't find records of those shipments, I won't know what's happening to them. That Baron is keeping me so distant from everything on such threatening orders to the men doesn't make me feel any better about my suspicions.

Frustrated, I stomp back to the palace. Servants bow out of my way so quickly, I wonder what my face must look like. Instead of using the elevator, I take the stairs.

But when I reach my floor, my feet carry me up another flight. I don't realize where I'm going until I face Baron's door. I can't get into the fort, but I can get into his suite.

Glancing up and down the hallway, I knock lightly on the door. If he is there, I don't want to just walk in. And I can come up with a quick excuse for being there.

No one answers.

Testing my luck, I turn the knob and slip into his suite.

If I'm caught sneaking around in his suite, the punishment is whipping. Not that it would be my first, but I seriously hope to avoid ever laying under the whip again. It makes my back itch just remembering the last time.

I hustle to Baron's desk. If he is hiding anything, it will be around the desk. The surface is covered with reports on the changing tides, fort preparations for the winter... Nothing of note.

A tiny replica of the old St. Louis arch sits on Baron's desk. I have seen this so many times in my life, but never truly understood what it was before now. I brush my fingers over the smooth surface. Why would he keep something like this?

It strikes me for the first time. Baron would have been Captain of Tides when my mother was chosen as Tribute. He was the one who took her from old St. Louis and brought her back here. Did that mean he was the one responsible for the destruction of the community? I shake my head. Baron is dedicated to his job, but he isn't cruel like my father. *Funny, I'm considering him for treason, but I can't imagine him destroying a community.*

Mom has an arch just like this one on her bedside table. Did Baron give it to her to remind her of her family?

I slide open drawers in the desk and shuffle through stacks of papers. One catches my eye and I pull it out.

Round Island Activity Report

Before I have time to read the report, a noise in the hallway freezes me. I slide the report back where I found it and ease the drawer closed. Then I hold my breath, waiting for the door to open. When it doesn't, I tiptoe to the door and peer through the eyehole.

Servants are busy readying the rooms down the hall for the girls' arrival.

After taking a few more minutes to rummage through the desk drawers and coming up with nothing else of note, I decide it's time to go. Before Baron makes an appearance.

Using the eyehole, I watch the hallway until I'm certain it's clear. Two servants grab a stack of clean towels and disappear into a room down the hall. Moving quickly, I slip into the hall and make my way down the back hallway to avoid detection. Being in the area isn't a crime, but if I'm caught sneaking around and Baron realizes someone was in his room, it's only another step for him to conclude it was me.

The day has left me with more questions than answers. Round Island is uninhabited territory. Only wildlife roams the tiny, forested island. So why is Baron receiving activity reports from the island?

Unable to process everything, I grab a bottle of whiskey from the bar on the main level.

Something pulls me to the treehouse near the cottage. As a boy, this treehouse became my favorite hiding place from my father. I even began stashing supplies inside. A weathered Adirondack chair. Pillows. Blankets. A lamp. A few books that I've read dozens of times now.

The floorboards creak under my weight as I duck inside. My old blankets are neatly folded in a pile under the small table. I wrap myself in two and position the chair near the window overlooking the cottage.

Even from a distance, I can feel the pull of Paige's magic. It's intoxicating all on its own. I drink the whiskey to warm my insides as I stare out at the cottage, willing Paige to step onto the balcony. I can't explain why I need to see her, but the compulsion is so strong it consumes my breath.

Darkness settles. The bottle nearly empties. My vision blurs.

Then she emerges.

Paige hugs her arms close despite the puffy coat. Her gaze is fixed on the road, searching for something. I try to figure out what she sees, but my vision is so blurry I can barely make *her* out well enough to be certain it is her at all.

I watch her forever. Until I can't think straight any longer. Until my bottle is empty. Until my eyelids droop.

------------ ❈ ------------

T HE RUINS OF THE old St. Louis arch tower over me. Warm air blows off the nearby river, caressing my face. *Why am I here?*

I stalk into the underground ruins beneath the arch. They are just as I remember them from my visit. Collapsed. Charred in places. Signs of a community linger in corners, but cobwebs cover everything, long since abandoned.

One of the white elevator pods sits open. I duck inside and settle on a seat, brushing my fingers over the vacant seat beside me.

"A curious place to sit."

The voice draws my gaze up sharply.

Paige leans against the doorway, watching me.

"Why are *you* here?" I don't mean to sound harsh, but her sudden appearance leaves me unsettled. Why does this keep happening?

"You tell me." She ducks into the pod and settles beside me. The warmth radiating off her body charges my insides.

I close my eyes and lean my head against the wall of the pod. "Nothing I say matters."

She shrugs. "Just say it."

I open my eyes, staring at her. The intense umber of her gaze pulls me in instantly. She has a point. If it doesn't matter, why hold back?

"Fine." My fingers inch toward her hand. "I'm drawn to you, but if I don't keep my distance, it will end badly for both of us." The tips of my fingers touch the top of her soft hand. Her fingers wrap around mine. I stare at our hands, enjoying the feel of her hand in mine. "I think someone killed my father."

"What?" Paige jerks back, startling me. Her wide eyes peer at me in shock. "The last king?"

I nod.

"I'm sorry, Zephyr."

"I don't care that he's gone." I shrug. "I am worried about why, though. And I think my uncle is hiding something from me."

"Your uncle would be...your father's brother?"

I nod again.

The two of us fall silent, holding hands. Minutes pass. Or hours. Or seconds. Then Paige clears her throat. "Would he be in line for the crown?"

"No. I mean, not unless..." Terror rips through me.

"What?" Her grip on my hand tightens.

"If all of us boys died." Baron wouldn't kill us all, though, would he? Except Alric died with Dad, and Cypress was there, so he probably was supposed to die. And the men mutinied against me. Which only left Dominic, the softest and easiest of all to pick off. Nausea turns my stomach. My mind is reeling at this. Baron was just as much a father to me as my own father...maybe more so.

Paige shifts closer to me, bumping my shoulder with her arm. "I'm sure there must be another explanation. Someone else must stand to gain power if the whole family falls."

I roll my head to the side along the wall and stare at her. Paige has a point. Just because Baron is the most likely suspect doesn't make him the only one. I need to step back and put more thought into it.

My gaze drifts down, fixating on her lips. They pull me in like a siren's call to a sailor. I wonder what they feel like. I want to kiss her. It's all I've wanted to do since I met her. Something about those lips calls me. A deep desire to know what they feel like, taste like. Dangerous thoughts. But I can't resist the draw. I lean closer, ready to seize this forbidden moment.

Paige pushes me away and surges to her feet. "What are you doing?" Her eyes crinkle in confusion.

I groan inwardly. "Great. Even in my dreams, I get rejected." *My dreams?* Those words came out without me understanding them, and now they feel strange in my mind. I rise to leave, but she blocks the only exit.

"Zephyr, I don't know you."

"Who cares?"

"I do! The only boys I've ever kissed have meant something to me."

"Like Easton?" I hate myself for snapping the question at her, but her rejection stings.

Paige's face sets in angry lines. Her jaw twitches. "Just further proof that you don't know me, either." She ducks back out the door.

I heave out a sigh. "Paige, wait."

But by the time I duck out after her, she's already disappeared. I spend days wandering old St. Louis, trying to find her.

———❈———

MY NECK ACHES AND I'm bone cold. I groan as I blink blurry eyes, trying to focus on my surroundings. As I shift, I nearly fall out of my chair, making my head hammer in agony. It takes a moment for me to realize I'm still in the treehouse. I hug the empty bottle against my chest.

"About time," Bronwyn says. She stands beside me, arms crossed. My dear, sweet sister, always looking out for me. "I was worried I would have to get your mother's help."

"Wh—what are you doing here?"

"What are *you* doing here?" Her pointed look makes my stomach twist. Does Bronwyn know? She's a Telepath. But no, her magic doesn't work on me. *Don't be an idiot, Zephyr. It's coincidence.*

I rub my eyes. "I don't have a suitable answer for that."

Bronwyn drops her hands to her sides. "Well, your skin is terribly pale. Come inside and I'll get you some coffee and a hearty meal. You need to warm up."

There's no point arguing. I allow my older sister to guide me away from the cottage, but I cast one more glace toward it, remembering the dream. Pain lances across my chest. Dumb that a dream should hurt, but all the same, it does.

10

GAVIN

EVERYWHERE I GO, PEOPLE watch me from the moment I step out the door to the moment I close it again. With each passing day, I grow more paranoid. Are they spying on me for the Elders, reporting my activity? I've tried making myself useful, fixing broken equipment, helping restore crops that look close to failure, completing odd jobs for people at their request around the homes. Still, their curious eyes make me nervous everywhere I go.

As I help a young family by creating a small bedroom for their young child—a bedroom that's little larger than a broom closet—Elder Carmen corners me.

"You've been busy since arriving, Gavin," she says, leaning casually against the narrow doorway of the small apartment.

I'm crouched beside the door to the new room, palm pressed to the stone to smooth out the ripples and jagged edges along the floor. My Power easily pulses outward. "I'm just trying to be useful." I don't spare her a glance, focused on my task.

The young couple sits off to the side on a hard bench that serves as their sofa, clutching the young child close to keep him out of harm's way while I work.

"These matters are brought to the Elders before action is taken," Carmen says. Though her tone is pleasant enough, something about it stiffens my spine. "We can't have you walking around here doing as you please. There is a way we do things for a reason."

"What reason could there be for not helping this family? Didn't you once have an Expansion Elder who oversaw tasks like this?" I ask.

"Gavin." The sharpness in her tone startles me.

I stop working and ease back to my feet, turning to face her. My questions are reasonable. I don't see why she's upset with me.

Carmen's brows draw tight. "You aren't an Elder."

"These people need help..."

"And they get it. In due time. From the Elders."

"How long does it take for requests like new lights or expanded quarters to fulfill?" I ask.

Carmen's jaw twitches. Is she angry? "We have dozens of families in line for such requests ahead of this one. We do our best to fulfill requests as soon as possible. But when you pick and choose who to help on your own, it creates problems. Others are *demanding* you help them next."

"Then I will."

Carmen huffs. It sounds so much like Paige's frustrated huff I know I've overstepped somewhere. "If you want to help, then you come to us, and we will put you where you need to be. But how long does a task like this take?"

I peer at my handiwork, at the small room without a door. "This one has taken me about forty minutes."

Carmen blinks repeatedly, lips parting. It takes a moment before she responds. "And then you're spent, I'm sure."

"No. It isn't hard. I could do this for hours. How many are on the list? I could probably manage seven per day, depending on how rested I am."

The couple whispers to one another, watching the exchange with intense curiosity. What are they whispering about, staring at me like that?

"Fixing the broken lights is different," I continue. "A quick fix only takes a few seconds. If there's a lot of damage, it might take me about fifteen minutes. Those I can do without really thinking. I probably could do it off and on all day long." I shrug.

Carmen eyes the couple, then gathers herself in an air of command. "If you want to continue your work, you will come to us, and we will give you daily tasks. No more helping at your will."

She spins on her heel and marches out.

I finish the room in a few more minutes. The couple offers me thanks and a small trinket from a long-lost era. I feel odd taking it. Is it like payment? I didn't ask for anything.

Unnerved, I head out to find Drake. The encounter with Carmen leaves me with a ton of questions. And it isn't my first elder encounter since arriving. Elder Julia has cornered me several times to ask questions about medicines back home—questions I carefully answer. I want to be useful and let them know Elpis has something to offer, but I don't want to put Elpis at risk either.

My trust in the Elders is waning. I hate to be suspicious, but something about the way the Elders act reminds me of the stories Dad has told me about his time in the Protectorate—people with the best intentions but the worst execution, whose very plans caused the deaths of thousands, who constantly offered Dad kindness and support while putting innocent people in danger.

Items have gone missing from my pack, too. I don't realize it until a week into my stay, but my notebook containing the notes I made before encountering Drake in old St. Louis is missing. It can't be a coincidence. I didn't write anything in it that would condemn Elpis or give away too much information. Mostly, it's full of my observations of the world during our trip. My biggest fear is that those observations might lead the Elders straight to Elpis.

I catch up with Drake as usual on his way back to his room from the shared washroom after work. I tell him about my fears.

"I think you're overreacting," Drake says as we walk. Each day he finds time to spend with me, most often later at night when he has finished with his work in the resource department. These walks are the highlight of my day.

"So what, my notebook just up and vanished?" I shake my head, hands stuffed deep in my pockets. "I don't lose things. And I don't believe in coincidence, before you even mention that."

Drake glances sidelong at me, offering a weak smile. While he has shared some of his thoughts about their religion, he knows I don't share his belief. "I'm sure it will turn up somewhere, Gavin." He pauses, drawing me to a stop in the empty hallway as well. "This isn't just about the notebook, is it?"

I flush and stare at the floor. Lines of thin cracks show through the floor, too narrow for anyone without a Power to notice, but they stand out starkly to me. My fingers itch to touch them, to smooth them out. What will the Elders say if I do?

Drake steps closer, tipping his head to force me to meet his gaze. "I know you miss your family and you're worried about your sister. But if she's anything like you, I think she is doing just fine."

I draw in a deep breath and let it out slowly, just like Paige and Dad coached me so many times. "I dream of her sometimes. It's strange, but the dreams don't feel like dreams at all. They feel...real. Like she is really right there, offering me comfort, putting her arm around me."

Drake places a reassuring hand on my arm. "Take that as a good sign. Maybe, somehow, the two of you are reaching out to one another in your dreams."

I snort and roll my eyes. The corner of my mouth twitches upward. But all the teasing dies on my lips. There are Powers where people can see the past or future through dreams. This was not the same, but it wasn't entirely dissimilar either. And Paige often suffers from insomnia, waking from horrible dreams she can't shake because they felt so real. Has she been a Dreamer all along?

Drake pats my arm, then resumes his stroll, misinterpreting my silence. "See? Sometimes, it's good to believe in something beyond yourself."

My feet hustle across the cracked floor to catch up. "Don't start with that again. There are scientific explanations for such things."

His shoulders shake ever so slightly. *He's laughing at me!*

"I don't appreciate being the butt of your amusement."

"Are you calling yourself an ass?" Drake teases. Mischief shines in his dark eyes, and my heart skips.

Heat rushes to my face. "Maybe."

We both chuckle as we carry on.

Something about being with Drake is easy. I can be myself around him, and he isn't judgmental of me. He pokes fun, sometimes, but only in endearing ways.

As we approach the door to the Minister's house, I want to turn away, ask if I can stay with Drake instead. Not that I don't appreciate the hospitality of the Minister, Pip, and Mrs. Garraty. But I am far more comfortable around Drake.

I chew my lip, nearly asking him if I can stay with him for the second time this week.

Drake remains close to me as we stand outside the closed door. His proximity has my heart beating faster. And the way he looks at me. My heart aches as I stare into those beautiful dark eyes. Not in the same way it did with Aron. Aron was agonizingly good-looking, but I never really felt so close to him. More of a tertiary amusement. But Drake... He *sees* me when he looks at me. I don't want to ruin our friendship or misinterpret anything. It wouldn't be the first time I'm made that sort of mistake.

"I don't think they will ever let me leave," I breathe. Those were not the words I had intended to share. Not even close. Though it is a relief that my mouth didn't get me into trouble again. I often say the wrong thing at the wrong time.

"Who?" Drake whispers, not even flinching.

"The Elders. They told me I'm a guest here, but they also said I can't leave the Haven." My gaze sweeps over his face, committing it to memory. "Emil said they wouldn't let him out the door for seven years. Now they won't even let me do anything without peering over my shoulder every second of the day."

A lump climbs up my throat, cutting off anything else. I quickly avert my gaze from Drake's captivating stare, not wanting to appear weak.

"Emil was a bit more rebellious than you," Drake says with a low chuckle. "I heard rumors that the Elders were worried he would expose the Haven to the Kingdom. It's not the same for you. From what you said, it sounds like they just want to be sure everything is done fairly."

I swallow and nod, but I don't believe him. Emil's motivations weren't so different from my own. And the Elders are wrapping reins around me like a broken horse.

"Hey." Once more, Drake dips his head to slip into my line of sight. "You are...different."

Different? What does he mean by that?

Drake takes a step back and clears his throat. "I'll see you tomorrow, Gavin." He flashes me a shy smile, then pivots and hustles away.

I rush into my room, closing the door, and throw myself onto the mattress.

Idiot. Drake is a friend. Just a friend. Just like Pip. The plush pillow presses against my hot face. I growl in frustration. Drake stirs something inside me. Something that I've never really felt before. My first crush was Liam. And he had seemed interested as well, but that had ended poorly. When I tried holding his hand at school the day after we kissed in my room, he pushed me away and threw some nasty words at me. Shortly after, he had a girlfriend and never spoke to me again. The entire incident burned into my memory, haunting every relationship I might have had since.

Aron is still in Elpis. Aron, my friend from work. The unattainable source of my most recent desires.

But Drake... The warmth and familiarity we have around one another, the way his touch awakens everything inside, terrifies me.

"You alright, Gavin?" Pip's gentle voice pulls me from my inner turmoil.

I roll over and offer a forced smile. "Yeah, I'm fine."

She raises a disbelieving brow and slips into the room, closing the door behind her. A moment later, she perches on the edge of my bed. "You don't look fine."

"I just miss my family." The lie slides off my tongue far too easily.

She nods, then curls up on the bed next to me so we face each other. It reminds me so much of Paige, how she would curl up on my bed like this to offer me comfort.

For the next half hour, she listens to me telling stories about my sister. I miss home desperately, and she commiserates. She even offers me hugs and tender reassurance. Normally, I wouldn't enjoy such familiarity with someone I have only briefly known, but Pip's comfort is so easy that I let it slide.

It almost feels like home.

11

Paige

S OMEONE WILL DIE SOON if I can't get away from these girls. The Admiral told me they locked us in this cottage for quarantine, especially after Ivy was taken away sick. None of the rest of us have shown symptoms of whatever plagued her. While quarantine makes logical sense, I can't help but wonder if this is a sort of psychological plotting as well. Some girls have drawn lines in the sand.

If the Kingdom hopes that by locking us up like this, we will become eager to jump at their king just to escape quarantine, they are sorely mistaken. Even Layla's eagerness has waned. How can any man be worth all this?

I'm wondering if we will ever even meet the King at all, or if he will just review information on a tablet based on our physical exams and make his selection that way. I've spent time outside, as much as I dare, and heard a couple of guards chattering about King Cypress. Mostly, their comments were about not envying that he would have to choose between some of us. Then they ranked us based on physical qualities, like January's massive chest and Layla's slender curves. One even *dared* to mention that my muscles weren't womanly enough. I had to resist the urge to drop in on them and knock him right out. Jerk. Let him see what he thinks of my unwomanly muscles after my fist breaks his jaw.

I have to get out of here. There must be some way to escape this place, this island.

I press my palms against the white railing of the porch and peer toward the road over the tops of the trees. I've tried to gain access to the roof, but the peaks and valleys are too numerous and none of the windows make it as easily accessible as I had hoped.

It's getting dark out. About half a block down the road, a tavern emits a warm glow of lights from within. It's a popular place for the guards to frequent when off-duty.

I watch every night, praying to see Easton stumbling through the door. I would give anything to lay eyes on his dumb face—something familiar in this foreign place.

Even Zephyr's face would be welcome at this point. But I have yet to spot him. He has not come to check on us since we arrived. It saddens me a little. I dreamed of him a few nights ago. In old St. Louis. That same night, I felt him close by. His Power does something to me I can't quite find words for yet. But I can feel him nearby. Was he watching me?

The porch offers me a chance to observe the comings and goings on the island. So far, my best escape plan is to slip the guards in the middle of the night when the palace has the least protection and the men around the cottage are waning in the dark. I have to wait for the bar across the street to go dark, though, otherwise I risk someone stumbling out and spotting me. I can find my way back to the dock easily enough. It's only a block or two off the main road leading to the palace.

The problem is, I don't know how dangerous the lake is at night. Nor do I know how to operate a boat. Do they have rowers, or are they all motorized? I think I spotted a few smaller vessels in the harbor when we arrived, but I can't be certain, and I can't see the harbor from here. I'll just have to take my chances when the time comes. And if I'm caught, maybe they will eject me from this dumb pageant and let me leave.

Very little comes this far up the street, but we aren't too far from the stables. I've made a habit of spending time out here seeking patterns, trying to get a good feel for how big the island guard is and when the best time to slip away might be.

I hate this place.

How long will they will force us to remain isolated in this cottage like Rapunzel in her tower?

12

Zephyr

When my leave ends, I head to the fort first thing in the morning. If I can't see Paige, I have a few questions for Easton. But an inspection of the barracks turns up nothing. I ask around, but no one seems to know whom I'm talking about. I can't help wondering what happened to him. Did they torture him? Is he dead? The very idea turns my stomach. *Paige would never forgive me.*

That rogue thought comes unbidden as I entered the tearoom—which serves many drinks, none of which resembles tea. Long ago, the tearoom operated as a tourist attraction in the fort. When the fort was converted back for use, the tearoom became the bar for soldiers to enjoy away from civilians. It's a fantastic place to hide—from my brothers, mother, sister, *people*—except Baron.

I spend my days burying myself in instructing the new recruits. The days blur together, as training often does. I break recruits into groups based on their magic and assign them officers who can teach them how to use their magic in a fight. My area of expertise is educating them how to man the ships—which is only taught to the recruits who have passed their first rounds of loyalty tests—or how to use a sword without harming themselves or others. The swords are only a last combat resort when their magic fails them, yet a critical skill.

After six nights in a row passing out drunk in the officers' quarters in the fort, Baron forbids me from entering the tearoom for two weeks. As if that will stop me from drinking.

One day—I couldn't tell you what day it is anymore—during a sword fighting lesson, I freeze. A cluster of officers marches across the hilltop nearby. Someone is in the center of their cluster, but from my lower ground, I can't get a good look at him. It must be nearly all the officers.

Except me.

Why was I not included in whatever urgent business they are on? Is it punishment for disobeying commands? Or have I lost Baron's trust? This bothers me most of all, which is ridiculous since I spent a week investigating him for treason—which bore no definitive proof.

I must find out what's happening.

"Swords away," I command. "We are done for the day. Go see your squad leaders for magic training."

The recruits dutifully follow my commands, but I keep my gaze on the cluster of officers. I expect them to enter the officers' quarters at the top of the hill, but they march past. Only two buildings are in that direction. The west watchtower and the medical building.

Once I have my sword tucked safely in my belt, I hustle up the hill, watching them flash in and out of sight through the trees. The hill slows me a little—it's a steep climb—and by the time I reach the top and round the trees, I can no longer see the officers.

I peer around the medical building toward the west tower, but they never emerge.

Then I hear a familiar voice inside the building in front of me. The words are hard to discern.

I crouch there for so long, waiting for something to happen or someone to emerge. Just when I fear I'm going mad, the doors open. A small cluster of men stroll out with the physician close on their heels.

"...really think it could be genetic?" a familiar voice asks. *Why can't I place that voice? I know it!* "Or infused with others?"

I hold my breath and dip a little lower, afraid that one of the emerging officers will spot me spying.

"Maybe. We just need a little more time to examine the samples." The physician wipes his hands on a cloth, staining it with blood. *Whose blood is that?*

"I will buy you as much time as you need," another man says. "But I would suggest moving as quickly as you can. Our leader is getting impatient."

My stomach clenches. What are they up to? And who is their leader?

I wait in the shadows of the trees until the coast is clear.

Moving with cautious steps, I edge toward the front of the medical building. A quick scan of the open field in front of the building reassures me I'm alone. The officers have disappeared elsewhere on the grounds for now.

Gripping my sword to keep it from making any noise, I slip through the wide-open doors of the medical building.

The building is open all day, in case there is a training exercise gone wrong and someone needs to be rushed in. And there is always a physician on duty.

Today, one bed at the far end of the building has a curtain drawn around it.

A groan from the back of the room freezes me in my tracks. I hold my breath, hand around the hilt of my sword, and sneak deeper to find the source.

"I'm telling you. I feel fine," a gruff voice snaps at the physician.

I freeze, trying to place that voice. I've heard it before.

"You will be dismissed shortly to your new quarters," the physician says. "But we will follow up regularly."

I hold my breath, worried that they will catch me listening.

The patient grunts but says nothing more.

A few minutes later, the physician closes himself in the office. I edge toward the far bed. Who could it be?

By the time I make it to the curtain, the office door jerks open. I dart back, using the curtain as cover. It flutters from the movement, and I pray he can't tell.

"Stay put. I'll be back to show you to your quarters shortly." The physician marches past. I can't breathe again until the door closes behind him. All he had to do was turn around and he would have seen me standing there.

"I know you're there," the man on the other side of the curtain says. "I can't touch my Power."

Power. Not magic.

Does the physician know I was there as well, then? Surely, he felt it, too.

I pull back the curtain, gasping at the sight of Easton perched on the edge of the bed. There are angry cuts and bruises all around his bare torso and arms. They replaced his nice pants with a set of scrubs. The corner of his lip is swollen and one of his eyes is an ugly shade of purple.

Something in him fractures when he lays his dark eyes on me. "Where is she? Is she okay?"

"Shh..." I glance toward the closed door. Whoever is in charge doesn't want me to know what's happening to him. I don't intend to let them know I found him. "Keep your voice down. She's fine."

He chews his bloody lip and nods.

"What happened to you?" I knew they would question him, but now that I have a better look, I can see entire patches of his skin missing. His muscles twitch and his thick neck pulses with fierce life. This isn't questioning. They are experimenting on him.

Easton squeezes his eyes closed tight. "It doesn't matter. As long as she's safe. As long as they...he..."

I avert my gaze to give him a little pride back. He is obviously trying not to cry, fighting to contain his emotions. Funny that someone so strong is having such a hard time fighting.

"Come with me," I whisper, glancing at the closed door. I reach for him to help him up. "I'm not sure what's going on here, but I won't allow it."

There must be somewhere on this island I can hide him until I learn more about what is going on. I'm not sure why I'm compelled to help him. Maybe because of her.

Easton shakes his head. "No. No, I can't... They will hurt her."

"Who will?" I ask.

Easton jerks away from me. "The captain."

"*I'm* the Captain."

He stares at me in wide-eyed shock, working his jaw. "The...General? A leader..."

We don't have a general, but I don't tell him that. Because the chill running down my spine tells me the terrifying truth.

My uncle did this. Here is the physical evidence that Baron is up to something, and I still can't accept that reality. There must be some explanation.

"I will see what I can do to help you," I reassure him.

He shakes his head, each movement jerky and unnatural. "I will do what I must do here. And when they let me train, I will be the best damned recruit they've ever had. I have to..." Something passes through his dark eyes, a suspicion that he might have said too much already. Instead, Easton shifts gears. "You protect her. *Please*. Protect her, at least until..."

I want to ask until what, but something about the fear in him prevents me. "I will." They won't hurt Paige. Cypress will want to get to know her first.

Paige's threat jumps to the surface. The harsh words she spoke to me when we first met. *"Take me to your leader. I dare you."*

Has she been biding her time these past weeks, waiting for her chance to get her hands on Cypress? Easton knows her better than I do. Is he worried she will keep true to her threat? If she acts out against Cypress, I'm not sure even I could protect her.

And in just a few days, we will find out.

I edge back. "I won't leave you here, Easton. I will find out what's going on. I will get you out of here."

But as I make my way toward the door, he repeats the same words with fevered determination. "Protect her."

I WAIT FOR CYPRESS to finish his meeting with Dominic, pacing the hallway outside the council chambers on the second floor. My gaze continually flits to the closed door, then down the hallway. I don't want Baron to find me. I need this to stay between Cypress and me.

At long last, the door opens, and my brothers emerge, grinning. Their conversation stops short the moment they lay eyes on me.

"Zeph, what's wrong?" Dominic asks, edging closer.

"Cy, can I have a minute?" I hate turning Dominic away, but until I talk to my brother, I can't have anyone else hearing.

Cypress frowns. "Sure." He pats Dominic on the shoulder. "Get those boards ready. I'll take a closer look at each of the girls' reports later."

Dominic dips his head and hustles away, leaving the two of us alone.

Cypress stuffs his hands into his pockets. "I'm listening."

I swallow and slip past him into the council chamber, easing into one of the gilded high-back seats. Cypress closes the door behind us and perches on the edge of the table, watching me. I don't know how to start or what to ask, exactly. I lean my forearms against the table, grasping my hands tight together. The muscles in my shoulders strain.

"You're making me nervous, Zeph."

With a forced breath, I launch into it. "Have you sanctioned experiments on Easton?"

"Who's Easton?"

The question catches my breath. My eyes dart up to meet his. Cypress' brows are knitted together, his lips scrunched in confusion. He crosses his arms over his chest. He really doesn't know.

"He's the one who volunteered as a recruit when we found Lady Paige," I explain. "In old St. Louis..."

Cypress chews on his lip, deep in thought. He shakes his head. "I barely even remember who he is. What experiments are you talking about?"

"It's..." I falter. "Something about genetics and infusions." I wish I could just show him like anyone else could. Cypress can read memories by touch. But my negation magic prevents him from using it on me. Instead, I attempt to break everything down for him. My observations. What I heard. Easton's condition.

By the end, Cypress slipped into a seat beside me at the table. "I will see what I can learn. But I promise you this is the first I've heard anything about it."

"Thanks," I murmur.

He gives me a reassuring pat on the shoulder. "Anything for my favorite brother."

I chuckle. It's a blatant lie and we both know it.

"Now." He stretches languidly in his seat. "Let's talk about girls."

13

PAIGE

A TEAM OF SEAMSTRESSES flit in and out under guard to take our measurements for new wardrobes once the quarantine is finally lifted.

Stylists trim our hair in ways that are quite flattering to all seven of us. They give Layla and Alice highlights to enhance their natural color. The effect is stunning.

Cosmetologists examine each of us and offer pallets of colors, instructing each girl on how to apply the makeup. I don't need the tips, but I don't bother bringing attention to the fact that I've used makeup in the past. The girls are already upset to learn I know how to read.

By the end of the third week, the transformation in all of us is striking. They erased Alice's dirty face and matted hair, revealing a gorgeous girl beneath it all. She is, without a doubt, the most beautiful out of all of us—something I never would have predicted before the makeovers. Layla has noticed, too. She throws sweetly coated barbs at Alice as much as she can. January's blond hair has been trimmed up so that when it cascades around her pale shoulders the tips stop short of her chest. It only draws more attention where she *really* doesn't need more attention.

River's wild red curls gleam with a natural sheen and falls in perfect ringlets framing her face. Summer plays with one of them, marveling at the look of the hair. Summer's dark skin has taken on a natural shimmer that River compliments.

Holly's arrow-straight black hair now hangs in layers that make it even more dynamic. She flips it constantly, and it quickly shifts and settles into new positions with ease. Despite her makeover, Holly's eyes remain dull. No amount of makeup can cover the sorrow burning her away from the inside.

Like most nights, I watch the tavern where the palace guards frequently drink. For more than a week, I have plotted my escape from the island. I've timed everything out but have been waiting for the right night. Three days would have been ideal. The guards on watch that night are more likely to nod off, giving me an opening to slip away. I will sleep in my old clothes beneath my pajamas and leave my coat near the door with my boots. The part I can't prepare for is rescuing Easton from the fort. I can't leave without him.

With a new dress arriving in the morning and all of us under-going makeovers, I'm forced to reconsider my plans. I may not be here in three days, and the guards on watch these next two nights are much more alert. I would have to knock them out, and if they are discovered before I make it off the island or back to the mainland, I'm certain I won't escape. I need a new plan.

As I breathe out the frosty night air, watching the tavern, I think about Dad. He told me so many stories about his youth. When he was taken in by the Protectorate and not allowed to leave their underground sanctuary, he knew he was trapped. So how did he escape?

He made friends with the Protectorate members. He infiltrated their upper ranks and waited for the right moment to slip away and take back control of his own destiny.

Instead of running away in the darkness of night, I know what I need to do. Even if it takes a little longer. I need to be patient.

I must infiltrate the upper ranks of the royal family. Just like Dad did to the Protectorate. I need to earn their trust and wait for the right moment to strike.

Invigorated by this plan, I smile to myself.

Freezing wind knocks the air from my lungs as I continue watching the tavern and the street. The trees are almost barren of leaves now. Winter is here. Which also means holidays are coming.

My fingers are going numb despite the gloves. The lights from the palace illuminate the surrounding street, making it easy for me to monitor the comings and goings. None of the cottage bedrooms offer a good view of the street or the palace. This porch is my only way to learn anything.

For weeks, I've been watching, waiting, slowly dying inside. I miss Gavin. I miss home. Hell, I even miss Easton. Will I ever return?

A chorus of voices fills the tavern. I close my eyes and imagine myself at home.

During the holiday, everyone comes to the house. All of Mom and Dad's closest friends. Bianca and Levi. Alex. Lily and Sho. Gram. After Alex has had a few drinks, he launches into a chorus of holiday songs, dragging the rest of us in with him as if warding off his own demons through song. He hasn't been the same since his partner, Jayme left. We don't ask him what happened. It only makes him irritable.

I remember the year Gavin and his best friend Liam spent the entire day in Gavin's room playing video games. That was the last time Liam came to our home for the holidays. Not long after, he and Gavin got into a fight. Gavin wanted more and thought Liam did, too. But Liam most certainly did not. Liam's rejection changed Gavin.

The only friend Gavin has had since is Aron, a guy he works with at the Department of Science and Technology. Are they reunited yet? I know Aron is interested in Gavin, but Gavin refuses to accept it. He is still wounded by Liam's reaction.

"...Zeph!"

I snap my eyes open at the call down in the street.

Zephyr stumbles away from the tavern, weaving back toward the door. I would recognize that gray overcoat anywhere. Does he wear anything else?

"Tomorrow, then!" he calls back, but his words slur together.

Seeing him drunk and staggering across the street to the palace sends a shock through me. I'm not sure why it surprises me so much to see him in this state. I smelled alcohol on his breath a couple of times before. Despite the smell, he was so calm and level-headed on the way to the island. Nothing rattled him. Why would he get so drunk? Uncle Alex only did it to drown his own sorrow. What did Zephyr have to be sorry about?

He nearly disappears. I have to crane my neck to see him through the trees. He pauses, as if sensing something. I hold my breath. Will he turn and see me spying on him? Just when I'm certain I should hide to avoid detection, he shakes something out of his coat pocket.

A flask.

He tips it back and takes a generous drink. *Seriously?*

"Again?" a woman's voice says from somewhere ahead of him. I try to get a look at her but can't see more than the hem of her red dress. She mutters something I can't hear.

Zephyr waves her off. "An' wha'z he gonna do 'bout it?" He staggers forward. His boot catches on the curb and he pitches forward.

The woman catches him, but I can only see her arms as she smooths the hair away from his face. The touch is very familiar, affectionate. A sister or mother, perhaps? Does he have a girlfriend or a wife? I'm only now realizing how little I know about him.

The two of them disappear, speaking in hushed voices to one another.

What could have pushed him to drink so much?

Unable to withstand the cold any longer, I sneak back inside and ease the door closed.

January stares at me with cold eyes, arms crossed over her ample chest. "Have you been sneaking out?"

I laugh and shake my head. "If I were, why would I come back?"

January rubs her eyes and follows on my heels as I head toward our shared room. "I suppose. If you are sneaking out to meet someone and the King finds out, he might have you executed. We aren't supposed to leave the cottage."

Executed. Is that what would happen if I tried to escape?

I roll my eyes and yank open the bedroom door. "Relax. I only go as far as the balcony." I shuck off the coat and rub my hands together, then slide under my blankets.

She lingers in the doorway, but I roll over on my side, back to her.

"Two days," she says. "I overheard the seamstress today. They are moving us into the palace in two days."

"Hopefully, we get our own rooms," I mumble.

Two days. I won't be able to escape from the cottage. I have to enact my backup plan. Infiltrate the King's inner circle and with their trust to get a ticket home. Hopefully for both Easton and me.

I DON'T RECOGNIZE THIS room. It's dark. Something ominous hangs in the air. I can't identify what it is, but it fills me with overwhelming dread. Tears well in my eyes. I edge deeper into the room, across the checkerboard tiled floor.

Then I hear the voices. I can't make out the words, but the sentiment is clear enough. Rage.

My heart hammers against my ribs. Some foolish part of me moves closer to the source, even if my brain is telling me to *run!*

The biggest man I've ever seen in my life towers over a huddled mass on the floor. The whip in his hand drips with blood. A shuddering breath slips past my lips. I've seen nothing so terrifying. It doesn't just send chills down my spine. It freezes the marrow in my bones. *Run, Paige. Run!*

"Keep your nose out of business that doesn't involve you!" the massive man growls at me. His voice is animalistic, feral.

I edge closer, wondering if my reflexes will allow me to seize the whip. His fist must be as big as my head!

The cowering form dares a glance up. *He's just a boy!* Perhaps only twelve or thirteen years old. But there is something familiar about his dark eyes.

Then the boy sees me, and his eyes widen.

Zephyr. He reminds me of a younger version of Zephyr.

The whip cracks in the air. I flinch. The boy cries out. An angry red gash bleeds on his back. Anger pulses within me. How could anyone do this to a child? I rush forward as the monster pulls back the whip for another lashing, forcing myself between the two of them. The whip turns to ash and crumbles from his giant fist.

"No!" The boy reaches feebly for me as the monster seizes the collar of my shirt and jerks me off my feet.

Our noses nearly touch. "Look at you." His lips peel back. Fire burns in his eyes. "Pretty thing."

The boy stumbles to his feet, trying to pull the monster's arm away from me. I admire his bravery but wish he would leave.

Some inner compulsion encourages me. My palm presses against the monster's chest, over his heart—if he even has one. Intense heat rushes through my body and out of my fingertips. Red mist wraps around the monster's chest. The boy stumbles back.

"You will no longer haunt this boy."

His hot breath rolls over my face like fire.

The red mist tightens around him. It pinches him in a vice grip. He tips his head back, and darkness escapes his mouth in a silent scream. My feet hit the tiled floor with a thump. The monster crumbles to ash and flutters to the floor.

When I turn, it's no longer the boy standing beside me.

Adult Zephyr trembles in his flayed gray waistcoat, bleeding. I step closer and place a hand on his arm. He flinches, then falls against me. I hold him as he cries.

14

ZEPHYR

AS THE RECRUITS GEAR up for a hike across the island in the snow, I count heads.

Cypress reassured me that Easton has been released to join the recruits in regular training. Baron insisted he knew nothing about the experiments on Easton, and that his interrogation injuries have all healed. I'm not sure either of us believed Baron fully.

But training is an excuse to talk to Easton again. I've always enjoyed training. The chance to work my muscles and avoid sedentary fatigue. Breathing in the crisp air. Getting to know the recruits.

The hike isn't terribly difficult. I can usually make it from one side of the island to the other in an hour or less, but our pace won't be a casual walk. The other officers and I intend to push these recruits at a fast pace, intending to weed out the weak from the strong.

My intention is to get some time to speak with Easton without the eyes of the fort watching.

I glance at him from the corner of my eye as he checks the straps on his pack. His height is hard to mask among so many younger boys, so I had to increase the size of the group to include older recruits still in training. The best way to do this is to empty the fort of anyone not too injured to hike. It also requires several officers to join us. I can't take them all on my own.

Easton puts on a tough face, but I can't stop remembering how broken he looked in the medical building. I want to make sure they stopped the experiments, like Baron claims.

Which means I need to talk to him. It isn't as if I can ask Baron if he lied.

"Line up and move out!" I call.

The recruits all hustle into place. Nat stops beside me on his way to the head of the group. I've given him the trail heads to take and asked him to lead the group so I can talk to Easton at the rear. Nat's an old friend. There isn't anyone else I can trust, and it's the only way to keep me from leading the hike.

"I hope you know what you're doing, Zeph," Nat hisses. He eyes some of the other officers—men I watched huddle into the medical building the other day. *They* know something.

"Just follow the path." I tighten my gloves around my fingers and flex them.

Nat nods once, then jogs to the head of the massive line of recruits.

I march toward my position at the rear of the group, not slowing as I pass Easton and mumble to him. "Fall to the rear in three hundred yards."

He doesn't indicate that he heard me, but I'm certain he did. Easton strikes me as a clever guy.

I reach position as the recruits begin their march out the northern gate.

The entire trail should take us close to four hours at a fast pace. I expect many of the recruits to trail behind by the first hour. That doesn't give me a lot of time to talk to Easton.

The company curves left out of the gate, then right past the active-duty soldier quarters. After three hundred yards, Easton begins gradually falling back. I monitor his progress from my rear position. By the time we reach Custer Trail, the company thins out to fit on the narrow path. Easton hit the last lines.

A few of the younger boys at the back eye Easton in alarm, obviously assuming he would make it to the head of the company. He probably would under normal circumstances.

"Pick up the pace, boys!" I bark. "Unless you want to miss dinner in the mess hall."

This motivates them to jog ahead.

Easton remains with me. I can't tell whether he is acting winded, or if he really is. I assumed he was extremely fit, but after what he has been through recently, I suppose anyone could be taxed.

The lines of the company snake through the barren trees lining the path as the officers keep the recruits moving. Yesterday was sunny enough to melt the ice and snow from the trail, so we don't need to worry about sprained ankles. Instead, the trees look skeletal, dead against the leaf-covered forest floor. The smell of damp soil carries on the breeze. It's not my favorite smell—damp soil has nothing on the smell of the open water—but it reminds me of my childhood, the time I spent on these very trails to escape the palace.

"How is she?" he asks, keeping his voice low so the boys ahead of us won't overhear.

"Fine. The girls are leaving quarantine tomorrow." I jog a few steps to close the gap between us and the others. Looking suspicious will do us no good.

"That's all I get? *Fine*?" He grunts. I don't have to look at him to sense the irritation.

"What else do you want from me?" I snap. "I haven't seen her either." Except from a distance. And in my dreams. I can't shake the memory of her banishing my monster father from a nightmare. Or the way her arms comforted me in that moment of weakness. But it was just a dream.

"Then how do you—?"

"I just do. Trust me."

He grimaces and glares at me from the corner of his eyes. He falls silent for a few yards, breathing even and well-paced beside me. "I dream about her sometimes."

I hope his dreams are better than mine. "I didn't do all of this so we can talk about girls," I say. The sharpness of my tone is unintentional. I can't help myself. I don't really hope his dreams are better. I'm a little angry that he dreams about her at all. My own might be more nightmares than dreams, but I wanted it to belong to me. Dumb as it sounds.

Some boys fall back again, as if the pace Easton and I keep at the rear is the acceptable minimum standard.

"Stop dragging your heels!" I bark at them.

One boy eyes the two of us with a scowl, but he increases his pace with the rest.

"You know they'll badmouth you later tonight," Easton says, sounding mildly amused.

"I don't care." The path reaches a fork. We follow the group along the right trail.

"Is it true that only officers are allowed to marry?" Easton asks. "I heard some guys complaining. They want change."

The questions alarms me. "Yes, it's true. Families have proven to be a distraction to soldiers. There are several reasons. Anyone can become an officer, though, so it isn't as if it can never happen."

Easton shrugs it off.

"I have questions for you, Easton, and I need you to swear on her life you won't tell another soul."

The corner of his mouth tips down. His jaw twitches. "I'm sick of the questions."

"We won't have much more time here," I hiss, glancing at the boys. "Please. This is important. It might even help me protect her."

I don't know if that's true, but I need him to understand the urgency of wasting no more time. And she is his weakness.

He gives a tight nod.

"I need to know what you told the others during interrogation," I say.

"Ask them."

"Easton…"

He refuses to elaborate. I huff. "Fine. Were those bruises their work?"

"Who else's would they have been?"

"And the skin?" I glance at his arms, but they're covered. "Who did it?"

"Does it matter?"

"Yes, dammit!" My outburst draws some gazes back our way, but a glare from me rights them again. I lower my voice. "I can't tell you much, but I need you to trust me."

He snorts. "Is that a joke? We are here because of *you*. As far as I'm concerned, you're the enemy."

"Then why ask me to protect her if you don't trust me?"

Easton slows his jog, then stops altogether, forcing me to stop with him. Pure rage turns his face red. He clenches his hands into fists at his sides. "There's a lot about our past you don't understand, and I sure as hell have no intention of telling *any* of you about it. But I know what they were doing to me, and I know why. I'm not a dumb meathead. But if he thinks for a second that his experiments on me are warranted, I am terrified of what he will do to Paige when he finds out what she is capable of. I can't get it out of my head. And I can't get out of the bloody *fort* to warn her." His gaze twitches to the forest at my back. Is he considering running? He won't get far.

"Unless you can get me out of there," he continues, "I need you to watch over her. He can't know. *Ever*. It's too dangerous."

"Who?" I take an urgent step toward him. "Tell me who to protect her from or I'm working blind here."

Easton opens his mouth, then falters.

"Everything alright back there, Captain?" Officer Cante has noticed the two of us falling behind. He eyes us from fifty yards up the trail.

"Fine. He just needed a moment to catch his breath. We will catch up in a minute. Carry on, Officer."

Officer Cante eyes the two of us, then nods and turns back up the trail. He will report that for certain. What will Baron say when he finds out?

"We are out of time here, Easton," I say, turning to him with more urgency. "Give me something to work with."

Easton throws his hands up. "I don't know who he is. The doc only calls him 'sir'."

"What does he look like?"

Easton works his jaw but can't seem to find words. His face turns red. After a minute, he clenches his jaw.

"Easton, you can tru—"

"I can't, okay?" Easton shakes his head in frustration, then runs up the path to catch up to the company, leaving me trailing behind.

I take even breaths, trying to wrap my head around what is happening, but none of it makes sense. Why can't he tell me? What is it he doesn't trust me with? Anything he can tell me about who did this to him will help me identify the culprit. I should've seized the moment and asked Easton if Baron is responsible, but if he can't give me a name... *He must know who Baron is by now.* Besides, I'm not sure I can handle the truth.

By the time I catch back up with the company, Easton has worked his way farther up in the group. He is clearly done talking to me.

⁂

IT'S NEARLY DARK BY the time the company returns to the fort. Easton had slogged his way to the front of the pack, then held pace with Nat. But Easton's pace was so punishing he might have left everyone behind if he knew where he was going.

I enter the fort, looking for him, but he vanishes before I enter the north gate.

15

GAVIN

Each morning, I report to the Elders for assign-
ments—fighting off the irritation at how short my list is
each day. It's almost as if the Elders don't want me to help these
people. The tasks they give me are few and petty. Check the water
filters, which I've already purged. Fix very specific lights here and
there around the Haven, lights that don't seem urgently in need
of fixing.

Worse yet are the people I must refuse to help when their requests are so simple. Mend a crack in their wall or tighten the
weave on worn-out clothes. I can do these things, but if I don't
obey the list the Elders give me, I don't know what they will do. If
they are testing my ability to follow their orders, I'm passing with
flying colors. If they're testing the limits of my Powers, they are
grossly underestimating what I can accomplish. The frustration
often sends me into dark moods by the end of the day.

Pip has become a fast friend. Her vibrant personality fills the
room. Her quick humor often turns some of my darker moods
bright again. I spend most evenings with her, talking and playing
ancient board games. She hates how frequently I win, often toss-
ing up her hands and complaining that I never let her win. But she
does it with a smile on her face. She reminds me a lot of my sister.

I haven't forgotten about Paige. I tell Pip stories about our
childhood—careful not to give away too many details about Elpis.

It has been weeks since we arrived. With each day that passes, I miss my sister more, worried about what she is doing, what the Kingdom is doing to her.

I sigh, reaching the end of my paper. I've only gathered a few small scraps to make notes on since I arrived. First, I noted the trek from Elpis to the arch where Paige was stolen from me. Then I expand the map along the river, recalling what little our drones had recorded and the old maps from before the Collapse. If my calculations are correct, we are only about five hundred miles west of the island. If Paige or Easton still have their radios, I could contact them, but something tells me those were taken away.

The others should have reached Elpis by now. How are Mom and Dad taking the news of our disappearance? I wish there was some way to communicate with him, but we are well out of radio range of Elpis this far north, and I don't have any other means of communicating. Regardless, I can't let go of hope. I spend several nights fiddling with the radio in my pack, hoping for some signal or sign that someone is out there.

I sit back and fold up my used paper, adding it to the stack hidden in a secret cubby hole I've created in my wall.

Drake left on another mission days ago. His absence grows more painful with each day. I can't stop thinking about him, so much that I often yearn for his telltale knock on my door.

I sink back into my desk chair. Without something to write on—without Drake's visits—the days here drag. Pip does her best to fill the space, but her presence doesn't satisfy me the way Drake's does.

A familiar rap on my bedroom door makes my heart surge with excitement. Did I summon him by thought? *Get a grip.*

"Gavin?" Drake calls before ducking in, just like he always does. When he sees me at the desk, his face splits into a grin. "Miss me?"

"Only a little," I lie, grinning back at him like an idiot.

Drake glances through the door, then closes it behind him. "Is that so?"

"Stop smiling about it." I drop the pencil on the desk and cross my arms.

He shuffles deeper into the room, both hands clasped behind his back. There's something charming about the way he looks. Even in his grubby Haven clothing, he's attractive. Soft strands of dark hair fall across his forehead. My fingers twitch to move them aside.

Play it cool, dummy. "I can't stop thinking about my sister," I mutter, examining my nails. *Too cool.*

Drake perches on the edge of the desk. "I'm so sorry, Gavin. I wish I could help."

"You can." I turn my desperate gaze up to meet his. "Help me get out of here. My dad will know what to do to help her, but he needs to know where she is and what he might be up against."

Drake chews his lip. "I'll see what I can do, but if you plan on encouraging a war with the Kingdom, the Elders will want no part."

"I can't leave her. Not after what you told me!"

Girls taken to the Capital as Tributes are forced to compete for the King's hand. Paige would never submit. But according to Drake, girls who refuse vanish. I'm petrified that her stubborn streak will be her downfall. Not that I want her to give in, either. But she's alone, probably terrified. Who knows how she will react?

According to Emil, even the girls not chosen are never released from the island. No one knows what happens to them, but they never come back. Emil's sister was a Tribute to the last king, and he knows she was not chosen as the Queen. Yet no one has seen or heard from her since.

"I will see what I can do," he says again. "But I don't exactly have a lot of sway here. You probably have more than me."

I nod, staring at my hands, unable to meet his gaze. Not that I feel like I have much sway.

Drake shifts a little closer. "I got something for you on the mission."

He pulls his hand out from behind his back and sets a notebook on the desk. I have to do a double-take, certain I am seeing things. A smile slowly builds and spreads across my face. My stomach flutters as I brush my fingers over the black and white cover.

"Drake...how?"

"I don't want you to be miserable here," he says. "And I know how much you like writing. I just thought, if I could get a hold of one, you would owe me."

I narrow my eyes at him.

The cover feels familiar. Like home. It reminds me of Dad and the notebooks he is always writing in. Even with the technology in Elpis, he prefers his notebooks. I want to hug it close, smell the paper, feel closer to home, even if only for a moment.

But I can't accept. Not if it means I owe anyone favors. Considering my situation, that feels like treacherous ground to walk upon. I swallow the lump in my throat and push it back toward him.

"Thanks, but I can't accept this."

Disappointment mars his face. I hate seeing that look on his face and knowing it's my fault. It makes my stomach twist with regret.

"Why not?" Drake doesn't make a move to pick it up. "Because of what I said?" His hand falls on my shoulder and gives it a squeeze. The touch sends my nerves into high gear. "I was only joking with you. You don't owe me anything."

Once more, I brush my fingers over the cover. "Are you sure?"

"Just a friendly gesture. A peace offering for keeping you in a hole in the ground, I suppose." A shy smile tips the corner of his mouth. "Please take it."

Does he have any idea how much this notebook means to me? "I won't get in trouble for having it, will I?"

Drake releases my shoulder and stands. "No, it's fine. It's just a notebook." He nudges it toward me with the tips of his fingers.

I sweep the notebook up reverently and flip through the blank pages, breathing in the smell of paper. It's a little musty, but it will do. I allow memories of home, of my parents, to sweep me away. Their warmth and love. I hadn't realized how good I had it back home—not really—until I saw how others lived outside of Elpis. It's my duty to record life beyond the borders and use my knowledge to help everyone. If I don't do it, who will?

"Glad to see you like it." Drake chuckles. "Pip is hoping you will join us for dinner."

My eyes snap open. "Uh, sure."

But not without the notebook. I scoop up the pencil and tuck it safely in the first pages, then follow Drake out toward the square for dinner.

The hallways are always lively, much like the streets of Elpis' neighborhoods. Everyone is kind to one another, and their conversations are very typical of what I've heard back home, though under slightly different circumstances. As I pass, the people either fall silent or lower their voices, watching me go. The looks aren't the same as when I first arrived, not as guarded, but I can't place why it still unnerves me.

The hallways are as wide as a one-way street, lit with the same round LED lights. Some are burned out. My fingers itch to fix them as I pass.

I learned in my first few days here that the Haven differs from Elpis in one critical aspect.

Not everyone has a Power.

In fact, only about a tenth of the population does. Those who don't have a Power depend on the others to keep their water supply and food safe—among other expansion tasks. According to Drake and Pip, there hasn't been anyone like me in a couple generations. No one can shape the earth to help create new homes and expand the community. And the Elders won't allow me to do it.

Pip's face lights up when she sees the two of us enter the square where everyone occupies tables over dinner. Drake chuckles and shakes his head at Pip's reaction.

She smooths her dark braid over her shoulder as we approach with our bowls. Another stew. They eat a lot of it. I've never been a fan, but under the circumstances I don't feel it is appropriate to complain.

"I see you gave him the notebook," Pip says, nodding toward it.

I remove it from where I pinched it under my arm to avoid spilling on it as I walked, setting it on the table delicately. "He did. I love it. It's kind of like having a piece of home here."

She reaches across the table and pats my arm. "Good. I'm glad to hear it."

"He tried to refuse it at first," Drake adds, smirking at me.

I flush and tuck over my bowl to eat, hoping to cover my embarrassment. I hadn't meant offense and hope that no one sees it that way.

Neither of them makes further comment, talking about winter and hunts as we eat.

"Mom says they will probably send up another hunting party soon," Pip says. "The deer are out in force right now, so it's a good time to collect meat before the snow comes."

Deer.

I remember Paige petting that white-tail doe so long ago now. The awe on her face had filled me with warmth, despite my uneasiness at being anywhere near the creature. Paige loved it. Just like she would love the woods here.

"Are you okay, Gavin?" Pip startles me from my thoughts. "You sister again?"

"Hmm?" I glance up at her across the table and realize I'm crying. Quickly, I drop my spoon and brush away the tears. "Sorry. I'm fine." I clear my throat. "Did you say something about snow coming?"

I've only ever seen snow in the mountains near Elpis. It hasn't snowed in the city since before the Collapse.

"It always comes a little early this far north," she says.

Drake bites into his bread, talking around it in a way that would have made my parents lose their minds. "I hate the snow. Cold, wet crap."

I grin, amused by his complete lack of table manners. He's clearly comfortable around me. Either that or he has no manners to speak of.

"Chew and swallow first, you heathen," Pip teases.

I laugh. Maybe I can't go home yet, but these two have a way of making me happy.

"Will you be joining us at the temple this week, Gavin?" Pip asks.

I've avoided it per Emil's direction for weeks. The way Pip's eyes light up as she asks makes it hard to refuse again. I find belief systems fascinating, but mostly because the structure of them adheres followers to a rigid form of right and wrong that is not always best. Having studied science as much as I have, believing that some ethereal entity controls our fates and created the world feels like grasping at straws. Powers are one thing. I can explain the genetic nature of our DNA and how they work. But religion gives these Powers a reverence I don't agree with.

But I can't refuse again. Not when the Minister himself opened his home to me. Not when it could kill the hope in Pip's eyes. Even Drake appears hopeful.

So I agree...very reluctantly.

16

PAIGE

THE STYLISTS ARRIVE EARLY in the morning, ushering all eight of us through showers, hair, and makeup. They squeeze each of us into a floor-length black sleeveless dress that hugs our hips and accentuates our chests. It's far too difficult to breathe in these torturous things. January nearly pops out of the top of hers. If King Cypress is a chest man, none of us stand a chance beside her.

As they fasten my dress closed in the back, I focus on the mission. Get close to the King and his family, learn about the Kingdom, and find some way home again. If there is any hope for peace with Elpis—slim as I am certain it will be—I hope to at least not burn the bridge completely. Dad won't thank me for that.

To get what I want, I must play this game. On the ship headed toward the island, Zephyr informed me that the King enjoys a challenge. I will use that to my advantage.

Once we are all ready, they loaded the seven of us into two beautiful horse-drawn buggies. The ride is ridiculously short, taking us to the main road in front of the cottage, then around to the front of the palace. The entire ride only takes about two minutes. We could have walked.

A butler in a severely starched suit opens the door and January steps out first. It seems they will march us right up the stairs and through the front door. A luxurious, bright red carpet beneath an impressive awning covers the steps all the way to the massive front doors.

At the top of the steps, the Admiral waits with his hands folded behind his back.

The seven of us climb. Thankfully, we were not forced into heels. Some of these girls look like they would fall right back down the stairs. No doubt, none of them ever wore shoes like these before. Layla manages well enough, though, practically elbowing the other girls out of the way to get to the front of the group.

I'm one of the first to reach the top, with Layla only moments behind. Feeling eyes on me, I scan the area. To either side, a covered promenade with pure white pillars at regular intervals stretches the length of the long palace. Doorways and windows offer glimpses inside.

My gaze drifts up.

Above the red carpet, a long balcony overlooks the entrance to the palace. Five people occupy the balcony. An older woman with a commanding air peers down at us with icy blue eyes. The crown on her head is a bejeweled golden piece, clearly marking her as queen. A girl our age with shiny brown hair whispers something to one of the three boys. His piercing blue eyes meet mine and a charming smile lights up his face. Soft curls frame his face. He is dangerously handsome. The other boy appears close to Blue Eyes' age. His gentle blue eyes examine all seven of us.

The final occupant makes my heart stutter. *Zephyr*. And for once he isn't dressed in that gray overcoat. He wears the same stuffy formal uniform as the Admiral greeting us on the red carpet. When our eyes meet, I offer him a smile, but he averts his gaze and whispers something to the Gentle Boy, then disappears into the building. The girl watches him go with a frown.

I can't be sure which of the other two boys is the new king. Neither wears a crown. Both are certainly handsome, but something about Gentle Boy feels...off. I can't explain it. A perception of déjà vu accompanies the sensation.

"Welcome to the palace, ladies," our greeter says, drawing my gaze back. The other girls follow him through the doors, and I hustle to catch up. "I am Lord Baron Strong, Admiral of Tides.

The others have already arrived, and the Queen is eager to get matters underway."

Others? January and I exchange perplexed glances. We didn't know there were others. Was there another cottage full of girls?

We pass into a lobby that stretches hundreds of feet in either direction. Stunning shades of red and green in varying hues cover the walls and furniture. The carpet is black with green leaves and red flowers in repeating patterns in all directions. Lord Baron leads our group deeper into the palace.

Some girls tilt their head all the way back to stare in awe at the chandeliers lighting the lobby. Others swivel their heads as they look this way and that, stunned into silence by the opulence. This sort of place must be like a whole other world. Nothing like it exists outside these walls anymore. Even in Elpis, this sort of thing would be lavish.

"Are those books?" Alice asks Layla.

I follow her gaze right to what appears to be a library behind bay windows.

"I've never seen so many in one place," Layla murmurs. "Paige should like that." She throws a devilish smirk over her should, clearly thinking she has insulted me.

Why do they think I enjoy books? I read in the cottage to pass time, but I can think of a hundred other things I would enjoy more. Like a fitness center, for starters.

Lord Baron climbs a short flight of steps straight ahead and motions for us to take a seat on the green-leaf sofas.

Four other girls are already seated, studying us with a mixture of fascination and—in the case of one girl—disgust.

I settle beside January, hiding my awe at the surrounding luxury. If I intend to play this game to earn the King's trust, I'm aware that it has already begun. The four girls already here do not show the same awe as the rest of us. They have been to this place before, which means they are from this island. They probably already know King Cypress.

Over the past few weeks, I got to know the six girls housed with me. Now, I take a moment to study the four newcomers. They wear the same black dress as the rest of us, which tells me this must be a customary thing for all Tributes.

Each girl is beautiful in her own way, but one of them is absolutely stunning. Her dark hair shines walnut brown in the light, piled perfectly on her head. A red flower matching those on the rug outside adorns her hair. Her sharp brows highlight her deep blue eyes. The makeup makes her cheekbones really pop. She must have won the genetics lottery.

She catches me staring at her and offers a kind smile that only makes me more worried. I don't really want to marry the King—or anyone—but if I am going to play this game, I already know she is my primary opponent for the King's attention. That smile is not only beautiful, but so warm I believe her to be friendly. A dangerous assumption, I'm sure.

Lord Baron steps in front of the closed doors beside the sofas, clearing his throat. All eleven of us turn our attention to him.

"Before we begin, I must give you a few ground rules," he says. "You are here for one reason and one reason only—as a potential future spouse to our new king. Should you refuse to participate, you will be removed from the premises and left to your own fate on the island. We will arrange no accommodation for you. We will make no payments. No one will take you in. You will be as you were beyond the Capital. Alone."

I can't help but wonder how many of these girls would prefer that over playing this game. I could handle myself on my own. Could any of them?

Lord Baron continues without missing a beat. "You are not, under any circumstances, to fraternize with *anyone* besides the King until you are dismissed. From this day until he lets you go, you are his."

A chill runs down my spine. *Nope. Don't like that.* They can't honestly expect us to accept this. I don't *belong* to anyone.

"Breaking the fraternization rule is punishable as treason," he says. I get the idea clearly enough. Treason equals death. "The same punishment applies if you assault His Grace or any members of his family. King Cypress, and only he, has the authority to dismiss you from the palace. Should that happen, we will help you transition into life on the island, and we will give you a generous payout to help you begin your new life. Should you reject him, we will dismiss you without these benefits."

I glance at the beauty from the corner of my eye. She remains calm, attentive, demure, holding her chin high. I would bet she doesn't need any of the benefits.

"You are forbidden to leave the palace grounds without permission from His Grace, King Cypress," Lord Baron continues. "This includes crossing the road and venturing down into the garden, or to the stables. This building and the side garden are your home."

Or our prison. I fold my hands in my lap to keep from fidgeting.

"It is not unheard of for a king to select a consort or two, as well as a queen," Lord Baron says. "So even if he does not choose you as his queen, he may still choose you as his consort. This decision is his and his alone."

Nope. I don't like that either. It means that, if I'm not careful, he might want to keep me as a plaything.

With a flick of his wrist, he commands two servants up the shallow steps. Each carries a long wooden box.

"Each of you will receive a bracelet clearly marking you as a Tribute," Lord Baron explains as the servants hold the box in front of each of us.

I reach in and pull out a bracelet, a series of gold links inlaid with emerald stones. It reminds me of the Power stone my dad found beneath Elpis a few years ago. That stone kills people with Powers. I don't want to put this bracelet on.

"You are to wear these bracelets at all times, both in your rooms and on the grounds," he says. "Removing the bracelet without

King Cypress' permission will cause immediate dismissal without benefits."

My fingers tremble as I clasp it around my wrist. A familiar yet uncomfortable sensation settles over me. I have only felt this a few times before. Around Zephyr. Instinctively, I reach out for my Power and hit a barrier. The block between myself and my Muscle Memory is invisible, but solid. Perhaps I should rethink my plan. It sounds easy enough to be dismissed. Will I be free to move around the island as I please if I am dismissed? I need a little more information before taking that step.

They are worried about us using our Power against King Cypress. I almost laugh. Wouldn't it be assault and punishable by death as well? Though I suppose a determined girl might kill him before being killed herself.

The stunning girl grimaces as she clasps her own bracelet. *Even her grimace is beautiful.*

"Today, you will meet one-on-one with the Dowager Queen," he informs us, drawing my attention back toward the closed doors. "She will ask you no less than one question, which you must answer. She will know if you lie, so I suggest honesty. Then you will be allowed to ask her *only* one question of your choosing. Once you are done, we will escort you to your new room. Dinner will come to you tonight. Tomorrow, you will all dine with the King and his family."

Each girl is called into the chamber beyond the doors in alphabetical order. I only catch glimpses inside at the green and salmon-colored room beyond. Once, I think I spot the head of a lion statue, but the door closes so quickly I can't be sure.

The stunning girl sits across from me, watching the lobby with intense patience.

Alice goes first, followed by one of the island girls named Bella—the same one who looked at us with disgust—then another islander named Everly. I struggle not to fidget, examining the red nail polish. Black and red seem to be dominant colors here, along with green. I wonder if these are the colors of the crown.

No one dares to speak as we wait our turn. Not with Lord Baron standing only feet away.

Two more girls disappear inside—Holly and January. Servants arrive with hors d'oeuvres and drinks for those of us remaining. I try to pick at a few, but my stomach is a mess. In fact, only the stunning girl and another with a plump, round face and broad shoulders eat with any level of calm.

Two more girls disappear—Layla, and the round-faced island girl, Maeve.

The stunning girl offers me a kind smile. "I promise he is a sweetheart," she whispers conspiratorially.

"I'm not worried about him," I admit, glancing at Lord Baron. Either he doesn't hear us or, more likely, pretends not to.

Something about her voice tickles my memory.

"Lady Nora." Lord Baron's voice calls the girl to her feet.

She winks at me as she makes her way to the door. "We will speak again later."

The door seals her inside, leaving me alone with River and Summer. I smile at them, but it's fake, and they can probably tell.

It hits me where I know Nora from. She was the one who found Zephyr drunk outside the palace two nights ago. My stomach twists. If she knows him that well, she probably also knows the King well.

Nora's time in the room is significantly shorter than any of the other girls. So much so that when Lord Baron calls my name, I jump in alarm and wonder if I've inadvertently done something wrong.

He opens the door. Up close, I can see the stark set of his jaw much more clearly. He reminds me of Zephyr.

The door clicks shut behind me softly, but the sound seems much louder in my ears.

At the head of the room, atop a small dais flanked by not one, but two bronze lion statues, sits the Queen.

"Lady Paige," the Queen says, motioning to an empty armchair across from her. "Or should I call you Princess Powers?"

My eyes widen. Zephyr clearly told her about my teasing. Is this woman his mother? I don't see any resemblance.

"No, Your Grace," I say, hoping I've used the correct title. "Just Paige is fine."

"Lady Paige," she insists as I settle in. "For now, at least."

The queen is a gorgeous woman, if a bit severe. She can't be much older than my mother, but unlike my mom, who prefers lounging in her PJs, the Queen appears at ease even in her elaborate red dress. An air of command and confidence surrounds her. She controls this room. I almost envy it.

"It is my understanding that your father is a community leader," she says. "And a powerful man."

"Where did you—?" But I cut it off, already knowing the answer.

Easton. How much did they force out of him? Questions about him dance to the tip of my tongue, but I bite them all back. I am only allowed one question, and I can't waste it on him. Not right now.

I smooth out my skirt and shake my head. "Never mind. It doesn't matter."

"What makes you think you would be a suitable candidate for the King's hand?" Her question sounds innocent.

I want to tell her I'm *not* a suitable candidate, but this is my chance to lay the groundwork for what I want down the road. Everything I do and say will all be part of their game from this point on.

"As you already know, my father is a powerful community leader," I say carefully, hoping she can't see my hands shaking in my lap. "I feel I could bring a potential alliance to the table."

She trills. "Oh, my sweet, we don't need alliances. We rule all."

I raise my chin. "I suppose you must. After all, your Captain of Tides found me hundreds of miles from home, where we have never heard of the Kingdom."

A flash of anger strikes her eyes, and her smile freezes menacingly. She leans closer. "If you wish to continue here, be careful how you speak to me. I am Dowager Queen to King Cypress. And my son adores me."

"As most boys do to their mothers," I say. "I mean no disrespect. You asked what I offer. I gave you an honest answer. More power, unlike anything you have here."

She sits back, pursing her lips. Have I made a misstep? I've never spoken to royalty before.

"What about your mother? Is she just as powerful as your father?"

"Not in the same way. My mom prefers her plants to politics."

"They both have magic?"

Magic. Zephyr called it that as well. I hesitate, then respond slowly. "No. There is a difference between commanding power and having Powers."

The queen eyes me for so long it takes all my strength not to squirm. Her icy eyes weigh me like a pound of flesh on the scales of justice. I suppose I can't fault her caution. One of the eleven of us will become her daughter.

"You have one question, Lady Paige," she says at last.

I almost sag in relief. This must be a signal to the end of this conversation. I can't wait to escape her.

Eager to be done, I straighten in my chair and meet her gaze with a steady one of my own. "Yes. I have one. If I am dismissed, will I be allowed to return home?"

Her eyes widen in shock, and her gaze sweeps the grand room. "Why on earth would you want to? There is nothing for anyone beyond this island. Even if you are dismissed, your life here will be better than it ever would on the mainland. We have given you a *gift*, rescued you from bandits, starvation, and terrible storms. No one ever wants to go back."

I lick my lips. "I just want to return to my family. I only want to know if I would be allowed to do that upon dismissal. My life before this was pretty great." Well, except for Tudor being a jerk and dumping me out of spite.

Silence settles. The queen gawks at me like I have something hanging from my nose. I resist the urge to rub my nose subconsciously.

"We will take it into consideration, Lady Paige," she says at last. "You are dismissed."

She waves me to a side door where a guard awaits. As I walk away, I can feel the Queen's gaze burning into me. Before slipping out the narrow side door, I glance at her.

That woman is terrifying.

17

ZEPHYR

"IT'S WHAT SHE WANTS," Cypress told me this morning. "At least you won't be stuck in the same room with her all day. Take your breaks where you can, Zeph."

Cypress had a point. Queen Elena isn't my biggest fan.

Cypress made Queen Elena's demands perfectly. Each girl will spend some time alone with Queen Elena. She will ask them questions to learn a little more about each of them and why they should be considered for this position. I am *not* to be in the room during any of this. Queen Elena intends to use her Polygraph magic to ensure the girls don't lie to her. If I'm in the room, her magic won't work. After her questions, each girl will be allowed to ask the Queen one question.

My job—my *only* job—is to escort each girl to her new room once she finishes the interview and try to determine the magic strength of each for a report afterward.

Now that the girls are in the palace, they are chatty. Far more than I expected. Alice tempers her curiosity, only asking me how I enjoy living in the palace and asking how Ian and Finrik—the boy recruits who traveled with us—are faring. I keep my response short.

Most of the other girls want to know about my brother. It's natural, under the circumstance. I try to give him as many glowing marks as I can without telling lies.

If they knew Cypress was listening to them from the small lobby outside his suite, catching glimpses of them as we round the landing and continue climbing the steps, they might not ask so many questions about him.

"Is he dreamy?" Layla asks as we reach her floor. "I bet he is."

I press my lips together. "I'm not sure how to answer that. Sorry."

"Well, other girls talk about him, right? What do they say?"

I stop outside her door, motioning toward it. "Your room, Lady Layla."

She pouts as she steps inside. "Not even a clue."

"I think an air of mystery is a good thing. I need to get back." Despite walking away, Layla continues asking questions I ignore.

She will get on Cypress' nerves quickly. And her magic is hardly impressive. Class three, at best. Chemical manipulation, from what I can sense. Hardly an exciting magic.

Maeve is next. Her father is one of the more influential men on the island, running the farmlands. Her class is borderline four organic mutation. I've watched her revive dying trees and turn grassland lush.

Most of these girls have passable magic. Which only makes Paige stand out like a blazing sun in comparison.

Nora's interview is so quick I don't make it back downstairs before she is waiting outside the door for me. She slips her arm into mine and we climb the stairs together.

"She's very pretty," Nora says as we pass Cypress' floor. Of the eight girls I've already escorted up, she is the only one who remains silent until we are past Cypress' floor. She probably knows he is there.

"Who?"

Nora trills, patting my arm endearingly. "Oh please, Zephyr. I heard you hid in the treehouse to see her. Paige. The girl you brought in."

My face heats. "It isn't like that."

"If you say so. Just be careful."

We round the next landing in silence. What does she mean? Do I want to kiss Paige? Yes. So badly. Will I? No. Desire isn't the same thing as love, and I'm not about to confuse the two.

Nora slips her arm out of mine and waves me off. "I can find my way from here. If you change your mind about her, just say the word. I'll make sure she's dismissed swiftly."

"Nora..."

She rolls her eyes and nudges me away. "Go. I'm joking. I'm not about to share."

Those five words carry me down the steps with a bit more haste. Not about to share? Is she talking about Cypress...or me?

I don't realize Paige is next until the door opens and she stumbles out as if someone pushed her out the door.

She glares at the door, smoothing out her skirt, then spins around and jumps in alarm upon seeing me. Her hand darts to her chest, drawing my gaze to the low cut of her dress. I glance away.

"This way," I grumble, nodding toward the steps. Thank goodness I'm in good shape. All this up and down the steps is exhausting.

"Not even going to *act* like a gentleman, I guess." Paige marches past me toward the steps.

I quickly match her stride, just catching the end of a mutter. "...drawn to me."

My heart stops. *No. She can't know that. It was a dream!* Mortification heats my face.

I step ahead of her, not bothering to offer my arm as I did for the other girls. The prospect of touching her both terrifies and thrills me.

When we round the landing near Cypress, I peek through the opening. He sits in a chair by his door, glancing up from a book as we pass. He frowns and cocks his head when he sees me. What must I look like? Red as a rose. Not holding her arm. Not talking to her.

His gaze flicks to Paige, sweeping over her. If I could turn any redder, I would. I don't want him looking at her like that. Then a hint of amusement crosses his face, and he returns attention to his book.

I peer back at Paige. Her own face is set with angry determination, as if the steps have offended her personally. If I could climb two at a time, I would. The faster she gets to her room, the faster I can get away from her.

"Zephyr, slow down," she snaps at last as we near the final landing. "I can run upstairs as well as anyone else, but not in this."

I freeze, hand on the railing.

Paige rounds the landing, squaring off in front of me. "Why are we racing?"

"I have a job to do. I'm doing it. But if I don't get back down there soon, it will leave the next girl standing there waiting. So, let's go." I brush past, launching myself up the last flight of stairs two at a time.

She growls. A moment later, she passes me, dress shoes in her hand and skirt gathered over her arm. I have to call her to stop before she passes her floor.

Paige plants her hand on her hip, glaring at me. "I don't know what I did to piss you off, but I would rather clear the air now."

"Nothing. You're in room 348. Right there." I point at the open door, then spin to sprint down the steps.

Paige seizes my arm. Her grip is powerful even without her magic. It brings back the memory of the nightmare she rescued me from. My father whipping me. Paige arriving and turning him to ash. Her arms around me. *It was just a nightmare.* A nightmare fueled by a combination of worry over the questions plaguing me, my ever-lingering fear of my father even in death, and my need to be close to her. *It was nothing.*

So why is my heart racing? She needs to get her hands off me.

"This could be considered assault," I say calmly.

Paige immediately withdraws her hand, paling. "Sorry. 348?" Sorrow shimmers in her umber eyes.

I swallow and nod. I hate how much that statement scared her.

Before she can stop me, I jog back down the steps, eager to put distance between us before I say or do anything stupid.

18

GAVIN

PIP CLINGS TIGHT TO my arm, as if worried that if she loosens her grip, I will change my mind and turn back. It certainly has struck my mind. I've never been religious. *Why did I agree with this?* Pip practically gushes with happiness as we make our way to the temple. *Oh right, that's why.*

Crowds of people flood the halls, headed to the same place. The murmur of friendly voices in hushed conversations and parents calling to small children reminds me a little of home.

I expect Pip to lead me toward the main square—that seems to be where most hubs of business are for the community. Instead, we turn away, following a maze of street-like tunnels. As we go, the passages to the temple imprint in my mind. They can go in the notebook later just in case I need them. The first thing I added to the pages were coded directions back to Elpis—just in case anyone snooped—then a map of the Haven.

This community's so much larger than I expected. The organization of the tunnels makes logical sense to me. Everything is in quadrants—blocks of homes in organized rows; food, water, and facilities clustered together. I'm certain there is still a lot I have yet to see here.

Pip and I follow the crowd toward the largest set of open arched doors I have seen here, deep in the belly of the Haven. I gape in awe at the massive carved doors gleaming in the LED lights. The carvings depict a scene of ancient biblical proportions. The doors must be two stories tall!

On one door, a man holds his arms high as the world around him changes—as if he is recreating the very surface of the world itself. On the other door, another figure stretches a hand toward the first man. The head is tilted toward the sky. And in front of this figure, flames engulf a massive tree.

The two carvings give me chills. No good beliefs can come from these two images.

We pass through the enormous doorway.

The interior of the temple is gigantic. I had wondered how so many could fit within the walls of the temple. Now, it's clear the temple could fit thousands. It reminds me of Fitness Stadium, but underground. The resources and dedication it must have taken—not to mention the Powers—to create a place like this had to have been impressive. And very much by design.

At the head of the temple, a wide wooden stage on a high platform of carved stone holds the podium and a box to the side where a choir waits. The two figures from the doors stand guard over either side of the platform, holding up the three-story ceiling with their outstretched arms. If I thought the doors were big, they have nothing on these two statues.

Fanning out from the platform, stone benches form a bowl of risers. Pip guides me down the steps of the center aisle toward the front rows closest to the platform. My steps become more stilted and I drag my feet, wishing now more than ever that I had not agreed to this. There's a one hundred percent chance I will find holes in this religion, and I worry I will say or do something to offend the only two friends I have in this place. I was so much better off remaining ignorant of all of this.

Emil warned me to stay away.

I failed.

Pip makes friendly conversations with dozens of people in passing. Her sweet, patient disposition would be endearing if I weren't so eager to flee.

Paige would hate it here. Underground. Surrounded by hundreds of people. As my chest tightens, I suddenly have a deeper appreciation for her claustrophobia.

"Gavin," Pip's mother, Mrs. Garraty, says, drawing my gaze away from the massive statues. "We are so honored to have you join us today."

I force a smile. If she can tell, she gives no sign.

"Today's sermon will be a great one," Mrs. Garraty continues.

My gaze sweeps through the crowd for Drake. I spot him nudging his way toward us. He waves at me, twisting to squeeze between two families talking in the middle of the aisle. Seeing that dumb grin on his face eases some of my tension. Having him close makes all this more bearable.

Mrs. Garraty guides us to our seats in the front. I turn as Drake takes a seat in the row behind us.

"Sorry," he says, breathless. "I had to finish some work before service. Almost didn't make it! Glad you're here." He pats my shoulder. "I hear the Minister has prepared a whopper of a service today!"

Minister. I know the title differs from my dad's—one is religious and the other is governance—but it still makes me uneasy. Would they misunderstand who my father is if I called him the Minister?

"Yes," Mrs. Garraty says. "Once he heard our guest would attend, Charles spent hours reworking his sermon. He wants to put our best foot forward today." She winks at me.

My gaze slips to Pip, who stares at me almost reverently. What has she told her father about me? About Elpis?

I press my back onto the bench and fold my hands in my lap, clasping them to keep from fidgeting.

Mrs. Garraty asks Drake some question. I can't make myself listen to the conversation. What kind of situation have I walked myself into?

Back in the city, Emil told Drake that Haven stuffed nonsense down their throats about someone coming to save them and rebuild the world. Drake seemed to think it was me. Emil called the whole idea garbage. If these people are fanatics for this religion they have created, there is every chance I have walked myself into some sort of religious cult. If I can talk to Emil about it, maybe he can shed more light on their beliefs. He certainly gave me the impression he doesn't believe in any of it.

I scan the crowd, but if Emil is here, he blends right into the hundreds gathered on rows of benches. *I need to get out of here.*

A piano plays a gentle song. Something about the sound sooths my unease. I watch the pianist for a moment, but doubt she is using a Power. Perfect Pitch is a real Power, but no one can create music that influences feelings directly through a Power. *Can't they?* It isn't something I've heard of before, but who says Elpis has a perfect knowledge base of everything that is possible?

Drake leans closer, whispering in my ear as he nods at the pianist and choir. "Acolytes."

As if that changes anything.

The choir voices hum into life. Their harmony is well-practiced, but not perfect. Every slight off key makes me wince. I've never been one for music, but the sound of their voices still stirs something inside of me. A sense of peace, or maybe hope. It must be a Power. Not the music itself, but the people singing it. There must be at least one Influencer in that choir. I don't like that they can use the music to influence the masses. It makes my gut churn.

How deep do the roots of this religion go? How zealous are the believers? The more fervently one believes, the greater lengths they will go to fulfill their convictions. I have read numerous ancient books about long-past wars founded on religious beliefs. The Haven wouldn't be like them, would they?

The Haven.

That name alone should have been a clue, but I saw it as something more innocent. A refuge from danger in the broken world. A haven of safety. What if my entire perception was wrong? What if they call it the Haven *because* of their zealous beliefs?

These realizations only make me more uncomfortable beside Pip.

The Minister approaches the podium in pure white robes. The same six-spoke wheel with the six-pointed star in the center from his chair is embroidered in the breast of his robes in brilliant golden thread that shines in the temple lights. This close, I can see how much Pip resembles him. The same angular face and eyes. His gaze meets mine and I glance away.

Seeing Mr. Garraty in these ceremonial robes settles oddly in me. Usually, he wears plain clothes like everyone else. Over the past few weeks, he has made rounds speaking with citizens. I assume it was just part of his job as Minister.

A hush falls over the masses as Mr. Garraty takes his place on the platform. That he commands the room effortlessly does nothing for my churning stomach.

"Followers of the Prophet, true believers of the Idols, I have spent the last week in quiet contemplation, reviewing the reverent words in the *Book of the Prophet*, reading the Signs." His voice carries through the massive temple, lifting and falling with his words in perfect rhythm. The effect is almost spellbinding, and I can see why people would listen to him, even if I don't believe in religious idols. "The Day of Glory approaches."

This pronouncement draws a series of murmurs of delight from the masses. The Minister presses onward.

"More than a century ago, the Lord rose again," the Minister says, his voice undulating with enthusiasm. "When the world fell into deeply seeded sin, He came. He looked upon the peoples of the world with profound sorrow and vowed to restore balance. But to do this, He first had to cleanse the world—such was the depth of depravity that the only way to reinstate glory was to remove all those guilty of sin and allow the earth to reclaim control."

I shift in my seat, tightening the grip on my clasped hands. None of this bodes well. They believe the war and collapse came because of *sin*?

"And so, He sent His son once more!"

The congregation ripples with praise. I feel sick.

"His son, the Champion, brought mountains to the sea, consumed the worst dens of sin into the oceans, poisoned the lands of the non-believers, until only the strongest and most devout remained."

The Minister speaks of the war and collapse as if some divine power brought it about. But history tells a different story. One of a young man named Atmos whose Power was so strong he changed the atmosphere of the world. His Power instigated a chain reaction of nuclear explosions and natural disasters that altered the surface of the world forever.

Until recently, the people of Elpis believed we were all that remained. People with Powers founded the city, and only those with Powers survived the apocalypse. Nothing existed beyond our borders as far as we knew.

Or at least, that was the case until Dad came along. He refused to accept that we were all that remained in the world. He never stopped looking for answers. Then, five years ago, he found them. The Founders of Elpis left behind evidence that there were others, people who had been blocked out by a Power-created barrier—aggressive men who stole, killed, and kidnapped.

I left the city with my sister and four others to find other communities like the Haven. In Elpis, we have proof that this religion is built on a foundation of misinformation and twisted truths.

Pip flashes me a smile that tells me she fervently believes every word her father preaches to the masses. I offer her a fake smile in return, not wanting to offend her.

"Those who persisted remained scattered, struggling to survive, falling prey to illness, poison, and starvation," the Minister continues. His voice rises to a fevered pitch. "But then, the Prophet came to us in our darkest hour. He gathered us, sheltered us—" He motions to the surrounding the temple, indicating this Prophet helped found this underground city. "—and filled our hearts with the promise of a new day. 'Support one another,' he said, 'protect each other, work as a community toward survival and one day, you will be rewarded with a new garden of Eden.'"

The masses chime in with a well-rehearsed, "Praise be the Prophet."

"On the Day of Glory, the Lord will send His Idols to liberate us and bring humanity and the world to the promised paradise." The Minister speaks with his hands, allowing his enthusiasm to show. Were I not so certain this was all a load of misinterpreted nonsense, it might sway me.

A glance at Drake reveals the same reverence as Pip. He is drawn into this just as surely as everyone else. I can't explain why it upsets me so much to know that *he* believes this. Maybe I had hoped that Drake had more sense than this. I will have to set him straight. Privately and quietly.

"The Idol of Desolation shall appear to us, cleansing the world of the last remnants of Man's sin. Then, the Idol of Creation will rebuild the world, welcoming us forth into a purified world of unity and security."

The sermon continues, explaining all the signs that brought him to the conclusion that the Day of Glory approaches. Some signs tie so closely to my arrival that I feel the eyes of the masses on me, as if I'm a link to the coming salvation. That He will come from the west, promising to rebuild the broken world with knowledge and power beyond understanding.

"He will be powers Himself."

My gut sinks. That must be coincidence.

Then the Minister connects the dots much more clearly. "We are blessed to have a new member in our congregation with us today."

Pip grips my arm with an enthusiasm that makes me sure I'm about to be sick.

"Pippen, please bring our visitor forward."

Me. He means me. I shake my head. "No," I hiss urgently in her ear. "I'm not comfortable with this, Pip."

She gives my arm a gentle tug. "It's okay, Gavin. My father doesn't bite." She tugs me to my feet.

"It's not him I'm worried about," I mutter.

But there is no arguing. If I refuse to comply with this, these people—hundreds of them—will turn against me. A moment in the spotlight can't be that bad, as long as I can melt back into the shadows when it's over.

He will be powers.

Pip escorts me up the steps toward the podium. Her face beams with delight as surely as the sun shines. We reach center stage and face outward.

Powers.

Hundreds, perhaps a thousand, all focus on me. My face heats and I dip my gaze away, only to be greeted by the faceless Idol statue. A lump lodges in my throat and no matter how many times I swallow, I can't dislodge it.

The Minister's hand falls solidly on my shoulder, clamping down as if holding me prisoner. The sensation of the walls closing in only amplifies the impression of being trapped.

"What is your name, son?"

He already knows my name. He wants me to say it, to announce it to everyone. My voice limps meekly past my lips. "G-Gavin."

"Gavin...?" He is pushing me to speak my last name. I know what he is doing, trying to force me into one of his signs.

But I have no escape. "Gavin Powers."

A murmur ripples through the crowd. The Minister puffs up as if my declaration just proved some mystical point. And to these people, it probably did.

"Gavin *Powers*," he says, adding extra emphasis to my last name. "Where do you come from?"

There isn't a chance I will give away anything in front of every member of the Haven. But he doesn't expect me to. He wants me to check off another box. My blood pumps in my ears. "West."

"West," he repeats. Again, the crowd murmurs. "By hundreds of miles, we hear."

I swallow and nod. The affirmation creates another ripple of awe in the masses.

"Pippen tells me you are special." Though he talks as if speaking to me, his focus is clearly directed at the people. "And I have heard from a few members of the congregation that you put on quite a display of power in old St. Louis, son."

Another box checked.

I close my eyes. My jaw twitches. *Stop calling me son!* My heart aches for Dad. He would know what to say or do right now. He always does.

Slowly, I open my eyes, turning a challenging stare at the Minister.

"I wasn't the only one," I admit, referring to Drake's Silencer Power that allowed us to escape without making a sound. Or April's Wind Dancing that helped the boat sail quickly upriver. Or Dani's Transmutation Conversion that allowed the Havenites to bring critical resources they otherwise would not have been able to move safely back home again.

"I heard." His affirmation doesn't reassure me at all. If anything, I detect a hint of something else hidden underneath. Some mysterious meaning. "And I've spoken with several of our citizens about your miraculous help these past weeks."

No. He's using my kindness against me. Kindness he tied a rope around to trap to his will.

"Just doing my part," I mumble.

His grip on my shoulder tightens even more. He turns his attention fully to the crowd. "The Day of Glory approaches!"

Bile climbs up my throat. He is turning my words into prophecy fulfillment.

I don't want this attention.

19

PAIGE

I WOULD HARDLY CALL my new room grand, but it certainly dwarfs my room back home. And I have a private bathroom. The wallpaper leaves something to be desired. Giant yellow roses surrounded by green leaves on a white background. The bedspread isn't much better. Whoever designed this palace clearly loved flowers.

Despite the unappealing design, I can't complain about the view. A balcony connects to the room, overlooking the palace grounds and the lake beyond. I stay on the balcony to watch the sunset. What would Gavin think of this place?

I've only dreamed of him a few times over the past few weeks. Each time, I felt like I was really sitting with him, really talking to him, really holding his hand. I never realized just how much I adored my brother until he was gone. If I have Dreamer Powers, those dreams might have some foundation in the truth. And if that's true, then Gavin is alive.

But it also means he isn't home either. Which means Mom and Dad must be beside themselves with worry. Dad is probably blaming himself for allowing us to leave, as if he could have stopped us.

Tears sting my eyes. I blink wildly to fight them off, rushing back inside to get some tissue to wipe them away. Dreaming. If I can control it, maybe I can use this Power to send messages to Easton...to home.

Which means I also need information. I make a mental list of everyone I have met—short as it is. There is Lord Baron, the Admiral, who I spoke with once before. He's a stern man. Zephyr, of course. The two curly haired, blue-eyed boys on the balcony—one of whom must be King Cypress. And the girl who was there with them. Is she a princess or perhaps a wife to one of them? I need all their names.

The Dowager Queen gave me chills earlier. That woman is a force to be reckoned with. I hope I never have to go toe-to-toe with her.

I also commit as much of the layout of the palace to memory as possible. So far, I haven't seen too much, but it was enough for me to at least know how to get out quickly. The stairs are right by my door. They come out three floors down in the main lobby by the red carpet steps outside. Once I'm out, there's nowhere to hide. If I need to make a run for it, I need to find a better escape route.

The race up the steps with Zephyr left my mind spinning. I don't understand why he is suddenly distant. All the way to the island, he was friendly. He even told a few jokes and laughed when I made fun of him. Now, that boy is gone. He seemed so eager to get away from me. Nothing like the dream where he tried to kiss me.

Was that dream real like the ones with Gavin? It could have been. Or maybe the dream was me projecting some deep need for companionship. They locked me up in that cottage with only girls, after all. And I kissed Easton in my dream once. Was that real as well? I have to learn how to tell the difference between actual dreams and Dreaming.

Voices in the hallway draw my attention. Some girls have gathered in clusters, showing off rooms and chatting amicably with one another. I drift toward January, Layla, Alice, and one of the new girls, Bella.

"—have danced with him before," Bella admits. "Last year at the Christmas Ball. It's open to the public, and people come and go all evening from the palace grounds to celebrate. He was just Lord Cypress then. His brother, Alric, was the crown prince."

"What happened to the crown prince?" Layla asks.

"He died recently, in the same accident that killed the last king, Alric the Third." Bella shrugs as if their deaths are no big deal.

"Not a terribly dedicated lady to shrug off the death of a king," I say.

Bella peers over her shoulder at me. Her gaze sweeps me over, quickly calculating my threat level. I'm not worried about this girl. In a fight, I could take her down in two seconds. "Don't assume that because I shrug, I don't care. We all mourn in our own way."

My lips thin.

Layla waves me off, eager to devour as much as she can learn about King Cypress.

I march back toward my door and notice Nora lingering in a doorway beside my own.

"Don't let her bother you," she says conspiratorially. "Bella is an entitled little prat." Lines of sorrow crease Nora's face. "She wouldn't know genuine compassion if it slapped her in the face."

Unlike Bella, I can read Nora's grief. *She* cared about the former King and the prince. It only reinforces just how close she must be with this family.

"I'm happy to try," I whisper back.

Nora gives me a half smile.

I want to ask her about Zephyr's odd behavior today, but worry that asking questions about him will get me into trouble.

"Layla's kind of the same," I whisper back.

"I get that sense." She nods stoically. Nora crosses her arms, glancing past me at the cluster of girls. "Sit with me at breakfast. I will be sure you get a proper introduction to Cypress."

I raise an amused eyebrow at her. "No titles necessary, huh?"

She smirks. "You'll get there." Then she winks and slips into her room, closing her door.

I feel like I have a friend. I also worry that Nora will arm herself with anything she can to win this pageant.

Strolling into my room, I grimace. I don't care. If I can befriend her, I can learn everything I need to know about this king and his family so I can find my way home. She can have him. I will even help her.

If she helps me.

20

ZEPHYR

NOW THAT THE INITIAL meeting with the Queen is over and the eleven girls are all tucked away in their rooms, the entire family convenes in the second room attached to the King's suites. I'm not sure who designed the color schemes for the rooms in the palace, but they certainly liked green and salmon.

Over the years, they have transformed this room several times from an office to a nursery to a spare bedroom. To prepare for the Tribute season, all beds have been removed and replaced with a long, wide table accompanied by two desks and several white-boards on easels. Twelve boards, to be exact. On each board, a picture of one girl with her name.

One is already crossed out. Ivy. Her tests revealed illness that disqualified her from contention. Last I heard, she was still in the hospital, but getting better. Not that I can say I've paid her a lot of mind.

My eyes are drawn to Paige. So much mystery surrounds her. When we collected her, she had fine clothes and a radio in her pack. And guns. The intensely raw strength is not only in magic, but her spirit is like a magnet. According to the stylists, her fingernails hadn't had decades of dirt under them like the other girls. She is unlike any girl I've ever encountered on the mainland.

Not to mention her desire to return home. Sure, most of the girls hadn't wanted to come along at first, but once they discover what life here could be like, they wouldn't want to return to the mainland. No girl has ever wanted to leave.

Yet Paige insists her life had been nice and she wants to return to it. Where did she come from? Paired with Easton's admission that he understands what their experiments on him mean... Are they more advanced than the other communities? Are they more advanced than *we* are?

"—dumber than a stack of bricks," Queen Elena says sharply, drawing my attention away from the image of Paige. She paces the green rug, shaking her head. "Unless you want an idiot at your side, I don't think she has anything to offer you that any of the other girls can't."

Who was she talking about?

I swallow and continue my task, writing the class of each girl's magic on their boards. All of them respectful—though I can already see a few falling short of the finish line.

We don't really care what anyone's magic *is*. But the class of it determines how strong it is. Previously, girls would have to show off their magical abilities. With me here, that isn't necessary. I can just sense their strength and skill.

Most of the royal family members are a four or five, which is above average and the entire reason we continue this Tribute tradition—to keep the magical bloodline strong. Aside from soldiers, few islanders have magical abilities beyond level one, if they have any at all.

High Houses keep their bloodlines as strong as they can so that their daughters can compete for the King's hand. In fact, it isn't uncommon for Tributes to marry an island lord if the King dismisses them. These girls are more desired than ordinary girls are. The High House daughters are somewhere between two and four. Nora is a rare six, which makes her a clear standout in magic. It's blood magic, which she could wield to impose her will on others. But classic to Nora, she uses it to help people.

But even Nora doesn't compare to Paige's class. We don't even *have* a class for someone like her.

"I will decide for myself what I think of each of these girls," Cypress says. I can hear how exhausted he already is with his mother. "Which one was Alice?" He glances at the boards.

I point at it, two boards from where I stand. "There. She may not have been terribly bright, but she is kind and sweet. That must count for something." Not that her magic does. She's barely a three.

Cypress strolls to her board, peering at the image. The image does little to reveal her natural beauty. Dark hair—like most of the girls. A smattering of freckles across the bridge of her nose and cheekbones. She wouldn't be my first choice, but she can turn heads.

My gaze returns to Paige. Her eyes stare out at me from the image as if peering into my soul. I edge toward her board, unsure how to write her class. What will they say when they see?

"I remember her." Cypress smirks at the image of Alice. "I will decide after I meet her."

Queen Elena rolls her eyes and huffs. "I'm telling you, she will bore you quickly."

The only sign of Cypress' irritation is a subtle thinning of his lips. He stops at Maeve's board and purses his lips. His nose scrunches. "This one bores me already."

Maeve is hardly a beauty by any means. She's short and wide. I suspect it's more bone structure than a weight problem, but it's hard to compete with some of these other girls.

Queen Elena marches over and crosses her arms. "Lady Maeve? She's an islander, and her father oversees the farmlands. You can't afford to anger him." She brushes past him to Nora's board. "I think your choice is clear."

My stomach clenches. I knew Nora would put herself in the running as Tribute, but the idea of her with Cypress unsettles me. That he reveals a hint of a smile as he gazes at Nora's board is of no help at all.

"If I won't dismiss any of them without meeting them first, I certainly won't make a choice until I do," Cypress says.

His answer irritates Queen Elena. Not that she expected him to choose Nora so quickly, but that he dismisses her comment so firmly. I wish that meant he would dismiss the idea of choosing Nora, but I know better. And if I could only free one girl from Cypress' bed...

I stare at Paige's board as the two continue their discussion about the other girls. The moment I write her class on this board, the entire game changes. Just what would they do if they knew the truth? Would Cypress take back everything he just said and choose Paige immediately? The strength of magic bears heavy influence on the final decision. How could he say no to someone as strong as she is?

"I liked January," Dominic says from a chair near the window.

Queen Elena snorts. "You just like staring at her chest. Don't think I didn't notice."

"And Bella," he adds.

His mother snorts and rolls her eyes.

I glare at Paige's board as if it should have answered this dilemma for me.

Were Paige a homely girl, I might convince Cypress to reconsider her inclusion in all of this despite her strength. But she isn't. And it isn't just the surface beauty—the flawless tawny skin or intense umber eyes; the shape of her hips and lips—there's also a fierce air around her that is alluring all on its own.

I know I must write something on her board soon as the conversation moves closer to her. The other girls are between class three and class six—respectable numbers. But to equate Paige to a number is impossible. We have seen no one over class seven. I chew my lip, debating how to go about this.

Even from where I stand, two floors down from her room, I can feel the push and pull of her magic fighting to break free. And that's with the bracelet on to limit her contact with the magic. Sweat beads on the back of my neck and I resist the urge to wipe it away.

Baron watches me. He hasn't said much, only adding a word here or there based on what he read in the psychology reports for each of the girls.

The conversation with Easton when we were trapped in the carriage surfaces. I explained to him the different classes, and how the two of us were class four—though he's borderline five. Then I had pointed at the ceiling of the carriage to show just how off the charts high Paige's class is by comparison.

What number does she deserve? *Fifty?* I can't write that. They will think I've gone mad.

Though if I give her a high enough number, Cypress might choose her over Nora. I almost reach out with the marker to write a number, anything high enough to impress but not seem crazy. Ten? It's hardly anywhere near accurate, but not insane.

Easton's pleading voice breaks through the chaos of my thoughts. *"Protect her."*

He could have insisted on help, release, but he didn't. Easton only asked for one thing. One thing I promised to deliver.

"Protect her."

I can't write class ten on the board. Even that will be too much. If Easton is borderline five and they are treating him like this, what would they do to her if they found out?

Cypress debates with his mother about River. Time is running out. I must write something.

On impulse, I write seven. It's a high enough number for Baron to know to be wary of her strength, but not so high that it over-shadows Nora. I lick dry lips, marker twitching in my hand. I nearly reach up to erase the seven and lower her number, but I can feel Baron's eyes digging into me. I've been uncertain for too long already. Erasing her number and lowering it will only raise more red flags.

I step back and cap the marker. When I meet Baron's gaze, he is frowning at Paige's board. Then I wonder what Easton has already told him. He already knows what she did in the woods—turning the men who mutinied against me to ash. Does he know my number is seriously skewed? Sweat rolls down my neck and trickles along my spine beneath my pressed white dress shirt.

There is no alternative. I told Easton I would protect her, and if they knew the truth, she would be in danger.

"Seven?" Cypress emits a low whistle. "Is she the one you were running up the steps to escape? The one whose friend volunteered as a recruit?"

"She is," Baron says, edging closer. He gives me a curious look at the mention of the incident on the stairs. I can't help flushing in embarrassment all over again. "She was with the group that killed more than half of our men in old St. Louis."

Cypress eyes Paige with an interest that makes my blood curdle. I should have given her a lower number. "What did we learn about her community from him?" Cypress asks Baron.

I perk up a little. Baron hasn't shared anything with me regarding Easton's questioning, and I would love to hear what he has to say about Easton's current situation.

"Nothing as clear as I would have liked," Baron admits. He joins Cypress in front of Paige's board. "He held out extremely well under pressure. We learned they are from quite a way west of the river, deep in the heart of the Wastelands. How far, he wouldn't say. Nor would he give me an idea of how large their community is, aside from calling it substantial and nothing compared to our island. I'm not sure if that means it's larger or smaller. For the moment, I think it's best if we assume it's larger."

Queen Elena scoffs from the chair she sank into a few minutes ago. "How could anything in the Wastelands grow so large? How did they survive in the first place? Lady Paige made it sound like a paradise and insisted she wanted to go back if she isn't chosen."

I resist the urge to look at Paige's number again. There was another boy in old St. Louis who was just as strong as she was. He escaped along the river. Baron already knows as much from my final report. It wasn't a detail I could conceal when so many men were there to witness it, and so many were lost because of it. If he knows how strong Easton is, he is putting the pieces together, just as I did...

Wherever these two are from, their magical reserve is much greater than ours. Even if their community is half our size, with magic that strong, we wouldn't stand a chance. And if Baron already knew, did it have anything to do with the experiments on Easton?

"It was all broken down in that report I sent to you," Baron says.

"She might be a greater ally than any of these other women," Cypress says. He smirks a little. "Not bad on the eyes, either." He turns his gaze on me, wiggling his brows to punctuate his point.

I humor him with a chuckle, but truthfully, I don't want him any closer to her than I do to Nora.

"Lady Paige?" Queen Elena's regal bearing presses down on us from across the room. Her scowl digs into Cypress with an authority that makes me uncomfortable. "No. Cypress, we know nothing about her or her people."

To my brother's credit, he squares his shoulders as he stares her down. "Then I will take my time getting to know her, earn her trust, and learn as much as I can."

Queen Elena rises, gliding across the green rug like a predator ready to devour its prey. "Listen to me, son. That girl is too dangerous. She put up a terrible fight, killed dozens of our men, and refused to comply with the blood tests upon arrival. She is hiding something. If it were up to me, she would never have come here."

"Good thing it isn't up to you then," Cypress says calmly. His strength is admirable. I would have backed down under Queen Elena's stern gaze.

"I don't want you spending time alone with her until we know more about her." Queen Elena strolls toward the door, declaring the conversation over.

Baron heaves out a sigh once she is gone. "That was tense."

"She won't choose for me." Cypress stalks into the parlor, to the wet bar, like a petulant child. I almost laugh.

Baron follows, waving off an offered glass of whiskey. "She isn't wrong. You need to be cautious with Lady Paige. I will see what else I can learn. Just...be careful until then."

He leaves the two of us alone. Is he going to interrogate Easton again? Maybe I should follow.

Cypress downs his whiskey and pours another, then offers Baron's glass to me. I take it without a second of hesitation. The whiskey should help take the edge off this day.

"Maybe they are right about her," I admit. If it keeps Cypress and the others away from her a little longer, then I will steer him in another direction.

He flops down on the plush green sofa and rolls his eyes. "Does Mother really think that forbidding me to spend time with Paige will stop me?" He takes a sip. "If anything, it only encourages me. She should know better by now."

I down the whiskey in a gulp, relishing the burn. I swipe a sleeve across my mouth and set the glass down. "I suppose you have a point. Instead, she should let me tell you how terribly dull Paige was all the way here. Never said more than a few words. Dreadfully prudish, too."

He chuckles. "Liar."

I grin back. "You don't have to ignore her, but maybe caution is wise. For now."

He turns the glass in his hand, eyeing the amber fluid. "Is she really a class seven?"

My breath catches. I cover my discomfort by marching to the wet bar and setting down the glass. "She is strong, Cy. And I can't really tell just what she can do. Honestly, she scares me."

"I noticed. And if that's not motivation to keep her, I don't know what is."

21

GAVIN

I F THERE IS A hell, this must be it. A parade of endless torture.

The sermon ends with a crescendo of praises from the congregation, followed by a song of elation. The itch to flee the temple overwhelms me. My throat is dry, and my palms are sweating. My insides are in critical mass.

The moment it ends, I surge to my feet and turn toward the aisle.

Before I can reach the end of my row, a crowd of people presses toward me. Eager faces form a wall between me and the exit at the far end of the temple. The distance seems to stretch away from me with each hammer of my heartbeat. The mass of bodies edges me backward toward the platform and farther from the door.

Questions hammer at me.

"Where are you from?"

"How far west is your home?"

"What can you do?"

"How long before the Day of Glory comes?"

My head spins, making me dizzy. My knees weaken. I'm not sure how much longer I can stay on my feet.

An arm slides around me. I'm about to jerk away when Drake whispers in my ear. "It's just me. Let's go."

I lean against him, overwhelmed, relieved to have him at my side. I draw from his strength.

Drake flashes a kind smile at the crowd still crushing forward to meet me—the same people who just this morning wanted nothing to do with me—then Drake pulls me toward the platform holding the podium.

"If you will excuse us," Drake says loud and clear to the crowd. "He has asked to see the acolytes."

No. I'm done with this. I don't want to see anyone else that has anything to do with this religion. I'm about to refuse when Drake hisses in my ear to play along.

We cross the platform to an alcove, then exit through a back door. Behind the temple is a series of hallways. The first doorway is the office of the Minister. Light inside glows, but Drake quickly ushers me past.

"Where are we going?" I ask, breathless. This entire ordeal has me unable to think straight. Is this what Paige feels like when she has her panic attacks underground?

"There are always a few empty rooms back here," Drake answers. "Most of the people aren't allowed back. Only acolytes."

Now that we are away from the crowd, his arm slides off my waist. The withdrawal sends a pang of disappointment through my chest.

Drake slips through an open door, then waves me in after him.

The room is tiny. Only twice as wide as the narrow single-person bed. A small nightstand with two tall drawers sits beside the bed.

The mattress is hard and uncomfortable, but it makes a suitable enough seat for me to catch my breath.

Drake crouches in front of me. "Can I get you anything?"

"Home. Get me home. I don't want to be here, Drake." My voice cracks.

He flinches. Sorrow creases his brows. Or is that hurt? "I'm not sure I can help with that."

"Have you even tried?" The venom in my tone makes him sink back against the wall opposite me.

"That's not fair—"

"No." Anger and hurt burn in my chest. "It's not fair. Not to me. I wanted to meet your Elders, not be propped up as some...what? What do they even think I can do for them?"

Drake rests his arms on his knees and stares at his hands. "You know, this life isn't easy for us."

"Life isn't easy for anyone! But how would you feel if I took you to my home and my council said you couldn't leave? That you could never go home." My hands clench and unclench in fists in my lap.

"They never said that."

"They may as well have."

Silence falls between us, thick and stifling. I hurt Drake. I'm not good with emotions, but that much I can read plainly on his face. Is he aware that his people hurt me?

Some great chasm has opened between the two of us. My feelings toward him don't matter when we come from such different worlds. We will never agree. This would never work.

Pip slips into the room, still beaming brightly. "There you guys are. Gavin, that was brilliant!"

Her. It's her fault Drake and I are at odds. It's her fault her father used me as a religious tool. I surge to my feet, rounding on her. "Don't *ever* do that to me again."

She steps back, and all her enthusiasm slips away. Her face sags. Her arms hang limply at her sides. "What's wrong?"

I sneer. Fury quivers in my limbs. "You knew I didn't want to go up there, but you dragged me along. You forced me to play puppet to the Minister's game."

"Game!" Her cheeks heat. "This isn't a game; this is our lives!"

"He doesn't get it, Pip," Drake mutters.

No. I don't. I don't understand how anyone could buy into this load of garbage. Emil was right. About all of it.

I step over his feet and edge toward the door. Pip presses her back to the wall as if afraid of me.

"Where are you going?" Drake asks miserably.

"I need space. From all of this." I wave my hand around.

The motion encompasses the two of them as well. Both flinch as if I slapped them. Neither moves to stop me from storming out the door.

I can't handle being around either of them right now. They knew this would happen. They fed the Minister information about me.

I've never felt so betrayed.

22

PAIGE

I PAD BAREFOOT OUT of my bathroom across the plush red carpet to choose an outfit for the day. A large white wardrobe takes up an entire corner of the room. When I peeked inside last night, the number of gowns alarmed me. All of them in varying hues of the rainbow. Apparently, the black dresses were only for the first day, a way to enter the palace on even ground.

My old clothes from home have disappeared completely. In fact, there isn't a single pair of pants in my entire wardrobe. I grimace, flipping through the colorful options.

According to Nora, we will be shown around the palace grounds, then each have a meeting with Prince Dominic, the King's younger brother. It's our chance to impress him and stand out from the others. Part of me doesn't care at all what they think of me—this entire process is demeaning—but if I want to open the lines of communication or go home, I need to play their game.

And I need to do it well.

I chew my lip as I consider the dresses. How big should I go coming out of the gate? Noticeable, but not so much so that I anger the other girls. Not that I think I could anger Nora. She has the patience of a saint.

A knock on the door startles me from my thoughts. I peer through the eyehole to see a handful of anxious girls and an older woman all in plain black and white uniforms. Maids? Housekeeping? I open the door a crack and flash them a winning smile.

"Can I help you?" I ask.

"We are here to help you get ready, Lady Paige," the older woman says. She taps the handle of a wheeled bag beside her.

I step back, waving them in. Two of the girls are young, perhaps fourteen. One is about my age. The fourth is the woman with wrinkles in the corners of her eyes. They all bear a striking resemblance to one another. Is this a family?

"Have you chosen a dress already, Lady Paige?" the eldest girl asks.

"No. Please just call me Paige." I glance at the open wardrobe doors, wringing my hands.

She offers me a kind smile, then marches over and flips through the dresses.

"I was thinking something understated, but that also stands out, if that makes sense?" I edge toward her.

She gives a quick nod and yanks a deep purple dress out of the selection. The neckline is modest enough, but the flimsy material plunges down the back. A ribbon of sparkling clear stones catches in the light as the skirt moves.

The ladies set to work, helping me dress, applying makeup, accentuating the natural waves in my hair down my back. I take the time to get to know each of them a little better. My initial assessment proves correct. The woman is Ingrid, the mother of all three girls. She has worked in the palace since she was a little girl, serving the King's grandmother during her Tribute.

Her oldest daughter, Mariah, is a whiz with a sewing machine and has a good eye for fashion. The two younger girls, Helen and Maddy, are twins. They begged to help their mother with this Tribute season.

"Did you serve during the last season as well?" I ask while Ingrid pulls the top layer of my hair away from my face.

She cocks her head, examining my espresso locks. "I did. I served Lady Emry."

"But she didn't win?"

Ingrid tenses, glancing at Mariah. The two share a knowing look that I don't much care for. They are hiding something. "She did not become queen, but the King had affection for her. She remained as the King's consort."

Consort. So he married the Queen and kept Lady Emry as a bonus prize. My stomach twists. Would King Cypress follow in his father's footsteps?

"I heard what happened to the last king and his heir," I say, hoping to seem subdued. "Sounds like it was a horrible shock."

All of them sober, but it's Ingrid who answers. "It was quite a shock. King Alric the Third was still in good shape. He had years ahead of him yet. And everyone adored the Crown Prince Alric the Fourth. Lady Nora most of all."

Nora was in love with the Crown Prince? Was she engaged to him, or would he have still called for Tributes like his brother?

Ingrid continues without missing a beat. "We were fortunate that King Cypress survived. We would be lost without him. Prince Dominic swore himself to life as Keeper of Tides, so he cannot marry without royal dispensation."

I soak up every ounce of information they give me. Cypress was not meant to be king.

"What about Lord Zephyr?" The question slides out the moment it comes to my mind.

Mariah giggles. Ingrid tsks, then sets to work fastening my hair in place. I sit patiently and wait for an answer.

"He is not the Queen's son," Helen says, fiddling with the makeup brushes as she puts everything away. "He can't be king."

I frown at this. "He called King Cypress his brother."

"He is," Ingrid says patiently as she works. "King Alric the Third was Lord Zephyr's father."

Mariah mutters something that earns her a glare. She flushes and looks away.

"His mother is Lady Emry," Ingrid finishes.

"Oh." The pieces click into place quickly. Zephyr serves in the military because he isn't eligible for the throne. The king kept two women from his Tributes, but only one could be queen.

And apparently, only her children can take the throne. Part of me wonders if Zephyr is okay with this arrangement.

As Ingrid finishes her work, I fiddle with the emerald-encrusted bracelet. How does it work? Lord Baron made it clear taking it off would be considered a serious offense, but what about just at night, when I sleep? Would they even know if I did?

"Oh, Lady Paige, you look amazing!" Maddy gushes as I rise from the chair.

The full-length mirror to my right shows me a girl I didn't even know existed beneath the Specialist uniform. My exposed arms reveal the muscles I had been hiding up to this point. What will the King think of those?

I step out my door while the girls finish cleaning up in the room. Nora joins me from her own room next door. Her gaze sweeps over me, and a broad smile lights up her face.

"Lady Paige, you look incredible." She matches my long strides effortlessly, floating over the carpeted hallway toward the stairs.

Her emerald dress makes the dark pools of her eyes pop, and every infinitesimal movement is so graceful it fills me with envy. She makes it look effortless.

"Thanks. So do you."

She frowns at her dress. "Maybe."

The two of us descend the stairs, though I admit I'm unsure where I'm headed. Nora seems to know her way around. Part of me wonders if I could ask her questions about the family, but another part worries she won't tell me the full truth. I am the competition, after all. It benefits her to see me fail. If she is so familiar with the family already, she probably has already set up her plan. Does she have a say, or was she forced into this like the rest of us?

Before I make my proposal—helping her win if she helps me get home—I must get to know her better.

We reach the next floor down, and I pause at the sound of raised voices behind a door at the head of the steps. Both are men, but I can't make out what they are saying to one another. Regardless of the words, the meaning is clear enough. They are not happy with one another.

Nora notices my steps have slowed. She pauses, glancing at the door, then shakes her head at me and motions down the stairs. We continue our descent in silence.

Once we reach the main floor and turn left along a long hallway, Nora leans close and whispers, "Baron has really been running Zephyr through the press since his return." She glances around to be sure no one else is listening. "I heard a rumor Zephyr ignored a command to return, then ended up losing almost all his men. You were in his group, right? What happened?"

My heart sinks as I recall the battle. *We happened. My brother happened.* How Gavin pulled so much Power, I cannot understand. He accomplished alone what teams of Naturalists can only do together.

I debate telling Nora the truth, but decide against it. Either she knows and is fishing for false trust, or she doesn't know and there's a reason the Admiral is keeping it quiet. Training kicks in. Skirting the truth in these situations is best to maintain the integrity of the chain of command.

I shake my head. "I spent most of the time in a carriage. Aside from a mutiny, I can't say much more."

Nora's eyes widened. "Mutiny!"

I wince. Maybe that was too much, but I assumed something as big as that would be hard to keep quiet.

Nora's mind churns, processing the information so clearly on her face that I almost feel bad for her. She absently turns into a café along the hallway.

We are the last two to arrive. My gaze sweeps the girls gathered. I can already weed out those interested in putting forth a genuine effort from those who would rather not be here at all. There's an almost obvious line separating the two groups. The girls with interest and those who are ready to be dismissed already.

The café offers cozy comfort. Two large, two-panel doorways overlook the promenade along the front of the palace. Several white tables with red metal chairs cover the checkerboard floor. At the head of the space, a small buffet table loaded with food awaits. None of the girls eat, though.

"Are we waiting for the family?" I whisper to Nora.

She shakes her head, then detaches from me and heads toward the girl from the balcony yesterday. I consider tailing her, curious about this new girl, but my stomach takes over as the smell of bacon tantalizes my nose.

After collecting a generous plate of food, I choose a seat at a table beside Bella. Her eyes bore into Nora's back as she speaks with the new girl.

"You might want to dial back your hate," I say softly to Bella. "If you want it to be less obvious, that is."

Bella's gaze snaps away from Nora and quickly sweeps over me. "Who even are you?" She doesn't like me. Not a big deal. I don't think I like her either.

"Paige." The dress forces me to sit upright as I eat my eggs.

Her nose slowly curls as she watches me eat. "You know he can see you, don't you?"

I shove more eggs in my mouth, then take a bite of bacon before swallowing the eggs. I grin at her. Though I can't help but wonder *how* he watches us if he isn't here. It doesn't matter if he can see me. I'm hungry, so I eat.

She mutters in disgust and looks ready to get up, but the new girl calls all eleven of us to attention.

"I know that the circumstances of your arrival are not all ideal," the girl says. There's an air of innocence about her. My gaze flits to her wrist. No bracelet. "My goal today is to help you find some way to be comfortable here in the palace. We want you to be happy and open to the Tribute process. King Cypress desires, above all else, for you to be interested in the idea of joining his family. Please eat breakfast. Once we are done, I will escort you on a tour of the grounds. Everything within these walls is open for your use."

The other girls exchange uncertain glances. Four of the girls—the four who were not quarantined in the cottage with us—don't hesitate to move toward the buffet. Nora pauses only for a moment to say something more to our hostess.

The girl approaches me while the others all fill their plates. With a sweep of her hand, she tucks her skirt and sits across from me.

"Lady Paige." Her voice is so sweet I can't help but wonder if she is faking. "I have heard about you already. My brother is impressed."

Brother. Is that Zephyr or King Cypress? The maids didn't mention a sister at all.

She must read my uncertainty. "Princess Bronwyn." Her hand presses against her chest. "Zephyr mentioned you are quite strong-willed and well-trained as a fighter."

I chew on my toast slowly, forcing her to talk more. The more I can learn, the better.

"I also hear you are eager to return home, should King Cypress dismiss you."

I freeze. Can she make it happen? How much influence does the princess have if the maids didn't even mention her?

I swallow the mouthful of food, take a careful sip of coffee, then smooth my hands over my dress. "I have heard no one ever goes home, and I'm worried that isn't by choice. My family will be beside themselves with worry. They don't know what happened to me. I miss Mom. And my dad..." Just thinking about our fight, how much he didn't want me to leave the city, how stubbornly I fought against him...and how right he turned out to be...it all makes my stomach churn. Will he assume I am dead? Tears well in my eyes.

Princess Bronwyn quickly reaches across the table and squeezes my arm. "I'm so sorry! I didn't mean to upset you. We just...well, we have never had a Tribute ask so insistently before."

Hard to believe, but I figure pointing that out will reduce my odds of success here.

"I only hope you will give my brother a fair chance," she adds. "He is very passionate and focused. I think he is hoping to find a wife who is as much of a force as our mother. From what I hear, that makes you a good contender."

"I look forward to meeting him," I say. "I only hope he can understand just how much my family means to me."

She pats my arm, then rises. "I'm sure he will, in time."

In time.

Those two words renew the ache in my heart. How long will I be stuck on this island? How long will my parents think the worst? All I can do is hope that Gavin makes it back to Elpis and explains the situation to them. What will Dad do? He is smart enough not to attack. Nor would I want him to launch an invasion because of me.

The only hope I can cling to right now is the sympathy of the royal family. King Cypress won't know what hit him.

After we conclude breakfast, Princess Bronwyn escorts our group through the palace grounds. The building looks massive from the outside, and the inside is no exception. We tour the throne rooms—because apparently there are two for different purposes—the formal and informal dining rooms, a library, arcade, daycare, salon, seamstress, and tailor.

Those of us from beyond the island take in the grounds in awe. It's hard to mask under the circumstances. The princess explains that the palace was a popular resort before the Collapse, with well over a hundred suites, several meeting rooms, ballrooms, restaurants, and more. The building was established in 1887, pre-collapse. Not that I have a sense of how long ago that really was. None of us do.

We pass a hallway along the tour that disappears deeper into the palace, but Bronwyn doesn't bother mentioning the hall at all. I pause, peering as far as I can until Nora catches up from the rear of the group and encourages me along. When I ask her what's down there, she shrugs and says it must be for the King and his advisors only.

The hotel has six floors. The first is a lower level, partially built into the hillside. The main level where the grand staircase enters is the main floor, and each floor after that is numbered accordingly—one through four. Those are the floors with the guest rooms and royal suites.

As Princess Bronwyn climbs the stairs toward our rooms, she informs us that from this moment, we are welcome to go anywhere we want inside the palace, except for the first floor of suites. That is off limits unless they invite us. I assume that means the King's suite is on that floor.

We reach the third floor of rooms, where she informs us they will select us one at a time to talk with Prince Dominic.

"When will we meet the King?" Layla asks.

Princess Bronwyn smiles sweetly at us. "My brother is quite busy getting other matters in order so he can focus more on each of you in the weeks to come."

Weeks?

"It won't be long, I promise."

Nora ignores this and heads straight to her room. I take a cue from her and do the same. I don't feel like wandering the palace right now. Later, after meeting with Prince Dominic, I will try to find the best means of exiting the building. During the tour, I noted a few possibilities. I just have to find my way back to them.

For now, I'm content to be left alone.

--------⊗--------

T HE SAME STARCHY-SUITED BUTLER leads the way down a long, wide walkway through a massive restaurant barren of life. I trail along, the hem of my purple dress whispering for me to run with each step. I heard the other girls chatting in the hallway after returning from their meeting with Prince Dominic. Alice had called him a sweetheart. Bella couldn't stop smiling. January shrugged and told us he only wanted to know her family history.

I had assumed they were once more working in alphabetical order, but River and Summer were both summoned before I was.

Best for last, I suppose.

I take in the lavish dining room. White cloth-covered tables. Fancy place settings. Did they leave this dining room like this all the time? Didn't the dishes collect dust or were servants forced to clean this room every day? Chandeliers hang from the tall ceiling.

The butler enters a round private dining space at the far end of the massive dining room. The boy with the gentle face sits at a table alone. Well, alone except for the books stacked on the table beside him. I can't help but smile. Something about him reminds me of Gavin, and it makes my heart ache.

"Lady Paige, my lord," the butler announces from the doorway.

I slip past him and wait, hands folded in front of me. I'm not sure whether I'm supposed to approach him or not. Better safe than sorry.

He rises from his chair, a bright smile lighting up his face. Is that what Zephyr would look like if he were more open and happier? "Thank you, Alfred." He motions toward the empty chair across from him. "Please, Lady Paige. Join me."

"You can just call me Paige," I say.

"And you can just call me Dominic."

A small feast awaits us on the table. Cranberry and walnut salad. Bacon-wrapped asparagus. Golden-brown dinner rolls heaped in a cloth-lined basket. Butter shaped like a whale. A platter with a variety of savory meat cutlets.

I settle into the seat, eyeing the feast. My mouth waters.

"I wasn't sure what you prefer for your meat, so I had them bring us a few options," he explains. "I hope you don't mind."

I breathe in the delicious smells and almost sigh. "Not at all." I can't decide where to start. "What did the other girls choose?"

He cocks his head to the side and eyes me curiously. "I didn't dine with them. I had hoped to be finished before dinner, but my stomach had other ideas. Only you, Paige, get the privilege of joining me tonight."

As we dig into the meal, he opens a book, making a note in it. I try to spy on what he is writing, but I can't make out his handwriting.

"Tell me a little about yourself, Paige," he says, pouring each of us a glass of wine from a bottle on the table. "I would love to know more about you."

I chuckled, peeling open a dinner roll. "Is this a date? Because I think the Admiral made himself *very* clear on fraternization."

He also chuckles. Dominic rests his forearms on the edge of the table. Everyone here usually has their sleeves down and dapper, but he rolled his up. "No. I am the Keeper of Tides here, and the keeper doesn't date or marry."

"How sad." I pat his arm in consolation. "That must be lonely."

"Not really." He shifts back in his seat, drawing away from me. "My job is my companion. It keeps me busy, especially during the Tribute season. My brother is depending on me, and I don't intend to screw any of this up."

I smirk. Getting him to open up to me was much easier than I expected. "You are like his right hand, yes?"

"I am his right hand. And sometimes his left." His blue eyes twinkle in the lights.

"Did you do this for your father when he was king as well?"

The smile on his face flickers. His gaze dips to his lap as his hands smooth out the napkin there.

"I'm sorry," I say quickly, worried I've somehow made a horrible misstep.

He clears his throat, then sighs. "It's alright. Have you ever lost someone close to you?"

I shake my head. "Not exactly. I mean, I'm here and my family doesn't know whether I'm dead or alive. And I'll probably never see them again. But they *are* all alive." Pain clenches in my chest as I imagine what it must be like to lose any of my family. "I can only guess what it must feel like."

"Who are you closest to in your family?"

"My brother." I tell Dominic stories about our childhood, careful to skirt some of the more specific details about our family and Elpis.

Something about Dominic puts me at ease. His big, open heart is apparent almost immediately, but he genuinely seems interested in everything I have to say. Not because he must be, but because he wants to be.

Conversation continues as we eat. I tell him as much as I dare about my family—that is what he wants to know after all—and he even shares some insight into his own childhood with three brothers and an older sister. I hadn't figured Princess Bronwyn was the second oldest. It strikes me then that their names are alphabetical by birth. Alric. Bronwyn. Cypress. Dominic.

So why did Zephyr's name start with a Z?

I also impressed Dominic by how much meat I eat. I explain that my Power also increases my metabolism, so I consume more calories than most.

"I know that sometimes the circumstances that bring the Tributes here are less than ideal," Dominic says as we finish. "And I hear you had extra difficulty on the way. Some men attempted mutiny?"

I swallow a forkful of prime rib, eyeing him warily. I wash it down with a drink of red wine. "I assume you already know what happened."

"I do. We are looking into it still, but we just don't understand *why*. We are hoping you can shed some new light on the incident for us. Did they say anything to you when they...you know...dragged you away?"

Memories of that evening are spotty for me. I remember being ripped out of Easton's arms and dragged away. I remember how one man nearly raped Alice, and how I fought to give the girls a chance to escape—which they didn't do. But what happened after that is...gone.

"Nothing I want to repeat in the presence of royalty," I say flatly. "One of them said they should have killed the captain and first mate, but another one said it didn't matter because by the time they reached the Capital, it would be too late."

Dominic turns ashen. "Too late for what?"

I have no answer for him. All I can do is shrug.

He nods sadly. "Thank you for your candid honesty."

"So no one knows why it happened?"

"Not so far, no."

That makes no sense. The mutiny had to be coordinated. And if they had a plan for this island, then they couldn't have acted alone.

Who else wants to see the crown fall?

Or just Zephyr...?

23

ZEPHYR

THE OFFICERS TAKE TO Easton quickly. Not only does he excel at *everything*, but he helps with training and offers advice when he thinks it might be welcome. He even volunteers for shifts in the mess hall. I can't help but wonder if he is angling for something.

Officers Cante and Ody join me in the tearoom for a drink once the sun sets. We all crowd around a table over mugs of ale. The bartender regretfully refuses to serve me, on Baron's orders, but Officer Ody takes pity on me and gets me a drink. Weak ale, but better than nothing.

"You didn't really find that guy in old St. Louis, did you Cap?" Ody asks.

I stare into my mug. "I did. But he claims to be from much farther west."

"In the Wastelands?" Ody's brows climb his wide forehead. "Rumors are going around about that. We thought nothing could survive out that way."

Officer Cante snorts in response, nearly choking on his ale.

"I don't know what to tell you. I only know what he said." I take a gulp.

"Easton said the girl trained with him, wherever they are from," Ody says. He leans forward urgently, meeting my gaze.

I don't know what to make of this comment. "So?"

Cante joins Ody in leaning against the table with urgency. He keeps his voice low. "So, doesn't that worry you a little?"

I frown, setting down the nearly empty mug. Ale goes down too quick and does little else. "Why?"

"She's a Tribute." Ody and Cante exchange glances for a moment, then Ody eyes me again. "That means she will be close to your brother. If I were you, I would be worried about his safety."

Paige's warning rings in my memory. *"Take me to your leader. I dare you."* I shake the voice out.

"She's too smart to do anything that foolish." But even as I say it, I'm not convinced it's true. It doesn't matter either way. Whether she is at Cypress' side or on the other side of the island, she can still destroy us all. We have no way to stop her.

Cante shrugs. "If you say so. But their training is impressive. Easton already has the skills to be head of the royal guard."

A position in the palace? Baron wouldn't allow it with Paige still there. But maybe Easton believes if he does well enough, he could earn a place closer to Paige. Then the two of them can plot their escape. She keeps saying she wants to go home. No doubt he wants to take her. Suddenly, Easton's go-getter attitude here makes much more sense. He's trying to get back to *her*.

I finish my mug of ale and rise. "Thanks for the drink, guys. I will keep your concern under advisement."

Cante snorts. "Now you sound like the Admiral."

I pause a few steps from the table. Should I ask what they know about the Admiral's secret designs? Why is he keeping his experiments from the rest of us? From me? Is he the one responsible? I can't figure who else would have had access to Easton when he arrived on the island. Digging these men for information will only get us all into trouble. I won't drag the men I trust into this. The more people who know, the more dangerous it is.

Restless, I return to the palace and head straight for Dominic's suite at the end of the fourth suite floor. I can't tell everyone, but I trust Dominic. I need someone to help me.

Dominic sits at the desk he placed by a window, pouring over mountains of books. As I enter, he glances up at me.

"Trouble, Zeph?"

I glance at his wet bar, eager for something stronger than watered down ale, but I know Dominic frowns on my drinking. Stuffing my hands in my pockets, I make my way to the sofa and slump down.

"You know me."

He chuckles. "I do."

"How did the meetings with the girls go?"

He leans back in his chair and crosses his arms, fixing me with a pointed stare. "You mean how did Paige's meeting go?"

I don't take the bait. He wants a reaction. Instead of meeting his stare, I unbutton my coat as if his comment doesn't even phase me.

"They all went about as expected, though Layla likes to talk. So does Bella." Dominic grimaces. He doesn't mind a good, spirited conversation, but he can get bored with empty conversations quickly. I almost chuckle at his reaction. "I got a lot of good information about their histories. Did you know Alice's father left her community to find the Haven? Her mother refused to go with him."

The Haven. That place is little more than a cult, from what little we have learned about them. Their existence drove my father crazy. Mostly because he couldn't stand not knowing where they were located when it had to be within the Kingdom.

"Paige's father is a Minister, which apparently makes him the leader of their community," Dominic continues. "So her goading you into calling her a princess might not be too far off. But some of her answers were evasive. I asked how her parents met, and she said it was in a forest."

"How is that evasive?"

"That's *all* she would say. I asked what she thought of their love story, and she just shrugged it off and told me they love each other now. The rest doesn't matter."

I fight off a smirk. "Maybe that's a good thing. If she is going to accept her place as a Tribute, it could mean that she understands that love can come later. It means she might come around."

Not that I want her to. I want her to reject Cypress.

"I asked her about the mutiny."

Images of the ash and fire that surrounded her rush to the surface. Fear grips me. "Yeah?"

"I can't quite get it out of my head," Dominic admits. His shoulders slump. "She implied those men had some plan here on the island, but she didn't know what it was. Do you think they were working with someone else?"

I scratch the stubble on my chin. They couldn't have been working with Baron. He wouldn't encourage that kind of behavior. But so many things about him are no longer stacking up. The burned community. The missing supplies from the ships. The reports from Round Island. Keeping Father's and Alric's bodies from viewing. Experimenting on Easton. What if he wanted me out of the way before I returned to the island? Dying on the mainland happens from time to time.

"Those men wouldn't tell me anything," I admit. "They said it would spoil the fun."

Dominic shuffles toward me, anxiety bleeding off him. Concern creases his brow. "Zeph, I'm worried. What if we have a traitor right under our noses and we don't know it?"

24

GAVIN

SINCE THE INCIDENT AT the temple, I have mostly kept to my room. No more daily chores to help Havenites. Not when they all look at me like a savior.

There's no lock on the door, but pushing the dresser in front of it is effective enough to keep people out. Mrs. Garraty knocks. I ignore her, pretending not to be in my room. She tries the door, making me thankful I've put the dresser there. After a moment, she gives up and leaves me alone.

The next morning, I return from my shower to find a binder sitting on the desk, tied closed with a ribbon. As I inch closer, I see a note tucked under the ribbon. When I pull it off, the title on the binder strikes me.

The *Book of the Prophet.*

My insides twist in a knot.

Biting my lip, I sink into the hard wooden desk chair and unfold the note.

Gavin,

I'm so sorry. I feel terrible about upsetting you. I had no idea you felt so strongly and realized that part of the problem might have been that you don't understand the Book of the Prophet. So, I am lending you my copy. Maybe if you read this, you'll understand why it is so important to us.

I hope you can forgive me.

Pippen

It isn't in me to forgive her. Not yet.

I slide her note in my notebook, then flip open the binder. Nothing on these pages will make me a believer. Religion isn't my thing. But Pip has a point. I can't expect to understand their point of view until I know where their beliefs come from.

The pages in the binder are handwritten. Nearly a hundred pages of verses. With nothing else to do, I lean forward and begin reading, dissecting.

Over the next few days, this becomes a ritual. I eat breakfast, then spend time re-reading the pages, ensuring I understand the details right.

But something is missing. There's no way this is the entire book. Did Pip copy these pages herself from the actual *Book of the Prophet*? The order of the pages is haphazard, as if she wrote them from random excerpts and just stuck them all in the binder together.

I rearrange the pages in a more logical order on the fourth day. *The Last Age. The New Age. Faith. Signs. The Coming. The Idols. The End. Days of Glory.* All the pieces are here, but as I sift through a hundred pages of her copied text, I can see the missing fragments. Does she know what those pieces are?

Once I've arranged them all in what I assume is a more logical order, I read through the *Book of the Prophet* again. What I can be sure of is that they believe the pre-collapse world was full of sin, which is why it ended. One day, two Idols will arrive—Desolation and Creation—to restore the broken world and create a new Garden of Eden. I studied the Bible from pre-collapse. A few people in Elpis still believe in it. But this *Book of the Prophet* is different. While I can see parallels between the two, the ideals of faith and salvation are different.

Who wrote this book? I wish I could see inside their mind. And I don't mean Pip's horrible handwriting. I mean the mastermind behind this collection of fear-mongering faith dependence and doom.

One thing I know for certain after reading these excerpts is this:

The Minister is setting me up as an Idol, using some coincidences—such as my name and where I come from—as signs that I could be one of the two. But it's unclear which he believes me to be. Or what either of them means to me.

Without a doubt, this work is incomplete. I need to see the entire book. Without all the information, I can't prepare myself for what might come next.

At dinnertime, I emerge from the cocoon of my room and knock on Pip's door. But she isn't here. Maybe she headed to the square for dinner.

Everything inside of me twists in a knot when I step into the main hallway. Eyes follow me with strange reverence. People whisper to one another. It churns my stomach. I can't move fast enough.

Ever since the incident at the temple, everything I do—and everything I don't do—has some significance to these people. I wish I could make them see how flawed their beliefs are. Most of what I have learned from the *Book of the Prophet* so far has a logical, historical, or scientific explanation. Even if it's layered in zealous faith.

A hush falls over the square, like a collective breath awaiting my every move. It makes my skin crawl. *"One day he will come with Powers beyond our understanding. He will promise to remake the world."* I shudder, recalling what Drake implied in old St. Louis when I mentioned the mission Dad sent Paige and I on...to find survivors and fix what was broken. His face lit up with enthusiasm and hope.

Now I understand why.

I fed Drake lines from his *Book of the Prophet* nearly word for word. I had inadvertently insisted I was there to fulfill this prophecy without knowing what my words meant to Drake. It's no wonder he and Pip are convinced I might be this promised Idol.

Pip sits at a table with a few other girls. When I approach, all the girls stare at me with wide eyes. A few of them blush. Their reaction makes no sense.

"Pip, can we talk?"

She chews her lip, then nods. "Of course, Gav."

Using my nickname makes the nerves writhing in my stomach even worse. I don't correct her, though. What's the point?

When I step back, she rises, then slides her arm through mine.

"Have you seen Drake?" I ask, escorting her away from the table of girls, self-conscious of the way they watch the two of us.

"Not today. He's been busy with work, though." She glances at me through her long lashes. "Gavin, I'm sorry."

We make our way back to her family quarters. People practically bow out of our way, calling me Mr. Powers. I don't like that at all. Dad is Mr. Powers.

"I know."

"Did you read the *Book*?" she asks shyly.

I nod.

"What did you think?" The apprehension is thick in her voice.

"I think most of the *Book* is missing. Where can I get a full copy?"

Pip falls silent for so long that I'm worried she won't answer. But then she says, "There is only one complete copy in the temple. Only the Minister and the acolytes have access to it. He selects the passages for the sermons to share with the rest of us. The acolytes organize pieces of it each week for the children."

I flinch. "What do the children do with it?" Religion is a heavy topic for most children to digest.

"It's part of their education. We all learn about the Prophet and the coming Eden in primary courses."

That they use their religion as a basis for their education explains a lot about why she and Drake see the entire *Book* differently from Emil, who grew up outside of the Haven. Emil's comment about "shoving it down their throats" makes more sense as well. The *Book of the Prophet* is as etched into their young minds as the idea that Elpis was alone in the world. The difference is, we left Elpis to learn the truth.

We enter the apartment and I pull away from her, headed toward my room.

I flip the binder closed and offer it back to Pip. "I reorganized the pages in a more logical order. I hope you don't mind."

"Not at all." As she takes the binder, her fingers brush against mine. "What did you think?"

I shake my head. "I don't think you want the answer to that. And I need more information. Is there any way I can read the entire book?"

Pip bites her lip, hugging the binder against her chest like a cherished object. "Not unless you become an acolyte. It's a sin for those not chosen to look upon the *Book*."

Of course, it is.

The Minister holds his secrets close to his chest, just as surely as Pip and her binder. Now I *have* to read that book. Especially if he intends to prop me up as an Idol.

Pip inches nearer, gazing timidly up at me. "Can you forgive me, Gavin? These past few days have been unbearable thinking you hate me."

Can I? Nothing has been the same for me since. But she is one of the few friends I have in this place.

"I don't hate you. But I have to be honest. I felt betrayed, Pip. I'm not... I don't do well in crowds, let alone in front of them. Now people won't stop staring," I huff, scrubbing a hand over my hair. "But I'm not angry anymore. I can forgive you if you promise never to make me do that again."

"Cross my heart!" She does just that with a finger. Then she edges closer, brushing her fingers along my arm. Her big, bright eyes peer up at me. "I will *never* betray you again."

Something about her proximity makes the hairs on my arms and neck rise. I'm about to pull away when she leans against me. Her fingers hold tighter to my arm. Her lips brush over mine. Everything inside runs cold. My limbs lock in place. As she kisses me, I don't kiss her back. How do I even handle this? I don't want to hurt her the way Liam hurt me years ago. But I can't let her get the wrong idea either.

My fingers grasp gently at her shoulders. She presses closer. I nudge her back, leaning my head away.

Her eyes flutter open, gazing adoringly at me. My stomach clenches.

"Pip..."

"Gavin..." She slides her hand up to my neck.

I draw away, prodding her farther back and putting as much space between us as I can. "I'm not... I can't."

Her happy smile slips. "Is there someone back home?"

"No." Aron's grinning face flashes in my mind. "Maybe. It isn't that."

She retreats a step toward the door, flushed. "Oh. I'm... I thought..."

"I consider you a close friend, but I can't give you any more than that."

Tears brim in her eyes, making me miserable. This isn't what I wanted to happen.

"Pippen, you're a pretty girl, I'm sure, but..." How do I tell her? Is it a sin to be gay in their culture? "You're more like a sister to me. I enjoy our time together, but it can't be anything more."

"Ever?" Her voice cracks.

I sag. "I'm sorry."

25

PAIGE

I HATE HEELS. WHOEVER invented them was a sadist. Thankfully, my boots are still in my wardrobe. I slip them on under my dress and grab a coat, then explore the halls of the palace.

Though the building is massive, everything seems to be lined up along a main hallway on every floor. I make a mental map of the layout, noting where the exits are, where each elevator can travel, and where the emergency alarms are located. I even check corners for cameras. The lack of them surprises me. I would think that, in the palace of all places, they would want to watch the hallways.

Eventually, I find myself in the library. It is impressive, but nothing near as large as the smallest libraries in Elpis. I scan the books on the shelves. Old encyclopedias, which are centuries out of date now. Books on the history of Michigan—what had once been a state in the old world was little more than a dusty recollection now. A few romance and mystery thriller books. A book about sailing and nautical knots.

Curious, I pluck it off the shelf, wondering if I can take books from the collection. Learning about sailing certainly will be useful if it comes down to my fleeing. I flip through the pages as I continue meandering around the small room. The book offers only a few cursory bits of information that might prove useful. Most of it seems self-explanatory.

I set the book down on a baby grand piano and slide onto the bench. The lid is closed to keep the dust away from the piano keys. I ease it up and test a key. A perfect B whispers in the air.

When my Muscle Memory kicked in, I wanted to try *every-thing*. Piano had been one of the easier activities to start with. In a matter of weeks, I was playing like a maestro and then promptly lost interest, switching to ju-jitsu.

Dad loved listening to me play. He said it was one of his favorite ways to pass time. I think he was just humoring me, but right now I want to be closer to him.

Slowly, my fingers tickle the keys, but the notes don't sound right. My gaze settles on the bracelet. I chew my lip, glance out the open door, then surreptitiously slip it off, setting it on top of the book. Just for a few minutes so I can lose myself in my Muscle Memory.

It only takes a moment for me to get lost in the music. Like most things I can do physically, playing piano comes back to me as naturally as breathing. I don't even have to think about it as I play. My body just knows what to do. As the song carries through the room, I feel like I am at home again with Dad sitting on the bench beside me and Mom curled up in her armchair. Gavin listens through headphones to dull the intensity of the sound on his ears. I can feel them around me.

As I glance around the library, it becomes home. I can see it as clearly as if I were there right now.

As the song ends, I close my eyes and take a moment to revel in that lingering sensation of home.

"That was incredible."

My eyes snap open and I spin around on the bench to see the boy with curly hair sitting on a bar stool in the back corner of the room. Not just any boy. By process of elimination, he can only be one person.

The King.

I rise too quickly, worried that I'm supposed to curtsey to him or something, but my boots catch on the hem of my dress, and I pitch forward, catching my balance easily as my Muscle Memory kicks in.

My eyes widen as I realize I've just been caught without my bracelet on.

By the King.

He is on his feet, ready to catch me, and a little surprised when I don't need him. No. Not surprised. Dismayed. He *wanted* to catch me.

"I'm so sorry," I say quickly, reaching for the bracelet. "I just wanted to play and...well..."

"That bracelet stopped you." The corner of his mouth tips up in the same charming smile he flashed at me the day I arrived. That smile could melt a steel heart. "Far be it from me to stop you from playing something so beautiful. But you should put it back on before Baron catches you. He can be a real bear."

I quickly snap it back on. "I heard."

He winks devilishly. "I won't tell."

I flush. "Am I supposed to curtsy or something?"

He chuckles. "A little late for that, Lady Paige. I was just headed down for a bottle of wine. Would you care to join me?"

"Down where?"

He waves at the small bar in the corner. "There's a larger wine cellar hidden behind that really mysterious door." He nods at the very obvious and not at all mysterious door connecting to the bar.

"Is this allowed?" I ask as I shuffled toward one of the empty barstools.

He strides around the bar—each movement self-assured—and crouches in front of the wine racks on the back wall. The shoulders of his white-collared shirt strain over his muscular shoulders. King Cypress must be close to my age—and fiendishly handsome. I don't mean to check him out while his back is turned, but it's impossible not to. The orbit of the room naturally gravitates toward him. It must be a Power. No one is that strong of an Influencer without the Power to back it up.

"Well," he says slowly as he reads a couple of labels, "we might need permission from the King, but I think he'll let it slide."

I can't help but laugh. Maybe charm is a Power of his. Because he certainly has it in spades. "He lets a lot of things slide."

He stands with a bottle and grabs two glasses from the rack. "I know. This entire kingdom is doomed. Or at least that's the rumor."

My smile freezes on my face. Is he still joking, or is there something serious beneath the jest? I can't help thinking about my conversation with Prince Dominic over dinner. Does King Cypress know someone is plotting against him? I school my features calm before he sees my uncertainty.

He opens the bottle and pours each of us a glass. His sleeves are uncuffed, rolled up to expose his forearms. Again, I don't mean to look, but can't help myself. My eyes have a mind of their own.

"That's not what I hear," I say, smirking slightly as I turn the wine glass in my hand—*not* looking at his hand.

"Now I'm intensely curious." He leans against the counter between us.

It strikes me he looks nothing like Zephyr. Paler skin. Perfect wavy chestnut hair. Piercing, heart-melting, blue eyes. Longer face. He must get all his looks from his mother.

I lean closer as well, lowering my voice. If he wants to play a game, I can match him. "I hear he is a man of passion."

His brows climb his forehead. "Really?"

"Yup." I take a slow sip of the wine, watching him over the rim of my glass.

He watches me intently, gaze locked on my lips against the rim of the cup. Inch by inch, he leans a little closer, captivated. This is almost too easy. I suppose when he sees the Tributes as little more than breeding pods, it would be easy to entice him.

I lower the glass, leaning in a little as well. His blue eyes lift to meet mine, burning with intensity.

"I also hear he enjoys a challenge." I lurch back and hop off my stool, swaying toward the door. "I should probably take this glass to go. Thank you, mysterious sir."

He says nothing as I leave, but I can feel his eyes on me all the way to the elevator.

When the doors close, I sag in a way that is very unladylike. As first impressions go, that one was pretty good.

26

Zephyr

Mom now sleeps soundly in her room across the parlor from mine. The physician slips out of her room and eases her door closed silently.

"How is she?" I ask, eyeing the ice in my whiskey glass.

He sets his bag beside the hallway door and folds his hands in front of him. "Not good, my lord. Her illness is progressing. Nothing I do will help her. It will only ease her suffering. We don't have healing for this sort of problem. At this rate, I'm not sure she will make it to summer."

I twirl the glass, watching the ice spin in the bottom. With Baron's motivations questionable and Mom on her deathbed, my allies in the palace grow thin. Bronwyn and Dominic will still be in my corner, but Queen Elena will want me out. She never wanted me here in the first place. No doubt she has already begun sowing her seeds of doubt in the two of them. How hard would it be for her to sway her own children against me? I would like to think better of them, but I'm not sure they would dare stand against her. And Cypress won't.

I knew this day would come. Originally, I thought Dad would kick me out once Mom died. Funny that she outlived him.

"My lord, is there anything I can do for you?" the physician asks, drawing me out of my contemplation. "A sleeping aid, perhaps?"

My gaze darts to him. Does he know about my dreams? The ones with Paige? No. How could he? I down the whiskey in a gulp and turn to pour more.

"If I may, my lord." He edges toward me. "I have medication that will help your mental health much more safely than drinking."

My grip on the glass tightens. *Who does he think he is?* No medication can dull the pain like alcohol. And his presumption that I need pills infuriates me. Heat builds beneath my skin.

"You can go now, Doctor."

He shuffles half a step closer, then stops. "I will be back in the morning to check on Lady Emry." His steps recede, then the door whispers closed behind him.

"Jerk," I mutter. I down a second glass and pour a third before stepping out onto the balcony.

Cold night air blasts my face. I drink it in, welcoming the sting. It reminds me of being on the lake. The peace of the water. The complete control and complete lack of control the water bestows at its mercy. I lean against the balcony rail and stare out at the lake in the distance. There will be no sailing for a while as winter traps us here.

Frustration takes hold. Succumbing to the tides is one thing. Succumbing to anything else is a whole other monster.

Mom is dying and there is nothing anyone can do to help her. Accepting defeat is not within my nature. I can't fail her again. Not like I did when Dad beat her instead of me. How much of her condition is my fault? Would she be this damaged if I had stepped in to defend her? How many times did she use her healing on me when she shouldn't have?

At this time of night, the world is peaceful. No carriages lumber along the road. No servants or visitors wander the grounds. Everything is perfectly still. I breathe it in, revel in the isolation.

Everything seems to be going wrong. Dominic's concern only amplifies the worry already brewing in me. Was Baron plotting to seize the throne? Is he still? Someone else might stand to gain something if the royal family falls. Lord Greene, for starters. He and my father had a falling out a few years ago that Lord Green holds onto bitterly.

And Lord Tucker controls the farmland. He could starve us out if it came down to it. Both have daughters in the palace right now. It doesn't have to be Baron. In fact, Lord Tucker could also falsify the contents of the goods bags sent to the mainland. For all we know, we have been delivering empty sacks. Is he storing it up somewhere? If he is angling to tear down the crown or undermine us, he could starve us out, then swoop in with his stolen goods as a hero.

My head aches considering the possibilities.

A melody carries on the breeze. I can't hear the words, but the sound captivates me. Something about the sad rhythm tugs at my heart. As the song winds down, I realize it is coming from the balconies above me. One of the girls.

Is it a lost love song? Or perhaps a lament of unrequited love.

Love songs never really touched me before. I'm not even sure I can love another person. Perhaps Mom, but that's different. My affection for her and my siblings is deep. I would defend and protect them. But I've had no one I would charge into a fire for. Maybe because no one has ever done the same for me. How could I ever understand what love is when I have never known it before?

This lack of love doesn't leave me bitter. It's simply a way of being. Some people have it. Some don't.

Maybe it's better this way. I care about others, but no one can break me if I don't submit every part of me to them. Love makes people weak.

Just because I'm not bitter doesn't mean it comes without frustration. Mostly because I *want* to understand, even if I don't want to feel it. Why can't I grasp a concept others bow to so easily?

Annoyed by my inability to understand something everyone else takes for granted, I march back inside, down the whiskey, then head for the door. I'm not sure where I'm going, but I can't stay still. My feet carry me onward.

The halls are quiet. At the right time of night, even the inside of the palace is still. For a few hours, all the servants are gone. Until the cleaning shift begins in the wee hours of the morning, no one moves. It's my favorite time of day in the palace.

I climb the stairs to the third-floor suites where the girls have rooms above my own. Baron thought the proximity might be a useful extra layer of security to keep the girls from using their magic in their rooms. Though the bracelets contain magic, they aren't perfect. Someone as strong as Nora or Paige could easily still break out. Or they could just take the bracelets off in their rooms. With me so close, it's that much less likely they will use their magic. If Cypress wants a display, he can request it. Otherwise, those bracelets are meant to protect us from whatever these girls can do.

Last night, I heard the girl in the room above me pacing the floor relentlessly. It hadn't taken much to figure out it was Paige's room. Her pull is like gravity.

The third-floor hallway is just as quiet as the second. I peer up and down the hallway. Bronwyn has a suite at the end of the hall, but she is no doubt sound asleep at this hour. Baron's also in that direction. All he has to do is open his door to catch me loitering out here.

Outside Paige's door, I hesitate. A churning in my gut causes great discomfort and my chest tightens. *Why am I here?* If I'm caught, Cypress will send her away, and who knows what the Queen will do to me. Worse yet, maybe he won't send her out. Maybe he will tell the others they sent her out, but she will end up in the same experiments as Easton. Sudden sickness swells in my stomach.

I pause, fist raised to rap on the door. Even just this noise could wake someone and gather attention. Seconds tick by slowly as I debate the brilliance of this plan. Or lack of brilliance. *What am I even doing here?*

I'm sure she wants information about Easton. Not that I can tell her what I know. Not for either of our sakes. Who knows what she would do if she found out? And then Baron would know that I know...

No. I can't do this. I drop my fist and pivot. Maybe a trip to the King's Observatory Bar atop the palace is in order.

"Your lordliness." Paige's voice draws me up short. "Running off?"

Crap. It's too late to turn back now, but if she wakes someone else, we are in trouble.

I spin back around and slap a hand over her mouth, nudging her toward her room and pressing a finger to my own lips. Her eyes widen in alarm at first as she stumbles backward, but she seems to understand and gives a small nod.

After easing the door closed, I turn to find her standing in her nightgown. This is a terrible idea. I'm in her room now. No good can come of this.

She says nothing. Instead, she just stares at me, waiting for an explanation with her hand on her hip and brows raised.

I don't have one.

I edge closer and notice her balcony door open. Isn't she cold? *Wait...was that her singing?* I slip past her and close the door, hoping to seal off our voices from anyone else who might wake.

"What—?"

I hush her. "Keep your voice down."

"Why?"

"Because this isn't safe."

"Then why—?"

"I don't know."

She takes my hand and draws me to the green loveseat, pulling me down beside her. Our knees brush as we angle toward one another. "Okay. Let me ask you a question then. Why did you just dump me in that cottage with no explanation?"

"That's my job. I don't owe you an explanation."

"Fine. Then tell me why four of the girls didn't have to stay in that cottage with us."

"I don't owe—"

"Like hell. What makes them special? If I'm to be part of this, I have a right to know what I'm up against." That stubborn intensity burns in her eyes.

Paige made it clear she had no interest in participating in any of this all the way here. What changed?

I lean back and cross my arms. "Fine. They are from the island. They went through their own vetting process before you arrived."

She nods as if she already knew this. Her gaze drops to her hands as she fidgets with the bracelet. "Nora mentioned you've gotten into a fair bit of trouble because of me."

Nora. I stiffen. What else has she told Paige about me? "I find trouble on my own. I don't need you as an excuse."

"I just wanted you to know I'm sorry. I guess."

"Some apology."

"Well, you abducted me." Fire burns in her eyes as she glares at me.

I fight off a chuckle. Once more, Paige has stripped me of my guard in an instant. It happened several times on the way here.

"Is that a smile?" Paige bites her lip, not bothering to hide her own amusement.

"Is that all you wanted? To reprimand me for abandoning you, as if you're entitled to my presence at all, ask about a few girls, as if I owed you an explanation, then offer me a backhanded apology?" Why did I say all of that? I need to get out of here. I rise.

Her eyes flare and the amusement vanishes. "You came here. I didn't ask you to come into my room."

She's right. I'm getting too close. I need to put distance between us for as long as possible. "You're right. It was a mistake. I shouldn't have come. Don't tell anyone else I was here. It will get you into serious trouble."

She surges to her feet. "You know, I had a dream where you were much friendlier than this."

I freeze.

Paige inches closer, taking my hand. Hers is warm and smooth, but not as soft as other girls. She's worked these hands. I draw my gaze to her lips, remembering my dream. I've been dying to kiss her ever since. Something is psychologically wrong with me, wanting something just because it was denied to me...and in a dream, no less. A dream she clearly knows about.

Paige stares up at me through long lashes. She's toying with me. I know it, but I can't help getting sucked in. "I need to know how Easton is doing. I understand I must stay away from him, and it's safer for both of us." She gives a small shrug. "Which is honestly for the best. I think he and I would be toxic. But we have worked together for over a year now. I may not be in love with him, but I care about his wellbeing."

I can't tear my gaze away from her hand in mine. My heart is hammering so loud I'm worried she can hear it. All I can think of is that dream. My brain is screaming *Danger*, but my legs won't move.

She takes another tentative step closer. "Please, Zephyr. Any news. I just need to know he is okay."

She smells like roses. The scent is familiar, inviting. My resolve trembles like a lonely leaf in a winter breeze, clinging to the branch, to hope.

Go. Now. I jerk my hand out of hers and march toward the door. She is doing this on purpose. *Fool!* I knew better than to come here. "He's alive."

"Wait!" She rushes toward me.

I jerk open the door and close it behind me before her fingers can brush my arm.

Without checking to see if anyone heard the outburst, without giving her a chance to catch me, I climb the steps two at a time, headed for the King's Observatory Bar at the top of the palace.

I need another drink. A lot of them.

27

PAIGE

ZEPHYR'S STRANGE RETREAT LAST night left me perplexed. I know he's interested, and I feel somewhat bad about using that interest to get information from him, but I didn't know what else to do. Now, I keep replaying the encounter in my head as I sit in the private dining room across the hall from the café.

It had started as toying with him, digging for information, but something in his eyes struck me. I *wanted* him there. There was a moment, as he stared at our hands, when I thought I might want him to kiss me.

Then he pulled away and stormed out just when I had been certain we were on the same page. What did I do wrong?

The other girls occupy two of the three round tables in the private dining room. They buzz with conversation. Today, we will finally meet King Cypress.

Some girls at the other table express their anxiety about this king we have not yet seen. It's hard to get excited about the prospect of marriage to him without knowing what he looks like. I don't bother telling them about my encounter with him last night. It will probably cause envy in some girls—like Layla and January in particular.

Bella and Maeve don't bother hiding the fact that they already know him, flaunting their association at every opportunity as we wait. The way Layla snaps at Bella makes me certain that keeping my trap shut is for the best.

"No man is worth this," Holly mutters under her breath.

I glance at the other girls at my table. Of the six of us, four are island girls. Clearly, they prefer sticking together. Do they think of themselves above us? Like we are gutter trash while they are noble? I covertly watch each of them as we wait. There is certainly an air of importance around each of them that the other girls don't carry. Like they own this room.

Most of the girls slouch over their drinks, eyeing the covered plates. They gave us strict instructions to wait for the royal family to join us before beginning. I can smell the pancakes and bacon. My mouth waters.

River watches all of us anxiously. I notice her fingers sliding covertly under the cover on her plate. A moment later, she slides them back out again. No one else seems to notice. I avert my gaze as her own sweeps the room. Using peripherals, I watch as she slips a small piece of bacon into her mouth when no one is looking. *Smart girl.*

"Nora, you know him, right?" January asks from the other table, turning in her chair. "Is he handsome, or a frog?"

Nora flushes, eyeing the open doors and the windows along the hall. "Even a frog can transform under the right circumstances."

Alice snorts and rolls her eyes. "Way to not answer."

"He has an easy smile," I say before checking myself.

All the cottage girls freeze, eyeing me.

"When did *you* see him?" Layla asks sharply.

"They were all watching us when we entered the palace that first day," I say quickly, thankful for an excuse to cover my slipup. "From a balcony right over the entrance. Princess Bronwyn was there, along with the Queen. Lord Zephyr was also there, and Prince Dominic was talking to King Cypress."

A few jaws slacken. Eyes widen. Hands fall into laps. Then they all look at Nora again.

She remains aloof, taking a drink of her coffee.

"I would rather go home," Holly says softly.

We all fall silent as the family glides through the door.

Princess Bronwyn sweeps in first, giving all of us that innocent, reassuring smile. She can't really be so harmless. Prince Dominic escorts her to the head table, giving all of us a polite nod as he passes. As he settles beside his sister, his gaze runs over the gathered girls, lingering a touch too long on Bella. He swore himself to a position that prevents him from marriage, but he clearly still has eyes.

Zephyr and Lord Baron trail behind them. I straighten upon seeing Zephyr, willing him to look at me. As he examines the small room, he looks everywhere *but* at me. All I wanted to know was how Easton was doing. Alive is hardly an adequate answer. Alive does not mean unharmed.

As the Queen enters, the native girls stand. The rest of us pick up the hint quickly and rise as well. She breezes past us as if we aren't even there. Once she reaches the head table, everyone settles.

"King Cypress will be a little late this morning, but he insists we get started without him," the Queen announces.

Servants rush forward, removing the silver lids from our plates.

The only girls who speak at all during the meal are the natives. How many meals have they had in the palace already? How much time have they spent around the royal family?

Halfway through the meal, chairs scrap the floor. The girls facing the door are halfway to their feet when King Cypress gives his command.

"Please, ladies, don't let me interrupt your meal."

I turn slightly in my seat, cursing the position. I can't see the door and can hardly see the head table.

The atmosphere among the girls shifts almost immediately. Those who had expressed doubts earlier or slouched in their seats sit straighter. The transformation is amusing.

"He's gorgeous," Alice whispers under her breath.

I don't crane my neck to look at him like some others do. He and I had a very good look at one another last night. Instead, I keep my focus on the meal.

On the way to the island, Zephyr warned me that his brother enjoys a challenge. If the other girls plan to fall all over him—a fact I cannot understand considering the circumstances that brought them here in the first place—I will present him with a challenge. I need his attention and trust to get home.

A few minutes after entering the room—and after a whispered conversation with Prince Dominic—King Cypress joins the other ladies' table. I still can't see much more than the side of his head, the brown curly mass of hair.

The conversation itself is bland. How are the ladies settling into their rooms? What do they think of the palace? His charm clearly wins over the giggling mass of girls. All but Holly, who remains silent, studying her breakfast. River and Summer offer smiles and kindness his way, but there is something guarded about their interactions. I can't say I blame either of them.

He excuses himself politely and walks over to our table. The only open seat is directly across the table from me, between Nora and Bella. Was that by design?

His cool blue eyes sweep over the six of us. As he engages with the four native girls first, I act as if none of this matters to me and continue focusing on the last few bites of my last pancakes, surrounded by a moat of syrup—just the way I prefer it.

An easy air surrounds King Cypress, reminding me of Tudor—my ex in Elpis. Everything about him exudes comfort and familiarity with his surroundings and the girls at the table.

"What about you, Lady Paige?" he asks.

I look up from my empty plate. All five girls are staring at me.

King Cypress leans back in the seat, his ankle resting on his knee and hands resting casually in his lap. A hint of amusement flickers in his blue eyes. Other than that, he doesn't show we spoke at all last night.

"I'm sorry, I'm afraid I missed the question," I reply. "These pancakes sent me to a whole other place."

He chuckles. "Quite alright. They do that to me sometimes as well. I suspect a very coordinated chef plot, distracting us with perfect pancakes as they take over from the shadows."

That's the second time he joked about a plot against the royal family. Does he suspect some truth to any of it? Maybe not chefs overtaking the Kingdom, but some sort of secret coup.

"I was just wondering how you are settling in. Do you like your room?"

I fold my hands demurely in my lap and straighten. "What's not to love? A balcony with a lakeside view. My own bathroom. More dresses than I would ever dare to wear in a lifetime. Is it forbidden for a lady to wear pants these days?"

Maeve fights off a giggle—surely at my expense. Nora smirks as well. But the King's amusement is quite different.

"It is...atypical."

"Well, that one word describes me perfectly." I force a smile onto my face and add a lilting laugh for good measure. Charm and mystery. That should do the trick.

"I fear that might be true." He taps a finger on his pants, then smooths out the material and rises. "It was a pleasure, ladies." His gaze lingers on me a touch longer than the other girls.

As he strides away, Layla sighs. The other girls at the table are glaring at me. Except for Nora, who fails at hiding her pleasure. I resist the urge to roll my eyes as he returns to the head table.

Zephyr's gaze bores into me, his expression hard. What is he thinking? Hoping to disarm him, I wink. He grimaces.

As I look away, I notice Lord Baron also watching me. His lips thin into a tight line so severe it makes me flush in shame. His dangerous eyes turn on Zephyr. I've just gotten him into even more trouble.

28

ZEPHYR

MY AFTERNOONS WITH EASTON in a private sword fight-ing session proves fruitful. His ability to pick up new fighting techniques and adapt is remarkable. I've only had a couple of sessions with him outside of group training, but already I can see what my lieutenants were talking about. Easton is far more intelligent than I initially gave him credit for. Which worries me. Someone as smart as him has a plan. Maybe my initial reaction is correct.

We wrap up our lesson, both covered in a sheen of sweat despite the cold air around us. Easton slides his practice sword back into place on the rack.

"You're doing well, Easton," I say, placing my sword beside his. If I can get him talking, maybe I can figure out what he's up to. "I've heard rumors that your time as a recruit might be short."

"You think so?" The hope in his eyes worries me. "Where do you think they will put me?"

I shrug, trying to act casual. "Where do you want to be?"

He slips on his coat. "Do I get a choice?"

The response is clever. He's fishing for information just as sure-ly as I am. "Not usually."

Easton grimaces and tugs at the bottom of his coat, straighten-ing it. "I want to be wherever I'm most useful."

A clever answer. I watch him ready the zipper on his coat. The way he scowls at the zipper tells me more than he realizes. It isn't the coat he's frustrated with. It's the entire situation. I slip my coat on as the bitter winter air turns the sweat to ice.

"Have you been placed under any further interrogation or experiments?" I ask, hoping to switch tactics.

"The fact that you have to ask worries me. You don't know what happens in your own fort."

"That's not an answer."

Easton jerks the zipper up roughly. "Is there any way you can get a message to Paige?"

The sudden shift in subject startles me. I blink, hesitating to answer. I narrow my eyes on him. "Why?"

Easton stuffs his hands into his pockets, raising his chin stubbornly as he glares at me. His broad shoulders rise, then fall. "I just want her to know how I'm doing."

"So that's the message?" I stalk toward him, wary of what he will say next.

Easton squares his shoulders. "No. Just... Can you get a message to her or not?"

I cross my arms. What will Baron say if he finds out I'm passing messages between them? "That depends on the message."

Easton grimaces, but nods. He knows this already. I expect he wouldn't ask me to deliver anything that might get any of us into trouble. "Just tell her my training is going well. It begins with a single step."

"What does?" Something about his wording has my teeth on edge.

His smile is sad. "She will understand."

After a bit more coaxing, he pulls an agreement out of me before I leave for the night. I can't stop turning the words in my head all the way home. What do they mean?

Sweat rolls down my back beneath my shirt despite the bitter cold. The first snowfall created a blanket of white over everything last night. Teams of horse plows spent hours clearing the roadways in the wee hours of the morning. Now, in the evening's darkness, moonlight reflects off the snow, lighting up the way home. It's beautiful.

On a normal day, I would ride to the fort and stable my horse there. This morning, I worried about how slippery some hills might be for her, so elected to walk instead.

The walk back to the palace is only about fifteen minutes. I march along Market Street, head down against the wind and hands tucked deep in the pockets of my coat. Only a few people are out under these conditions, and they hedge away from me, heads down against the cold. Most are tucked away in the small houses lining the narrow street. Island shops are dark. The guard house is quiet. They shut the stable doors to protect the horses inside from the elements.

I peer up at the lights of the Medical Center. No matter how dark the rest of the island is, the Medical Center and the palace always have lights on. There's something cozy about the island on a winter night. Warm lights glowing in homes. Glittering snow.

But tonight, I'm distracted by my own thoughts.

Easton's training is nearly complete. We can only train recruits so far before they are ready for placement. Easton's proficiency with his magic upon arrival paired with his military background has allowed him to bound through our training program. He will be an officer before we know it.

But Baron won't let Easton leave the fort. Not if Paige remains a Tribute. Their connection is dangerous. Not because they might be romantically involved—both have clarified that isn't the case at all—but because their history could pose a threat to all of us.

What would Baron do if I broke Easton out of the fort? I don't know why I consider this. Maybe because Easton won't give me a straight answer about what is or isn't being done to him. Is he worried someone in the fort is watching or listening? Does he think they will retaliate if he speaks out?

Not that I know where I would take him. There are a few buildings on the island, and most of them are near the palace or within view of the fort. None are unoccupied.

As a child, I searched for all the best hiding places on this island. But my father's men could find me anywhere I went. I even tried camping out in the forest in the middle of the island when I was thirteen. They still found me and dragged me home. That was one of the worst beatings my father ever gave me.

That was also the first time I ever had alcohol. Baron gave me whiskey and forced me to finish it. He insisted it would help with the pain. And it did. For a time. When it didn't, I went looking for more.

I round the corner. Within a block, the palace comes into view.

One lesson I learned quickly as a child is that this island is small. Not only is there nowhere to hide, but I can walk anywhere in an hour or less. And I have. I know this island inside and out, which makes me certain any attempt to hide Easton would be pointless.

The men respect me. If I ask for help, most of them would jump at the chance. They are also just as likely to confess everything should Baron ask questions. They respect me, but they admire him a great deal more. None of them would dare keep secrets from the King, should he ask. I'm not even sure my friend Nat would keep my secret.

I stomp off the snow on the soles of my boots as I enter the side door. They still drip, so I crouch and remove them to carry. The checkerboard tiles are pristine. The servants have enough to do without cleaning up the snow I track through the palace too.

Instead of heading straight to my suite, I take the elevator to the girls' floor. The sooner I deliver the message, the better.

Glancing up and down the hallway, I knock as quietly as possible on Paige's door. I keep a keen eye on Baron's door at the far end of the long hallway as I wait. Seconds tick by slowly and I worry she won't answer at all. I set my boots down. Just as I'm about to try knocking again, the door opens.

Paige's brows are high on her forehead as she stares at me. For a moment, I'm rendered speechless as I take in the glittering red gown that hugs her curves. She sticks her head into the hall, glancing in both directions, then jerks me inside.

I stumble helplessly behind her.

She closes the door and rounds on me, hands on her hips. "Is this how it will be? You ignore me all day, then come to my room for clandestine visits at night?"

My heart is beating way too quickly. I take a step back from her, needing to add space. "No. I'm just here to deliver a message."

The two of us stare at one another. I can hardly think straight with her in that dress. It occurs to me in this moment, as my heart is racing and my stomach is rolling in a way that makes me extremely uncomfortable, that the lieutenants may have been right about her. If she is as skilled in combat as Easton, but looks like that in a dress, Cypress isn't the only one in danger.

"Well?" She taps her fingers on her hips. I can't help staring at the manicured nails along those curves.

I clear my throat and force myself to move away. "From Easton. He says his training is going well—which it is—and that it begins with a single step."

Paige's shoulder sag with relief. She glides across the carpet and sinks into the armchair. The way she slumps makes the top of her tight dress slip a little. I quickly avert my gaze to the floor.

"I don't suppose I can see him," she whispers. She already knows the answer.

"Not without Baron's approval, and I don't expect that to be forthcoming." I stuff my hands deep in my coat pockets.

"Do you see him every day?" she asks. Her voice is so gentle it doesn't seem to fit with her usual tough attitude.

"Nearly."

She nods, fiddling with her hands. "Good."

I'm dying to ask what the message means, but she won't tell me. Just another question in a long list of unanswered questions.

I bid her goodnight and turn to the door.

Paige jumps to her feet and takes my hand as I pull open the door. A rush of electricity races up my arm, then spreads through my entire body. Without meaning to, I tighten my grip on her hand.

"Thank you." The sincerity in her eyes is disarming. I need to get away. Quickly. "For watching over him. And for delivering his message. It means more than I can express."

She leans closer. I freeze. The warmth from her body soaks through my clothes and burrows into my bones. Paige kisses my cheek. Her lips burn their mark in my flesh.

I step back, dumbfounded. I want to hold her hand tighter, pull her closer. But the danger of those treasonous thoughts bears down on me. Her hand slips out of mine. She wipes a hint of her lipstick off my cheek and the touch nearly undoes me. Then she closes her door in my face.

I stagger back a few steps, staring at Paige's closed door.

For a moment, I remain there in the hallway, unable to pull myself away, feeling her on the other side of the door. The warmth of her touch, her kiss, lingers on my skin. The overwhelming urge to go back and throw caution to the wind rushes through me. I shake my head and grab my boots from beside the door.

I need to walk away. Now.

I grimace and turn, heading back downstairs. Heat engulfs me, and I rip off my coat as I go. None of this is fair. Cypress gets whatever he wants, and I must stand by helplessly and watch.

I need a drink. A *lot* of them.

I drop my coat on a chair and march straight for the wet bar in my parlor. My hands tremble as I pour a glass of whiskey. I need something strong tonight.

Voices from my mother's room draw me toward her bedroom door. I down the whiskey, then set the glass on the counter and edge into the entryway outside her door.

"...soon." Baron's voice rumbles through the closed door.

I press closer to the door and hold my breath, listening.

"I know." Mom's voice is so weak, defeated. "I'm worried about what it will do to him."

Are they talking about me? About her inevitable death? I peer back at my abandoned whiskey glass.

"Trust me," Baron says. I want to burst in and tell her to do anything but trust him, but I wait for more. "Please, Emry. You have done so much for me since the moment we met. Let me do something for you. I can help him through this. I *want* to help him through this."

She murmurs a response I can't make out through the door. I slowly wrap my hand around the handle, but some part of me resists. I don't have any right to spy on them. Baron, maybe, but not Mom.

Nor do I have the energy to try. My hand trembles on the handle. I step away before they catch me eavesdropping.

Then I pick up the whiskey glass and bottle and close my bedroom door.

29

GAVIN

THIS MORNING, THE MINISTER forced his way into my room to confront me. The Elders are unhappy with my sudden withdrawal from my duties. People are begging for my help. *"You need to step into this position you carved out for yourself,"* he told me. But I don't want to. Not any longer. Not when everything I do seems to prove to these people that I'm one of their precious Idols. I don't want any of this. I just want to open communication with Elpis and get my sister.

I sleep with the radio tucked under my pillow. I prefer sleeping with it there. It brings me closer to home. Not that it ever makes a sound. Nor do I expect it to.

The few times I have left my room—usually in search of food—I return certain someone has been snooping. Thankfully, I hide the radio and notebook in the cubby I created in the wall whenever I'm not around. When the hole closes, the wall is seamless.

Whomever sneaks into my room executes their search with great care. Did I not have Perfect Memory, I wouldn't even notice the subtle shift in my clothing stacks or how my bed is made. For now, I will let them believe I'm clueless.

Whoever it is, they have access to the Minister's quarters. Unfortunately, that doesn't narrow the list down too much. I don't know who the Minister allows in and out of his home. And there's always the chance that it's him.

Or Pip. She hasn't said much to me since I rejected her advances. Her smiles are tight-lipped. Her conversations are stilted and brief. Hopefully, she just needs a little time. I definitely don't want to lose her friendship.

The radio from Elpis has become a pet project. I pass time fiddling with it. I can't boost the radio signal any farther than five hundred miles. The materials on hand can't extend the range any farther. While that leaves me within range of the island where Paige was taken, I'm twice that distance from Elpis. Unless Dad sends out another team to track us down, I won't hear from anyone.

My parents probably assume the two of us are dead. I close my eyes, picturing their faces. Picturing my sister's face. How is she doing in the Kingdom? I haven't Dreamed with her in a while.

I lick my lips and press the button on the radio, sending out another desperate call to home—or anyone from home who might be searching. Nothing comes back.

With a sigh, I click it off and tuck it back into the hole in my wall.

I need to see Drake. I've only been to his quarters once. It's a small place, but functional for him alone.

The walk through the Haven halls sends my gut into a frenzy, as always. The eyes that follow me bring heat to my face. My steps hasten along with my pulse.

As I round a corner, I nearly collide with Elder Ally. She grabs my arms to keep me from stumbling off balance.

"In a hurry, Gavin?" she asks, smiling sweetly at me.

I swallow. "Just...going to see Drake."

"Can we expect you to report for a repairs list in the morning?" While she is only a little older than me, Ally gives off a commanding air that sends a pulse of fear through me. She oversees the Guardians, the security force that protects the Haven. If she wanted, Ally could have them force me to do any number of tasks.

I want to tell her no, but fear the fallout of another refusal, so I hedge. "Maybe."

Her keen eyes pick me apart as if determining the level of threat I pose. It makes my skin crawl. "I hope you understand how special you are to us, Gavin."

A lump lodges in my throat. I couldn't answer her if I wanted to. Not that I know what to say. Her words feel layered in hidden meaning. Or maybe it isn't so well masked and anyone but me would pick up on it. All I can do is nod stiffly.

Ally steps aside. "Tell Drake I say hi."

I can't escape fast enough.

A small cluster of people congregates in the hallway near Drake's door. I pause. Should I turn back? I don't want to talk to these people, and the interaction with Ally has me rattled. I pivot, but before I can take a step, Drake's familiar voice calls me to a halt.

"Gavin?"

It's been a week since we spoke, and my last words weren't exactly polite. Is he angry with me?

I slowly turn as Drake edges his way through the cluster, patting another boy on the shoulder as he turns his body to slide past. A flare of jealousy surges through me. Unsure what to do, I stuff my hands into my pockets. My gaze drops to the floor.

"I'm so sorry about what happened at the temple, and that I disappeared on you," he says when he reaches my side. "I wanted to give you the space you needed. Figured you would come when you were ready." He shrugs. "Then the hunting party needed my help. My Silence gift is helpful for sneaking up on animals. The team leader was determined to get as much as possible to help stock up for the winter."

Hunting. That makes sense, I suppose. I nod, glancing past him at the boy he touched. It was probably nothing, but I can't help wondering.

"Can we talk in private?" I ask.

"Absolutely." Drake takes my hand and pulls me toward his door. His hand is warm and sends a jolt through me.

Drake nods politely to the people near his door, then closes it behind the two of us.

Unlike Pip's bright room, Drake's quarters are a cluttered mess of trinkets he has collected on scavenging missions. A black orb that looks like a speaker. A snow globe of a city now in ruins somewhere in the world. A wooden heron statue with a broken beak.

I pick up a pair of rope bracelets with a face like a watch. But instead of hands, one has the mountains and the other has a wave. The moment I make contact, the sensation of electronic components pings my Power.

"I just liked them," Drake says.

I glance over my shoulder to see Drake strip off his shirt. Heat rushes to my face. I can't help but appreciate the way the muscles in his back move. I clear my throat, mouth suddenly dry. "Where did you find them?"

"There's an enormous shopping center in old Minneapolis we go to sometimes." Drake slides a fresh shirt over his head.

I must look away as my heartbeat quickens. Instead, I funnel all my attention into the bracelets. The components inside are a little degraded, but still functional. I turn them over in my hand, sliding my thumb over the back of the face on each. The devices are so small I don't need to open them to make them work again. It only takes a few seconds. The atoms respond to my energy, shaking off the rust and reconnecting.

My love is and will always be yours. The words engraved on the back of the face feel personal. What were these for? I can sense all the components inside, but it isn't until I depress the face on the mountain bracelet that it makes sense. The other one vibrates.

"How did you do that?" Drake whispers.

I dare a glance over my shoulder, only to find him directly behind me, his face inches from mine. My stomach burst with excitement. Every part of my body comes alive in a way I've never felt before. Not with Liam. Not around Aron. *This is bad.*

He pulls his gaze from the bracelet. His dark eyes peer into me. Then he takes a quick step away as his cheeks turn pink.

Once again, I clear my throat. "I just kick-started the components inside. They are designed to communicate. I feel the messaging connections, but I think we need an outside source to make it work."

Drake pales. "So...they're technology? From the old days?"

"Seems like it. We probably have something back home that could help them communicate."

Drake shuffles back, shaking his head. "No, Gavin. Turn them off."

"What's wrong?" I turn to him, holding both devices in my hand.

"Technology is forbidden. It's one of the original sins." Drake swallows.

Technology is a sin? I don't remember that from the pages Pip shared with me. "But the water treatment and air filtration...the lights..."

"Necessities for survival are allowed. *Those* are frivolous." Drake waves a trembling hand at the bracelets.

My heart sinks. If this is true, there is nothing Elpis has to offer the Haven that they will accept. If anything, they will see us as heathen sinners. "You don't really buy into all of this, do you?"

Drake sags, raising a tremulous gaze to me. "I don't know how else to explain what happened."

I set the bracelets in the box on his shelf again, then join him on the edge of the bed. "I do. Back home, we have detailed records that tell us exactly what happened. Even if a few of the details are wrong, which I admit is likely, the overall truth remains the same. No deity came and cleansed the world. Humanity did."

He flinches as if I slapped him. "But there are still too many unanswered questions."

"Religion is founded on unanswerable questions."

Drake gives me a flat stare, shaking his head. "How could the Prophet have predicted *you*? Gavin, I was in old St. Louis. I saw what you did. You wielded so much power in the fight against the Kingdom. I've seen nothing like it. I've never even *heard* of anything so powerful!"

I don't just want him not to believe in all of this. I *need* it. Maybe it's selfish, but his ability to use logic and think through this without the Minister's sermons swaying him is important to me.

"Drake, there are perfectly reasonable scientific explanations for what happened." The more I explain, the more animated my voice becomes. "In Elpis, we have teams of people who have dedicated decades to studying Powers and how they work with our genetics. They can prove beyond a doubt how and why we are the way we are. Even me. Given enough time, they could even explain why so few people in this community have Powers. We know how all this works."

Drake smirks slightly, though it's weak. A dimple forms on one cheek.

"What?"

"That's the first time you've named your community."

My heart stills. What can the Haven do with that information? Will it lead them to Elpis? What will they do when they see all our technology? I need to steer him away from home.

"Don't you see?" I surge to my feet and begin pacing, unable to remain still. "Your religion is based on the idea that you should blindly follow the faith while you wait for some savior to come rescue you. But change happens through action." I spout words I've heard Dad use before.

Drake rubs his chin. "Okay. Let's say for the sake of debate that you are right. That doesn't make the *Book of the Prophet* inherently wrong."

"How do you figure?"

He straightens as if bracing himself for a fight. "Just because you can prove how we are what we are does not mean the Prophet was wrong about what comes next. At some point, all of this must get better. We can't stay in the dark forever. And then there's *you.* 'He will come from the west.' 'He will wield unfathomable power.' 'He will have the power to remake the world.' I *saw* it. Regardless of what you can prove, the Prophet was right."

How can I argue with that logic? Coincidence? "He was a Precog."

"What?" Drake's face twists in confusion.

"The Prophet could see the future. That was His Power."

"Which makes Him right."

Again, I falter. The Prophet could see the future. He wrote it down, and it became the religion it is today. Does that mean he was right about the Idols? *It's science, not religion.* His Power is explainable through science. Right or not, faith isn't what will save these people.

Something desperate flashes in his eyes. "Besides, is hope such a terrible thing to cling to?"

I rub my neck. "No. But you don't need a savior. You need your own strength. If you want things to change, *make* things change. Take ownership."

Drake's brows draw together. He rubs at his ear, then drops the hand in his lap. "What do you mean?"

"Our entire social structure was deeply flawed when my dad was a teen. It hurt some people and propped up others." Just like the structure here in the Haven. "But no one had the guts to make change. No one knew *how.* My dad saw the flaws in the system. He saw the need and knew he couldn't wait around for someone else to rescue them. He banded together with the people and *made* those changes happen."

Drake shakes his head. "We aren't as strong as you. Most of these people have no gifts."

"My dad doesn't, either. He didn't do it to flex his Power muscles. He did it because it was right. It was what needed to be done."

Drake draws back. "I don't see how this all connects."

I inwardly groan. How can he *not* see? It's so clear to me. I take an urgent step toward him. "Drake, something here is off. The Minister controls everything and the Elders bow to his will. When

I tried to help people, they stepped in and shut me down, then gave me a bunch of menial tasks way below what they know I'm capable of."

"So you admit you are capable of great things."

I wince. He's twisting my words to fit his beliefs. "That isn't my point right now. Drake, the Elders are hiding something."

He shakes his head in fervent denial.

"You don't need these imaginary Idols to save you. *Be* the change your people need. Claw your way out of the earth yourselves."

"Imaginary..." Drake mutters. Irritation flashes in his dark eyes. His jaw twitches, and the vein in his neck throbs.

I press on, praying he will understand. "Make change happen while working toward fulfilling the Prophet's vision for your future on your own. Why can you not have your faith and *be* your faith? These two things are not mutually exclusive, are they?"

He heaves out a sigh, shoulders sagging. "No."

Relief washes over me. He gets it. He must.

Drake rises, closing the distance between us, hands stuffed deep in his pockets. The hard set of his jaw makes me ache. I've made him angry. I didn't want this. Let anyone else be angry with me except him. I'm not sure I can handle it if he turns against me. That might destroy me utterly. I would accept Liam's rejection a hundred times over this.

"You don't understand what life is like here." The pain is so acute in his tone that even my socially hopeless brain catches on. "You never step back from yourself to look at anything else. To look at me."

If only he knew. "I *do*." All the time.

He shakes his head, sadness pouring off him. I ache to fix it. "You live in your own bubble. And that's fine. It's you, and I love that, but sometimes it hurts. Gavin, you constantly talk about your family. You drone on about how much you miss them. How much you love them. But you have never asked about my family."

I blink, opening my mouth to retort. But he's right. I haven't. Not once. Shame flushes through me. Not only have I never asked, but I have only heard a passing reference to his father since my arrival. My gaze sweeps through his small quarters. Cozy. Comfortable. Fit for one.

"Drake, I'm sorry."

"I don't doubt it."

I lick dry lips. My limbs tremble. *Please don't hate me.* I have never needed acceptance from anyone as wholly as from him.

To make matters worse, I don't understand how to connect these dots between religion and his family, which only increases my frustration with myself. "How does this relate to our debate?"

Drake stops so close the toes of our boots nearly touch. I can see the flecks of green in his dark eyes. "Life in the Haven is hard. Most people don't live past thirty without a gift. Somehow, gifts extend our lives here. But people die from illness, injury…childbirth." He swallows, dipping his head away. "Mom died giving birth to me. Dad was crushed in a tunnel expansion project when I was ten. I barely remember him."

The revelation punches me in the gut. Pain catches in the back of my throat. I can't even imagine what that is like to lose one's entire family. And here I've been lamenting not being able to see my own since the moment I woke up on that boat. What kind of pain have I caused him? I'm not sure I've ever hated myself so much. My apology comes out thick with grief and regret.

Drake draws in a breath, steeling himself, then raises his chin. "The point is my story isn't unique. There are so many kids here who only know their parents for a few years, if at all. Some people live their entire lives without ever seeing the surface." His voice tenses with a pain of his own. "The *only* thing that gets us through that darkness, that gives us hope, is faith. Our dream that one day things will be better."

The passion of his speech, the emotions he puts on display with each statement, each word, draws the strength from my limbs. I can't meet his gaze any longer. I stare past him at nothing and release a long breath.

Drake has a point. Historically speaking, people cling hardest to religion during the worst periods of global strife. It's inherently human to seek hope when all seems lost. I don't have the right to tear away his hope. Nor do I want to. I just want him to understand that there are answers out there, that not everything the Minister teaches is true. That something here is *wrong*. But I need to see the actual *Book of the Prophet* to prove anything.

I can't force this on him. He needs to get there on his own. I can help him find the path to see for himself, but he must be the one to see it.

"I have a proposal for you," I say, taking a step back. While I enjoy being so close to him, I don't want to give him the wrong idea—or set myself up for another bitter disappointment. "We agree to disagree. Don't ever try forcing me into another position like what happened at the temple. I'm not a savior of anything. But I will keep an open mind where your feelings are concerned."

Drake raises a skeptical eyebrow, stuffing his hands into his pockets. "And?"

I hold out my hand to shake. "And I won't try to convince you that your religion is wrong, as long as you keep an open mind to other possibilities."

Drake hesitates, staring at my hand, then nods. "Deal." He slides his warm hand into mine, shaking briefly before pulling me into a hug.

My heart hammers against my ribs. Can he feel it? This means nothing. It's just a friendly hug. But no amount of repeated reassurance can conquer what engulfs my senses. Drake smells of fresh earth and charcoal. If someone stuck a match right now, I would be consumed in his flames.

30

PAIGE

*I*T BEGINS WITH A *step*. I keep telling myself this as the days crawl past. To learn about the world and the royal family, I must take things one step at a time. Easton warned me not to be hasty, to take things slowly. I hate how long it's taking to make progress, but I can't deny that it's working.

Two girls are dismissed in a matter of days, both island natives. The departure seemed amicable as Maeve and then Everly are carted away in a royal carriage. I'm not sure I understand how he could know so quickly, but Nora explains that both girls have weak magic compared to the rest of us. She says King Cypress likely worked out a mutual agreement with their fathers before dismissal to avoid any fractured relations between the royal family and the two lords.

King Cypress spends the next week gathering the girls for group activities. A brunch where the girls all vie for the closest position to him. A handful of us—Nora, Summer, River, Holly, and I—allow the other girls to fawn over him. We're content to permit it without comment. That night, Layla and January launch into a bitter argument in the hallway. I ignore their cattiness.

Another day, he takes us horseback riding. A man King Cypress calls a jockey teaches each of us the basics of riding. Only four of the girls—myself included—mount without needing help. I've never been on horseback before, but catch on quickly. Alice and Holly both struggle with their horses. When King Cypress attempts to help Holly, she refuses to look at him or touch him.

Layla seizes that as an opening to fall off her horse. While the girl had shown no riding skills, part of me believes she wants to put on a show for the King to get his attention. And it works. She loses control of her horse so many times that he guides her alongside him, holding the reins himself. But I'm not so sure the attention she receives from him is the kind she wants. King Cypress strikes me as someone who likes a girl to be confident and in control.

Curling proves far more entertaining than I expect. King Cypress instructs each girl on how to play individually, guiding arms and legs into position, holding their waists to temper the speed. By the time he reaches me, I already have the stone in motion. He observes as I hit the center of the target after the third attempt...then on every attempt thereafter. I'm pretty sure it disappoints him that he couldn't direct me like he did the other girls, but I relish the surprise on his face. Though, if he knew I slid the bracelet off and into the pocket of my coat, he might not smile so much.

Most of the girls are terrible at bowling. A few times, when I'm certain no one watches me too closely, I loosen the clasp on the bracelet, breaking the harness around my Power. Each time I sneak it off, I bowl a strike. The other times, I'm close enough that it still earns me praise. At the end, after I beat all of them, King Cypress shakes my hand and offers congratulations. But as he does, his finger brushes over the clasp on the bracelet. Thankfully, it's clasped tight when he does. He suspects what I did but says nothing.

The more days that pass around him, the more I grudgingly respect him. King Cypress isn't a tyrant. He doesn't abuse his power over others. Under different circumstances, I might even seriously consider this entire ridiculous pageant.

One chilly afternoon, King Cypress escorts the eleven of us down to the ice rink alongside the inactive fountain across from the palace. They erected a dome with semi-transparent walls alongside the rink. Each of the girls wears colorful sequined dresses with short skirts and long thermal leggings. The sleeves are warm and soft enough that we don't need to wear coats.

Inside the dome, tables covered with sweet treats line one side, with a setup for hot drinks at the far end. Benches for changing our shoes line the other side of the dome. Heat pumps in from somewhere above.

I lace up the skates and press the gloves tightly around my fingers. My maid, Maddy, had braided my hair back intricately to keep it off my face, obviously aware of what the plan for the day was. The ends of the braids stop just past my ears, leaving the rest of my hair hanging in loose waves from the bands around the braids.

As the other girls finish preparing, I covertly unfasten the bracelet under the sleeve of my dress. The sleeves are tight enough to hold the bracelet there as long as I don't jostle it too much.

I step out into the bitter cold air and approach the rink. Several guards wait beside the half wall, observing not only me, but every-thing around us.

Last time I went ice skating had been indoors with my family. Mom and Dad were terrible at it, but they had laughed and clung to one another as they carried on around the rink. Gavin had only skated briefly after I coaxed him out onto the ice. To him, this endeavor was too dangerous. He has spouted the statistical probability of injury and wasn't satisfied until I reassured him that my Muscle Memory would protect us both. Even then, he only stayed on the ice for a few minutes.

Thinking of my family makes me hesitate beside the open doorway into the ice. *One step at a time.* I want to go home, but I need to approach this one step at a time.

And today that means skating—as ridiculous as it feels.

I step out, easily gliding across the surface. The smooth ice beneath me and the rhythm of my movements make it easy to fall into old habits. By the time the other girls emerge from the dome to join me, I am deep in a trance. Rocker turns. Spins. Jumps. Everything floods back from my lessons. I finish with a series of spins that would make anyone else dizzy.

Applause takes me by surprise as I stop spinning and glide out to skate around the track. The other eight girls are lined up at the half wall with King Cypress, staring slack jawed as he offers his praise. I flush. A few of those glares are more cutting than the blades on my feet, particularly from Layla, January, and Bella. My performance will probably result in some cattiness once we are back on our floor later. *Great.*

King Cypress glides out to greet me, taking my hands. "Is there anything you can't do?"

"Go home." The words slip out before I can stop them. My face twists in horror. "I'm sorry."

"It's okay." He nods at the ice. "I would like to take a spin with you."

After what I just said, there is no way I can say no. I nod.

King Cypress beams. He clings to my hand—the hand with the loose bracelet—and the two of us move around the ice together. Reluctantly, the other girls join us. Some of them stick to the wall as they go, unaware that it only makes it harder for them to skate that way.

"I understand you and your family were close," he says. "I wish there was something I could do to help."

"You're King," I say, eyeing him. How does he not see the obvious?

"I answer to more people than you realize." King Cypress glances toward the palace. For a moment, I'm sure I see the Queen watching from a balcony. Does she pull his strings?

"They don't even know if I'm alive or dead." I hold tighter to his arm as if I need his support.

The two of us fall silent. The muscles in his arm tense. Then he pats my hand. "Maybe I can send them a message on your behalf. Let me know what to send and where, and I will see it done."

Does he really think it will be that easy to learn where Elpis is? I'm not about to tell him where to send a message, no matter how badly I want to send it. What will the Admiral do on his orders once they know where I'm from? But I can't outright say no either. King Cypress is trying to offer me an olive branch, underhanded as it is.

"I will consider it," I say carefully. "Thank you, King Cypress."

"Just call me Cypress." He loosens his hold on my hand and I release my grip on his arm.

We skate together for a few more minutes before he moves on to join Nora. I make my way to the exit, then awkwardly walk on the skates into the dome to grab a snack. Someone beautifully crafted the cookies and fudge. I can't resist sating my sweet tooth.

I finish a few cookies, then pour myself hot cocoa. When I turn, Bella pushes past my shoulder. The move throws me off balance in the skates and I fall back, spilling scalding hot cocoa on my shoulder and neck. A scream rips from my throat.

Bella slaps her hand over my mouth, muffling the sound as she crouches over me. The hate in her eyes is so pure it makes me tremble. "Stop showing off and give the rest of us a chance, Paige." She throws a wad of napkins at my burning neck. "Or next time will be worse."

A guard bursts through the door, but before I can speak, Bella is pressing napkins over my mouth.

"What's happening in here?" he asks.

"Get a physician!" Bella calls back, her voice trembling. "She tripped on the skates and burned herself with the cocoa."

The guard rushes out the door.

Bella leans so close I can smell her sugary breath. "I have connections in this palace. Breathe a word of this to anyone, and it will be the last thing you say."

Something flashes in the sparkling fairy lights. A knife in Bella's hand. I can easily disarm her, but doing so will reveal my unclasped bracelet, which could get me into serious trouble. Bella can slip into my room and kill me in my sleep. As this reality sinks in, I close my eyes.

I don't want any of this. I just want to go home. Heat rushes through me, making every part of my body burn with embarrassment. How did I get caught like this?

"You can't kill me," I say breathlessly. "What will they do to you if they find out?"

Bella pouts mockingly at me. "Oh, you poor dumb girl. My father controls the horses on this island. I'm valuable, protected. What do you think will happen to me?"

The truth sinks in. *Nothing.* Unless King Cypress knows how to replace her father.

"The Queen is pushing for me," she says. "And she holds more power here than anyone else. Including our King."

Where is that help?

The heat in my body squeezes me tightly in a vise. I can't breathe as reality weighs down on me. The men in the royal family are dangerous in their own way, and I have looked at them as pieces on a chessboard. I knew the girls were vying to be chosen by the King, but I never considered how far any of them would really go. *Fool, indeed.*

"Remember," she hisses in my ear. I can feel the blade press against my neck. "Your life is at my mercy."

The heat inside of me bursts outward. I whimper and scream. Bella flies back across the dome, hitting the far wall. The entire structure trembles. Tables topple and food rolls across the carpeted ground.

King Cypress rushes in. "What happened?"

A sob crawls up my throat as fear and grief take hold. The dome collapses.

King Cypress throws himself over me, shielding me from the weight of the building.

------◈------

I WAKE IN MY bed, head hammering like a drum. When I move even the slightest, intense, blinding pain shoots across my skull. I groan, pressing a hand to my forehead as if that alone could silence the war drums.

My Power is locked away behind a wall again. Not that Muscle Memory would help me. What happened to me in that dome? Some Power I don't understand exploded out of me. I felt it but can't connect it to any of the Powers I know of.

Hushed voices emit from the doorway. I try to open my eyes to see who is there, but the brightness of the room is too intense. When I try to roll over, my stomach lurches and I nearly vomit on the floor.

A warm hand wraps around my own. I blink cautiously. "Lights," I groan.

Someone turns the overhead lights off and closes the curtains. It takes a moment for my eyes to focus well enough to see King Cypress kneeling beside my bed, cradling my hand in both of his.

"Thank goodness," he breathes. "You've been out for hours. I was worried."

"Bella...?" She was in the dome with us when it collapsed. I remember how her back hit the wall with a sickening smack. She may have threatened me, but I don't want to kill her.

"She'll be fine," King Cypress reassures me. He brushes a hand gently across my forehead, moving my hair aside. "Minor concussion and a few bruises along her spine. Nothing more."

Bella is fine. I hate to admit it isn't a relief to hear. Not wanting to kill her differs from not wanting to maim her.

I try to ask what happened but can't get the words out quite right. King Cypress seems to understand the intention well enough.

"Your bracelet was loose," he says. "Lady Paige, did you unclasp it?"

My heart thuds. Removing the bracelet results in severe punishment. I don't want to know what that might be. "No."

King Cypress' lips twitch, but he offers me a nod. He doesn't believe me. Does he know I've been removing it for days? Surely, he suspects.

"Unfortunately," he says, "because of the incident and your surge of magic, there is some concern that the bracelet is not strong enough. We are working on a new one for you. One that won't have a faulty clasp."

One that likely will not be so easily removed. My heart sinks.

"Meanwhile, my brother will keep watch over you."

Before I can ask which brother, Zephyr steps around the foot of the bed and plants himself near the door, arms crossed over his chest. I don't even know why I wondered. Of course it would be the one who can hinder my Power.

"Lady Paige, do you know what happened?" King Cypress sounds so patient, so much like my father when he is digging for an answer he expects I already have. But I don't know how to explain.

"No. Not really."

He rises and perches on the edge of the bed, still holding my hand in his. "When your bracelet came loose, you had a surge of your magic. Maybe because it was contained for so long and it needed to break free. Maybe because something caused you stress that triggered it."

The emphasis on the last sentence makes it clear he knows something was amiss in the dome. But I can't tell him about Bella's threat. That dangerous glint in her eyes told me she means business.

I frown. "My Power? But...Muscle Memory..." *Denial, Paige. You're falling deep into denial. You've felt that Power before.* This realization makes the hammering in my head intensify.

He shakes his head. The chestnut waves shake with him. "That wasn't Muscle Memory."

He's right. Something is happening to me. First Dreaming, now this...

If Gavin was here, or Dad, they could explain it. Instead, my mind falls desperately into denial. I can't have a Power I can't control. It couldn't have been me. They're wrong. "Maybe Bella—"

"She can grow flowers," Zephyr says. "She can't create energy like that."

Create energy...? Does that mean I can do what Uncle Alex can do, manipulating energy? Gavin has more than one Power and I've always felt like less because I only had one. But what if there was something else beneath the surface that I just haven't had a reason to use?

It couldn't have been me.

Testing should have identified any additional Powers. While testing isn't what it was when my dad was a child, it's still used to a lesser degree to find out what Power each citizen has. Knowing how to use one's Power helps prevent disasters.

Like an entire building coming down on our heads.

My eyes widen, sweeping over King Cypress. "It fell on you! Are you...?"

"All fixed up. Don't worry about me." His thumb brushes my cheek. I want to pull away, but don't want to offend him. I hope he doesn't mistake any of this for interest in him in that way. While I don't loathe him as much as I once did, I don't feel *that* way about him.

King Cypress leans closer and kisses my temple. "Rest well, Lady Paige. Zephyr will be here if you need anything, and I have already instructed your maids to monitor you, but give you space to rest."

I want to wipe away the kiss. Instead, I curl my fingers into the covers and hug them tight to my chin.

King Cypress leaves me alone.

With Zephyr.

31

ZEPHYR

PAIGE DID IT AGAIN. She used a fraction of that magic hiding dormant deep inside of her. Cypress could have died. I should tell him, but still can't bring myself to confess the truth.

She could destroy this entire island.

While I understand the need for me to remain close to Paige until they can fix her bracelet, I loathe the execution of the plan. At first, it isn't so bad. Paige rests on and off. I make sure she has water or food beside the bed when she wakes. Recovery from her magical surge takes time.

That night, I leave the room to return to my own. But before I take three steps out the door, Dominic appears with a handful of servants and a rollaway bed. My stomach sinks. I don't have to ask what's happening.

Cypress isn't taking any chances. He told me to stay close to her until they fixed her bracelet, and he meant it literally.

I shake my head just outside her door as the servants quietly enter the room to set up the extra bed. "This is a terrible idea," I tell Dominic.

He shrugs. "Hey, at least you get to sleep with one of them."

I scowl. "That's not funny.

"It's kinda funny."

The grin on his face chips away some of my irritation. My shoulders sag.

Dominic pats me on the shoulder. "It's just one night. We should have her bracelet ready tomorrow."

Should. I don't like that word. But I don't complain. It won't do any good.

After the servants drift out of the room, Dominic hands me a small packet of pills. "Just in case she needs *help* sleeping." He puts extra emphasis on the word help. I know what that means. If her magic goes out of control, I have to get these in her system somehow to keep her from overloading.

I pocket the packet and nod. He doesn't even realize a fraction of what she is capable of. What happened outside was only a drop in the bucket.

We say goodnight.

When I tiptoe back into the room, Paige remains asleep in her bed. There's nothing charming about the way she sleeps with her head tipped back to the sky and her mouth gaping. I almost laugh.

They squeezed the cot between her bed and the massive wardrobe. I strip down to my t-shirt and boxers, monitoring her all the time to make sure she doesn't wake. Then I climb into the cot and rest my head on my arm, watching her.

Seeing Cypress tend to her bedside, kissing her temple, holding her hand, made everything inside of me want to haul him away. And the way he looked at her... Cypress likes her. Which also signifies that any feelings I have are meaningless.

I drift off as I observe her sleeping.

And I dream I'm in a locker room. The metal lockers are painted a dark shade of gray and the tiled floor is damp in places. A bin full of dirty towels rests in one corner.

Voices drift to me from deeper in the room, somewhere just beyond sight. I edge closer, listening to the anger in the boy's voice.

"...gone for months," he snaps. "Which tells me you never should have been sent on this mission in the first place."

I reach a corner and peer around. Paige and a boy I don't recognize are tucked away in an alcove leading to a door.

"Why are you here?" Paige asks. Her voice trembles. I'm not sure I've ever heard her scared before. *Who* is *this guy?*

He stalks closer, forcing her against the concrete wall. His breath ruffles her hair as he speaks. She shrinks—literally growing inches smaller—beneath his force. "To remind you that you are in this alone. Sink or swim, Powers."

Fury pulses through me. Who does this guy think he is? I barrel into him, slamming him into the far wall. His head smacks the concrete. I pin his neck to the wall with my forearm, applying all the pressure my body holds. His face turns red as he struggles for air.

I bare my teeth in a feral snarl. "Leave her alone."

"Zephyr!" Paige rushes over, pulling my arm back. "Stop!"

As our eyes meet, the other guy vanishes. She reaches up and touches my cheek. I jerk away. What is going on? Is this a dream or real? Why can't I tell anymore?

My eyes snap open, heart hammering against my ribcage. The feel of her fingers against my face lingers.

Paige stares at me in the darkness, studying me in a way that makes my insides twist. "You were there, weren't you?"

I swallow. It was a dream, but did we share it? How? Were those other dreams shared as well? *That means...*

I swallow, only able to answer her question with a nod. "How?" I croak.

She shakes her head. Confusion wrinkles her forehead.

For several minutes, we lay in silence, studying one another. I can't make sense of what happened. If it was Dreaming magic, she shouldn't be able to use it around me, let alone on me. But the strength of her magic presses against my own. It pushes me away. It pulls me close. It leaves me alone and cold. It envelopes me and holds me tight.

"Who is he?" I ask, breaking the silence.

"No one." But her heart isn't in it.

I raise my brows at her. "Didn't seem that way to me."

Paige picks at the hem of her comforter as she considers her answer. At last, she licks her lips. I watch the motion, thinking of the dream where I tried to kiss her. Does she think of that dream, too? She must know about it.

"When my team left home, we were chosen because of our specific skills sets," she whispers. "Our council wanted to keep the team small, so they had to be careful whom they selected. Tudor and I were in training together. We were sort of seeing each other."

The words are as good as a shot through the heart. "Sort of?" But he acted like such an asshole in her dream. Did that really happen?

She gives half a shrug. "There are rules against dating people on your team. Which is also why Easton didn't tell me how he felt, and why he won't, even now, allow any kind of association. We would lose our jobs. Once our superiors found out…" Paige sighs. "Anyway, they couldn't let Tudor and me both on the team because of our history, so they chose me."

"And he didn't like it." I know men like that. There have been a fair few who think we should choose them for certain missions and lash out when they aren't. "So, he threatened you."

Paige shakes her head. "Not exactly. He basically called me a selfish princess and told me he wouldn't carry me anymore."

Were it not for the pain in her eyes, I would have laughed. Not only because she introduced herself to me as a princess, but because I can't imagine her being selfish. How any man could treat her like that and not swear to wait for her return with open arms, I don't understand.

"Did you love him?" I hate asking. I don't want the answer, but I need to know.

Paige chuckles. "No. I'm not sure love is in the cards for me. I seem to hurt everyone who cares about me. Tudor. Easton. Cypress…" Her list trails off, her umber eyes locked on me.

A dull ache in my chest spreads to my gut. If she is implying me on that list…it's probably closer to true. Nothing can happen between us.

"Cypress is fine." My feeble attempt at reassurance—and changing the subject—does nothing for her. I can see it written plainly even in the room's darkness. A lump climbs up my throat and I struggle to swallow it down.

"I know he is. And Cypress has been kind and affectionate enough..." Paige huffs out a strangled laugh and rolls on her back. "I shouldn't be telling you any of this."

"But you don't feel that way about him."

She closes her eyes. "Goodnight, Zephyr."

I lay awake, watching the steady rise and fall of her breathing. The fact that she didn't respond tells me what I need to know, but she also knows that telling me can lead to her dismissal.

So why does she want to stay when she's been so eager to get home?

And do I want her to stay when her dismissal could open the door for me?

32

GAVIN

THE HAVEN BUSTLES WITH activity as citizens move about their ordinary day. The atmosphere is warm, inviting...almost a little too inviting. The longer I stay here, the more off everything feels. I've never been one to follow gut instincts, preferring facts and science to feelings. But I can't let this go.

And it all leads to one place.

If the Minister discovers I am angling to see the *Book of the Prophet*, he will shut me down. Possibly even make me a prisoner among his acolytes. I need to find someone who has answers. Or at the very least, who has enough knowledge that I can find the answers for myself.

Unfortunately, I cannot move through the halls of the Haven without notice. I stroll as inconspicuously as I can manage, keeping my head down, hands in my pockets, avoiding eye contact. But people still stare at me, still whisper, still offer greetings with tremulous voices.

Men and women in Guardian uniforms eye me as I pass. Acolytes in their cream-colored robes bow their heads to me, a keen sense of some understanding in their eyes.

Acolytes are the most devout believers in the *Book of the Prophet*. Everyone else in the Haven defers to them with reverence. I don't fully understand what they do—aside from indoctrinating children—but I have learned from Drake and a few other Havenites that every acolyte has a gift of some sort. No one outside of the temple seems to understand exactly what they can do, but they wield Powers for certain.

I promised Drake I wouldn't press him further about his religion, but if I find irrefutable evidence, he has agreed to keep his mind open. The desperate need to make him see reason continues driving me. I don't want to take his faith away, but I need him to be open to other possibilities. Pip might not tell me the whole truth—if she even knows what that truth is. She is fully indoctrinated in this religion, blinded by it.

Only one person might see matters from my point of view and have insight on how to proceed.

I need to see the original *Book of the Prophet*.

Emil can help me.

That Pip's binder was so incomplete has chaffed under my skin for long enough. I can't stand not knowing. My mind is like a universe-consuming demon, always hungry for more, never satisfied without all the knowledge it can collect.

When Dad was my age, his curiosity got him into endless trouble. His need for answers led to a rebellion. I don't want matters to become so dire in the Haven, but the suppression of knowledge smothers me.

"Gavin."

My steps halt the moment I recognize the Minister's voice. I turn slowly, my heart pounding. He is the last person I want to see. "Mr. Garraty."

"I don't think I've ever seen someone so lost in thought before," he says, edging closer. "And that's saying something when Luke is constantly thinking about something."

Elder Luke oversees education, which means he is part of the system that encourages indoctrinating impressionable minds like Pip at a young age. My jaw twitches.

"Dad tells me it's a perpetual state for my face," I say, hoping to inject some of Dad's trademark wit. Not that I've ever been as good at it as he is.

"You're too young to be so pensive." Mr. Garraty places a hand on my shoulder.

The move is meant to be fatherly, reassuring. Instead, it's like a vice. His bright eyes—the same eyes as Pip—bore into my soul.

I've never stopped to consider what his Power might be. All the Elders have some kind of Power that affords them their position. What would a man in his position benefit from? Telepathy? A chill runs down my spine.

"I am happy to offer you the same services I offer the other members of our community," he says. "Tell me what bothers you, son."

I'm not your son. I have a father.

The truth would be so much easier to garner directly from the source. Telling him what bothers me would lift a burden from my back. No one knows the *Book of the Prophet* as well as the Minister. All the answers are right here in front of me. All I need to do is ask. My lips part, the words on the tip of my tongue.

"I just...was thinking..." A wave of cold surges over me, as if someone dumped a bucket of ice water over my head. My lungs compress. My heart stops.

And I see the moment with striking clarity.

Influence.

He's an Influencer.

Mr. Garraty can encourage people to confess anything to him...or be moved to action by his words. He can change minds and hearts with the right touch, the right words. *He can influence their minds.*

"It's alright." He gives me an encouraging nod.

How did I snap out of it?

Gram. I swallow, taking a moment to steady my racing heartbeat. When Dad was a boy, Gram placed a psychic wall around his mind to keep people from reading his mind or influencing his decisions. Five years ago, when Dad confessed how Paige and I differ from others—our genetics are more evolved, allowing us the potential to control multiple Powers—he insisted we allow Gram to put up the same psychic wall on our mind to protect us. No one can enter without permission.

The Minister's Influence has no control over me.

But I can't let him know that.

"I just want to find a way home," I say, the lie sliding past my lips. The slight narrowing of his brows tells me he might not believe me. "And ever since the sermon, people treat me differently, look at me strangely. It makes me uncomfortable."

Mr. Garraty's hand drops off my shoulder and he nods with sage understanding. "It can be hard, I'm sure. But the people are only curious about you. No one knows where you came from, so they are naturally interested. And you've helped the Haven in ways no one has done for quite some time. Our balance here is tenuous, and you've shaken up the status quo. But if we follow the path set forth in the *Book of the Prophet*, we remain safe here in the Haven. I'm not sure how things are done where you come from, but we have rules here that are necessary to maintain our tenuous balance."

My jaw twitches. His incessant need to repeat the importance of their tenuous balance only reinforces my belief that their social system is just as broken and repressive as Elpis once was. Does he know how many lies he is feeding to these people? Does he *care*? The Minister isn't just part of the problem. He *is* the problem. He and the entire Elder council.

Once more, the drive to uncover answers creates an unquenchable thirst for the truth. I must find it, and the only way to do that is to get my hands on the original *Book of the Prophet*.

"That actually makes me feel a little better." I'm getting good at lying. "I was also looking for Emil. Do you know where I might find him?"

Mr. Garraty frowns. "Why do you need him?"

I swallow a lump that jumps into my throat. "He lost his sister, just like I did. I thought maybe he would understand and help me...you know...with the despair."

He studies me for a moment, then nods. "He works in the scrapyard."

"Thanks." *Now, where is the scrapyard?* I turn away, eager to put distance between the two of us.

"Gavin!" The Minister calls after me. I glance back over my shoulder, but don't stop. "I sincerely hope we will see you at the next sermon in a few days."

My stomach drops. Instead of answering, I dip my head away and turn the first corner.

It didn't sound like a request. Whatever I plan on doing, I need to finish before the next gathering at the temple.

Because I have no intention of ever going back there.

33

PAIGE

THE NEW BRACELET IS twice as thick as the last, and somewhat heavier. The stones are larger as well, which increases my worry that they are some form of Power stone—a stone that can slowly drain the Power of the wearer and eventually bring about his or her death. I don't want it on. I want to shove Prince Dominic away when he arrives to wrap it around my wrist and secure it with a strange locking mechanism and key.

Zephyr lingers at Prince Dominic's shoulder. We haven't talked about the dreams further. Not what happened in them, nor what we discussed in the dark. Unloading some of that on him had helped me sleep better, but it's created a tension between us. Can Dominic tell?

As Prince Dominic finishes locking the bracelet in place, his hand delicately cradling my arm as he works, Zephyr and I stare at one another. He seems worried. I can't figure out why. But the longer we stare at each other, the harder my heart beats.

"All set," Prince Dominic announces as he slides his chair back away from where I'm perched on the edge of my bed.

Zephyr and I both yank our gazes apart. I examine the new bracelet. It's snug, making gentle contact with my skin. There is no clasp. Just a lock that disappears almost seamlessly. *No slipping this one off.*

"How does it feel?" Prince Dominic asks, genuinely concerned. "It isn't too tight, is it? I can loosen it a little. But we need to be careful that it doesn't slide off, for your own safety."

I shake my head, rubbing a hand around the emerald-encrusted band. *For my own safety my backside.* "It's fine. Thank you, Prince Dominic."

He winks at me. "You can just call me Dom."

He rises and rolls up the leather wrapped jeweler tools. As he marches toward the door, Zephyr follows. My heart sinks. I want Zephyr to stay, though I can't say why.

Prince Dominic stops at the door and nudges his brother back. "Cy wants you to stay here until her maids arrive for her fitting."

Zephyr's face droops. His arms drop limp at his sides. He works the muscles in his jaw as if chewing on what he wants to say. *Is he so eager to leave me?*

Prince Dominic leans closer and whispers something to Zephyr, then pats him reassuringly on the arm before turning out the door. I didn't hear what he said, aside from the words "all night" and "dry". I don't understand what it could mean.

Once we are alone, Zephyr groans and buries his face in his hands, then drags them up through his messy, dark hair. I pad over and rest a hand on his shoulder, hoping to offer some reassurance.

Zephyr jerks away, glaring at me. "Don't touch me."

The animosity in his dark eyes makes me recoil. I glimpse Nora wandering away from Bella's room in her nightgown. She cocks her head at the two of us curiously.

"Go shower before your maids arrive," Zephyr snaps at me.

I scowl at his back, then march into the bathroom and slam the door hard enough to rattle the wall. I thought we were making progress last night, but it seems I was wrong. I don't know who was talking to me last night, but it certainly isn't the same guy lingering in my doorway. I actually liked the Zephyr who spoke with me last night. The daytime Zephyr is a jerk.

By the time I emerge from the bathroom wrapped in a towel, Zephyr is gone, replaced by my four maids. All of them beam at me. Ingrid—the mother of the three girls—motions to the vanity chair.

I sit without comment.

"The Winter Festival is a few days away," Mariah says as her mother fusses with my hair. "King Cypress thought it would be nice if we gave each girl the option of designing a dress that represents your community." Her eyes drift to the larger bracelet on my wrist.

At that moment, I notice that all four of them are forcing smiles. None of it's genuine. What kind of rumors have surrounded my Power surge? I pull the bracelet close and fiddle with it self-consciously.

Instead of lingering on what rumors surround my surge, I focus on the chance to design something representing Elpis. But how does one do that? And how can I make it show-stopping enough that I can barter with King Cypress to get a ticket home?

Mariah listens attentively as I detail a dress my mother once wore to a gala with Dad, but I add a few Elpis embellishments. Elements of a crow, the infinity symbol, a twisting helix. As I carry on, Mariah draws on a pad nestled in her lap. When I add additional details, she erases, then adjusts.

The final sketch is far more stunning than anything I had in my head. "You have a gift," I say.

Mariah gives me a weak smile. "Only if I pull it off. Some of these materials might be scarce."

"It's okay. Just do the best you can."

They finish dressing me for the day. Ingrid informs me that Princess Bronwyn and Lady Emry have requested tea with me, and the King will wait in the lobby for me afterward.

I swallow and smooth my hands over the burgundy dress I've selected for the day. Hopefully it's satisfactory for whatever is in store.

With the room number in hand, I step into the hallway to join the princess and Lady Emry. Bella stands near the elevator, speaking in a low voice with someone I can't see. He responds just as quietly, then strokes her cheek. A shy smile spreads across her face.

Was King Cypress flirting with Bella? A flare of anger surges through me. I'm not envious, but after what happened between Bella and me, I don't understand how he could be interested. Is he just toying with her because of who her father is? Bella seemed to think the Queen was pushing for her to be chosen. Maybe the Queen offered King Cypress counsel he couldn't ignore.

I dip back in my doorway as Bella turns and marches away toward her room, a far-off look in her eyes.

"It's clear," a girl whispers from down the hall.

At first, I think she is talking to me, but when I peek out, I see Summer leaving River's room. They didn't want to be caught together. Why?

River reaches out and takes Summer's hand, pulling closer. My cheeks heat and I duck back in my doorway once more. Summer and River. What would happen if King Cypress found out? I vow to keep their secret, even if I think their sordid affair is foolish. Nothing good can come from this unless they can both find some way to be dismissed by the King. Does the Kingdom welcome same-sex couples? We don't think twice about it in Elpis.

Ever since the cottage, Summer and River have been close. They even shared a room there and spent a lot of time in that room together instead of out in the parlor with the rest of us. Does this relationship go that far back? Maybe that's where it all started.

I make my way to the room on the next floor down. A servant stands outside the door. The moment she sees me, her face lights up. She offers a curtsy, then opens the door.

"...shouldn't be doing this." Zephyr's familiar voice drifts through the open door. He doesn't sound angry. He sounds desperate. "Mother, you need rest."

"I don't think sitting in my parlor having tea will tire me out," a woman says. "And if it does, my room is right there. You get to work."

The servant clears her throat and announces me. I take my cue and turn through the entryway, gliding into the parlor.

Zephyr stands ten feet away, stiff as a board as he meets my gaze.

Beside him, an older woman sits in a blue velvet chair. She narrows her eyes at him, then her gaze sweeps over me. Zephyr has her eyes.

"I need to get to work." Zephyr snatches his coat off the back of another chair and storms out a door on the other side of the parlor. It rattles against the frame behind him.

"Lady Paige, please forgive my son," the older woman says. I assume she must be Lady Emry, Zephyr's mother. Which also makes her a consort to the former king. "Please, join us."

Princess Bronwyn beams at me and nods, motioning to an empty chair at the table with them. "Yes. My brother has had *quite* a bit to say about you."

I nearly ask her which one, glancing at the door Zephyr stormed out of as I settle. But asking will only cause more trouble.

"Zephyr can be quite stubborn," Lady Emry says.

The servant pours my tea and offers me a plate of breakfast sweets. I take a pastry with murmured thanks.

"I get that sense from him," I say, trying to relax. Should I relax around these two?

Why am I here? Something about Lady Emry feels terribly familiar. Not only because she has Zephyr's eyes—or I suppose he has hers—but there is something else. A sense that I've met her before.

Lady Emry laughs, but something about the way she studies me makes me uncomfortable.

"Cypress has been very worried about you since the episode yesterday," Princess Bronwyn says. She holds her teacup in her hand but never drinks from it. Nor does she touch her food.

I set the pastry down on a plate and wipe my fingers on a napkin. "I feel terrible."

Lady Emry and Princess Bronwyn exchange amused glances. I hate not knowing enough about these people to read into those looks.

"Don't feel terrible." Lady Emry reaches over and takes my hand, giving it a gentle squeeze. "You would blush if you knew what I did during my time as a Tribute."

"Were you from the island?" I ask.

Lady Emry's eyes turn sad, and she looks away, withdrawing her hand. "No. My community was in old St. Louis."

My heart stops. That's where Zephyr found us. He came back to his mother's community to find new Tributes. Instead, he found me.

"Did you ever want to go back?" I ask timidly.

"Sure. They separated my brother and I that day. I never saw him again. But I fell in love here."

A stab of pain lances through my chest. I swallow thickly. "My brother and I were separated as well." I hate how the emotions climb to the surface, but if I want the royal family to pity me enough to let me go home, I need to show these emotions. So I let the tears slip out. "I can't bear the idea of never seeing him again."

Lady Emry nods in commiseration. "It gets easier."

I shake my head. "I can't accept that. No man who loves me would keep me from my family. And I don't think I could love someone who does." The words are dangerous, yet true. King Cypress could dismiss me for that statement alone. Without him, I don't know how to get home. I need to make him the man who loves me enough to send me home. Even if I still couldn't love him.

Princess Bronwyn gapes at me, stunned by my blunt confession. I blush and stare into the depths of my teacup. "You are admitting you could never fall in love with Cypress?" she whispers, as if the words themselves are treasonous. *Are they?*

"I suppose that depends on him." I raise timid eyes to each of them. "Do the royals truly believe that abducting girls from their families and bringing them here for this pageant will lead to love? When was the last time a king chose a queen not from the island?"

Lady Emry's gaze turns inward, likely recalling her own abduction and time as Tribute. How could she fall in love with a man who did these things?

Unlike Lady Emry, Princess Bronwyn stiffens her spine. Her eyes harden as she stares at me. "It sounds to me, Lady Paige, like you *are* saying you could never fall in love with my brother. I suppose it's better that I tell him this now than allow you to string him along."

Great. I've made a terrible mistake. "That's not what I meant. I just mean that maybe, if a king wants love, there might be more peaceful ways to go about it. Some of those girls would have come either way."

Princess Bronwyn sets her jaw. "But not you."

"I think I've already made myself clear."

She surges to her feet, setting her cup down on the table. "Excuse me. I think I've had enough. Thank you for inviting me, Lady Emry."

Panic grips my lungs. I can't let her leave, but I don't know what to say or do to fix this. Lady Emry exchanges a worried glance with me.

I rise, spinning to face the princess as she marches toward the door. "Princess Bronwyn, please let me explain."

She doesn't stop. "You've already made yourself clear."

I flinch. "I thought so as well, but you are angry with me, so clearly I made a mistake." I walk around the chair to cut off her exit.

Princess Bronwyn huffs, but halts.

"Just because I didn't want to come here, and just because I want to see my family and want him to care enough to let me, doesn't mean I don't have great affection for him." I plant my fists on my hips. "Your brother has been gentle, tender, and caring. And I can see that he wants to find happiness and not just pick a girl from a lineup. Each of these outings has been a test, whether those other girls realize it. He wants someone who can enjoy the same things as he does, connect with him, and care about him. I'm not saying I can't do that. I'm just saying..."

My arms fall limp at my sides. A pit of sorrow opens wide in my gut. "I'm just saying that I miss my family. How would you feel if they ripped away you from your family, knowing you may never see them again? Could you love the man who did that to you if he never helped you reunite again?"

Princess Bronwyn fiddles with her necklace. The features of her usually smooth, innocent face turn downward. Her eyes shimmer with unshed tears. "I'm sorry. You're right. It would be hard, and I understand what you mean as well. I would want him to love me and trust me enough to let me go. Or at least take me."

I nod, relief flooding through me. "That's all I'm saying. Did I want to come here? No. But I'm trying to remain open-minded. It's just so hard when my world has turned upside down."

She chews her lip, fighting back her tears, then lunges forward and pulls me into a tight embrace. The move is so sudden that it throws me off balance. I hug her back briefly, casting a pleading glance for help at Lady Emry, who watches us with an affectionate smile on her face.

When we break apart, Princess Bronwyn sniffles and swipes away a few rogue tears. "I have a few things to attend to today. You enjoy tea with Lady Emry."

I nod, stepping out of her way.

The moment the door closes, Lady Emry's voice sends my world head over feet. "My son is quite smitten by you."

The confession drives all the air from my lungs. I try to gulp down deep breaths, but it does nothing for the weight pressing down on my chest. I can't move. The bracelet around my wrist feels like a hundred-pound weight dragging me down.

"Please sit with me, dear. I'm too weak to talk to your backside."

My limbs move stiffly back to my seat. I sink in, hands folded in my lap, unable to meet her gaze.

Zephyr. But he is so hot and cold.

"You must have noticed."

I shake my head, but even if I don't speak the denial, it doesn't make the lie any less real. A dream I had weeks ago resurfaces. Zephyr and me in that pod in the old St. Louis arch. How he was drawn to me. How he tried to kiss me. It was only a dream, but it felt so real that even in the dream, I jerked away and rejected him.

But if last night had been real for both of us...

I swallow a lump the size of the moon in my throat. Does he realize this, too?

Lady Emry nods. "You've noticed. I want to tell you a story, Lady Paige, of another girl taken from her family and brought to the island by a handsome but restrained captain. And how dangerous it became for that girl when the Crown Prince discovered the truth. The Crown Prince found new, creative ways to impose his wrath."

My gaze flits up to hers, expecting anger or sorrow. Instead, her dark eyes gleam with worry. Though who for, I can't be sure. I swallow again, unable to clear the lump lodged in my throat.

A few of the pieces click suddenly into place, and I find my voice at last. "Wait. You said you came from old St. Louis." I remember the burned ruins inside the underground arch. And Emil's story about the Kingdom coming back to destroy them. "Your brother! I know where he is!"

She flinches as if I slapped her. "Emil?"

It is *him!*

I shift to the edge of my chair and take her hands. I push all my certainty into her, wishing I could share what I saw with her. "He was in old St. Louis with us when the Kingdom struck." I close my eyes. Someone needs to tell her the truth. "He lives in the Haven. And he never stopped thinking about you, either."

Her hands tremble in mine. Her already pale skin drains of color. Lady Emry sinks back in her chair. "Lady Paige, that is the best gift you could have ever given me."

"*My* brother is with him," I say, clinging to her hands. This might be my chance. Maybe she can help me. "He will come for me. Gavin would never leave me, and he can track anything anywhere. If I can get this bracelet off, I can send him a message. I can send Emil a message!"

Her gaze drops to the bracelet, then she yanks her hands out of mine as if I've suddenly turned vile. "Be careful. This is treason." She glances toward the doors.

"But we can all get out of here, together," I say urgently. "We can reunite with our brothers and go to Elpis, where we will be safe and together."

"What is Elpis?" Her dark eyes narrow.

"It's the city I come from. My father is in charge there and he will protect all of us. I promise you that."

Lady Emry shakes her head, then closes her eyes and presses a palm to her temple. "I need rest."

She rises on shaky legs.

I rise with her. "Please. This can work. I have a friend here. In the fort. His name is Easton. He can help us, too."

"No." Her voice lacks conviction. After a few steps, she stumbles. I try catching her, but with the damned bracelet on, my Muscle Memory is useless. We tumble together, her body falling over mine.

"Help!" I call.

The servant rushes in, eyes wide when she sees the two of us.

"Get help. Now!" I hate snapping at a girl who probably deals with it all day long, but something tells me this is urgent.

She rushes out of the room. I struggle with a limp Lady Emry, trying to slide my body out from under her to drag her toward what must be her room.

Guards rush into the room, followed by the Admiral and King Cypress. The guards lift Lady Emry with the Admiral's help and carry her the rest of the way to bed. I stand and turn to King Cypress, shaking from head to toe.

"I didn't do anything. I swear it."

Will they kill me if they think I caused her harm? Striking out at a member of the royal family is treason. Tears well in my eyes.

King Cypress pulls me under his arm, tight against his chest. "I know you didn't." He ushers me to the exit. "They will take care of her."

We reach the elevator, King Cypress holding me close to his side, and he presses the button for the elevator.

"What did she do?" Admiral Baron storms out of the suite toward us. Pure rage twists his face.

King Cypress raises his chin. "You and I both know Lady Emry has been sick for some time. Lady Paige was just in the wrong place at the wrong time."

Admiral Baron's jaw twitches. Despite the rage on his face, I can see the anguish in his eyes. *The handsome, restrained captain.* I feel like this should make more sense, like there is something I can't quite place, but I'm too shaken and scared to think straight.

"I will have answers," Admiral Baron snarls through his teeth.

"You will remember that I am your king, and you are an admiral. Learn to restrain yourself, or perhaps it's time for retirement." King Cypress' tone holds a firm air of command the likes of which I have never heard before.

Admiral Baron points at me as the elevator doors open. "Your Grace, I hope you have enough sense to ask her what happened before the Collapse."

King Cypress guides me into the elevator protectively. "I have enough sense to run this kingdom. I think I can handle this."

The doors slide closed between us and the Admiral. I can no longer hold my composure. I sag against King Cypress and cry. I can't tell them the truth about what happened, what we were discussing. Lady Emry called it treason. What will they say if they know I was trying to plot an escape with her? I got caught up in a moment of desperate hope. I pushed too hard, too fast, not knowing she was in a fragile state. Easton tried to send me a warning. *One step at a time.* I should have walked. Instead, I tried to run.

Now they could very well kill me.

The only thing standing between the Admiral and my punishment is King Cypress.

The elevator doors slide open. I stumble alongside King Cypress into another suite. He eases me down on an ivory loveseat and settles down beside me.

"I didn't do anything," I say, voice thick with terror. "We were talking, and she said she needed rest. When she stood, she just...collapsed."

King Cypress sweeps my hair back from my face. His hands cup my face tenderly as his thumbs stroke away the tears. "Shh. It's okay. I'm not angry."

"But the admiral..." My gaze flits to the door.

"I told you he's a bear, but he will come around to reason." His blue eyes gaze at me, and the sincerity and concern for me are all over his face. I feel safer with him. What will happen the moment he leaves me alone?

I reach up, clinging to his arms as he holds my face. "I don't want to be alone." Zephyr will hate me. He will blame me. I can't bear his anger. A fresh wave of tears hit.

"You won't be." His forehead kisses mine, just like Gavin often did when he tried comforting me. I cling tighter to King Cypress' arms.

Then his lips brush mine. My entire body seizes. I want to push him away but am too terrified of what will happen if I reject him right now. Does he know this? Is he using this weakness to his advantage?

My lack of response draws him back. His blue eyes pierce me, displaying feelings I don't share.

"Too soon?" he murmurs.

I nod.

Disappointment flashes in his pure blue eyes, but he voices none of it. He mimics my nod, then rises. "Come with me. You can rest in my room. I won't let anyone enter."

His room... If I just told him the kiss was too soon, why does he think this is a good idea?

He stops beside the door as I gaze at the large four-post canopy bed. Fear and anxiety knot in a ball in my chest. Does sleeping in his room, in his bed, imply consent? I don't want to give him the wrong impression. And what will the other girls say if they find out? Bella already threatened me. What will *she* do if she finds out I slept in his bed?

King Cypress places his hand on the small of my back and gently encourages me into the room.

I spin around, eyes wide, as he eases the doors closed. I don't want to be here. My legs tremble and my muscles tense.

He offers me a reassuring smile that in no way reassures me at all. "I'll be right out here. It's all yours."

Then he seals me inside.

34

ZEPHYR

I'VE HARDLY BEEN AT the fort for more than a couple of hours before a messenger from the palace arrives to summon me back. News of my mother's collapse sends a bolt of fear through my gut. I rush back to the palace, where a strange storm cloud brews over the sprawling building. Baron's work, no doubt. He's furious. Terrified for my mother, I dash straight to her room.

Baron paces outside her closed door, fury burning in his eyes.

"What's wrong? How is she?" I ask in a rush, ready to burst through her door.

Baron holds up a hand to stop me. "Resting. She woke briefly and insisted she only misjudged her state and stood too quickly, but something isn't right. I think that girl did something to upset her."

I frown, momentarily confused, before remembering that she insisted on having tea with Paige. "What did Paige say?"

Baron's jaw twitches. "I haven't been allowed to talk to her. Cypress swept her away swiftly and in no uncertain terms made it clear I was to stay away." Red fiery anger makes the muscles in his neck swell. He clenches his fists at his side. That storm was definitely his work.

Protect her, Easton said. But she isn't more important than my mother. We need answers.

"I'll see what I can do." I pivot to leave, but Baron's hand clamps down on my shoulder.

"Zephyr, be careful. That girl is dangerous."

I can only nod stiffly. If he only knew...

As I descend the steps two at a time, I wonder how much Baron really knows about Paige. All the girls had to give blood samples when they arrived on the island. Those were supposed to be used to make sure they don't carry any illnesses that might affect Cypress or any potential heirs. But what else can they learn from those samples? Can the physician use that blood to detect the strength of Paige's magic?

I'm still suspicious of Baron's motives, and who he might be working with. Could he use this event as an excuse to convince Cypress to dismiss Paige so he can sweep her up in his experiments?

I burst into the King's Suite, ready to confront Cypress and question Paige about what happened. I need the truth to protect her from Baron—and to protect my mother from her.

Cypress' bedroom door is closed.

"Over here."

I spin around.

Cypress stands on a tailor box with his arms outstretched as the tailor checks the fitting of his holiday suit. The dark blue material of the jacket is clearly meant to highlight his eyes, and the cut fits his form immaculately. As the tailor makes a few more chalk lines on the suit, Cypress grins at me.

"What do you think?" he asks.

I enter the parlor and cross my arms over my chest, squaring off against him. Who cares about a suit right now? "What happened with my mother?"

His gaze flicks to his bedroom door. "Keep your voice down. She's resting."

Paige is in his bedroom? My stomach hardens, and I fantasize about punching his pretty face into something much less attractive. My fingers dig into my arms. I focus on breathing evenly, telling myself it doesn't matter. But no amount of false reassurance will calm my aching chest.

"Why are you looking at me like that?" Cypress asks, his nose curling up.

"I'm worried about my mother, and you are protecting the only person with answers," I say through my teeth.

He snorts and rolls his eyes. "We all know your mother was already sick. I spoke with Paige before she went to rest. They talked and Lady Emry announced she needed rest. Then she collapsed. It isn't Paige's fault."

Cypress is right. I know he's right. Mom has been sick for at least a year now, getting progressively worse. What happened wasn't Paige's fault. I was worried about Mom before I left for the fort.

The tailor announces he is finished, and Cypress slips out of the jacket and steps down. "You were right about Paige, though."

I comb my memory to figure out what he is talking about.

He changes out of the trousers into a clean pair. The tailor gathers the discarded clothes and loads his equipment onto his cart.

"She is dangerous." Cypress slides on a new jacket and smooths out the sleeves. I tense, worried about what he might say next, or what he might know. "I wanted to let her dangle to draw her in, but find I can't stay away."

The pain in my chest intensifies. Dark clouds edge my vision. Cypress pours us each a drink, but I'm too afraid of moving my arms to accept. He holds the glass of whiskey out to me, brows climbing his forehead when I don't take it from him. I look suspicious. He knows I never turn down a drink. I snatch the glass from his hand.

"What's the problem?" I ask a bit too sharply.

Cypress takes a generous drink from his glass. The ice clinks against the edges, and the sound is like thunder in my ears.

He casts a sorrowful gaze into the glass. "She doesn't seem interested."

A tight smile curls the corners of my mouth. I take a drink of whiskey to avoid giving too much away. Sudden lightness eases away the tension in my chest. Paige isn't interested in him. I asked her last night, but she never gave me a direct response. Has she given him a sign?

He is expecting a response, but I fear what I might say if I open my mouth. I take another drink to buy a moment of time.

"Did she tell you that?" I ask, hoping I sound indifferent.

"No. And maybe I was too forward too soon."

What does that mean? My hand tightens around the glass.

Cypress sinks into a chair as the tailor wheels his cart out the door and closes it behind him. His gaze drops to the cushion of the love seat beside him and brushes a hand over it. "All the signs pointed to interest, but when I kissed her, her entire body went rigid, like she wanted to push me away."

He kissed her. Those three words make my face burn with anger. My stomach writhes so madly I'm worried some of the whiskey might find its way back up again. I can't move, afraid one step in the wrong direction will start a fight.

At least she rejected his advance. That's something. Not that it should matter. He is perfectly well within his right to make advances on her.

I'm not.

If I were to touch her the wrong way, he could have us both whipped—or killed. His choice.

In all my life, I've only ever been mildly envious of Cypress. Usually when our father favored him. And that envy never burned so hot in my blood before.

I need to calm down or I will give myself away. I force my fingers to release their death grip on my sleeve and edge toward the other love seat. "Give her time. She misses her family. This is an adjustment."

Cypress nods forlornly. "I know she does. She has made that perfectly clear." Sorrow creases his forehead. "Do you think there's someone else?"

Yes! "No. She mentioned something about an ex in her community, but he turned out to be a jerk, I guess." I try to brush off the hammering of my heartbeat.

"What about that guy that was with her?"

I shake my head. "They both insist there's nothing there."

"Well, there must be *someone*." He watches me with sharp eyes. Does he suspect me? "I will give her time, but I need you to help me, Zeph."

I withdraw. "I'm not sure I'm the right person to help."

Certainty burns in his gaze. He suspects something now. *Great.*

"Yes, you are. I will give her space. I should spend some time with the other girls, anyway. At the ball, I'll let her dangle. But you will spend the evening with her. Talk to her about me. Make her see why she should give me a chance."

I recoil as if he tried biting me. My face twists in revulsion. "Cypress, I don't have any magic words that will change her mind."

He leans forward, resting his arms on his knees. "Then use her friend. Find out from him how to charm her. He clearly knows. I heard what happened in the carriage."

"Easton? But they never talk. They haven't seen each other since the *Wave Slicer*." I don't want to do this. Anything but this. Cypress wants me to make her fall for him. The very idea makes me want to rip out his eyes.

"They don't need to talk. You just need to talk to him. Find out what she looks for. Then use that information to pique her interest." Cypress nods as if it's settled. I heartily disagree.

"While you are at it, talk to Holly as well," Cypress says, waving absently, as if she is a tacked-on afterthought. "That girl has been distant from the beginning. Spend some time with each of them at the ball. Plant the seeds for me, brother. And keep the vultures away from Paige."

The last thing I want is to be near Paige talking about how wonderful Cypress is. But I can't refuse. How would I explain it? There is no justification that doesn't end in me being punished. "As you wish."

Cypress' face lights up.

But I know deep down I will ruin everything. It's my special talent.

35

GAVIN

I ENTER THE SCRAPYARD lobby, marveling at the numerous rooms branching off in all directions. A sign above each chamber door explains what I might find within: home goods, clothing materials, metals, jewels, tools. The scrapyard is not what I expected, meticulously organized and maintained.

I spot a map near the main entryway depicting the series of chambers and what I might find in each. They have been managing the scrapyard for a very long time.

A teenage boy sits at a wooden desk near the entrance. The moment I enter, he jumps to his feet, face lighting up. "Gavin Powers! I...it... How can I help you?"

His reaction pulls a grimace from my lips. "I'm looking for Emil."

The boy's smile falters. Is that confusion?

Maybe I assumed he could help a bit too quickly. "Do you *know* Emil?"

"I...yes." He shifts feet, averting his gaze. "He's in the tool room."

I thank the boy, glancing at the map to learn the way, then stroll away.

"I can show you the way," the boy offers.

"I can find it. Thanks, though."

Having the boy nearby during my conversation with Emil will probably cause problems. Whatever he hears may end up reported to the Elders, and I can't have that.

The scrapyard reminds me of a library, but instead of books, the shelves have artifacts from an age long gone. They have lined each series of chambers with shelves from floor to ceiling. Each shelf overflows with items scavenged from the surface.

Emil busies himself reorganizing a shelf in the tool room. As I approach, his shoulders tense. He pauses with a small artifact in his hand. "Gavin."

I peer over my shoulder to make sure the boy didn't follow, then edge closer. "Can we talk?" I whisper, worried someone will be listening from another aisle. Who knows how many people are here? There are at least a dozen places to hide.

He puts the artifact in a bin before I get a look at it. "What about?"

"You warned me, when I first arrived, to play the Elders' game."

Emil crosses his arms over his broad chest. "I also told you to stay away from the temple, but you ignored that advice."

My palms sweat. I scrub them against my pants. He's right. Deep down, I knew it was a bad idea, but I still went to appease my friends. "I had no idea."

He raises a brow like I'm an idiot. Something about him reminds me of my dad's best friend, Alex Miller. Alex was one of my biggest supporters when I struggled with my sexuality. He also has a no-nonsense attitude, just like Emil. Blunt in a way I can appreciate. It's so much easier than trying to guess what people feel.

"The trouble is, I can't play their game." Every part of my body is shaking in fear. I'm putting a lot of trust in Emil, who hasn't said much to me since dropping me off in the Minister's home. Can I trust him at all? I'm operating on the assumption that he is just as skeptical of everything here and might help me. It's a dangerous assumption.

I lick dry lips. "The Elders know the rules of the game and I don't. The Minister has made the people believe I'm some sort of sign of the coming glory days."

He shakes his head, grim-faced. "Not a *sign*, Gavin. I saw what you did. So did Drake. The Elders know, too. They don't see you as a sign. To them, you *are* the Idol."

Fear grips me by the throat. I knew it, but hearing him say it out loud makes it so much worse. The brutal truth only reinforces why I came.

"To play their game, I need to read their rule book." I hold my breath, hoping he understands. Emil gives no sign either way. "So naturally, I came to the scrapyard to find out where one might find such a relic."

He narrows his eyes. "In the temple."

"Obviously. But how would one get to it?"

His anxious gaze darts around the room, but if anyone else is here, we can't see them. Emil edges closer, lowering his voice. "What are you up to, Gavin?"

"Fulfilling my destiny, Emil." I can't help the mockery clipping my words. I won't be the Savior, but I *will* use the Elders' rules against them. "According to your Elders, that is. Not that it matters to you, right? I mean, you don't believe in this garbage they stuff down everyone's throats."

He grimaces. Every muscle in his body tenses as he scans the room for eavesdropping. "No, but I care about these people. I've lived in communities on the surface and none of them are as safe as this one. Don't mistake my atheistic skepticism for indifference. I won't swallow their Prophet pill, but I *will* fight to protect the people with my dying breath. If your actions put them at risk, the civility between us is dead. Are we clear?"

I swallow and nod. What else do I expect? Emil had been worried about the safety of this community back in old St. Louis. He made a home here.

He scowls. "If this is about your sister—"

"Of course it is." Heat rises in my voice, and I bite back a fit of anger. What does he expect from me? I made it clear weeks ago that my priority was getting to my sister and getting home. "But it's also about the blatant secrecy the Elders huddle over in the name of balance. I've heard of systems like this one before. I know what happens."

He sneers. "You know nothing."

A snort huffs out of me. He assumes because I'm young, I couldn't possibly understand. But I have read a lot of history books. My father is the Hero of Elpis. He *lived* through this sort of thing. "It would surprise you what I know. How does one become an Elder? I know there are vacant seats. I assume because no one with the right Power has come along."

Emil's jaw twitches. His nostrils flare. He motions between the two of us. "We're outsiders. No matter how well we infiltrate their culture and follow their rules, they never truly accept us. We don't fit nicely in their structured society. We are not one of them."

No, the Elders need all members to be indoctrinated from birth into their belief system. An outsider might shed light on the truth—that there is more out there, that the Collapse came from human interference and not divine power. That there's another way. The truth strikes me like lightning.

Control. It's all about control.

As long as the Havenites believe the surface is still too danger-ous, they will remain hidden beneath the surface looking to the Elders for guidance and protection. They will believe that only those with Powers can safely walk the surface. It's the same fear the old Directorate in Elpis used to suppress the people.

Fear of the unknown.

Safety in the protective hands of the government.

Or in this case, the Elders.

What would Dad do?

Collect allies. Gather evidence. Challenge those in power. But who is an ally when everyone in the Haven believes in the *Book of the Prophet*?

"Emil, I need your help." I straighten, gaining confidence. A plan forms in my mind like a lump of clay slowly taking beautiful shape. "If you help me, I give you my word that I will do every-thing in my power to protect these people."

He appraises me. Emil's Power is detecting lies. But he won't find any deception here. My heart is in the right place. My mind is clear and focused on the task ahead.

To destroy the system, I must become a part of it. I must infiltrate the Haven at the highest level. Excitement pumps in my veins.

Emil's lips thin into a tight line. The seconds tick by agonizingly slow. If he refuses, I have no one. I can't ask Drake for help. Not yet. First, I need evidence.

"I don't see how this won't end in disaster," he says at last.

"I need to read the *Book of the Prophet*."

He shakes his head. "It'll never happen. I lived among the acolytes for two years and never read it. I've only seen it from afar. They guard that book like rabid dogs."

"But you lived among them for *two years*. Tell me everything you learned about the acolytes."

Emil chews his lip, uncertainty creasing his brow. War wages in his eyes as he struggles with his own doubt. "Their training begins as children."

The two of us move deeper into the bowels of the scrapyard as Emil tells me everything he knows. Acolytes are children with the potential to develop gifts. They aren't taken from parents. No one really knows where they come from. The acolytes grow up immersed in strict adherence to the *Book*. They brainwash the younger Haven children on the ins and outs of the *Book of the Prophet* and why it is so important to the Haven social structure. Those who develop a gift move up in the acolyte ranks to help maintain the temple and organize the educational teachings for the rest of the population. Between the ages of sixteen and eighteen, they select acolytes for a secret program. At twenty, they select acolytes who qualify for military training to become Guardians. The rest of the acolytes learn how to use their gifts to help the Haven.

But so much still doesn't make sense. If they are there to help, then why have some matters fallen into such disrepair?

"You wouldn't stand a chance in a fight against Guardians," Emil says urgently. "They not only know how to defend themselves with deadly force, but they can use their gifts collectively. It's what makes the Guardians such effective defenders of the Haven."

"Are all the Guardians former acolytes?" Something about this doesn't make sense. A piece of the puzzle is missing.

Emil nods grimly. "Do you understand now? The Minister controls the Haven. There is no way you will get to the *Book* without being caught by the acolytes." He pulls me into an alcove in the back of one of the scrapyard rooms and leans close. "Gavin, something else happens beneath the temple. There's a thick steel door at the end of a hallway protected by some sort of security lock. You can't get in without the right code."

I chew on this for a moment, trying to connect the pieces. Then one of them falls into place. "Drake said that technology is considered an original sin. Which means if the Elders are running genetic experiments to learn more about Powers, they would need it to be kept under lock and key." Just like Paragon did. Why are there so many similarities?

My gut flips. There must be a more peaceful way to end all of this than what happened in Elpis.

"What happens to the acolyte children who don't develop a gift? You said they have the *potential*, but surely, not all of them develop one."

Emil scratches his scalp, then shrugs. "Who knows? Maybe they all develop."

I want to believe him, but statistically speaking, it's improbable. "Scavengers are ordinary people with gifts. Then there are the Elders, acolytes, and Guardians. How many others have a gift?"

"None."

Not even one? The odds of that must be astronomical. *Where do the Elders come—?* I groan. *All* of them were acolytes at one time. They must have been. But how do children like Drake slip through the cracks?

Pip told me weeks ago that only about a hundred people have Powers. If she includes the scavengers, Elders, acolytes, and Guardians in that number, it can't leave much space for others.

"How do I get in without notice?" I ask. Because I must go in.

Emil rubs his neck, watching the rest of the room at my back as he tells me about a secret tunnel the acolytes use to get in and out. Why they need a secret tunnel unnerves me, but I don't ask.

Getting into the temple to find the book isn't going to be that difficult. It's getting out I need to worry about. "I know what to do," I say. "Here's what I need from you."

36

PAIGE

"Oh, Mariah! You've outdone yourself. This dress is glorious." I slide my hands along the curves and marvel at the soft fabric. Dresses have never been my thing, but this one... It's enough to make me want to wear it all the time.

Mariah beams in delight. "Thank you, Lady Paige, but the design was yours."

I shake my head. This was not what I envisioned. It's so much better than anything I could ever dream up. The work of a master.

Helen and Maddy clap their hands in delight, gushing with their own envy.

I can't believe this dress is mine.

The asymmetric top wraps snuggling over one shoulder as the entire dress twists around my body. The black underlayer modestly covers what the rest of the dress exposes. Twin swathes of red and blue fabric wrap around my body, at a downward angle, connected by shimmering ribbons of blue and red. It's reminiscent of a DNA helix.

The mermaid style hugs my curves all the way to my knees. A narrow slit up one thigh allows for easier movement.

At my knees, the skirt flares out in stunning layers of black crow-like feathers all the way to the floor. As I turn in front of the mirror, the feathers almost seem to take flight. The dress itself is like a living thing. It's far more magnificent than the dress my mother wore to that fundraising gala with my dad seven years ago.

I turn around to spy the back of the dress. The strand of the helix dips low on my back as it twists around me.

"Let's talk hair," Ingrid says, easing me into the vanity chair. She gathers my mass of wavy dark locks and sweeps them up off my neck.

"How many of the girls will have their hair up?" I ask.

"All of them. It's a standard style for the holiday."

"Then I want it down."

Ingrid frowns slightly, but Mariah offers a sly smile. She understands. The dress will certainly make me stand out, but if I want to make a statement, I need to buck tradition.

Ingrid sets to work taming my hair and stressing the natural curls so they sweep my shoulders—a compromise between having my hair up. Helen and Maddy lie out the makeup to make the best selection for my skin tone and the dress color.

"Is it true you kissed King Cypress the other day?" Mariah asks. Her hands are busy with some kind of ornamentation they intend to hang in my hair.

My cheeks burn brilliantly. I haven't been able to stop thinking about that kiss. King Cypress is a handsome man. I won't deny that. But his kiss hadn't created any reaction in me except the desire to escape. That can't possibly be a good sign.

"I don't think you should put too much stock in rumors," I say, hoping they can't hear how worried I am that he might try again.

The younger girls exchange knowing looks and simultaneously say, "He kissed her."

I huff and try to sag, but the dress holds me firmly upright. I couldn't slump in my seat if I wanted to. "It didn't mean anything."

Mariah's brows knit together, and she looks utterly confused. "I don't know how a kiss could mean nothing."

"It means I don't want to talk about it!" I snap.

They all flinch. Immediately, I regret barking at them.

Everyone falls silent as they work. Guilt gnaws at my stomach the longer the silence stretches, but I don't know how to recover.

I don't want to talk about the kiss and give anyone the wrong impression, but I don't want these four mad at me.

Ingrid puts on the finishing touches, adjusting the black beaded headdress that reminds me a bit too much of a crown cradling my scalp instead of pointing at the sky. Will the Queen be angry that I wear such a thing on my head?

"Mariah, I'm sorry for barking at you," I say as the girl cleans her mess in the corner.

"I shouldn't have pressed, miss. It's not my business." She rises and heads out the door ahead of the others.

Clearly my apology didn't matter much, and the other three don't offer me reassurance as they finish up and pack their things.

My heart sinks. I keep making mistakes with these girls.

A knock on my door startles me from my misery. My stomach coils in a knot, worried about who it might be.

Ingrid opens the door and announces Lady Nora, then she and the twins slip out.

Nora steps inside, watching them with a curious frown on her face. "Are you harassing the help again?" She's teasing, but it hurts.

"I didn't mean to upset them. I will make it up to them later."

I quickly compare my outfit to Nora's. Her dress differs greatly from my own. The neckline highlights her ample chest. Long sleeves of green lace just brush the edge of her shoulder and sweep almost all the way to the floor. She wears a smooth red velvet A-line style that hugs her torso and has golden embroidered threads that shimmer in the light. The embroidering looks nearly identical to Queen Elena's crown, but it hugs her waist where the red velvet sweeps out. The dress is much more modest than my own, but still stunning on her.

As Ingrid predicted, Nora's hair is swept in a raised crown curly updo. Soft ringlets hang loose and frame her angular face.

"You look amazing," I say, rising and smoothing out my dress.

Nora's brows climb her forehead as she looks me over. "Wow. That is a style where you come from? I'm fascinated."

I flush, examining my feathered skirt. "Sort of. It's kind of like something my mother once wore, but different as well."

"I thought *I* would turn heads tonight, but I have a feeling all eyes will be on you." Nora's smile is kind. "I think I underestimated you, Paige Powers."

A tittering laugh slips out. "I get that a lot." I don't usually get along with many girls, but Nora is hard not to like.

"I thought I might offer my services this evening, as much as I can," she says. "The Holiday Festival is often a big event with several important members of the Kingdom's hierarchy. Lords and land managers. Ladies who control the gossip chain, that sort of thing. It will be a shark tank for anyone not able to navigate the waters. In the past, these men have courted girls dismissed by the King."

The idea of older men trying to fight for my attention if King Cypress rejects me is not only repugnant but also demeaning to women.

The idea of parading through a room full of such men in this dress has me regretting my design.

"I think I would be a fool to refuse your help," I say. "Shall we?"

37

ZEPHYR

THE PROSPECT OF SPENDING an evening with Paige has me trembling in my dress shoes. How can I survive an entire night in her company, talking up Cypress and not doing anything that will get us both into trouble? My palms are sweating already as I make my way across the parlor to Mom's room.

Commotion on the other side of her door worries me. I rap gently before easing it open a touch.

"Mom? Are you alright in here?"

"Fine," she says.

I peek inside to see her maids in a flurry of activity around her as she sits in her dressing chair in a stunning dark green silk dress. One maid applies makeup to cover her pale complexion and another fusses with her hair.

I thrust the door open and stride in. "What are you doing? You should be resting!"

"I will not skip the Holiday Festival. I've never missed one before and certainly won't start now." I know that tone. I've heard it so many times before. She's already decided and nothing I say will stop her.

"Mom, the doctor said you need as much rest as possible."

"I would rather die while living than never live at all." She glances at me, her gaze sweeping over my suit. "Where's your jacket?" She motions the maids to back away, then wobbles as she attempts standing.

I rush over and offer to help. "In the parlor. I must protest this."

"Noted." She fusses with my cuff links. "Now get your jacket and help me to the elevator. I won't let Elena use my absence against me." The sentiment brings her determination into clear focus. She is worried about what Elena will do to the two of us without my father to protect us.

A few minutes later, the two of us ride the elevator to the main level.

"Zeph, before we tumble into the chaos of the evening, I have something you need to hear."

I keep my arm around her. Mom's whole body leans against me, pulling from my strength to keep her upright. She shouldn't be doing this.

"I'm not sure now is a good—"

"Please." Her dark eyes bore into me. "I know I haven't been there for you like you deserve. It's a burden I bear with great shame."

"Mom..."

"Hush." She strokes my cheek. "Life has dealt you a terrible hand. I want you to find happiness in something. I want you to find love."

I grimace, averting my gaze. I can't bear that tenderness in her eyes, the earnestness.

"You may not recognize love," she continues. "Again, that is my fault. You may even try to deny love when it comes to you. I know how you like your walls. When the right girl comes along, she will slip through the cracks in your walls and see *you*. She will draw you in, consume your every waking and dreaming moment."

A chill runs down my spine. She can't possibly know about the dreams I've had of Paige...or *with* her. But this isn't love. Desire and love are *not* the same thing.

"When you realize you love her, you will risk everything to have her, hold her, protect her. Don't make the same mistake I did. Fight for it."

Mistake? What mistake did she make? I frown, the question on the tip of my tongue, but the elevator doors slide apart, opening us to the cacophony of voices as lords, ladies, and high-ranked men and women filter through the palace lobby.

The moment we step through the ballroom doors, Mom draws away from me and stands tall. All signs of her illness vanish as she glides across the open floor to a small hive of women.

The ballroom hums with life. Wealthy, well-connected locals mill around in conversation. The dimmed lights create a warm atmosphere. Red and green holiday accents bring the room to life, and twinkling garland wraps around the pillars. A massive buffet of hors d'oeuvres spreads across the far side of the room. Round tables with red and white poinsettia centerpieces frame the wood dance floor.

The buffet won't be the only food. The formal dining room along the front of the palace serves fresh dinner upon request all evening long. The people gathered in the ballroom are only a fraction of those wandering the main level to enjoy the evening.

The throne itself sits empty at the head of the massive room. I scan to find a cluster of girls huddled together in beautiful ball gowns, whispering and staring in the same direction. At Cypress.

He certainly strikes quite a figure as he whisks Bella across around the dance floor. Her golden dress twinkles in the dim lights, making her look like she's floating on a golden starry sky. The smile on Cypress' face as he speaks to her is warm and charming.

A second group of girls sits at a table together, barely bothering to even glance in Cypress' direction. Two of the girls—Summer and River—sit close together, clearly enjoying their conversation with one another and more than happy to ignore Cypress.

Nora's red velvet dress is crowned around the waist, making it clear she is here for one reason and one reason only. When she shifts her hips, the dim lights make the crown shimmer. The slender curve of her fingers around her wine glass or the way she moves her hips would have once enticed me. But they pale compared to the girl at her side.

Paige's dress leaves little to the imagination as it hugs her body so tight I can see every curve of her muscular frame. The feathered flare of her skirt seems to dance around her when she moves. Somehow, the strips of red and blue on her dress seem to glow with a life of their own. She smiles at one of the local lords, and it brightens the entire room.

A lump lodges in my throat. I can't do this.

"Pick up your jaw off the floor, Zeph."

I jump as Dominic joins me, unable to tear my gaze from Paige. "She looks incredible." That word feels insufficient to describe her.

"It isn't fair, is it?" He hesitates a moment, then grudgingly offers me a glass of wine. My hand trembles as I accept. "All these beautiful girls. All here for him."

"For now." Those two words slip out as I imagine, just for one delusional moment, that Cypress will dismiss Paige. I take a long drink to cover my blunder. "I think he is already weeding them out in his mind."

Dominic snorts. "You don't really believe that, do you?" The bitterness in him is new. Dominic is the gentlest, most patient of all my brothers. He isn't bitter often. "He told me to talk him up to two of the girls because they haven't shown him any interest. I'm supposed to find some way to make them fawn over him."

"Yeah, he asked me to do the same for a couple of them." I watch Paige grimace as she adjusts her dress. It almost makes me laugh. "But this is the way things are done. One of these girls will be our next queen." Just imagining Cypress and Paige wrapped around one another makes my stomach boil. I take another long drink.

"Slow down," Dominic mutters.

Lord Greene, Bella's father, approaches Nora and Paige. He flashes a charming smile at them and engages in conversation. I notice the way his gaze roves over Paige. My teeth grind. Lord Greene has been without a wife for nearly ten years. She drowned at the beach, washed up on shore dead and bloated. They say the tides dragged her under, but some part of me never trusted Lord Greene. He probably told her to walk off a cliff into the lake.

My chest clenches. What if Lord Greene is controlling Baron, manipulating him with magic to eliminate the royal family and setting Baron up to take the fall? I've suspected he might be involved, but knowing how he can control people, he could easily do so to Baron without Baron's knowledge.

"He will keep as many of them as he can, you know," Dominic says. It takes me a moment to pull myself from these horrible thoughts and figure out what Dominic is talking about. After giving a nod to the Main Street property manager, he lowers his voice. "He's always been selfish and spoiled. He thinks he's entitled to all of them."

I give him a flat stare. "He is." *Where is this coming from?*

Dominic matches my flat stare with one of his own. "You don't care at all that he already sees Nora as a top contender?"

I swallow, turning my gaze back to the two girls across the room. Both meet my gaze. Paige smiles shyly. Just for me. The churning mass from a moment ago becomes an intense heat spreading through my body. Lord Greene rests a hand on her arm, and I have a momentary fantasy about breaking his arm.

I haven't thought about Nora for some time. For now, it's best if Dominic assumes my reaction is because of her.

"Alric. Cypress. Does it matter?" A server passes with a tray of drinks. I set my empty glass on it. "Anyway, you swore off marriage when Dad made you Keeper of Tides. It isn't like you could have any of the leftovers."

Dominic smacks my arm. "Jerk."

I chuckle and rub the sore spot. "What? It's true."

"It doesn't make me blind." He stares at the table of disinterested girls. "I still don't understand why Dad put me in this position and not you."

Dominic has a point there. I hate to admit it, but the youngest is usually Keeper. Except I know why our father named me Captain instead of his other two sons. He called Cypress weak and Dominic soft. Not to their face—at least not as far as I know.

Dominic chortles. "We all know he had little love for you. What better way to punish you for existing than making you swear off women and never producing offspring?"

The words hurt. Dominic has always been the sweet, understanding one. I'm not used to this from him. My shoulders slump and my lungs compress. Is he trying to upset me? Why? I would expect a backhanded comment from Cypress, but never Dominic. *It must be the wine.* Dominic doesn't usually drink.

I clear my throat, clenching my hands into fists to keep from shaking. I need a drink so badly. "Our King gave me a task. I should get to work."

I march away, melting into the crowd. Instead of beginning my task, my shiny shoes carry me toward the bar. A few of the locals strike up pleasantries. I do my best to smile and disengage without seeming rude.

Dominic's words plague me. Worse yet, I understand the logic behind his reasoning. He has a point. So why did Dad name him the next Keeper of Tides instead of me? Just because Dominic was too soft for anything else? What would he be doing now if Dad had given Cypress the Captaincy and me the Keeper title? The lead position only recently became Dominic's, after the last Keeper—our Uncle Cole—died in his sleep two years ago. He was young. Only thirty-three. His death had been a shock to all of us.

Perhaps it was Dominic's gentle disposition that made him a good fit for the job. The Keeper serves the King and kingdom for life as their second hand and keeper of the histories and traditions. His job is to ensure positive local relations and the continuity of tradition—no distractions induced by having a family. Much like the soldiers in service.

As the child of King Alric's consort, I am not entitled to anything. He didn't *have* to name me Captain of Tides and next in line as Admiral. The only reasoning I can assume that kept me out of the Keeper position is that our father didn't think I was worthy of upholding tradition. Or maybe by making me Captain of Tides, he knew it was as good as sending me away.

I down a glass of whiskey, leaning against the bar, and signal for another. Neither of my uncles ever had children of their own. Uncle Cole had been denied the chance to marry and have children; Uncle Baron chose to be alone.

"Your brother struck the jackpot." Lord Greene steps up to the bar beside me and motions to the bartender for a drink. Then he turns his hungry eyes toward the girls.

Toward Paige.

"Do you think it's too early to get in line for a few of them?" he asks.

"Probably." I down a shot.

He takes his drink, then steps away from the bar, patting me on the shoulder. "I'll have to see for myself."

I snatch his hand, tugging it off my shoulder. The overwhelming urge to break his fingers washes over me. Instead, I let go, scowling at him. "Don't touch me."

Lord Greene frowns, then brushes his sleeve indifferently and marches away, muttering under his breath.

I call for another drink, trying to calm the fury pumping through my veins.

"Slow down, Zephyr." Queen Elena stops at the bar beside me, motioning toward a bottle on the top shelf. The bartender quickly jumps to fill her glass. She turns to me, icy eyes sweeping over me in her usual cold calculation. "I believe Cypress gave you a task to complete, and drinking yourself into oblivion will not make it possible." She smiles sweetly at the bartender. "He's cut off."

Those three words slice into me.

He bows in agreement.

I glare at her back as she strides away. *Fine*. I'll make my way across the floor and grab something off one of the serving trays.

Word clearly spreads quickly. All the serving staff turn the trays away as I approach, heading in a different direction and blending into the crowd. I clench my jaw in irritation. How will I make it through this night without another drink?

Paige is deep in a conversation with Baron. I'm dying to know what they are talking about. Is he asking her about Easton, or maybe what happened to my mother? I decide to leave her be for now. I'm not sure I have the strength to interrupt the conversation without a drink in my hand.

Holly sits at a table alone, a full drink resting in front of her. She toys with the stem of the glass, turning it slowly on the tabletop. I pull out the chair beside her and turn it to face her, then settle in.

"Can I give you some advice, Lady Holly?"

She looks up at me and resentment flashes across her face. I try to ignore it. "You will, anyway."

I lean forward, resting my arm on the table. "I know what you left behind, and I don't expect it will fade in just a few weeks. But it would be to your own benefit to embrace this situation."

When Holly joined me as Tribute, she did it to save the man she loves back in her own community. Her ability to see his actions before he took them made it clear at the time that she stepped forward to stop him from acting out. He would have died.

Anger burns in her eyes as she glares at me. "What do you know of love?"

"Nothing." I shrug. "And I freely admit it. You sacrificed your own happiness to save him. A noble endeavor. Thanks to you, he can love again." I peer over her shoulder at the edge of the dance floor where Cypress now speaks with Nora. The gentle touches and coy smiles make their flirting apparent even across the room. "Why deny yourself a chance at love as well?"

"You don't honestly think I could ever love *him*, do you?" Holly's lips compress. She sinks back into her chair and crosses her arms. Her dress sags on her shoulders. "When love consumes you, it isn't just a need. It's the air. The missing piece of your soul. The reason your heart beats. And when you lose it..." She swallows and shakes her head. Tears well in her eyes. "Nothing can fill that void."

"Again, I don't understand. I have felt nothing like that before. It seems pretty wretched, if you ask me." I can't stop staring at her full wine glass. If she doesn't want it, maybe she will give it to me. "My only point is, you won't be returning and reuniting. I think you already know that. If he will find love again, would it be so terrible to open yourself up to the chance, no matter how slim you think it may be?"

Holly smooths her hands over the tablecloth, forming a ring around the base of her glass. Her lip trembles, then she nods. "You're right." Her response lacks emotion. It would worry me, but perhaps she's only steeling herself to the truth. Her hand creeps across the tabletop, then settles over mine. Her gaze is steady, but something about her seems empty. "Thank you, my lord, for helping me see things a bit more clearly."

I raise her hand to my lips, then give it a pat. "Let me know if you need anything else. I'm at your disposal tonight."

Hopefully, given some time to think over what I have said, Holly will see reason. I know she left a deep love behind. If all I managed is planting a seed of hope for her own future here with Cypress, then my job for the evening is done.

I give her some space and rise, scanning the room. The sooner I finish with Paige, the sooner I can return to my room where a wet bar awaits.

38

GAVIN

THE URGE TO VISIT Drake before breaking into the temple consumes me. In the end, it's better for him if he doesn't know what I'm about to do. Once the acolytes get their hands on me, Drake will be in danger. If the Elders suspect he helped me, they will punish him for certain. Instead of turning right to head to his quarters, I turn left.

According to Emil, the best time to get in and out is in the middle of the night. The acolytes are mostly asleep, which gives me a chance to slip in and read the *Book*. Two guards will be on duty, but if I create a distraction, I can slip in.

I expect capture. That's the plan. Slip in through the secret acolyte entrance. Learn as much as I can from the *Book of the Prophet* so I know how to play the Elders' game. Get caught by the acolytes on guard—though I will have to put up a fight to make it look like I tried to escape capture. Then, during the sermon at the temple, I use the knowledge from the *Book* to break out and fulfill their dumb prophecy. Then everyone will listen to me, and I should have the sway to make necessary changes that benefit everyone.

If I want to get out of the Haven and get home, I need to bind the Elders with their own prophetic beliefs. They can't stop the Idol, after all. At least, that's my hope. Once I read the *Book*, I will be sure of my course.

Since they consider technology a sin, I'm not worried about any kind of Power-suppression like the cuffs Dad designed. In the past few weeks, nothing that might hinder my Powers even a little has surfaced.

Knowing I will fall into acolyte hands has my nerves on edges, strumming like too-tight guitar strings ready to snap at any moment. My heart has never beat so hard before.

Only three Guardians are awake at this time of night. But Emil knows where they are and gave me the paths to avoid. Their job is to make sure any paths into the Haven are secure, not to guard the depths of the hallways.

Emil's warning screams in my head as I tiptoe through the halls toward the secret entrance in the back of the medical center. *"The moment I think your actions will harm the innocent people here, we are no longer on the same side. Risk their lives, and I will end yours."*

While I have no intention of hurting anyone—this *needs* to be executed peacefully—no one can promise safety. Dad tried to protect people, but thousands died. That can't happen here. With only a thousand people in their community, even the slightest miscalculation will be catastrophic. I have no margin for error.

Which is why I won't fight back. Not really.

But I won't remain silent either.

The square is dark and silent. String lights usually illuminating the wide-open space have been turned off for the evening. Only a soft light from the medical center glows. I stick to the walls and make my way around the long way. If anyone stumbles across me in the square, I already have a list of viable tasks I could be completing.

The medical center always remains open, again, in case of emergency. I glance around the square before slipping in. Two doors against the back wall are closed. One leads to the office where the tunnel entrance is. The other leads to the sleeping quarters for the doctor on duty. I hold my breath as I tip-toe past the sleeping quarters. If the doctor catches me here, I can pretend to be sick, but the plan is ruined.

I sneak through the office door and breathe a sigh of relief. It's empty. I ease the door closed, then run my hands along the walls. Emil said the entrance is an illusion, which explains why I've seen so many acolytes moving in and out of the medical center. I assume the passage must be along the back wall.

My hand brushes a rough edge on the clay wall, then dips into nothing. I jerk my hand back, steadying my racing heart. This is it. The wall is there—or it appears to be there—but when I reach out experimentally, my hand slides right through. No wonder acolytes oversee the medical center. It helps keep this passage secret. Elder Julia does, as well. She must know about it.

My heartbeat drums in my ears. My pulse races. I take a tentative step toward the wall.

Then come out on the other side.

The tunnel is dark, but not pitch black. I lick my dry lips and edge deeper, using my tracking Power to sense where the last trail of footsteps leads. My fingertips slide along the uneven clay wall, worried about walking into it unknowingly. Each step is tentative.

Drake's Silence Power would be useful right now. I yearn for his presence at my back. This would be so much easier to handle if he were with me. *Get a grip, Gavin.* I can't risk his safety.

The tunnel winds onward for hundreds of feet. Emil couldn't tell me how long it went on for. He never actually traveled the tunnel, but he knew where it comes out on each end.

My breaths become more ragged with each step. Tremors that started in my hands, spread up my arms to my shoulders, then down my spine to my legs. Even my insides rattle in fear.

The silence of the tunnel is so deep I swear I keep hearing someone following me, only to discover the sound is me.

When I finally reach the other end of the tunnel, I nearly cry out in relief. Paige could never handle this. She would hate everything about this place. I hope she is doing well where she is now. We haven't spoken in Dreams for so long.

I pause at the exit and hold my breath, hyper-vigilant of any noise on the other side. Nothing comes back to me. It's been as easy as Emil expected so far.

The hardest part is yet to come.

The tunnel exit spills out into one of the main tunnels of the acolyte quarters. Where all the acolytes currently sleep. This is exactly why Drake would be useful. How light do the acolytes sleep? I'm certain my heart beats loud enough to wake them all.

I edge past the first series of doors, careful to touch nothing. Not even the wall. It's bad enough that my feet make sounds on the floor. Each whisper of my feet over the smooth stone floor makes me wince. If one door opens and an acolyte steps out, nothing I say will save me. What will they do to me when they catch me sneaking through their halls? Use their Powers to torture me for answers? Can they turn me into a puppet Idol? What are they even capable of?

I carefully measure each breath. Even my breathing could wake them.

A rustling from one room freezes me in my tracks. Should I run forward? Turn back? I hold my breath and wait for the door to open. All falls silent once more.

If the tunnel into the quarters felt long, it's nothing compared to the way these hallways stretch, twist, and turn forever. Emil gave me very precise directions to the room where the original book is guarded. But the taught nerves interfere with my Perfect Memory. For the first time in my life, I panic as something I know evades me.

Did I take a wrong turn somewhere? Surely, the tunnels along the quarters couldn't be this long. I must have turned right when I should have turned left. Doubt is not a friend of mine. I don't like it.

I pause at an intersection and close my eyes, focusing on Emil's directions. *Left. He said left here.* My eyes snap open and I turn into the hallway. A cry of relief catches in my throat when I see the door he told me about is cracked open. It takes all my self-control not to run inside and close the door behind me.

Hushed voices filter through the rush of blood in my ears. I press my back to the wall, unsure where to hide.

The acolyte night guards. What can I use to create a distraction without alerting the sleeping acolytes?

Down the hall, near the open door where the *Book* awaits, a boy and girl about my age linger in another doorway. They wear the same ivory robes as the rest of the acolytes. He leans his forehead against hers and slides his arm around her waist, then whispers something in her ear. She bites her lip. I flush. I shouldn't be watching this.

Her gaze flits along the hallway. I dip back around the corner, holding my breath and praying they didn't see me.

"We are supposed to watch the *Book*," she says, but her tone implies weakness.

"No one ever comes here at night," he whispers. "This is the most time alone we will have for a while."

She murmurs a reply I can't make out.

Then a door clicks shut.

I release a breath of relief and peer around the corner. The door to the *Book* remains ajar. *So much for needing a distraction.* Holding my breath, I tiptoe past the closed doors, unsure which one the couple disappeared into. How much time will their tryst buy me?

A giggle to my right freezes me. I watch the door a moment before daring to continue onward.

A dim light in the *Book's* room glows. I slip through the door, wincing when it creaks. *Please let them be too absorbed in one another to hear that.*

The book room is larger than I expected. A series of tables line the walls, reminding me of the tables in a library.

In the center of the room, an old tablet sits dark on a desk. A lamp glows beside it.

Technology? Drake insisted that technology is a sin. *Hypocrites.*

I rush to the table and sink into the chair. It only takes a moment to activate the tablet. No security lock. Why would they when it's meant to be read by everyone with access to it?

A few icons line the screen. I recognize many of them as older versions of apps used in Elpis for medical records, water treatment maintenance, solar panel electrical monitoring...and a journaling app. I tap it.

The name knocks the breath from my lungs.

Airen Mosheyev. One of the original twelve founders of Elpis. Mosheyev and Jonah Crow had a falling out over a new project meant to protect Elpis from outsiders. Dad uncovered the truth about our founding five years ago. Mosheyev and Crow disagreed about the use of the Power stone to create a protective barrier around Elpis—a stone that stole Powers from people and killed them. When those Powers were stolen, the stone stored them inside for gradual emission. It was how the barrier around Elpis remained powered for over a century.

Until Dad learned the truth and took it down.

Mosheyev led a revolt against Crow over the project, then disappeared with a couple of other founders. No one knew what happened to them. Did Mosheyev find his way here and create his own community? What would he think of the way the Elders run things now?

Eager to connect the dots and figure out how this religion started, or how I play into it, I read the journal entries as quickly as I can.

Mosheyev never directly mentions Elpis by name in his entries, though he alludes to it a few times. *That place farther west.* The initial entries are all about the mechanics of how the Haven works. I skim the info for anything useful, but none of it pertains to my needs right now.

There's also quite a lengthy report about the Power stone. How dangerous it is. What it can do. How it can't be touched by people with Powers or they lose their Power and die. How Powerless people can touch the stone and, theoretically, infuse the contained Power in themselves. His notes on how it might be possible are quite detailed and impressive, though some of his calculations are a touch off.

Some of the final hypothesis about the Power stone makes my stomach twist. How to harness Powers trapped in the Power stone—including human experimentation to deduce whether it can be injected into someone somehow. It's clear he was trying to find some way to give the Powerless some Powers at first. Is that what happens behind the locked door?

The more I read, the further off the rails Mosheyev's ramblings become, even mentioning that the "people" have begun calling him the Prophet, and how he embraced the title.

The Idol of Desolation is not what the Havenites are led to believe. Mosheyev rants that someone will come from the west to destroy them and take everything with him. My only assumption is that he started losing touch with reality and believed that someone from Elpis would come to destroy them. Then the Idol of Creation would come and save them from Desolation.

They will come one day. Not in my lifetime. But it will happen.

And I did. Just as Mosheyev predicted.

The more I read, the easier it becomes to see how this strange religion was born from Mosheyev's words. He rambles about the end of the world, how he saw the end in a dream, and how he walked in the new Eden. *It will come,* he writes. *When that happens, we will be capable of great things. Creation...or desolation. It will be unlike anything we have witnessed before.*

We will either remake the world...or annihilate it.

The Powers are a gift that allow us to survive, and we must use that gift to help those who cannot help themselves. But the Powers are also a curse.

I find extensive entries about the signs that the end is coming, that only together will they survive and be freed from the Haven. The more I read, the more it reads like a religious text and less like a journal entry.

The last entry has a unique feeling. Mosheyev did not write it.

The Prophet has passed from this world, but he leaves with us the gift of his knowledge. His last words. "It starts and ends with hope and powers." We will use his teachings to give our people hope until the Idols come.

Creation will be revered.

Desolation will be burned alive...for the sake of our survival.

I sink back in the chair, rubbing a hand over my face. *It starts and ends with hope and powers.* The Minister took my last name and used it to fulfill this belief. I knew that, but seeing the words as clear as day in front of me makes me sick.

Terror grips my heart. Emil called me an Idol...but which one do they see me as?

Creation...

Or Desolation.

Everything they do, everything they believe, is built on a foundation of one man's descent into madness, and possible Precognitive misunderstandings.

One man who came from Elpis.

Historically speaking, religion cannot be fought with force. If I want to help these people, I need to become what they want me to be. Which means I need to know the difference between these two Idols. Unfortunately, the text is vague about this aspect. One will save. The other will destroy. But perspective will decide which I am.

The only way I can control my fate in the Haven is by using what I learned in this journal to make all the people believe, without a doubt, that I am Creation. But if I fail, the Minister might brand me Desolation and burn me alive.

"What are you doing in here?"

I jump, tapping off the tablet and surging to my feet.

"Powers..." The boy's eyes widen. His hands tremble as he edges into the room. The girl follows him, flanking me.

This was part of the plan. Breathe.

I dart for the door, knowing the effort to escape is pointless. Even if I got away from them, where would I go? There's nowhere to hide in the Haven. Which is exactly why I planned on being captured.

The girl moves with lighting quick reflexes. She grabs my arm, twisting it back and pinning me to the floor. I press a palm against the solid clay earth and focus my Power on transforming it. A ripple moves outward, throwing the boy off his feet before he can help the girl.

Her icy hand presses to my temple, but the floor beneath me opens, dropping me inside. Her grip on my arm doesn't break. She holds tight to my wrist as I dangle in the hole I made. The boy climbs back to his feet and rushes at the hole. I thrust a hand up, creating a wall between us. He hits it with a solid crack.

"Stop!" she commands, using her strength to pull me up from the hole.

I brace my feet against the wall and push away, yanking her down with me. She yelps as she tumbles down. Her hand slips off my wrist as she catches her fall. I bolt toward the opposite side of the hole, away from both, and jump onto a landing that transforms out of the ground. It launches me out of the hole and toward the door.

The distraction will only slow them. It won't stop them.

But now that I've read the *Book*, I have one more thing to discover before they take me down.

Following Emil's directions, adrenaline pumping through my veins, I dart through the halls as their pounding steps pursue me. An alarm rings somewhere in the distance.

Then the halls burst with activity.

Five acolytes step in my path. I seize the wall with my Power and move it to my right so that the hallway forks away from them.

I glance back over my shoulder, thrilled to see the acolytes floundering to fix what I've changed. But when I turn course, I slam into a wall of muscle. Before I can recover, the acolyte throws a fist at my temple, sending me careening toward the wall to my left. I crumple in a heap on the floor. Dark spots float in my vision.

A black bag snaps over my head. Another punch lands at the base of my neck.

And I fall.

39

PAIGE

THE GRANDEUR OF THE evening seems too ridiculous for words. Does King Cypress truly think that holding a party and dancing with a few of the girls will erase what he and his men have done? And I am expected to put on a smile and charm the local lords. Lord Greene was charming, and more tolerable than most of the rest, but something about the way he looked at me leaves me feeling dirty.

Thanks to Nora's gracious offer to help me, I avoid several near disastrous blunders with those lords—and a few of the ladies.

All evening, I try catching King Cypress' eye. We haven't spoken since that horribly awkward kiss, and I feel like I need to explain myself. But as the minutes fade into hours, he never glances in my direction. Maybe I offended him when I rejected his advances.

When he at last approaches, I follow Nora's lead and produce the best curtsy I can manage in this tight dress. He holds his hand out to Nora and asks if he can steal her away. I get little more than a cursory glance, as if he only just realized I'm there and I'm completely inconsequential. It hurts.

I definitely offended him.

I cling to my wine glass, trying to tell myself it doesn't matter that he has whisked away Nora instead of me. It isn't as if I truly want any of this. She does.

Yet every day that passes makes it harder to imagine I can ever get home. Especially if he ignores me.

I don't belong here. I miss home. I miss Gavin and Mom and Dad. But until the King allows me to leave, I'm trapped. I'm not even certain I can get dismissed any longer. King Cypress knows I removed my bracelet on multiple occasions, an act that should have had me out the door, but he ignored every infraction. Now I can't even get close to him. How can I convince him to let me go if all I do is offend him?

I grimace, downing my glass of wine.

"Lady Paige."

I spin. The skirt of my dress flies outward as if it could fly away. I wish it could whisk me away.

A commanding air surrounds Lord Baron. Something about him reminds me of Dad at social gatherings. Relaxed, but observing everything. Not for the first time, I notice how much Zephyr resembles him. Zephyr has his mother's eyes, but if he looks like Baron, does that mean the former king did as well? They were brothers, after all. Cypress and Dominic look a lot alike.

"Lord Baron." I curtsy. My gut churns. Last time I spoke to him, he threatened me and was full of rage.

"No need of that with me." His gaze flits to the bracelet momentarily before meeting my eyes. "I hope that bracelet is working better for you. King Cypress was quite worried about your well-being after the incident."

I fiddle absently with the thick bracelet. Telling him I hate it and would rather crush it into a fine powder probably won't help my cause at all. Instead, I flash the best impression of a timid smile I can muster. "Yes. Thank you."

"My nephew mentioned you introduced yourself to him as a princess."

Nephew. My gaze falls on Zephyr as he crosses the room. I straighten, but even he doesn't pay any attention to me. He joins Holly. Does this dress have no effect on the brothers?

"Did he? I was mostly teasing him after he introduced himself as a lord." I flush, remembering that exchange. Knowing a little more about where Zephyr comes from, I suppose I understand why he called himself Lord Zephyr.

"I have spoken with your friend," Lord Baron says. "Easton."

My heart skips. No one ever talks to me about Easton. I worry about his wellbeing. Was Lord Baron part of Easton's questioning? What does Lord Baron already know about us? "Is he doing well?"

"Exceptionally well, actually. The lieutenants are impressed with his skills." Lord Baron waves it off as if it doesn't matter.

But it does for me. It means everything. Having Easton on the island—even if I never see him—offers some comfort. I'm not completely alone. Perhaps, if the lieutenants are singing his praises, he will be allowed to visit soon. I don't dare ask.

Lord Baron leans close. "He told me your father rules over your people. Like a king?"

His proximity doesn't make me uncomfortable, like some of the other lords here. I remember the maids mentioning that he had never married. Hopefully he isn't reconsidering. He's the same age as my father.

I grab a fresh glass of wine off a passing tray and take a sip. It does little for my parched throat. "We don't have kings. He is the Minister. Sort of like a governor or...well, a leader. Not a ruler."

"So, you are not a princess."

I laugh, hoping it sounds more lilting and less tense than it feels. "No."

The corners of his mouth curl down as if the news disappoints him. "A shame. That might have been in your favor with King Cypress. I would love to hear more about your community if you will share."

My heart picks up speed. Though his request sounds innocent enough, I know he is digging for information. I don't know what Easton told them and don't want to contradict anything. Nor do I want to give away too much.

"I'm not sure there is much of merit to say," I respond, averting my gaze to play timid. "We had a rough go of it for a while, but my father has made great strides in improving our lives since he took over. Our people adore him."

Lord Baron ponders this for a moment, then offers a gentlemanly smile. "That is good for our people, then. He must be a remarkable man. Easton spoke highly of him as well."

The last statement isn't meant as a threat—at least I don't think it is—but it stills my hammering heart. I have to change the subject. Quickly.

I glance over at King Cypress and Nora. They seem very familiar with one another. "May I ask a question?"

"You may, but I may not answer."

I nod. "Fair enough." I won't bare all my secrets. Why should he? "Have I offended the King? He hasn't even glanced my way all evening."

Lord Baron chuckles, swirling his drink in his hand. "King Cypress is not an easy man to offend. He has a lot of potential ladies here tonight. I wouldn't read into it too much."

A hushed commotion nearby draws his attention away. Every muscle in his body tenses. For just a moment, his entire body goes still. Swiftly, he excuses himself. I watch him hustle toward the small circle of activity. Lady Emry rests in a chair, her face horribly pale. Another woman stands over her, fanning her face.

Zephyr kneels in front of his mother, holding her hands in his as he speaks. Lord Baron lingers behind Zephyr like he wants to take over, but doesn't want to overstep. I edge close enough to hear clipped parts of the conversation over the music and din of the event.

"...me take her back," Zephyr says.

Lord Baron slides his arm around Lady Emry and helps her to her feet. "I can handle this. You..."

They wave their hands at one another. But at a gentle touch from Lady Emry, they both settle. Zephyr hangs his head, stepping back as Lord Baron escorts her out.

I can't stop staring at the abject disappointment creasing Zephyr's face. He takes a step, as if he has changed his mind and intends to follow them. Then he freezes.

One of the older women beside him places her hand on his arm and murmurs something to him. Zephyr yanks his arm away and turns, catching me staring.

I snap my gaze away, but it's too late. He noticed. I don't have to peek to be aware of his long, heavy strides as he approaches.

"Lady Paige." He stops in front of me.

"Lord Zephyr. Is she okay?" I peer past him as if I can still see Lady Emry, but she is long out of sight now.

He reaches for a tray of drinks as it passes, but the server turns in another direction. His jaw twitches. I swear I can hear him clenching it. Why are they refusing him a drink? He is part of the royal family. "No, but it's none of your concern."

Silence settles between us. He looks like he would rather be anywhere else than standing with me. Why did he approach if he doesn't want to talk?

I follow his gaze around the room. He is staring with glassy eyes at the drink trays floating around.

"Maybe you need this more than I do," I say, holding out my wine glass.

His chest rises and falls with heavy breaths as he stares at the glass. His hand twitches at his side, but he doesn't reach for it.

"I won't tell," I whisper conspiratorially, guessing that they ordered him not to drink.

Zephyr accepts the glass with a murmur of thanks. His hand brushes against mine, sending a surge of warmth through my fingers.

He takes a drink. A very generous drink.

"What's wrong with your mother?"

Zephyr scowls at me, then downs the rest of the wine in a single gulp. "Dance?" he asks, setting the glass on a nearby table.

"Is it allowed?"

"The king has given me special dispensation to be your escort tonight." Nothing about his tone shows he has any interest in this honor. He holds out a hand. "Yes or no."

I take his sweating hand. "Charming."

Zephyr sweeps me out onto the dance floor, not saying another word. We move together in silence. Each step is sharp, practiced. The distance he maintains between us is like a wall. There is nothing smooth or gallant about him. This dance is an obligation and nothing more.

I briefly consider asking him if I upset his brother, but quickly dismiss the notion. The idea of explaining the kiss, or even admitting it, to Zephyr sends my insides into a tailspin.

I edge closer to him, shifting his hand on the small of my back a little tighter. His fingers press into the thin fabric. The other hand sweats in mine.

"My people know a lot about illness," I say softly, afraid of breaching the subject of his mother, but knowing I might have something to deal. "Maybe I can offer some advice about your mother?"

He makes a sound of disgruntlement in his throat. "If the physician can't help her, why should I believe *you* can?"

I tilt my head, forcing him to look at me. His gaze is angry, but more than that, there is pain hiding underneath. I put forward my gentlest smile. "She is your world. I can tell. Would you discount me if there was even a slight chance I could help?"

The muscles of his back tense beneath my hand. War wages behind those dark eyes. Finally, his jaw twitches and he says, "She spent years looking after my father, healing him whenever he was ailing. Now..." His voice cracks, the first sign of a chink in his armor. He stiffens and draws in a breath to center himself.

"Now her Power is causing her illness," I finish, understanding perfectly what she is going through. "We have the same problem where I come from. It doesn't happen to everyone, but those who end up with Power-related illnesses used to die prematurely."

His dark eyes snap into sharp focus. "Used to?" Hope springs to life. He edges urgently closer. "But they no longer do?"

"It depends on individual situations." I carefully hedge around the truth. If his mother is so far advanced, it may already be too late. But this is also my chance to gain his ear and his trust. I must proceed with caution. "When my father was my age, my grandfather died of a Power-related illness. Not long after, Dad learned that one of his friends had it as well. He dedicated all of his time to trying to find a cure for several years. It isn't perfect, but it usually works to slow the illness. Jayme, his friend, should have died before I was born. But he still lives."

His breaths roll across my face in quick succession. His words rush out. "Do you know how it works? How to fix it?"

"*I* don't. But some of my people do. If we could get her to my people—"

"She would never survive the trip." Zephyr sags. All the hope has drained out of him. The intensity that burned in his eyes a moment ago winks out. "Her illness is advanced."

I chew my lip, hating the devastation on his face. His hands tremble against me.

"Zephyr..." What am I doing? This is too risky. I could put Elpis in danger. But the heartache he is trying—and failing—to cover makes my heart reach out for him. I release a shaky breath and lean closer to his ear, lowering my voice. "In my pack, there is a radio I can use to contact my father. I just need to be within five hundred miles of my community. In days, he would be here with people who can help. He knows what it's like to lose a parent like this."

As we continue dancing, he doesn't say anything. I've just told him how to get in contact with Elpis. What can his people do with that information?

"What you offer is impossible, Paige," he murmurs in my ear. "The shorelines are frozen. We can't go anywhere until the thaw. For the next few months, we are stuck on this island."

The news sends a bolt of disappointment and alarm through me. I jerk back, eyes wide, hoping to see some deception on his face. But the earnestness that greets me stills my breath.

He means it. No matter what happens with King Cypress and this entire dumb pageant, I am stuck on the island until spring.

"How long?" I loathe how my voice quivers.

"Three months. Maybe four, depending on the weather."

Grief grips my stomach in an iron grasp. Tears spring to life in my eyes. No, it can't be. Four more months? *Mom and Dad will think I'm dead!*

Icy dread pulses through me. Suddenly, I can't stop shivering. Nausea threatens to upend everything I've eaten tonight. I need out of here. I need to leave this room. This palace. This island. I drag in ragged breaths, unable to satiate my need for air. The room tilts. The walls and press of bodies close in around me.

"Paige?" I can hear the concern in Zephyr's voice, but all I can see is the distorted stretch of the dance floor toward the exit.

I pull away from his powerful grip and stagger a few steps toward the door. "I need air."

As heavy weight presses down on my shoulders, I make furtive movements towards the exit, cursing my heels. Just when I think I can't handle it any longer, when I can't take another step, an arm slides around my waist, holding me upright and helping me along.

I allow Zephyr to guide me outside. He helps me settle into an empty chair along the promenade, away from prying eyes. Then he slips out of his jacket and wraps it around my shoulders, tugging it closed in front of me. It's warm and smells of the lake. Just like he does.

"Slow, deep breath in," he says softly. "Then out."

For two minutes, he coaches me through the breathing exercise, crouching in front of me. I can't stop trembling. I'm uncertain if it's the cold or harsh reality. And I can't hold back the tears. A few roll down my cheeks and I briskly brush them away. Why am I crying so much lately? I feel foolish. Foolish, helpless, and alone. Easton is on the island, but he isn't *here*.

Zephyr is.

The chilly December air slaps my lungs with each breath. Zephyr settles on the bench beside me, putting his arm around my shoulders and rubbing me for warmth.

"I knew I couldn't leave, but I guess…" My voice cracks. I take a moment to regain my control before continuing. "I guess I didn't realize I would be stuck here for so long."

He remains tight against my side, offering comfort and warmth. "You really believed you would go home? Paige, no one has ever gone back. Why would you want to?"

I gaze up at him, tears still brimming in my eyes. "It's not as bad out there as you think. I'm not sure what they teach you here, but where I come from…it's comfortable, safe, beautiful, and full of life."

Though, if I thought about it much, our two ways of life are not so different. Elpis may not be a literal island on the water, but it is an island all its own. No one leaves. And they teach us all our lives that the world beyond our borders is a dangerous place.

I sniffle again. Zephyr offers me a clean handkerchief from his suit pocket. I murmur my thanks and dab my eyes dry.

"I guess I just assumed that if I played along, I could convince him to let me go home." I scoff at my foolishness. "Stupid. My dad begged me to stay home, not to go out into the unknown. But I was so determined. Too stubborn to listen. I thought I knew better. He told me he was terrified of losing me. He will blame himself, Zephyr. Another death in a long line of loved ones lost. He deserves better."

He tucks a stray curl away from my eyes. "You really thought you would go back?"

I nod. "Dumb, I know. But the idea that my parents, or even my brother, will suffer the loss when I'm not really gone…" My throat clenches, cutting off any further comment.

"Brother?" He stiffens his hold on me.

I bite my lip, staring into his dark eyes, praying he won't connect Gavin to the intense Power in that battle in the city.

"Yes. He's older by about a year and a half. Smartest person I've ever met." I shudder as an icy breeze whips past. Zephyr huddles nearer. "I'm closer to him than anyone else. If I never return home, he might do something drastic."

A shadow of sadness flickers across Zephyr's face. "My brothers wouldn't miss me. Dom, maybe at first. Cypress would get over it quickly. But my sister would be crushed." His fingers linger on my neck, just below the ear. I try not to think about how his touch heats my skin. "If anything happened to Bronwyn, I would probably tear the world apart looking for her. So, I guess I get where your brother is coming from."

I lower my voice, afraid of the answer to the question I haven't been able to stop asking myself since capture. "Do you really expect any of us girls to fall in love with a man who has us abducted and forces us to take part in this ridiculous pageant?"

He swallows, then whispers, "No, but it's the way things are done. No queen has ever not loved the King. The system might be flawed, but it works."

Some inexplicable force pulses with life between us. I stare at his lips. How many rules would we break if we kissed? Did he escort me out of sight of the windows on purpose? I want it. I want the kiss from him and not his brother. How broken am I?

He inches closer. A softness in the dark pools of his eyes draws me in, entrancing me. His fingers shift on my neck, back into my hair, cradling my face in his palms. My heart races wildly. The hair on the nape of my neck rises as his fingertips trace back and forth delicately. If he doesn't kiss me soon, I might lose control.

My hands slide up the cold front of his dress shirt, feeling the tense muscles in his chest. I want to grab hold, yank him closer, force him to kiss me, but the shirt is so well-fitted I can't grab hold of the material. Our lips are so close that his rapid, warm breaths fan out across my cheeks like wings. Once more, I wish I could fly away from here. But now I want to take him with me. I can almost feel his lips now as he inches closer, painfully slow.

We barely make a whisper of a connection when a loud thump shocks us both, breaking us from the trance. Zephyr jerks away. His sudden absence makes the cold air even more bitter. My entire body trembles—and I'm sure it isn't from the cold.

Both of us surge to our feet and rush to the railing along the promenade. As we move, I catch the swish of a golden skirt around the corner.

Zephyr curses so professionally it makes me flush.

Plastered against the concrete road, Holly's lifeless eyes stare at the red carpet leading up the stairs—like a final salute to being trapped. Her dark hair is matted in crimson blood that seeps from a crack in her skull and pools into her ivory and green dress.

My stomach twists. I slap my hands over my mouth and turn away, squeezing my eyes closed. Only to bring the vivid image back to life.

40

ZEPHYR

THE THUMP OF HOLLY'S body as it hit the metal roof over the entryway, then rolled to the ground with another wet smack, is enough to bring me back to my senses. My mind screamed at me, shouted for me to pull away, to leave Paige behind. But I couldn't listen, drawn into those umber eyes. Holly's suicide snaps me back to reality before making a terrible mistake.

With a quick command, I send Paige to her room. As she darts away, I call the nearest guards for the discreet removal of the body. It won't do to have guests seeing Holly's twisted body when they leave the party.

I deliver the news to Cypress as unobtrusively as possible, not wanting to cause a scene or disrupt the guests. He dismisses me from the event to investigate. It's best to allow the party to continue at least until the mess can be cleaned, which requires his presence in the hall. Word will get out eventually, but control of the situation is critical.

Once the chaos of the evening finally ends, I rush to my room to drown myself deep in my drink.

As I gulp down glass after glass of whiskey, my entire body trembles violently. The evening has rattled me to my core. It can't possibly get any worse. Holly's death is my fault. I knew she was unhappy, yet I tried to brush it off. And then there's Paige... We may not have kissed, but if Holly hadn't jumped, I know it would have happened. If anyone saw us, Cypress could still punish us for treason. Guilt gnaws at my gut, making the whiskey hit my stomach hard.

I wipe sweat on the arm of my sleeve, then pour another glass, shaking so violently the amber fluid sloshes against the sides of the glass.

Noise from my mother's room captures my attention. I can't quite make out what is going on, but there is no doubt something is happening. I can't afford to have anything happen to her tonight. It would be the end of me.

Trying to control my trembling, I set down the glass and edge toward her door. Worried that she might need help, I open the door.

Filtered moonlight drifts through the windows, curtains drawn aside. Two bodies are tangled in an affectionate embrace. Heat surges to my face. Mom has a male visitor? Who?

I step backward, ready to close the door, when Mom yelps. He turns his head toward the door.

"Baron?" My mind reels. I scrub a shaking hand over my face and groan. Unable to connect these pieces, to accept what my eyes have seen, I fumble for the handle on the door. I can't deal with this tonight. Not after everything else.

"Zephyr, wait!" Mom calls after me. Her voice is so weak it freezes me in my tracks, my back to them. I can't look.

My gut twists. No. This isn't right.

I can't do this. Not tonight.

"Please, Zephyr," she whispers. "This is important." Her voice is so frail, like the slightest breath could break her utterly.

"Mom, we don't need to do this now."

"We do," Baron says, a hard edge in his voice that grates against my raw nerves.

I glare at him—still clothed, thank the Tides, though his shirt is unbuttoned and loose around his massive chest. Tension builds in my shoulders. This is the man I suspect of torturing Easton in twisted experiments. Of stealing supplies meant for communities.

Of killing my brother and father and plotting against the rest of us.

And he's in my mother's bed.

All embarrassment at catching them in an embrace burns away as anger rushes through me. What would he have to gain by seducing my mother on her deathbed? After Cypress and Dominic, Baron has the strongest claim on the throne. Elena would be a better target than my mother.

"This is all part of your plan, isn't it?" I snap. My hands curl into fists at my sides. "I don't see how the pieces fit together yet, but I see them all. Now get away from my mother."

Baron sits up, cocking his head at me like an idiot, pretending he doesn't know what I mean. I don't even realize I've crossed the room until I'm yanking Baron out of the bed by his shirt. My fist cracks against his jaw. Were it not for my iron grip on his shirt, he would have fallen to the floor. I pull back for a second attack.

"Zephyr, stop!" Mom cries out.

I land another blow on his face, busting open his lip.

She pleads for me to stop, confessing her love for him. But rage has taken hold. The same rage my father bestowed on me for years. All the years of abuse at my father's hand. All the envy and rage toward Cypress for having what I want. My inability to protect *anyone* I care for. My hate for Baron. What he turned me into. What he's done to my mother. What he's doing to my family.

Mom continues crying, and her agony stabs the final knife in my heart.

Baron doesn't even try to fight back, which only fuels my torment. I want him to fight back, to stop me. After each punch to his stupid face, he lifts his chin like he is begging for another. What is his problem?

"Fight back," I growl at him.

"No," Mom whimpers. "He's your father!"

The words slowly soak through the cloud of torment and whiskey. All the breath punches from my lungs. As if this night weren't bad enough, she is choosing *now* to drop this on me?

The fight winks out of me. My iron grip on Baron's shirt slackens, dropping him on the floor. My fist trembles violently, knuckles pulsing in pain and spotted with blood.

My father's blood.

I shake my head and stumble away from them. If he is my father, then they have been hiding their affair all my life. *Why didn't they tell me the truth?*

Baron locks gazes with me, tenderly working his jaw. Mom trundles to his side.

What kind of monster did they allow the King to turn me into? All those years they let that man beat me bloody to hide their secret. Did the King ever know? Is *that* why he beat me? Tears sting my eyes. I clench my jaw so tight it aches. In a single moment of rage, I became him. They *made* me him.

"Zephyr..." Mom's voice breaks, pleading with that one word.

Zephyr. A Z name. Last in the alphabet. Last in line. Everyone's last choice. Alric was making a statement when he gave me that name. A statement he reinforced with his fists for years.

I stumble another step backward, listening to the way my mother dotes on Baron, much like she used to do to me after my father finished—no, not my father. The King.

Every part of me trembles violently with shame and hurt and rage and betrayal. Mom was the *only* person in the world I trusted completely. And she lied to me.

"Zephyr, stop," Baron calls after me. Even he sounds pitiful with heartache. *Good.* Let him stew in it. Let him hurt, ache, break like I did for years.

I march out the door, slamming it shut behind me. I grab the whiskey bottle, forgoing the glass, and stalk into my room, locking the door behind me.

Then I drink myself into oblivion.

But no amount of alcohol can make me forget.

DOMINIC SHAKES ME AWAKE. I roll over, covering my eyes with my arm.

"What?" I groan.

"Zeph, get up. It's your mother." Dominic rips off the knitted blanket I had haphazardly covered myself with last night.

His words plunge me into a cold as bone-chilling and thorough as a frozen lake. Pieces of last night resurface. I flex my aching fist, still speckled with Baron's blood. Dominic gives the knuckles a curious glance, but he doesn't ask questions. *Good old Dominic.* Did he know the truth about my father?

I force myself upright. Apparently, I passed out in my clothes with one shoe still on. Instead of searching for the missing shoe, I toe off the other one, then rise and run my hands over my rumpled suit.

Then I see the sorrow creasing Dominic's usually jovial face. His eyes are bloodshot. The veins in his neck cord tensely.

And I already know it's too late.

"No..." I jump off the bed, stumbling as my head spins and pulses in protest.

The parlor is crowded. Cypress refuses to look my way. Bronwyn stares at the floor, picking at her nails. Queen Elena glares at me as if her eyes could burn me alive. The physician speaks in a low voice to a bruised and bloodied Baron.

He meets my gaze, his jaw twitching, tears in his dark eyes.

Agony rips at my heart as I push my way through the crowd to Mom's room.

Sunlight streams through the windows, shining on her pale face. Her hands are folded over her stomach. Her eyes are closed. She looks so peaceful, as if she is simply sleeping.

But her chest doesn't rise and fall.

I can't move any closer. My legs quiver. My knees threaten to give out at any moment. It takes all my strength to remain upright.

Her last memory of me was rage. It breaks me.

A strangled cry climbs up my throat. I stumble to the empty chair beside her bed and take her hand as hot tears streak down my cheeks. Her fingers are icy. I press them to my lips, then sink my head against the bed and let the grief wash over me.

41

GAVIN

I GROAN AS I wake on a firm mattress. My limbs tremble with even the slightest movement. Sickness climbs up my throat. The tips of my fingers are like ice as I press them to my forehead. I've never felt so drained. The last thing I remember is fighting those two acolytes in the office.

Where am I?

I try sitting up, but my stomach heaves and my limbs refuse to comply. How hard did that Somatic Strongarm guy punch me in the head? It must be a concussion.

"Gavin, I am beyond disappointed in you." Mr. Garraty stands on the other side of a small window, peering into my cell.

My cell. I fought the acolytes and didn't stand a chance, just like Emil predicted. This is the next step in my plan. But something doesn't feel right. *I* don't feel right.

"I had hoped you would prove to be the Idol of Creation," he continues. "But your actions have proven you to be far too dangerous."

I swallow, then clench my jaw and muster all the strength in my quivering, weak body to sit upright. The room tilts. My head pulses.

"I had even hoped you might become part of my family," he says. "Pippen has talked about nothing but you since you arrived. What a blessing it would be to have her wed Creation itself."

I press the heel of my palm against my throbbing skull. That would never happen.

"I'm relieved that it hasn't gone so far yet," he says.

I can't see him clearly on the other side of the glass.

Green light pulses in the ceiling. I frown, glancing up. The brightness of the light temporarily blinds me. Then I see what casts the green light.

A Power stone.

Panic seizes my chest. Where did they get a Power stone? Did Mosheyev bring it from Elpis? No. He couldn't have. It would have drained him, killed him.

"But your arrival will not be without its merits. If you refuse to work with us, then we will create ourselves in your image."

I shake my head and clap my hands over my ears, as if that will stop anything. Terror runs through my veins like ice.

Power stones have one use in a situation like this. Absorbing Powers for gradual release. If the Minister has control over how those Powers—my Powers—are released, what could he do with them? Will I live long enough to find out? No one exposed to a Power stone survives.

I had a plan. It had been running smoothly. Get to the *Book*. Find answers. Get captured. Rise to fulfill their dumb prophecy.

The Power stone changes all of that. Mosheyev's theoretical human experimentation must have become a mission for the Elders.

Mr. Garraty has access to the calculations in Mosheyev's journal—wrong as they were—and a Haven full of Powerless people to choose from.

My nostrils flare in anger, though I'm not sure if it's directed at him or myself. I should have seen this coming when I read the journal. What an idiot, not preparing for this possibility.

The Elders probably already have someone lined up to use the stone.

My skin turns clammy. "You can't create yourself in my image, though," I say through gritted teeth. Nausea swirls in my stomach. "The stone will kill you."

He nods sagely. "*I* can't. Thankfully, my daughter has kindly volunteered. How fortunate I have such a selfless child—a giftless child."

Pip? If they screw up the calculations like Mosheyev did, Pip will die.

"Gavin, something else happens beneath the temple. There's a thick steel door at the end of a hallway protected by some sort of security lock."

No...

The acolyte children who don't develop a Power. Powerless children. The Elders don't have to pull Havenites for their experiments. They have a host of Powerless acolyte children to use with no one being the wiser. As I close my eyes, I see a clear image of what happens behind that locked door buried in these hallowed halls.

The Powerless rejects are used to test the Power stone.

Unless I swallowed their religious pill, I always would have ended up in this cell. The Elders just needed me to confirm my strength. Instead, I forced their hand.

"Thank you, Gavin. Your noble sacrifice will save us all."

All the fear and anger burning beneath the surface bubbles out. I surge to my feet and shout at him, but my limbs give out. My knees hit the hard ground, then my hands. Desperate, I reach out for my Power, but what comes back to me is a trickle of what it once was. Not nearly enough to save myself.

Mr. Garraty cocks his head and peers at me through the small glass window. "Even you are helpless against the might of the stone. Rest well, Gavin. Tomorrow, the acolytes will bring you to the temple, where I will be left with no choice but to declare you a false Idol. Your death will save us all. Then, Pippen will rise."

I claw toward the door, digging my fingers into the cracks around the edges. But there is little strength left in me.

Footsteps recede outside the door.

He's gone.

Frustration claws at my veins, fills me with fury. The walls of the cell shrink around me. Pain lances through my lungs, chest, and throat. A scream climbs up my throat, feral, raw, and full of terror. I can't die like this.

I scream until my throat is raw and there's no breath in my lungs. Then I curl into the fetal position on the floor and sob, hot tears streaking my face.

By tomorrow, my Powers will be gone.

I will be helpless to stop the Minister from burning me alive.

And the Havenites will bray for my demise.

⁂

M Y DREAMS ARE FLEETING. Moments in time, sacred memories of Mom and Dad, Paige. Alex reassuring me when I suffered my first romantic rejection. Bianca laughing as she tries to teach me to fight. Drake's green and brown eyes. The faces of those who love me fade in and out, creating such a deep agony that I fear my heart will shatter into a million pieces.

I failed them all.

My body is too weak to hold itself upright. Even the slightest movement makes my bones ache and my body quiver violently. The nerve endings are hot, yet my skin is cold.

Today, I die.

Not that it matters. I couldn't possibly face the shame of failing my family or friends. I'm too tired to even think.

A small team of acolytes flip off the green light before entering my room. They scrub my body clean to prepare for the sacrifice. I couldn't fight them if I wanted to.

Once satisfied that I'm clean and dry, they cloak me in black robes. The cloth is so heavy it's like carrying a mountain on my body. A more alert Gavin might have been able to figure out what makes these clothes special.

But I'm hardly able to keep my eyes open. The Power stone has drained me to a trickle of Power.

The two stronger acolytes sling my arms over their shoulders to haul me upright. But I can't stand. Instead, my bare feet drag on the cool stone floor while they carry me out of my cell.

A girl in blue robes slips into the cell with a metal box. I blink lazily at her, but my head dips to my chest. I can't even hold my head high.

My toes and the tops of my feet turn to ice as they drag along the floor, as if my skin is absorbing all the cold in the stone. I watch the smooth, red clay pass beneath me, remembering the cracks I saw on these floors before. Cracks I can't see anymore.

No one speaks. The only sound is of my racing heartbeat, the scrap of my feet against the floor, and the scuff of the acolytes' slippers.

We stop in front of a set of double doors. I groan as a wave of nausea rolls through me.

A warm hand grips my chin, forcing my head up. Elder Julia peers into my eyes, turning my head from one side to the other as she assesses me.

"We can't present him to the congregation weak and glassy-eyed," Julia says. A moment later, she holds a large brown pill to my lips. "Open up, Gavin."

I squeeze my lips tight and try turning my head away, but I'm too weak and her grip is firm.

"Open his mouth."

All attempts to fight back in this feeble state are pointless. The acolytes pry my jaw open, and Julia pushes the pill deep in my mouth. Before I can spit it out, the acolytes tip my head back. Water rushes in my open mouth. I cough and sputter, but my body's reaction is automatic.

I swallow the pill along with the water.

Julia gives the acolytes final commands, then stalks away.

What are the odds these acolytes believe any of this is wrong? Slim, if they are raised deep in the *Book of the Prophet*. Escorting me to my death is probably considered a position of honor, which means none of these men and women will want to help me.

The doors open and the acolytes escort me through. I've recovered enough to manage keeping my feet under me, though only slightly. The bare soles slap against the wooden platform as we cross the stage.

Two large six-spoke wheels are propped up on the stage. One on either side. The acolytes escort me to one wheel as a hush falls over the congregation. My heart races a mile a minute as I'm tied with thick leather straps to the wheel. At the base, carefully organized logs rest against each other like a giant bonfire waiting to be lit. The acrid smell of gasoline makes my nausea worse by tenfold.

This is where I die.

With no Powers to save me.

The stage is made of wood. Some acolyte probably has the Power to contain the fire, so it doesn't spread out of control.

Mr. Garraty's gaze is hard as he watches the acolytes tie me to my wheel of death. Though he speaks, I don't hear a word he says. The fear and grief are too overwhelming.

Tears prick the corners of my vision while I stare out at the crowd. Thousands of sets of eyes glare at me. No sympathy. No remorse. To them, I am evil, and I deserve this fate to preserve their precious world.

Among the masses, one man gazes at me with sorrow in his eye. The corners of Emil's mouth are turned downward. His brows kink together. I have never been good at reading people, but his profound sadness bleeds into my heart. He mouths an apology.

But there's nothing he could have done. No way he could have known. No way he could have stopped me.

My heart clenches in my chest. Somewhere in this crowd, Drake must be watching me. That he might support my death like the rest of these people breaks what little resolve I have. A sob climbs my throat. Hot tears roll down my cheeks. I close my eyes and hope that Drake will walk away.

"...as the false Idol dies, the Idol of Creation shall rise. Today, the Days of Glory make their approach!"

The crowd roars in delight. The sound is thunder in my ears, shaking the very platform of gas-drenched wood beneath me.

Pip steps forward, her hair elaborately braided away from her face and laced with tiny white flowers. As she passes me, the sympathy that shines in her eyes is not because she truly feels sorry for me. It reminds me of the condescending way that people offer me false sympathy, as if I deserved my fate. At school, when teachers punished me for being smarter than them. While I don't know a lot of looks, that one I've become an expert in.

She believes I deserve this punishment as surely as my teachers did.

The betrayal breaks another piece of my soul.

Her pure white robe glows with a light of its own as she glides toward the second wheel.

"Pip, don't do this," I mutter, but the noise from the crowd swallows my plea. I tug at the straps holding me in place.

Pip kneels in front of her father. "I humbly accept this sacred role and dedicate my life to the service of the people and the world. Righteousness, disease, war, and death will be pacified. The faithful chosen will survive to rebuild during the Days of Glory. They will be given new lands and kingdoms. Men will live in peace and prosperity in the new social order. They will lay their crowns at my feet and be granted entry into the new Eden."

I recognize those words. My brain just can't pull up from where.

The Minister places a hand on her head. "We praise you, Creation. We serve you, Salvation."

Pip rises and lifts her arms to the sides, a serene peace on her face as the acolytes strap her to the wheel. Isn't she worried about what might happen to her? Why am *I* the only one scared for her?

The blue-robed acolyte steps forward with the metal box as the others tilt Pip's wheel forward until she hangs beneath it.

My heart thunders against my ribs.

The Minister stops by her head, whispering something to her. Pip nods. He raises a knife up for everyone to see. *What is that for?*

I tug harder at the straps. "No! Pippen!"

"The moment has come!" the Minister calls above the din of the masses. I lose the rest of his proclamation to my panic.

I scan the crowd for Emil, spotting him right where he stood before, eyes wide, locked on the knife. "Emil, stop him!"

He doesn't hear me.

"He will kill her!"

"Even now, the false Idol fights to break free and destroy us from the inside out," the Minister preaches. "Creation will rise, but first, this false Idol must be cleansed. Light the fire."

With the last of my strength, I tug at the straps, trying to wrap my fingers around the ends to loosen them. The acolytes march toward me, torches in hand.

"No!" A single voice of anguish screams out from the crowd. "Gavin!"

My heart plummets as I lift my gaze and sweep the crowd.

Drake fights his way forward, but the press of bodies eager to get a closer look at the spectacle bar his passing. He pushes, pulls, punches, fighting through them. Fighting his way toward me.

I clench my jaw. I can't let him see me die weak and crying.

"Gavin!" he shrieks, nearing the head of the crowd.

The roar of spreading flames bursts to life around me. Heat prickles my forehead. My palms immediately break into a sweat. How long can I hold out without screaming?

Drake reaches the front of the crowd, pinned down by four acolytes. He bucks wildly against their grip. "Please! Let me go! Gavin...!" His voice breaks over my name.

I raise my chin. Anger burns hotter than the flames around me. Heat prickles my feet as the fire inches closer. Panic tightens around my chest, making my ribs ache, stealing away my breath. Smoke climbs toward my eyes like a vengeful serpent.

Fire licks at my skin. Smoke fills my lungs. Every muscle in my body tenses as sweat seeps through every pore.

Then agony consumes me whole.

42

PAIGE

TERROR MINGLES WITH GIDDINESS as the morning light streams through my windows. Holly's death shook me to my core last night. I had nightmares of her dead eyes following my every move. Of her blood coating my ball gown. Waking is a relief. Instead of focusing on the horrible trauma from the night, my mind drifts to Zephyr.

The feel of the almost kiss remains on my lips, a whisper, a promise. My fingers drift up to my lips, but I don't dare touch them, afraid doing so will taint the lingering sensation.

What would King Cypress do if he found out? While we hadn't followed through with the kiss, it had been so close.

Zephyr is nearby. I can feel his Power push against me.

As I climb out of bed, the whispers of the other girls in the hallway draw me toward my door. Nora meets my gaze.

"Holly is dead," she says, her voice thick with sorrow.

Telling them I know or that I saw might spur a series of questions I don't want to answer. Because all of them lead to why I was out there with Zephyr.

"Suicide, they are saying," she continues. While the other girls seem to chatter curiously about Holly's death, Nora is the only one who sounds sorrowful.

The excitement in the other girls as they whisper about the tragedy like some great event makes me sick to my stomach. Holly was like most of us, ripped away from her home, her family, her love, and forced into this ridiculous pageantry. How would her boyfriend feel if he knew how little these people cared about her? I don't even know what they did with her body, and I'm ashamed to admit I don't have the courage to ask.

Nora leans closer to me and whispers, "I heard a rumor that she was pregnant when she arrived."

My stomach drops. How did she make it through the examination without raising alarms? And how did none of us notice?

Bella meets my gaze, and the fierceness in her eyes sends a bolt of ice down my spine.

The elevator door dings and slides open.

Queen Elena steps out and all the whispered excitement in the hallway stills. The girls drop into a curtsy. I'm in my nightgown still, and do my best to curtsey as well, but I'm certain I look more awkward than Nora.

"To your rooms," she commands. Her voice carries along the hallway.

Each of the girls scrambles to obey.

Terror grips my insides. Why are we being sent to our rooms? I cross the threshold and am about to close the door when Queen Elena approaches. I freeze.

A knot of worry lodges in my throat. I barely have time to step out of the way before she breezes past into my room.

"Close it," she commands.

My hands tremble, but I do as I'm told. This woman is intimidating on a good day, but something about her today feels ten times worse than usual.

The punishment for fraternization is the same as treason. Did Zephyr and I commit treason last night? We didn't kiss, but we wanted to. We nearly did. That must qualify. Is she here to punish men? To question me?

"Sit." She points at the green velvet loveseat.

I obey, praying she can't see me quivering from head to toe.

For a moment, she says nothing. Queen Elena stands with her hands clasped behind her, studying me. Her scrutiny is unnerving.

I know her Power is Lie Detection and not Telepathy, but I can't help the dread that she *can* read my mind.

"I will only tell you this once," she says at last. "So be sure you hear me *very* clearly, Lady Paige."

Her icy blue eyes bore into me. Is she expecting a response?

"Of course, your Grace." Was that the correct response?

"I don't trust you. I don't like you. Since you arrived in our palace, you have been arrogant, disrespectful, and self-absorbed. But I gave you a chance because my son wanted me to do so." Queen Elena's words sting. They are far too similar to the words Tudor threw in my face before I left Elpis. But unlike Tudor, this woman could crush me at her whim. "The *only* reason I haven't dragged you out the door by your pretty hair is because my son is determined to keep you here. I don't understand why, but I suspect you are manipulating him to get what you want."

She glides a few steps closer, towering over me. It takes all my willpower not to shrink away. No doubt that's what she wants. And she isn't entirely wrong. I *am* trying to use King Cypress to get home again.

"I know what you've done," she continues.

My stomach drops out. This is it.

"Yet still, he refuses to dismiss you." Her jaw twitches in anger. Cypress knows and still wants me here? Why? "But rest assured, when this is all over, you will *not* be chosen." She says this as if she is delighted to tear away something she believes I want.

I don't want the King. He's been kind enough, but when he kissed me, I felt nothing. Not like with Zephyr.

"If Cypress keeps you as a plaything, I won't stop him." She waves dismissively at the very notion that her son might want me just for his bed. The idea sickens me. "But you are a danger to us out there in the world. Which means you will never leave this island. If you try to harm my son or use him to go home, if you try to escape, I will use your friend to inflict pain. I will make him suffer. And I will make you watch. Have I made myself clear?"

Agony tears through my stomach. Sweat beads on my forehead. If I had access to my Power, this woman wouldn't be able to stop me from leaving. But they have blocked me off with this dumb bracelet and Zephyr's proximity. Unless I can remove this bracelet, I'm a prisoner. It might as well be cuffs around my wrists. I wrap my arms around my belly, which draws a satisfied smile from her lips.

"Just send me home, and I won't be a problem for you any longer," I plead, a tremor in my voice. "Let the two of us go, and I promise you will never hear from us again."

Queen Elena sneers down her nose at me. "As I said, my son insists on keeping you here. If you disappear, he will certainly blame me."

Nausea swirls through my gut. All the muscles in my body cramp.

Queen Elena glides toward the door. "I won't tell you again. This is your one and only warning." Then she leaves, slamming the door closed behind her.

Tears blur my vision. There must be some way to rescue Easton and get out of here. If I can get him to leave with me, we'll be fine. We can go home.

Zephyr.

The way he looked at me last night implies he might have deeper feelings than he let on. Would he help us? He has access to Easton *and* to the boats. But can I trust he will help?

43

ZEPHYR

BY THE TIME I'VE finished grieving, a hollow pit has opened in my gut. My mother died thinking I was angry with her. And I *was* angry. They lied to me all my life. But I would give anything—*everything*—to have those moments back.

I dry my eyes and shuffle into the parlor. The whiskey bottle is empty. There must be something else that will help chase away the pain.

Cypress sits in one of the blue armchairs, a jacket across his lap. Everyone else has left.

"Your Grace," I mumble as I shuffle toward the wet bar.

"Have some coffee, Zeph." The sharpness of Cypress' tone gives me pause. "It's a little early for alcohol."

A tray of steaming coffee sits on the table beside him. He motions for me to sit in the chair across from him. I oblige. A servant brings me one of the coffee cups, black just like I like it. Cypress dismisses her with a sharp gesture.

In moments, the two of us are alone.

"I'm sorry about your mother, Zephyr." But his tone doesn't sound sorry. He sounds angry and hurt.

I blow on the coffee and take a sip. "Thanks."

His cool blue eyes bore into me. I try to act like it doesn't bother me, sipping the coffee as casually as I can. But the pain in his eyes haunts me. I knew he cared about Mom, but didn't realize it would have this effect on him.

"I gave you one job last night, Zephyr." He sounds utterly exhausted—and a touch irritable.

My gut twists. I already don't like where this is headed, and my head isn't in it. The sudden shift in subject makes his condolences stale.

"But instead of driving Holly into my arms, you pushed her off her balcony."

"I didn't push—"

"*That's not the point.*" He enunciates each word so sharply I shrink back. He rubs at his brow, then drops his hand with a sigh. For the first time, I notice the bags of exhaustion under his eyes. Did he sleep at all last night? "What did you say to her?"

I take another drink to collect my thoughts. Everything is a jumbled mess. What *did* I say that drove her to her end? Was it anything I said at all? I set the cup on the chairside table and lean forward.

"Cy, I did what you asked. I encouraged her to give herself a chance at happiness here." I scrub my hand over my face and groan. "When she volunteered to come with us, there was...a boy. In her community. She knew he was about to do something that would get him killed, so she volunteered to stop him from acting out. As my men escorted her away, she...professed her undying love to him."

Cypress' jaw tightens. "Then why did you bring her?" Again, his words are clipped.

My jaw slackens. It takes a moment for me to realize he's serious. "Cy, it's the law. She's too strong not to be brought in. If I left her, I could have been punished for treason."

"Treason." He snorts, and for just a moment his lips tremble. He takes a moment to collect himself. "Do you really think I would try you for treason if you left behind a woman who never would have had an ounce of interest in me?"

I want to tell him Paige doesn't have an ounce of interest in him either, but pointing that out right now might be in poor taste.

And it certainly is selfish. "Why do you even care? You've hardly even said hello to her."

Cypress hammers a fist against the arm of the chair. "Because the moment she stepped through those doors, she became my responsibility!"

"I only told her what she did was noble, giving him a chance to love again, and she deserved that same chance. There is no reason, if she opened herself to this, to *you*, that she couldn't be happy. I tried encouraging her to give you a fair chance."

"Sure you did." He tips his head back and scrubs his hands over his face. Something else is bothering him. Or is it just exhaustion? As he rights himself in the chair again, his blue eyes are full of pain. "Where were you?"

"What? When?"

Cypress surges to his feet, clutching the jacket in a white-knuckled fist. "When she jumped to her death! Where were you?"

His sudden outburst pushes me farther back into my chair. My face heats as the implication sets in. Paige and I were alone on the promenade, so close to a kiss it still fills me with shame. *Idiot.* I lick suddenly dry lips.

"I was doing what you asked me to do with Paige. She had an anxiety attack, so I took her outside to get air. We were out there when Holly..." I lean forward and press the heels of my palms into my eyes. This is all too much to handle. I'm reaching a breaking point.

"You were pretty cozy out there, I hear." His magic pulses against my own, a clear sign he is furious. Cypress is a reader, specifically the history of people. In his anger, he instinctively tries to read me, but it won't work. My magic stops him.

"Nothing happened. We danced—"

He clenches his teeth. "I saw."

"—then she needed air, and we sat and talked."

And almost kissed. I tried to resist. But desire waged war with logic in my mind. I didn't say much of anything at all about Cypress the whole time, which was the entire reason I was supposed to spend the evening with her. I can still feel the whisper of her lips on mine, a reminder of what can never be.

Cypress' face twists in betrayal. He paces a few steps, gripping that jacket so tight his hand must be going numb. "And kissed."

I flinch back. How could he know?

"Her maids brought this back to me this morning." He whips the jacket at me. I barely catch it before it hits my face. A jacket is hardly incriminating. But he doesn't look angry. Betrayal mars his usually smooth features. "They assumed it was mine. Can you imagine? I mean, who else could it belong to? I was too embarrassed to correct them."

My stomach sinks. I left my jacket with Paige in the chaos of Holly's suicide. But it was cold outside. Surely, he can't assume I'm guilty because she still had it. Unless he could sense what happened by touching the jacket... His magic allows him to trace the history of people—as far as I knew that was it. Not items. *But he did it with the crown, when he became the King.*

"And then one of the girls came to me this morning and told me she saw the two of you together." His voice cracks in misery. "What you did is punishable as treason. I could have you whipped for this, Zephyr. I could have you killed! Mother is furious. She is demanding I punish you."

I hang my head. There is no point in denying any longer. I didn't kiss Paige, but we certainly were close. If one of the girls saw and reported us, nothing I say in my defense will matter, but maybe I can help Paige. She shouldn't be punished for my weakness. I took her to a private space. I pulled her close when I should have left space between us. I touched her when I knew how dangerous it would be. This is my fault.

"Just don't hurt her. It isn't her fault."

Cypress takes a few steps back, shaking his head as horror and pain contort his face. He expected me to deny it. Maybe he even wanted me to give him a good excuse for what happened. But I don't have one.

A lump lodges in my throat. I'm not sure if I'm more concerned about punishment, or afraid of never seeing Paige again. "Cy, this is such a mess. I'm sorry. Is there anything I can do to make it up to you?"

"Yes." His voice turns hollow. "Leave."

I press my back into the chair, gripping the arms. "What?" There's no way I heard that right.

"I trusted you, Zephyr." His voice falters. I've hurt him worse than I ever imagined I could. "My mother is braying for blood. It's all I can do to protect Paige right now. If you value your life at all, leave."

My heart sinks into the pit of my stomach. Leaving now means missing my mother's funeral. Cypress wouldn't be so cold, would he? I meet his empty gaze and my stomach sinks like lead. He would. "Where will I go?"

The hollowed-out core of him hardens into jealousy and anger. "Jump off a cliff for all I care. Zephyr Strong, you are hereby stripped of your title and rank and banished from the palace. In the spring, you will go to the mainland on the first ship. Take today to say your farewells to your family. By dusk, I want you out." He skulks toward the door, yanking it open. "The Queen has given orders to use any means necessary to remove you from the premises at that time, and equal orders should you try to return without *my* invitation."

The door slams shut behind him. I wince.

In less than a day, I have lost everything. And I will never see Paige again. That hurts more than I expect.

———— ❖ ————

G OODBYES AREN'T MY THING. I don't want to face Baron. He probably supports this decision after the way I snapped and pummeled his face last night.

Queen Elena certainly isn't on my list of farewells. She has never liked me. I wonder now if she knew the truth all along, that I wasn't Alric's son. *Does Cypress know?*

Bronwyn offers me hugs and reassures me she will keep in touch. It's a nice sentiment, but once I'm banished from the island come spring, there won't be anything more from her. Her promise to talk reason into Cypress will probably only get her into trouble, but she won't let me dissuade her.

When I leave her room, I hustle past the girls' rooms on the same floor. I won't stop at Paige's door, no matter how desperately I want her to know what's happened. She should know the danger she is in now. But if I knock on her door, Queen Elena just might get her way after all and have Paige punished—or killed. Instead, I duck my head and turn toward the steps, bag slung over my shoulder.

"Where are you going?" Nora's voice halts my steps.

I turn slowly.

She leans against her door beside Paige's room. Not so long ago, Nora drew me into her like a moth to a flame. She doesn't have the same effect on me any longer.

"I'm sure everyone will talk about it soon enough," I say, unable to admit the shame of my exile.

For a moment, she just studies me. Then she nods as if she accepts my statement as an excuse. "Take care," she says, and starts swinging the door closed.

"Wait." I stride toward her door, placing a palm against it. I keep my voice low, afraid Paige will hear me ask. "Can you keep an eye on Paige for me?"

Nora hesitates. The corners of her full lips turn downward.

"It's important, Nora. I wouldn't ask otherwise. You know I wouldn't."

She glances at the wall between her room and Paige's, then sighs. "Of course, I will. But only if you tell me where you're going."

I hesitate. Words fumble on the tip of my tongue. "I—I...can't. Just tell her something for me, will you?"

Nora frowns, narrowing her eyes at me.

"Tell her they know."

She gazes at me as if expecting more or waiting for an explanation. I can't say any more. "Okay..."

I can tell she doesn't like my answer, but I don't have another to offer. Before she can ask further questions, I pivot and descend the staircase.

It's nearly dusk. Time to go.

Cypress wants me to stay away from Paige, but I'm worried they don't understand the danger we are all in if I'm not nearby.

Protect her. Stay away. I can't do both. Sadly, there's nothing I can do to protect her. Queen Elena will kill me if I linger. And I hurt Cypress enough that he won't stop her this time.

When I reach the lower level, I head along the checkerboard hallway to the side exit. My steps are sharp and quick. A churning in my gut pulls me toward Paige. When I reach the doors, I stop and peer up to where her room is several floors above. What kind of danger am I leaving her in?

"Not going to say goodbye?"

I jump.

Dominic approaches from a bench near the door, hands deep in his pants pockets. "What did you do, Zeph?"

I swallow and glance at the doors. The moment I step out, my exile begins. I edge closer to my brother. *No, he's not my brother. He's my cousin. We don't share parents.*

"Dom, I think you're right," I admit. "I think someone is plotting against the throne."

He stiffens, eyes widening. "Do you know who?"

I shake my head. "No. But I suspect Baron has something to do with it. He has access to the missing shipments, authority over the military. Lord Greene might have something to do with it, too." I chew my lip. Should I tell Dominic I suspect Baron might have had something to do with the King and Crown Prince dying? "I worry Cypress is in danger."

He nods grimly. "I will look into it."

"Be careful. If anything happens to you, there is no one left to help him."

"I'm not dumb, Zeph."

"I know."

Silence falls between us. I glance once more toward Paige's room. "Watch over Paige. With me gone, her magic might break free."

Dominic cocks his head, narrowing his eyes at me. "That new bracelet should do the trick. If the other bracelet holds Nora as a six, the new one should hold Paige at seven."

I bite my lip, adjusting the strap of the bag on my back. Along with clothes and Mom's old St. Louis arch statue, I packed Paige's radio. It might come in handy. Five hundred miles from her community. That's what she said.

"What are you not telling us?" Dominic hisses.

Once I admit the truth to him, there's no going back. "She's not a seven, Dom." Cypress will probably find out, unless I can extract a promise from Dominic. "Swear you won't tell Cypress unless she becomes dangerous."

He frowns. "I promise."

I lick my lips. "Her magic fights against my own. It's so intense I can feel her from here. She's not a seven. I only said that because...I don't know what she is."

Dominic studies me, weighing my confession. "Just how intense is her magic?"

How can I scale this so that he understands the danger? "If girls like Bella and Maeve are a single flame, then our magic is like a campfire, yes?" He nods. "She is the sun."

His face falls. His jaw goes slack. I can almost see the gears turning in his head as he comprehends the enormity of what I said. "That—that's impossible."

I don't flinch as he eyes me, waiting for a denial.

"Zeph, you need to tell him. You need to stay here if she's that strong!"

I shake my head. Cypress would never allow it. Nothing I say will change his mind. "Just watch over her."

"I will."

That's all I can hope for right now.

"Where are you going?" he asks.

"I'll check in with Nat and go from there." I shrug.

Before he can force me into some tearful goodbye, I push my way out the doors, walking away from everything I have ever known. Away from my mother and father. Away from the only home I've ever had. Away from Paige.

Despair clenches my stomach. Each step becomes heavier. No matter how hard each step away from the palace is, I force myself to carry on and not fall apart within sight of the grounds.

I don't dare look back.

44

GAVIN

"**G**AVIN, YOU DON'T BELONG here."

I spin in place, standing on smooth water in nothingness.

A man I've only seen in photos materializes out of the air. My grandfather. The man I was named after.

"I'm dead."

He pulls me into a fierce hug. I crumple against him, clinging to him as I sob. *I'm dead.*

"You don't belong here, boy." He pulls back, gripping my shoulders.

Then he punches me so hard in the chest that I fly back away from him.

<hr>

A TRICKLE OF EARTH and flame. A pulsing electric surge. It wraps around me, hugging me tight like a coiling snake. I suck in a breath—*am I alive?*—then the pulsing surge within intensifies.

The Minister's frantic commands to the acolytes fill me with fury. "Do something. Fix her!"

Pip. What happened to Pip?

I pull at the leather straps around my arms. They creak and strain. The flames wink out of existence in a heartbeat. Did I do that?

The mass of Havenites watching are utterly silent.

I clench my jaw and draw as much of the Power as I can reach. It fills me, overflowing, spilling out of every pore.

Blue light pulses outward from my body.

The straps around my arms unravel themselves, falling away.

I hover toward the second wheel. Toward Pip.

Acolytes rush forward to stop me, clawing at the hem of my weighted black robe. The Minister sputters, eyes as wide as cups, gaping at me in shock and awe.

Someone in the crowd cries out. "He has risen!"

Not just someone. An acolyte proclaims me with reverence.

I reach toward Pip's wheel. With a flick of my wrist, it rises in the air. Pip's body hangs limp from the wheel. Blood trickles down her neck and drips to the stage.

The masses cry out, scrambling in every direction as chaos breaks out. I reach for the Power stone. I shouldn't touch it. The stone will kill me. But I can't stop myself.

The green stone glows with life on the back of her neck. Instinct takes over. I slide my fingers along the stone edge, then slide it up and out.

My Power surges, no longer a blue light from within, but wisps that slide out from my body in all directions. The wheel holding Pip's body transforms into a lifeboat. The two of us float toward the floor of the stage. I crush the Power stone in my fist. It crumbles like dust. Then I blow the powder in my palm, unsure what that will do.

The powder floats away through the air, coating the screaming acolytes on the side of the stage, settling like a film over the massive Idol statues holding up the ceiling.

Acolytes hurry toward me. I brush my fingers along Pip's neck, searching for a pulse. Nothing. My heart breaks.

"I'm sorry, Pip. This isn't what I wanted."

I lean close, kissing her forehead. Tears drip from my eyes to her hair. I slide my fingertips across the hole they carved in her neck to embed the stone. If there was some way to bring her back, I would. She deserved better. She was misguided by the Elders, used by her own father.

I scoop Pip into my arms and march toward the edge of the stage. Her head and arms dangle limply. "See what your Elders have done!"

I hoist her body above my head until it floats over the masses. Her white robe, stained with blood, hangs limply from her lifeless body.

An entry from the *Book of the Prophet* comes to me at that moment.

One the day of His resurrection,
He will show us a piece of His true power.
He will move the immovable.
Change the unchangeable.
Tear open the sky to reveal the light
and bring about the Days of Glory.

Time to use their beliefs against them, to show them their wrongdoings and misguided ideas.

Step one: Move the immovable.

I leave Pip's body floating overhead so they can all see what their faith has done to her, then I turn to face the massive statues holding up the ceiling. Powder from the Power stone glitters on each. I close my eyes, envision them as giants, and command them to move.

When I open my eyes again, acolytes and Elders rush toward me, wielding their Psionic Powers to stop me, but my mind is behind an impenetrable wall, safe from Psionic mind traps. One of the Idol statues lowers a massive hand toward the stage, blocking off Somatic and Naturalist attacks. It closes around a cluster of acolytes like a stone prison.

Step two: Tear open the sky and reveal the light.

The other statue rises, ripping a hole in the temple's ceiling. Snow falls through the growing gap. Snow and earth. It rains down around everyone. The sun shines brightly overhead, casting light over a thousand Havenites who shield their eyes from the blinding brilliance.

As their eyes adjust, they all gape at the winter sky above. Drake told me many of these people live their entire lives in the darkness underground, never seeing the surface. That changes today.

The Power still surges through me, remaking the entire temple.

"Gavin!" Drake runs up the steps, now free from the acolytes as they gawk at the sky.

The Minister stumbles across the stage, dodging movements from the two massive statues as they continue their work reshaping the temple, then planting a tree that grows up and out from the stage toward the sky. He grabs Drake, wrapping an arm around Drake's neck.

"Let him go," I say. My voice booms around the temple.

"What have you done?" the Minister barks. Manic terror shines in his eyes.

Drake claws at the Minister's arm, then goes limp in the Minister's arms, turning mistrusting eyes on me.

He's using his Influencer Power on Drake to turn him against me.

Anger pulses through me. Is this what it comes down to in the end? "I'm doing exactly what you wanted of me. Becoming your prophecy; your creation."

The floor transforms into a series of wooden acolytes of my making. They drift toward the Minister. His gaze darts from them to the open ceiling and moving statues.

"Stop this!" he barks.

"Stand down, Minister. It doesn't have to go this way. I came here for peace." My gaze falls on Drake. War wages in his dark eyes. He is fighting for control of his own mind. *Fight him, Drake!*

The Minister glares at me. Acolytes surround him—wooden as well as flesh and bone. All of them are against him now. His grip slackens, then drops.

Drake tumbles to the floor, drinking in the air on hands and knees.

My Power finally wanes. The Idols no longer hold the temple roof up. Now they hold it open.

I rush to Drake, kneeling beside him with a hand on his shoulder. He lifts his green and brown eyes, studying me.

"It was you," he says, then throws his arms around me in the tightest hug of my life. I hug him back, burying my face in his neck, inhaling the familiar scent of fresh earth and charcoal. His warm breath sends a thrill through me. "I knew it was you."

Then he pulls back. For a moment, the two of us examine one another. Everything else vanishes, and only he and I exist. Does he know how I feel about him? Would he feel the same, or am I once again reading too much into his friendship? I wish I had the answer. My heart drums in my ears.

My gaze slides past Drake at the masses.

Everyone is watching us.

I lower Pip's body to the stage. Anger beyond understanding radiates from me toward the Elders who misguided Pip so thoroughly she would believe I should be burned, and that divine right chose her to be a vessel for my Power.

Unexpectedly, like a great rolling wave, the Havenites all fall to their knees, bowing to the stage.

To me.

To my left, the remaining Elders crowd together, glaring hate at me as acolytes drag the Minister away. But as the undulating praise from the congregation continues, each of the remaining Elders dips their head. I don't buy for a moment that they truly accept me. Deep in my bones, I know this isn't over. I have infiltrated the Haven's most deeply rooted convictions and seized influence from the Elders. They will not give in so easily.

Another fight is coming.

To win, I need to use my knowledge from the journal of Mosheyev to free these people from the Elders' control and create a system of democratic equality.

An insurrection against the old status quo approaches.

Then I will finally be reunited with my sister.

45

PAIGE

SOMETHING IS HAPPENING. I can't put my finger on what it is, but they have confined all eight of us to our rooms for the day. Servants bring up meals and take away dishes but refuse to engage in conversation. A general sense of fear and loss permeates their every move. Does it have something to do with Holly? Do they suspect foul play?

I spend the day pacing in my room, doing pushups, and stepping out onto the balcony when the walls of the room close in too tightly around me. At one point, I swear I hear Zephyr's voice in the hall, but when I open the door, no one is there.

At night, I toss and turn, sleeping restlessly. I can't feel Zephyr anywhere nearby. While I am used to him leaving the palace during the day, he always returns at night. I can't sleep, waiting to feel the push of his Power against me.

But it never comes.

I miss home. I miss my family and my bedroom and the trek to work. It all feels like a lifetime ago.

When my maids arrive in the morning to ready me for the day, I'm curled up on the loveseat under a blanket, staring at the sunrise.

The maids' mood is somber as they set up their workstations in my room.

"Lady Paige, why aren't you showered yet?" Ingrid asks.

"You can all go today." Sorrow bleeds in my voice. "I don't feel up to seeing the King."

They exchange worried glances.

"What?" I pull my hair over my shoulder, fidgeting with it.

"He insists on all the ladies attending the funeral this afternoon," Ingrid says softly.

My stomach sinks. "Holly?" *So soon?*

"Lady Emry."

Tears blur my vision. She's dead? Is that why I haven't felt Zephyr all night? Maybe he left the palace to carry out funeral tasks. My heart goes out to him. I can't imagine what it's like to lose a parent. It would crush me beneath the weight of a mountain.

I rise from the loveseat and drift toward the bathroom. "How is Lord Zephyr?"

At the bathroom door, the uneasy looks that pass between them freeze me in my tracks.

Ingrid clears her throat. "He's gone, my lady."

The floor tilts beneath my feet. I grip the doorframe to steady myself. "Gone?" *He left me?*

Mariah averts her gaze, fussing with the black dress she brought in with her. The twins focus all their attention on the makeup cases. Ingrid clutches her cool curling iron to her chest, staring at the floor.

"What?" I snap, unable to stand their silence.

Ingrid jumps at my sharp tone. "King Cypress and the Queen Mother banished him from the palace yesterday."

Banished...? All the air in my lungs escapes in one sharp breath. No matter how much I try to gulp down more, I feel empty. Queen Elena warned me about toying with her son. She threatened to drag me out by my hair.

"I know what you've done." How did the Queen find out about the intimate moment between me and Zephyr?

I need Zephyr to have any hope of escaping here. He knows the island. He has access to the ships. He can get Easton to safety. Without him, I am well and truly trapped. And God help me, I want him with me.

I close my eyes as sorrow squeezes my insides. Then I remember it. The flash of golden skirt disappearing around the corner.

Bella. Anger surges to life inside of me. It pulses against the bracelet, eager to break me free.

I open my eyes and hiss a command at the maids. "Get out."

The four of them blink dumbly at me.

I press a hand to my roiling stomach, unable to hold in my temper a moment longer. "Get out!"

Ingrid ushers the girls out the door, leaving behind the dress and makeup.

If the Queen Mother and King Cypress think they can control me, I will teach them a lesson they will never forget. And if Bella is angling to get rid of me, I will destroy her.

But first, I will attend the funeral for Zephyr. Because if they insist I attend, then he will be banned.

S UNLIGHT SPARKLES OFF THE snow, making the world blindingly bright as the caravan of carriages makes its way to the cemetery. Two for the Tributes. Two for the royal family. One carrying Lady Emry. I peer out the window from my spot beside Nora. She holds my hand tight. This loss is probably hard for her, having known Lady Emry much better than I did. We cling to one another silently. We've not had a moment alone since all of this happened.

On the bench across from me, Bella sits beside Layla. Bella studies me with harsh eyes. When I first arrived at the palace, those hateful glares had been directed at Nora. If Nora realizes how much Bella despises her, she is fantastic at ignoring it. A few times, Bella squirms under my vengeful gaze.

If she wants me to back off from the King—which I assume is the case since she was so eager to spill about my tryst with Zephyr—I'm more than happy to oblige. In fact, I would be thrilled if he never showed his face around me again. Her anger toward me must be fueled by the knowledge that her tattling didn't result in my punishment.

The cemetery is ancient, surrounded by a low stone wall and barren trees. We exit the carriage. Nora remains glued to my side. I'm not sure if her grip on my arm holds up me or her. Either way, I take some comfort from her presence.

As we pass headstones, my gaze sweeps over a few old, faded etchings. Some headstones date all the way back to the 1800's, centuries before the Collapse of the modern world. How old are these graves now?

A minister preaches at the head of the coffin, giving a moving speech about the selflessness and love Lady Emry shared with the royal family. Throughout the entire speech, he doesn't mention her son once, as if they have wiped Zephyr from their history. I clutch tighter to Nora's arm as anger pulses through me.

Afterward, everyone steps forward to place a hand on the coffin. I nudge my way into the crowd and lean close to the closed lid. "I'm so sorry your son isn't here. He cared deeply for you. But I'm sure you know that." I right myself and slide my hand over the coffin, then move out of the way for others.

Bella strolls over and stands beside me, her face a perfect mask of mourning, which belies her words. "Clearly, the King favors you." She keeps her voice low as she speaks, watching everyone else to be sure no one comes too close. "Otherwise, you would be dead."

A chill runs down my spine that has nothing to do with the cold. I want to shove this girl's face in mud.

"You'll use that favor to get closer to him."

"I will *not*." I glare at her from the corner of my eyes.

She raises a brow. "You will. Because the Queen isn't the only one with access to your friend in the fort. And if you do what you are told, when you are told, you *might* even return home."

"I thought you wanted me to stop hogging his attention," I hiss.

Bella places her hand on my shoulder as she turns back to the carriage. To anyone watching, the gesture appears consoling. But her manicured nails dig into my skin through the thick cloth of my jacket. "He exiled his brother to keep you close. It doesn't matter any longer if it's you or me close to his side. The result is the same."

I don't want to ask, but cannot hold my tongue. "What result?"

She pats my shoulder. "Just do as you are told. Keep him close. By *any* means necessary. Tell *anyone*, and you will both suffer horribly." Bella strolls away, head hanging low.

Pieces click into place. I don't see the full picture, but I have a much clearer idea. Dominic and I had dinner together and discussed the mutiny of Zephyr's men on the way to the island. Those men were convinced by the time they reached the island it would be too late for Zephyr to stop whatever they had planned. I knew the mutiny had to be coordinated, and they couldn't have acted alone.

Bella must be part of whatever resistance was in place. But Zephyr stopped those men and returned to the island. What would have happened if he hadn't? I had considered that they wanted Zephyr to fall, but with him banished, there would be no reason to continue the plan. So what game is Bella playing?

And why does she want me close to the King for it to work?

The others all head for the carriages. Nora strolls over to me, sliding her arm through mine. "Everything alright?"

I shake my head, but play it off as the funeral and not Bella's threat.

King Cypress helps his mother into their carriage. Before he climbs in, he pauses, meeting my gaze. Piercing sorrow and pain shines in his blue eyes. Is that because of Lady Emry's death, or because of my betrayal? He frowns, then ducks into his carriage.

Pressure builds in my chest. The bracelet on my wrist suddenly feels too heavy. Once more, the anger burns in my veins, threatening to consume me whole. I tense, offering Nora a brief smile of reassurance when she asks if I'm okay again. I appreciate her kindness, but I can't tell her the truth.

My anger spreads outward, then collapses under the pressure of a wall blocking me off. I nearly trip over the hem of my dress as I realize why. It isn't anger. It's that strange Power I felt in the dome with Bella. I shouldn't be able to feel it with the bracelet on at all, but even assuming there is a way, the sensation of being cut off is familiar. Comforting, even.

Nora climbs into the carriage. I pause, scanning the cemetery.

In the shadows of a tall fir tree, a cloaked figure hides behind the evergreen branches. But I feel his gaze on me, and I take great comfort from his presence.

Afraid someone else might notice Zephyr, I hike up my skirt and climb into the carriage.

When I left Elpis, I wanted to prove myself. I thought I could return home a hero worthy of my father's legacy.

Now I don't know if I will ever see home again.

**Curious what Ugene uncovered to make this mission possible? Wondering about the barrier?
Download the prequel, Revelation, only available at Starr ZDavies.com.**

The adventure continues in *Insurrection*.

I hope you enjoyed Paige, Gavin, and Zephyr's story. If you did,
please consider leaving me a review. I love hearing what people
liked about the book.

ACKNOWLEDGMENTS

I HAVE TO THANK Zephyr—my beloved Captain whom I tortured without end. You took it like a champ, even if you lost contol for a hot second there.

As always, I have to thank my husband for letting me dig into writing this book while our house fell apart, and for letting me spend my days living in a fantasy world instead of the real world. To my kids, who kept the dishes clean(ish) and their patience plentiful (sometimes). And of course, my family for the endless support and encouragement (even if you aren't really readers). To my daughter, sorry Easton isn't dead yet. I know how much you wanted him to die. Believe me, I tried.

This book wouldn't be where it is without the dedication of my beta readers: Kevin Mackie, TaniaRina Perry, Asher Jones, Jared Goldman, Kris Shotts, and Jennifer Garcia. Nor would it have been fit for print without the steady hand of my editor, Maddy, who always has the best suggestions, advice, and praise alike. The support from my fellow dystopian authors in the Dystopian Author League have helped me launch this series. You should read their books, too! I promise they're all amazing!

Cole R. Eubanks, thanks for giving these characters *amazing* voices for audiobook lovers to enjoy. I know I do!

And of course, I want to give a big thanks to you, my dear reader. Because without your support, my books would go unloved and unnoticed.

POWERS LEGACY SERIES

A POWERS UNIVERSE SERIES

A ROYAL ROMANTIC DYSTOPIAN FANTASY SERIES
FEATURING DIVERSE CHARACTERS,
POWERFUL FAMILY BONDS, DYNAMIC
RELATIONSHIPS, AND FORBIDDEN ROMANCE

WWW.STARRZDAVIES.COM/POWERS-UNIVERSE

POWERS TRILOGY SERIES

A POWERS UNIVERSE SERIES

A SUPERPOWER DYSTOPIAN SCI-FI SERIES
FEATURING DIVERSE CHARACTERS,
FOUND FAMILY, DYNAMIC FRIENDSHIPS,
AND POLITICAL CORRUPTION

WWW.STARRZDAVIES.COM/POWERS-UNIVERSE

About Starr Z. Davies

STARR Z. DAVIES is an award-winning author of over 20 tales that span dystopian realms, epic fantasies, and echoes of forgotten histories. Dubbed the "Character Assassin," she weaves stories where heroes are tested by fire—both emotional and physical.

From her woodland home in northern Wisconsin, she crafts worlds while surrounded by her greatest allies: a supportive husband, two imaginative children, and a curious menagerie of robotic pets. When not conjuring new adventures, she dabbles in home enchantments, swims like a siren, battles through video game quests, and devours books like ancient tomes of power.

If you want to become friends with Starr, dark chocolate, Doctor Who, Parks & Rec, The Office, and the MCU are all fantastic ways into her heart. That or a love for fantasy books by indie authors.

Learn more about Starr and her books.

Keep up with Starr by signing up for her newsletter.